The Stars of Scotland

by

Erica Mae

Scottish Stars Series

Dedication

To every woman searching for an incredible love that lasts a lifetime. This story is for you.

xo

Chapter 1

There's something about time. I used to think I had all the time in the world, then I got married and my time was shared. Then, we had children—two amazing, beautiful kids—and time clicked by quickly. Then, I got divorced and there's barely time for me anymore.

My wish: time.

Brielle blew out thirty-one glossy candles at her quaint dining table. Well, she attempted to, except the excited puffs from her three- and six-year-olds beside her beat her to the task. She laughed and was joined by a soft guffaw from her mom, AKA Mimi, in a whimsical, tangerine blouse that floated to her braceleted wrists, and a high-pitched giggle from her best friend, Andrea, with a hand cocked on a full hip across the golden, pine kitchen table. A flowery *Happy Birthday* sign scalloped across the glass slider, while hand-crafted arrangements of wildflowers and pale-pink roses perched in petite jars of various sizes on every surface in the family room. Warm notes of Southern California spring wafted through the screen.

Her son, Noah, pressed a wet kiss on her left cheek. "Happy birthday, Mommy."

"Thank you, sweetheart." She wrapped an arm around his slim shoulders and kissed him back, inhaling his little boy scent of cotton and a hint of dirt.

Climbing onto her lap from the opposite side,

Phoebe stared with mermaid green eyes speckled with bits of gold near the iris. "Make a wish!"

Brielle gazed at the homemade, two-layer birthday cake with swirls and globs of cotton-candy-pink, buttercup, and lavender frosting—thanks to her tiny helpers—and a rainbow of sprinkles. This cake was so much better than last year's when her ex, Ryan, insisted he'd purchase the dessert and then showed up late and empty-handed. The cake even smelled sweeter with notes of vanilla mingled with melted wax. Plus, celebrating with the four people she held most dear was just what she needed this year. "I wish for the biggest hug ever!"

Noah and Phoebe giggled and wrapped their small arms tight, snugging their heads into her chest.

As contentment washed over her, she closed her eyes.

SMACK!

Brie winged her eyelids open. Across the family room, the rainbow piñata pitched wildly back and forth, while colorful, pastel ribbons swished at the bottom.

Beside the candy vessel, Andrea held a powder-pink piñata bat like a sword. She pointed the bat. "That's not a wish. You need a good one this year. How about a hot guy?"

With a crinkle of her nose, Brie shook her head. "A hot guy? I don't think so." She didn't need a hot guy. She had her happy family of three and stability—both desperate wishes on her last birthday.

Twelve months ago, she finalized her divorce a week before her thirtieth birthday, severing seven years of marriage and breaking apart their family of four. Yet, her ex still insisted on attending her party. She'd allowed him in again, pasting on a smile to show her sweet babies they could still be a happy family despite the ache within. Yet, they weren't.

Ryan was more concerned with his cell phone and the woman on the other end than talking to their children, especially their oldest, Noah, who vied for his attention. And when Ryan finally put the device away and demanded a hug, he grew frustrated when Phoebe clung to Brie with tears swimming in her eyes and Noah stomped away.

At that moment, Brie promised herself she would do everything in her power to give her children a happy, stable life. She muddled her way through the last year—starting a new job as a Proposal Writer, balancing kid activities, and juggling more responsibilities than she could count—with lots of tears and willpower. And when the pain engulfed her, she wrote in her journal. A journal that has transformed into a work-in-progress memoir about her journey to finding happiness. Seeing the two smiling faces before her as they swiped fingerfuls of frosting off the cake in the quaint, powder-blue living room of her three-bedroom rental home in Lakewood, California, she had succeeded with her initial wish.

"Darling, make a real wish." Mimi's crushed orange and cobalt stone earrings swayed delicately below her earlobes. "Last year, I wished for one of my finished art pieces to be in a gallery. Now, I have two."

"Okay." Brie tipped her head and spied a pastel-pink notebook resting on the side table. "How about I wish for my memoir to be completed this year?"

"That's a goal, not a wish. Like how about a vacation?" Andrea walloped the piñata again, gathering

3

Noah and Phoebe's attention as the colorful candy holder pitched vigorously back and forth.

Brie gazed at the secondhand watercolor painting gracing the wall beside Andrea. "A vacation…" With delicate puffs of purple heather and towering, rolling green hills, the painting created a feeling of serenity in her family room. She'd love to go gallivanting in a faraway land, but she'd finally created permanency for her and her children. Stability. Something Noah and Phoebe could count on when their dad let them down time and time again. She couldn't just leave on a whim. Yet, she also couldn't deny something was missing. She blew out a breath and snuggled her children closer. "I have all I want right here, but I wouldn't mind a laundry fairy. Or, how about a dish fairy?"

Mimi laughed.

Andrea snorted and shook her head, shuffling brunette curls off her shoulders. She set the piñata stick down in exchange for the vintage server nestled atop a stack of pink, ruffled napkins.

"I can cut it," Brie said.

Andrea pointed the spatula. "Nope. It's your birthday. And besides, we have some surprises, don't we, kids?"

They disappeared into the kitchen, then reemerged a moment later with birthday bags filled with fluffy pink and cotton-white tissue paper.

Brie commented on the skill of the hand-painted, olive lizard rock from Noah for her tiny vegetable garden and "oohed" and "aahed" at the playful, fuchsia flower painting from Phoebe. "I love them! Thank you."

"Open more, Mommy!" Phoebe lifted another bag,

fingertips covered in purple marker.

As she gently lifted tissue, Brie unearthed a beautiful emerald dress, cream scarf, and clover green coat with polished, black buttons. "Oh, these are wonderful, but you spent too much."

Mimi shook her head, swishing her short, gray bob. "Nonsense."

"Just say, 'thank you.' " Andrea winked.

Brie rubbed her fingertips along the soft, knit dress and studied the elegant, thick coat. "Thank you. These are absolutely gorgeous. With summer coming in a few months, I don't know if I can wear the coat for much longer, but I can't wait to wear it next winter."

Andrea glanced at Mimi with a devilish look in her eye. "There's a reason for the coat."

"A reason?" Brie asked.

Mimi quickly ushered the kids outside to play in their shoe-box-sized backyard.

"What are you two up to?"

With a grin that winked dimples at Brie, Andrea didn't utter a word.

Mimi returned a moment later and handed Brie a slim white envelope. "We have one last surprise."

Lifting the envelope flap, Brie expected to find a birthday card. Instead, two, white-and-black plane tickets were tucked inside. And the final destination: Edinburgh. She blinked. "Scotland? You bought me a ticket to Scotland?"

"Yes!" Andrea threw her arms up. "And I'm going with you. We'll check out Edinburgh, castles, museums, stay in posh hotels, or quaint B&Bs, meet men in kilts and be lulled by their sexy brogues, drink whisky, write, and whatever else we decide!"

Brie always dreamed of traveling to Europe, especially to Scotland and Ireland where both parents had ancestral roots, but the stars never aligned. She glanced down at the tickets once again and the span of time between departure and return. "Ten days?" Her heartbeat quickened and mind raced. She'd never been away from her children more than a day. "This is an incredible gift, but I can't leave the kids for almost two weeks. They need me."

Leaning forward, Mimi gripped her hands. "They do, but they also need to know their mother can be away for a few days and still love them dearly. And as their mother, you need to show them it's important to take time for yourself to rejuvenate your mind, body, and soul. You need this."

Brie glanced at her kids again. Noah with his quick grin, soft blond hair ruffled by the summer air swinging in his big-boy swing, and Phoebe with her silky brown hair sparkling with golden highlights, twirling a bubble wand. She was the only one who knew how Noah liked his secret-ingredient jelly sandwich, and what about Phoebe's egg allergy? She'd been so careful.

"They'll be fine," Mimi said from behind. "They have school and will be with Ryan for part of spring break as planned and with me for the rest. We'll have fun, I promise. And so will you."

Shaking her head, she squeezed her eyes that stung with unshed, joyful tears. "But this is too much…"

Yet, how wonderful would exploring Scotland with her dearest friend be? Breathe in the fresh Scottish air, instead of the stuffy city air she was used to, or jog along the base of rolling green hills? She could even learn something. And, she could write. She could write more than the single hour after the kids went to bed and work on her in-progress memoir. She could actually finish—something she'd hoped for, but wasn't sure was possible.

This trip offered possibilities. Tingling ran up her spine as she glided her fingertips along the ticket's rounded edges, tracing the smooth curves. She pictured herself strolling through purple-tipped, heather-covered hills, flowers tickling her shins, and climbing stone-faced castle steps to towering heights. A grin tugged at her lips.

"Well?" Andrea tilted her head.

She gazed at her children once more—her happiness. Yet, Brie had forgotten what made her happy. Perhaps now was the time. "I'd love to. I just need to request time off work and organize a few things before I can say, yes."

And what's more, Brie had to discuss the trip with her ex.

****

The following evening, Ryan glared at her from the porch. "Two weeks?" He stood, hand on hip with his dark hair slicked back. "Who's taking care of the kids?"

Guilt tangled her gut, but she forced the feeling away before it consumed her. She wouldn't allow him to make her feel bad when she was the one juggling work, schedules, and children. Ryan traveled two or three times a month for work across the U.S. or to London, and when he wasn't traveling for work, he'd jet off to Hawaii, the Bahamas, or Greece with what's her name. When she and Ryan were married, they talked about taking family vacations when the kids were older, or maybe that was her, she couldn't remember. The good memories were now tainted with the bad like a dust-laden photo.

She lifted her chin. "You and my mom, remember? You're supposed to have them for four days beginning the Saturday before spring break and then my mom will take care of them."

"I recall saying I'd take them a few days."

"You always pull this." Shaking her head, she threw her hands into the air. "Promise them one thing and then do another. And I'm left to pick up the pieces! They miss you. Can't you see that? You're supposed to have them every other weekend, and you barely spend two days a month with them."

"I know." Ryan expelled a breath and then swiped a hand over his slicked hair. "I miss them, too. I'll spend more time with them, all right? But I have a new relationship I'm trying to make work and a demanding career. Things come up."

Anger bubbled and strained against her ribcage. "And, you have kids."

"So do you, but you seem to have forgotten that with your little trip planned."

She opened her mouth, then promptly closed it. Brie almost said she hadn't fully agreed to the trip yet, even though her boss granted her the time off, but standing there with a frowning Ryan, she grasped the Scotland trip like a brightly lit beacon. She didn't need his permission. Not anymore. He'd lost that right when he showed up at their family home with the buxom brunette in his sports car, waiting at the curb.

Leveling her gaze, she straightened. "I'm going on this trip, Ryan." And with that statement, a surge of confidence coursed through her. She pivoted on her socked feet. "I'll get the kids ready."

He jingled the car keys. "Actually, we're meeting Jasmine's family at the club tonight, so they won't be staying over."

Brie spun. "Fine. Enjoy the frozen yogurt and make sure Phoebe's is egg-free."

Ryan rolled his eyes. "I know, Brie. Jesus. She's my daughter, too. I know what she can and cannot eat."

"Stop it, Dad."

Brie glanced at her son. She hadn't realized he'd joined their conversation. Since Ryan left, Noah stepped in as Man of the House. Although she loved him for the newfound-role he, himself, assumed, she didn't want Noah to have to be anything more than a happy, healthy, six-year-old kid.

Ruffling his hair, she smiled softly. "It's okay, Noah. Your dad and I were just talking. Let's grab your shoes! It's frozen yogurt time." She left Ryan waiting on the porch. Brie didn't want his energy inside her house. This was hers. She'd sold the home they'd shared as a family ten months ago, unable to bear the memories. She also couldn't afford the beautiful two-story, even though her mom offered to help with what little money she made as a part-time art teacher and the child support from Ryan. Brie wanted to show Ryan she could stand on her own two feet, though she was drowning inside and barely scraping by with her Proposal Writer salary. Drafting persuasive proposals for potential clients about TechCo's recruiting software might not fulfill her creative urges, but the job provided independence.

"Okay, kiddos. Who's ready for some frozen yogurt?" She gathered Phoebe's jacket, lightly lifting her hair above the fuzzy hoodie, then bent down to help Noah tighten the last shoelace.

"I've got it, Mom." His fingers tangled in the laces.

Brie's heart exploded with pride. Her son was so determined.

With laser focus, Noah looped one lace and weaved the fabric around his pointer finger, then circled the other lace around the loop. "There!" He pulled the laces tight like bunny ears.

"Perfect, buddy." Brie leaned down and kissed his forehead. "Have a great time!" She waved good-bye until the sports car disappeared around the street corner. Closing the door, she leaned against it and inhaled, telling herself to breathe. She hated how Ryan could make her feel so diminutive. In one quick moment, he struck her happy mood down like whiplash. Yet, he wasn't always this way. Until that day in August, she believed he was the best husband, or at least, she'd convinced herself he was.

With one last inhale and exhale, she pushed away and spied her cell phone on the ivory entry table. She grasped the smooth device. She was going to do this for *her*. With trembling hands, she clicked the familiar bubble icon and created a group text with Andrea and Mimi. She hovered her pointer finger in the air as her breath shot out in quick puffs.

—*I'm in!*—

—*YES!!! Scotland here we come!*—

Andrea followed the text with a shirtless, Scottish hunk in a kilt, dancing some sort of jig, while flexing his impressive muscles.

Brie snorted and responded with a laughing face emoji.

Mimi texted a moment later with near a dozen heart emojis.

—That's wonderful! You'll have the best time. And don't worry about the kids, I'll take care of them and organize with Ryan.—

Brie danced in the entryway. She was going to Scotland!

Chapter 2

From Brie's window seat a month later, miles and miles of cerulean-blue transformed into emerald green, reminding her of the rich clover fields she'd played in as a girl behind her grandparents' farm in Pasadena and the familiar, earthy fragrance. She inched closer to the glossy window. "It's magnificent."

"What?" Andrea tilted her head with rose-colored earbuds perched in her ears.

The view, she mouthed and pointed outside the window.

With a giggle, Andrea removed the earbuds and peeked. "Yup, fucking beautiful."

She relaxed her head against the headrest. "I think that was the longest span of kid-free time I've had in the past six years."

Andrea snorted. "You slept for almost the entire flight and with only one glass of wine I might add. I'm impressed." She toasted Brie with the plastic champagne glass.

Brie sighed. She couldn't remember the last time she'd slept more than six hours. After she put the kids to bed, she'd finish dishes, fold laundry, clean a room or two, and prepare lunches. If she had energy left, she'd write for thirty minutes to an hour. Her normal routine ended with her in bed by ten p.m. "Did you sleep?"

Leaning in, Andrea leveled her deep, dark brown eyes toward her. "Heck no. Not when I can binge watch *Swords of Scotland*. Give me sexy, highland warriors in kilts with Scottish accents any day."

Brie peeked at Andrea's tablet and crinkled her nose at the gruesome battle scene. Men in kilts wielded large, silver swords at men in crimson red coats with splashes of mud and blood smeared across their faces and bodies. "Blood and guts? No, thanks."

"Of course, there's blood and guts during battle scenes like this one—the show's set during the Jacobite Rebellion. But there're also steamy sex scenes and romance. Can you imagine being a woman in the eighteenth century loved by a man who pledges his heart and sword at your feet?"

She hummed, but longing tugged her heartstrings. Did a man like that even exist in the real world? "I guess I'm not in with the in crowd. Although I can summarize highlights of kid shows, if you like."

Andrea snorted. "No, thanks. I'll keep my gaze on Alexander James Mackenzie's sexy ass."

She laughed. "Does that mean you didn't write that chapter you were talking about?"

"Nope." Andrea snugged herself into the seat farther. "My mind is full of sexy highlanders, and I don't feel the least bit guilty."

Grinning, Brie recalled the first time she ran into Andrea. Although she and Andrea didn't meet until a few months on the job at TechCo, they had formed an instant bond over their love of books and writing. One day, she overheard a director talking about how Vice President of Human Resources, Andrea Accardi, had a short story published. And although Brie had a handful of bosom friends before getting married, she watched them drop off one by one once she had Noah. She couldn't meet for Sangria Saturday's or girl getaways, not when Ryan worked fifty-five-plus hours a week. She longed for someone to talk to besides her mom.

"Hi." Brie stood at the threshold of Andrea's office and then introduced herself. "I hear you have a short story published."

With a document in hand, Andrea glanced up. "I do."

"I do, too." Brie inched forward. "And I'd love to start writing again—creatively, I mean."

Andrea smiled wide. "Come in and close the door."

They formed a *Secret Writers' Club* at work and became quick friends. At first, she jotted down children's stories she'd been telling Noah and Phoebe, but then with the divorce, she also wrote about her personal journey to finding inner happiness.

She still remembered the day she told Andrea about her memoir. Brie scribbled in a notebook on break beside the building's water fountain outside and heard a gasp.

"That's not a children's story." Andrea stood beside her.

"No. It's about me…and my marriage." Her voice caught in her throat. "I-I need to write it down. It's the only thing that's helping me get past this"—she swelled her hands from her chest—"this pain."

Placing a hand on Brie's shoulder, Andrea squeezed. "I understand. My parents divorced when I was a teenager."

When Brie shared her personal writing the following week during page exchange, she glanced at

Andrea, while her hands shook and heart rapped. She still remembered the first few lines.

I do. Two words we promised each other under an arch blooming with fluffy hydrangea and fragrant lilies and roses. More than two hundred family and friends attended to witness our exchange, but all I could see was you. That was seven years ago. Today, I signed the papers alone, finalizing our divorce...

Andrea smacked the pages down on the bench. "Oh, my God. It's a memoir. I love it. Keep going!"

Brie blinked. "It is? I never thought about it being a memoir...I'm writing this for me. I just need to get the words out, even if the results are terrible."

"It's not. I'd totally read it!" Andrea jutted a hand up. "I just read a memoir about that comedian, Abby Christina, and the writing was horrible. The publisher paid her to write this book, and I bought it, thinking it would be funny. Don't get me wrong, some parts were, but in other parts, she complained, literally in writing, about having to write the memoir. Yours has so much more heart and truth with a slice-of-life woven in. Women will read this, I promise."

But did Brie want to share her private life?

After deliberating for a week, writing, deleting, and re-writing, worrying if she was talented enough, she decided if she was going through this tough time, other women were, too. And maybe they needed to know they weren't alone in their journey. Maybe through her journey, they could find hope together.

Glancing at Andrea popping chocolates into her mouth as her gaze fixed on the screen, Brie couldn't help but feel grateful for her best friend. She'd urged her to keep writing, and now, Brie had near one hundred and ninety pages written. Still, she didn't know how her story would end.

With another glimpse out the oval, airplane window now encased in ethereal clouds, she retrieved the newly-purchased, floral notebook and set pen to paper.

April 24

The clouds drift by my window like snowy cobwebs, making me feel as though I'm still dreaming. With a single glass of wine, I fell asleep quickly after takeoff and slept for close to nine hours on this tiny, airplane pillow. Now I'm awake and officially on vacation. Vacation...can you believe it? My very first vacation in years.

Edinburgh will be our first stop—the nation's capital—before traveling west to Glasgow, and finally up to the highlands to picturesque Glencoe. Watching travel vlogs a few nights ago, I couldn't stop admiring Scotland's incredible variety—from bustling cities to historic castles, fascinating museums, breathtaking mountains, and magical fairy pools. I even saw a tutorial on basic greetings in Scottish Gaelic and had so much fun practicing pronunciations. I've always loved languages, even though I don't speak any fluently besides English. But Scottish Gaelic is spoken in Scotland and apparently making a comeback throughout the country, so I figured if I'm vacationing in Scotland for ten days, I should learn how to at least say, "hello," "good day," and "thank you."

Ten days...

Ten days of vacation and ten sleeps until I rejoin my babies. Ten days isn't long—not even two weeks when you think about it, but I know things will happen that I'll miss, like the way Noah hugs extra-long in the morning when he first wakes, and Phoebe's shining face when she wants to show me her latest artwork.

I miss them already. When I'm at work, I'm so focused on getting my tasks done that I don't have time to miss them. Plus, pictures of them pepper my desk as lovely reminders. When I'm at home, they're all consuming, and I love that. But at times, I can't wait until they're asleep for some time to myself, even if that time equates to a few minutes.

Speaking of sleep, my children are currently asleep in their beds at home. It's well past midnight in the states, and I hope they're having wonderful dreams. Yet, I can't deny the guilt that snuck into my chest just now, as well as when I said good-bye to Noah and Phoebe this morning, or the tears that soaked my sweater. I can still smell the faint notes of caramel pancake syrup as Noah slid his arms around my neck and nestled his forehead close to mine and feel the angel-softness of Phoebe's rosebud lips on my cheek. Even though I'm sure the tinge of guilt will remain throughout this trip, I'm going through with this vacation. For me.

Isn't that why I started this memoir? To help get me through the hard stuff and find myself in the process?

I'm taking my life back.

We have one, quick plane change in London, then we'll be on our second and final flight to Edinburgh. I know I'm in for an adventure. And I'm ready.

****

Before Brie placed a teal-and-pink running-shoed-foot on Scottish soil, she beelined through the terminal with one thing on her mind: the ladies room.

"Seriously? The plane had three toilets. I want to get out of this damn airport, into a hot bath, fresh clothes, and talking to a sexy Scotsman before the night is up." Andrea huffed.

"I know. I know. I'm sorry." Brie couldn't stand cramped spaces, and airplane bathrooms didn't help her situation. Leaving Andrea outside the terminal, she jogged over to a sign pointing to the restroom, rounded a corner, and proceeded another fifty feet. *Phew.* Three people ahead of her, and she'd be golden.

BLING! Brie's text notification chimed.

BLING! BLING! BLING!

"Who the heck would be texting? It's still bedtime in the states," she mumbled. Glancing in her purse, she caught sight of Andrea's name and multiple lines of text messages. Curious, she fished her phone out.

—Hurry! Someone spotted Alexander exiting the terminal next to us!—

Alexander, who? *Of course, Andrea's favorite character from the television show.* She wondered if anyone called him by his real name.

—Be there ASAP. I'm next in line!—

—Just hold it! —

—Go talk to him!—

Andrea could stalk the movie star, while she used the toilet. Besides, she wasn't into the show. She'd let her get her fill. Two minutes later, Brie swung through the bathroom door, relieved, and much more comfortable when more text notifications chimed.

—I'm following him!—

—I need a selfie!—

—Shit! —

—I lost him! —

Brie giggled. She hoped she didn't ruin Andrea's chance. Picking up her pace, she jogged around Edinburgh airport and rounded the corner toward their terminal.

OOMPH!

She flew backward. Her head smacked the tiled floor followed by her bum and not-so-funny bone rapping. "Ugh," she said in a strained voice. As Brie blinked back the stars filling her line of sight, a towering shadow filled her view.

"*Och,* Jesus," a rich, thick voice uttered.

"No, I don't think I'm dead yet. Tell Jesus I'm not ready."

The shadow morphed into a man, who knelt beside her clad in a light-gray shirt, leather jacket, and boots. "Can *ye* stand?"

Brie lifted her head, and the world spun. "Just as soon as everything stops spinning." Closing her eyes, she attempted to suppress the whirlwind.

He muttered something.

"What was that?"

"I hope *ye* don't have a concussion."

"No, I can't." Slowly, she opened her eyes. "I'm on va-vacation. I want to see The *Buachaille* in be-beautiful Glencoe when the morning mist burns off. I've even practiced the pronunciation and a few other phrases like…face-ker ma."

"Ah, you're a witty one. *Feasgar math* to *ye*, as well. *Yer* pronunciation is near spot-on," the voice said in a deep brogue with rolling *r*'s and a hint of humor.

Brie peered upward. He had startling, crystal-blue eyes that pierced hers from under a gray hat, dark lashes, and a couple of days' worth of golden-copper stubble edging his square jaw and upper lip perfectly. A clean, fresh scent fanned toward her, and she found herself breathing him in while she dropped her gaze to his lips, which were full and slightly parted. A sudden flash of warmth spread through her body. She hadn't reacted like this in a long time. And here she was, sprawled out on the ground like a starfish stranded on the beach. At least, she wore her favorite lavender running leggings, a flattering V-neck, and a swipe of mascara, thanks to Andrea's nagging. She'd thank her later.

"How are *ye*? Feeling okay to sit up?"

"I think so." She cleared her throat and smoothed a hand through her hair when she noticed people rubbernecking at her clumsiness. She didn't want to make a scene, so she sat up. Luckily, stars no longer cascaded before her.

He glanced over his shoulder, settling a hard gaze at something behind them, then redirected those blue eyes. "Can I call someone for *ye*?"

"I-I'm traveling with a friend. She's, well, she's back at our terminal, I think." Brie rubbed the back of her head. "Unless she's found the man of her dreams and is galloping into the sunset."

With a twinkle in his eyes, he grinned. "Is that so? I was no' aware Prince Charming frequented the airport, but I'll have to keep an eye out myself. How do *ye* suppose he managed the horse?"

Brie cracked a smile. "I suppose he checked it along with his giddyap."

Chuckling, he scrubbed a hand over his pants-clad knees. "Can I get *ye* ice? I'm sure there's got to be some around here. It's the least I can do."

"No, I'm okay. Really." She smoothed a hand down her sweater and then noticed his outstretched hand. She slid a hand into his, feeling sparks burst in her palm and spread toward her fingertips. With a gulp, she allowed him to help her up with a bulging, muscled arm. "Thank you." At five-foot-six inches, she barely came up to his shoulders, and she had to lift her gaze to meet his. His eyes were so clear and blue they magnetized her. When her heart began to pound, she glanced down at his broad chest where a faint outline of pectorals was evident through his T-shirt. She flicked her gaze back up, noticing a slight sunburn reddening the arch of his nose, while auburn waves not only tucked beneath his hat, but also weaved behind his ears and stopped a few inches below. She itched to grasp a curl. But she'd just met him. What was she thinking?

****

Bryce stared into gypsy green eyes with flecks of amber, reminding him of the Scottish Highlands in spring. As the weather warmed and the snow melted, hills burst into color invigorating the dew-soaked grass with fierce potency, while the sun's rays etched golden blades like embers.

"Sorry for running into you."

Her smooth voice drew him out of his thoughts, and he cleared his throat. " 'Tis I who should be apologizing. Em, sorry, I don't believe I got *yer* name."

"Brielle, Brie."

"Brie." A smile tugged at the corners of his lips. "Bryce, pleasure to meet *ye*."

"You, too." She smoothed her blouse down. "Are you Scottish?"

"I em."

Her cheeks tinged a rosy pink.

"*Yer* American then?"

"Yes. From Los Angeles."

He'd only just returned from Los Angeles where fans identified him easily enough, swarming for selfies. The paparazzi snapped pictures during his every move, though they didn't find him in the hills—his sanctuary. He'd hiked past sandal-wearing enthusiasts until he disappeared up the trail where orange-and-yellow-flamed flora, brush, and pine welcomed him with natural, earthy aromas. At the top, he'd taken his own selfie. Yet, Brie didn't recognize him. *Ach*, it was a strike to his ego, for sure, but also alluring. Someone who didn't have preconceived notions about him, someone who was equally as mysterious as he.

Yet, when he noticed someone with a mobile ready a few meters away, he clenched his jaw. Brie could be a fake—a reporter undercover. Though the fact he ran into her made the idea improbable, but not impossible. He swiveled. "Well, Brie, enjoy your visit."

"Thank you." She smiled warmly. "Maybe we'll run into each other again."

Even with his guard drawn, Bryce couldn't help but grin in turn. "Aye, hope 'tis not as painful next time."

Brie laughed softly.

Something about her—something inviting and warm—drew him in, which surprised him since he'd guarded his heart after the last breakup. A chime of a cell phone sounded again and again, reminding him he needed to get moving.

She extended a hand. "It was nice to meet you,

Bryce. Painful, but nice."

With a chuckle, he grasped her soft, smooth hand. "And *ye*."

"Try not to knock anyone else over today."

He laughed full and strong. "No promises. The day's no' over yet."

Flashing a bonnie smile, she jogged away.

Bryce watched her sprint on long, toned legs leading to a nice, round bum. He rubbed his hands together where her touch lingered.

She slowed and glanced back one last time before rounding the corner.

He was caught, staring right back. Truth was, he'd seen her a split second before he'd run into her, or she him. He wasn't sure how it happened, but the encounter still left him reeling.

With her gone past his line of sight, he shook his head and pivoted toward baggage claim. He should've gotten her number, but he was getting too old for flings, and he had to be chary. He didn't date to date, especially after his latest disaster relationship bit him on the arse. Kathryn Bailey got what she was after—a leading role and an in, thanks to him. A common trope—one he'd seen in movies countless times; yet, he'd pursued her initially, hadn't he? What he hadn't expected was for her to release pictures cataloging their time together with stories on social media about the *Real Bryce Fraser*. Scottish he was, but a warrior, he was not. As much as he celebrated fans responding to his on-screen character, he steadfastly safeguarded his privacy along with his family's. His sister, brother-in-law, ma, niece, and nephew didn't deserve to be splashed in the limelight. And Kathryn knew that, didn't she? She was privy to the breach of privacy that happened years ago.

With a grunt, he tugged his hat down and sidestepped oncoming travelers toward baggage claim, but he wasn't quick enough. He collided with another traveler. With an apology, he strode forward, but not before he noticed a few travelers with phones pointed at him. Tightening his fists, he strode ahead. He still remembered the headlines, information from his private social accounts, and personal, family pictures.

When they were on the hunt, the press and fans were vicious. Bryce supposed he wasn't prepared for the sheer magnitude of *Swords of Scotland*. *Och*, he was aware of the book series' success that was adapted for television, but he didn't realize how devoted the fan base was. While shooting the first few episodes, he, the cast, and crew traipsed around the highlands with little-to-no invasion. Bryce was sure his countrymen wondered what they were doing running, as well as riding on horseback, in historically accurate kilts and red coat costumes, but they were welcomed. During the third episode shoot, however, a small group of fans arrived with homemade baked goods—a tasty, far cry from the wee catering budget when filming first began.

Soon, a group of fifty to a couple hundred fans, along with members of the press, followed them location-to-location. The attention swelled the pride he felt for his role and appreciation for the series, especially after his first few movies didn't reach much success. But as an unknown actor, he discovered the press and fans were keen to discover his secrets. *Did he have a girlfriend? What was he like in his youth?* He'd always been private, but then pictures and stories appeared from his private social accounts—those shared only with close family and friends, and most recently, his new girlfriend. The lass had been paid by the media to uncover information to which the UK magazine splashed around for months, and even still, republished now and again. He'd seen red. He wished he could grasp the claymore that had become an appendage on set.

Clenching his jaw, Bryce thought back to the second personal betrayal. He should've listened to his colleague who told him Kathryn was a fake from the start. He wouldn't have wasted the wee hours he had. He'd worked tooth and nail cultivating a career in television and movies and recently was offered a leading role in a new superhero franchise with an eight-figure salary to advance his career even further. He was elated, but he also wondered if that was the best career direction. He'd put his career first for near fifteen years and was thankful, but he longed for something more—something real. His run-in with the American caught him off guard. Brie was refreshing and witty, and she'd charmed him. Yet, she didn't recognize him.

As he sidestepped a group of travelers clad in shorts and sandals, he retrieved his bag and chuckled. They'd be visiting a *mor-stor* for jackets soon enough. When he caught a throng of cameras outside the airport, Bryce tugged his cap low and strode toward the arrival door. He'd take heed and keep an eye out for Brie... if he wasn't spotted first.

Chapter 3

Brie gazed out the window of the double-decker bus in Edinburgh. Even with the second-level seat, she tipped her head toward the tall, narrow buildings, gray brick, and high, pitched gothic-style towers as the bus rambled over cobblestone streets, and dank air snuck through the window panels mingling with leather. So much character existed compared to her hometown, which was established in the 1950s. Yes, she loved her one-story bungalow and the safe city she and her kids lived in, but Edinburgh had been built centuries ago.

The city held stories from families who'd lived years and years ago, roads driven and trotted upon by horses, carriages, and now cars, and a skyline rich with history. Edinburgh had a story. A long one. Brie wished she had that kind of life story—that kind of connection. She'd grown up fatherless, and though her mom surrounded her with love, she always desired to find out more about who she was and where her family came from. Surrounded by history, Brie's story was just beginning.

As the bus ventured farther, large, sage-green trees dotted her view along with white-and-black-faced as well as tan-and-brown houses, and stone buildings. Yet, through the trees, she spied a castle atop a hill overlooking the city. Under the shroud of a thick blanket of mist, the castle appeared as though it was carved out of the Middle Ages. *Incredible*. She leaned closer to the window, breath fogging the glass.

As they winded around the curving streets, she let her gaze devour the city before her. Dark buildings juxtaposed fresh bursts of vibrant navy, red, jade, and golden storefronts on the street level that flashed before her like a colorful magazine spread, while an upbeat piper's lively music filled her ears.

After checking in and entering the apartment-style hotel that would be their home for the next two days, Brie strode over to the expansive living room window. Her jaw dropped. From the window, Edinburgh Castle perched atop what she now recognized as a volcanic-style rock, while mossy green grass highlighted the stone and curvature of the giant rock below. "Oh, my God! Edinburgh Castle is outside our window. Check it out."

Andrea slung an arm around Brie's shoulders. "Yup. That's why I booked this place. Plus, free Wi-Fi."

Fifteen minutes later, Brie donned a beanie, coat, and ankle boots and headed out the door with Andrea to explore. Tomorrow, they'd venture to Edinburgh Castle and take a tour of the Royal Mile. This afternoon, they'd explore on foot. When she saw Andrea remove an Edinburgh Travel Companion book from her red tote, Brie stifled a laugh.

Snapping her head up, Andrea sent spiraling curls in motion. "What? We could still explore and see a few things." She glanced back at the travel book and slid a finger down a few inches. "There's a free Writers' Museum close by at the top of the Royal Mile. Built in the seventeenth century."

"Let's check it out."

They wound up dank, shadowed alleys where gray-black stone darkened from hundreds of years of weather, and the cloudy sky swirled above. Feeling as though she'd stepped back in time, Brie tugged her jacket closer, gaze fixed on the passageway.

Ten minutes later, they arrived at the base of a towering, historic stone building where a black-and-gold iron sign with a writer seated at a desk, quill in hand, informed them they arrived at *The Writers' Museum.*

"Cool place," Andrea said. "Creepy, but cool."

"I couldn't have said it better myself." Brie strolled through the opening into a small, dark corridor and climbed the narrow steps where bold blue and red splashed across the walls. At the top, she gazed at detailed oil paintings of famous Scottish writers including Robert Burns, Sir Walter Scott, and Robert Louis Stevenson. She felt like a creator amongst creators. Next, she examined original pieces of work displayed in glass cases along with artifacts from the authors—a walking cane, pipe, and more. She strolled, gaze alighting on each meticulously selected piece until she paused at a case with books. First edition copies lay open for the curious, and she leaned in, admiring the vintage typeface, delicate, curled pages, and ornate illustrations. Tingling ran up and down her arms. Her first book, her memoir, was almost complete. She might not be famous, but she was doing it; she was writing.

When she stopped at Burns' writing desk, she envisioned the famous author putting lovely words and brilliant ideas to page like she was doing. Burns had a rag-to-riches story—one of a ploughboy to beloved writer. Since she began writing again, Brie started dreaming of a day when she had more than a desk job—more time for her children and herself. During college, she dreamed of being a writer, but shortly after graduation she met Ryan, and within six months, they were engaged and, nine months later, married with a baby on the way. After only working at the boutique magazine for a little over a year post-graduation, she submitted her notice to become a stay-at-home wife and mom. She hadn't touched her leather notebooks with ideas and chapters of novel aspirations since marrying—they lay buried in her desk drawer beside her degrees. She didn't look back with regret, though— seeing her babies take their first steps, sharing special moments, and watching them grow—she relished that time. But now they were off to school, and she found herself dreaming again.

When Andrea sidled close, she leaned over. "Can you imagine seeing our books on bookshelves one day?"

Brie flashed a smile. "Yes, I can."

"Quite the writing legend, huh?" Andrea swirled a hand around.

"Yes." She eyed various books on the shelf, remembering reading Robert Louis Stevenson's *Treasure Island* as a young girl, adventuring with Jim Hawkins in search of the infamous pirate treasure. Here in Edinburgh, she was on a similar adventure, albeit without pirates, a boat, and well, not really in search of a treasure. Yet, her first adventure abroad had just begun. They had a few scheduled tours and books to guide them throughout the country on independent expeditions. She couldn't wait to see what discoveries she'd make and also jot down every incredible moment after they returned from their first, self-guided tour.

Half an hour later, they exited the museum and ventured into a gift shop where Brie purchased a T-shirt for Noah, a Scottish princess doll for Phoebe, a scarf for Mimi, and a knit beanie for herself. When they sauntered back out, they meandered down Victoria Street gazing at the pastel painted shopfronts.

"So, what else do you want to do today?" Andrea asked.

"I don't know." Brie lifted her shoulders. "I'm up for anything."

Andrea stopped and arched a brow. "Come on. This trip is for you. As much as I'd like to play tour guide, you need to have a say."

"I know, and I'm grateful."

"Grateful schmateful. What do you want to do?"

Brie glanced down the street. She wasn't used to having so much time to herself. She couldn't even remember the last full day she took off that didn't involve one of her children being home sick. But here and now, she wanted to explore, taste, and experience all Scotland had in store. When subtle salty and savory aromas wafted from an unknown source, she rubbed her growling stomach. Brie glanced back at Andrea who studied a gold-leaf-painted sign on a teal wall that stated it was Scotland's *most photographed street*. "All right. I want to try some local food and then relax somewhere beautiful."

"That's the spirit!" Andrea weaved an arm through Brie's and skipped. "Let's do it."

A few meters down Victoria Street, the salty, fried aroma grew stronger, wafting from an open door of a shop. "Fish and chips?"

"Heck yes. When in Scotland!"

A few minutes later, Brie bit into steaming, flaky fish and sighed. The creamy texture of the fish with the salty bite paired perfectly with the lively rock music playing in the background. "Yum."

"I'm going for a chip." Andrea dipped a chip into the famous dark chippy sauce. "Oh"—she danced a happy food jig in her seat—"it's tangy with a little spicy bite."

After their meal, they meandered up Victoria Street toward Princess Street Gardens. The sun snuck through the gray veil over the city, igniting the clover-green grass and gardens vibrantly, while warming her back. Brie breathed, inhaling floral and grassy notes and listening to the musical lilt of Scots mingled with high-pitched sounds of children running freely.

A mother strolled ahead, hand-in-hand with a little girl with swinging, blonde pigtails, while pushing a pram.

Watching the little girl talk exuberantly, Brie grinned, thinking about Phoebe's mile-a-minute chatter. She'd only left her a day ago, but she already missed holding Phoebe's hand.

When the little girl skipped in her petite sneakers and yelled a name, she danced in place as a man with dark hair jogged toward them. He skimmed a hand over the mother's shoulder before placing a quick kiss on her cheek and then slipped a hand in the little girl's petite one.

"Want to sit by the fountain?" Andrea asked.

Brie nodded, yet her gaze rested upon the beautiful picture before her. She'd spent the last year getting over

Ryan and moving on with her life, but she couldn't deny the tug and longing within. She always wanted a family, a whole family, yet Ryan destroyed that dream. Gazing at the sweet family before her, she realized what she wanted even after failed love was to love again.

****

"Whatyawantin'?" the bartender asked with a salt-and-pepper beard, solid line between his brow, and cobalt tweed cap.

"A beer. You know what?" Andrea leaned forward, lips curling. "Surprise me! We've traipsed around this gorgeous city, and my feet are spent. I need a drink and a massage."

"I'll see what ah can do." He shifted his gaze. "And ye?"

Brie snugged a hip against the counter. "Cider, please."

Nodding, the bartender grasped a glass with one hand where three varied, silver-and-black rings etched with mountains and Celtic designs encircled, and then gripped a wooden-handled tap with the other. The glass filled with a warm, amber-colored liquid. Placing the glass in front of Brie, he busied himself filling Andrea's surprise order.

"Thanks!" Brie lifted the cider to her lips. Instantly, crisp notes of apple and a hint of tart lemon mingled with spices on her tongue. As she sipped, she trailed her gaze over the mahogany bar with golden hues from shaded lights above, while numerous, jewel-toned alcohol bottles created a colorful backdrop. All around her singsong tunes mingled with rich laughter.

"What brings you lassies here tonight?" A young man sidled up. He was as tall as he was thin with a thatch of curly, black hair.

Flicking her head, Andrea sent riotous curls flying. "Vacation."

"Ah, Americans." He hauled a barstool over, while another young man appeared with sparse blond stubble on his cheeks and chin.

"Yes, but I have some Celtic heritage, though. My last name is Irish—Finlay," Brie clarified.

"No," a gravelly voice carried from across the bar. " 'Tis not Irish, lassie. Finlays might have traveled to Ireland a century or two ago, but Finlay is one of the ancient Pictish clans of Scotland."

Brie swiveled. "Really?" She didn't know much about her dad's side of the family other than they were Irish. Her paternal grandparents passed when she was young, and she'd spent many years wearing green, toasting on St. Patrick's Day, and even had a short-lived fling with a redhead in college whose parents were from Ireland, but that didn't connect her to her roots. "Are you a historian?"

"Aye, as a pastime." He rubbed the end of his dark beard, streaked with wiry gray, and then lifted a short glass filled with a dark substance.

Brie scooted closer. "How fascinating. I always wanted to join one of those ancestry databases and see where my family came from before settling in America." She shook her head. "I'm sorry, where are my manners? I'm Brielle, and this is my friend, Andrea."

He extended his wide hand peppered with age spots. "Murtaugh Mackay. Pleased to meet *ye*."

Andrea acknowledged him briefly, then focused on the much-too-young men who were grinning and pouring their Scottish charm thicker than the whisky glasses in their hands.

"Can you tell me more?" Brie asked.

"The surname Finlay was first found in Banffshire, which is now the Scottish county divided 'tween the Council Areas of Moray and Aberdeenshire. Finlay descended from the Chiefs of the Clan Farquharson, one of the great Clans."

"Wow," Brie said. Unfortunately, the only knowledge she had of clans stemmed from a historical movie about William Wallace. Although the historical Hollywood drama fascinated her, she remembered more of the sexy actor who played Robert the Bruce than clan history. "Are there still Finlays in Scotland?"

"Oh, aye. Many." He lifted his glass for another drink. "I know some Finlays and Farquharsons myself."

Tiny dancers trotted across her chest. Brie always thought her family came from Ireland originally, but she had Scottish blood, as well.

Andrea inched forward. "So, she's Scottish."

"No." He shook his head. "She's American like *ye*."

With a shrug, Andrea swirled around.

He grinned and sipped his whisky. "*Ye* ken the show *Swords of Scotland*?"

"Not really, but"—she angled her head toward Andrea—"Andrea does."

" 'Tis an American show woven with history and, of course, fiction, but I hear tell the Jacobite rising includes some historical figures."

"Really?" She propped a hand below her chin. Perhaps she should watch the show, after all.

Bobbing his head, Murtaugh's bushy brows jutted

up and down. "Oh aye. And the Farquharsons were very involved in the Jacobite rising—the cause to restore the House of Stewart to the British throne. And on April 16, 1746, they fought alongside the Camerons, Frasers, Mackenzies, Macleans, and many others."

"Wow, I love how rich your history is here. Where can I visit to learn more about Clan Farquharson?"

"Aye. Invercauld and Braemar Centre are the ancestral homes of the Clan Farquharson. *Ye* can even see some artifacts in Braemar Castle. All are open to the public."

Tingling ran down Brie's spine. She itched to visit and learn more about the Farquharson history and perhaps some of her own heritage. With a quick zip of a fiddle, music started in the background. She inched closer. "Are they nearby?"

He fanned a hand. "A couple of hours' drive from Edinburgh. The Farquharson estate also hosts the Braemar Highland Games in September."

"Ole Murtagh's correct," a man said suddenly beside her with thick, dark curls and even darker eyes. "But if *ye* wish to see a real Scot in action, I'll take *ye* for a spin on the dance floor."

Scooting herself closer to the bar, she shook her head. "Thank you, but I'm enjoying my current company. Maybe another time." When she spied Andrea talking to the much-too-young lads, she added, "But my friend"—waving a hand toward Andrea—"would love a dance."

As he looked over a shoulder, he swept his gaze up and down Andrea. A devious grin flashed across his face, and Mr. Tall-Dark-and-Handsome strolled over.

"Aye, off wit' *ye* dobber," Murtagh added.

Brie giggled. "Everyone sure is friendly here."

He kicked up a bushy brow. "What I dinnae ken is why *yer* spending *yer* night talking to me. I see *ye* have no ring. A bonnie lass like yourself should be dancing."

Brie turned, catching Andrea kick her head back and laugh at something the handsome Scot whispered in her ear before he tugged her onto the dance floor. "I'd love to dance, but I'm"—she began and glanced at her ring-less hand where a sparkling solitaire encrusted with diamonds and a gold band used to rest—"I'm working on my own story."

"I can understand fine what *yer* telling me." He bobbed his head. "Just remember stories are meant to take unanticipated turns, and sometimes the people *ye* meet along *yer* travels are meant to be a part of *yer* story, *ye* ken?"

Brie smiled. "Like you."

He laughed. "Aye." Murtaugh lifted his glass. "*Slainte Mhath*."

"*Slainte...Mhath*." Brie raised her glass. He'd mentioned the Highland Games in Braemar were hosted by the Farquharson clan, and to be around people who might be distantly related to her sounded appealing. Brie grew up with her mom and maternal grandparents, but they were her only family besides an uncle she saw once a year. Her dad and his ancestry were as foreign to her as Scotland itself. She yearned to know more.

****

After splashing through the pouring rain running back to the hotel, Brie helped a stumbling, giggling Andrea into the room opposite hers.

"We can't go to bed." Andrea held up her phone, showing numerous notifications on social media. "Fans saw…Alexander…in Edinburgh at some…some," she slurred.

Brie kissed Andrea's forehead, then plucked the phone from her hand and plugged the device into a charger. "Well, if he's in Edinburgh, maybe we'll see him tomorrow."

In response, Andrea swan-dived into bed and muffled sweet-nothings into a fluffy pillow.

Brie peeled Andrea's jacket off and unzipped her heeled boots, then tucked her in. After a warm shower, she retrieved her notebook. Her plan was to end her memoir on the last day of vacation, but for now, she needed to write about her first day.

April 25

I'm in Scotland.

So far, I've crossed the Atlantic, aka "the pond" according to locals, ran into—literally collided with—a hunky Scotsman in the airport who stirred something in me, and…who am I kidding? I was attracted and completely arrested by his sincerity, sexy brogue, clear blue eyes, and scruff over his square jaw. I didn't even think I was ready to meet someone and then bam!

I doubt I'll see him again, but he was wonderful.

After settling into our hotel, Andrea and I strolled through the streets of Edinburgh, including Old Towne where I spent a few hours in the presence of writing geniuses, ate my first fish and chips, promenaded through Princess Street Gardens, and met a few locals at a bar, including a local historian who taught me about my last name's history.

When I got married, I took my husband's last name—what most women do. Though unlike most women, I didn't have a middle name. Instead, I added my maiden name. Brielle Finlay Hunter. Finlay. A name that stemmed from great clan chiefs of Scotland. Who knew?

Looking around the bar earlier, I wondered if my dad resembled the locals. But then again, the pictures I'd seen were black-and-white or discolored from age, though cherished for years by Mom and me. Then I thought about my son, Noah, and how much I'd always believed he looked like Ryan, but as I recalled the last picture taken of my father on our entry table, I remembered him standing in his army greens and couldn't believe I hadn't seen it sooner. Noah had Ryan's dark-blue eyes and stubborn nose, but he also resembled my father with soft, wavy hair and a wide, genuine smile. And that tiny bit of information gave me more of a connection to myself and discovering who Brielle Finlay Hunter is.

Chapter 4

The following day, Brie laced her running shoes up, feeling the smooth cords between her fingers and tied the final knot. She crept through the hotel room, careful not to wake Andrea, and silently escaped into the brisk morning.

Breathing in the cool air, she relished the feeling of freedom and eased into a jog. According to Andrea's Scottish Travel Guide, down the road was a trail. Eager to get back into nature, Brie pumped her arms and legs, gliding past empty restaurants and storefronts with metal screens and past a little café where two older gentlemen sat with caps and canes leaning against a table over conversation.

"Storm's comin'," one uttered.

Brie laughed. Of course, a storm was coming. She could even smell it—the subtle moisture in the air and dank pavement. She waved and continued. Turning down a narrow bend, she ran onto a road that encircled Holyrood Park. The cool air nipped at her shoulders and chest, and her breath puffed in front of her in ethereal, white flurries. Low clouds and fog rested on the towering rock hill—Arthur's Seat—as if hiding a secret from King Arthur himself.

She dashed around the shoulder, happy to run freely without crowds of tourists and just the road ahead. Although she ran a couple of days a week during her lunch breaks, she'd been busy with work the last few weeks, getting proposals out early in preparation for her trip, and she desperately needed to feel the freedom beneath her feet. She lengthened her stride and ran faster. A SUV drove past, as well as a boxed truck, but they didn't disturb her. Spying an opening to a dirt trail, she pivoted and ran up the brief incline past royal-yellow and forest-green shrubs.

Forty-five minutes later, a droplet of water hit her forehead, then another until fat raindrops consistently tapped her head and shoulders and blurred the curving path. At least, she had sense enough to put a long sleeve on. Within minutes, Brie was soaked through, and she hadn't even remembered her cell phone. She was so excited to get out of the hotel with no attachments and no responsibilities that she'd been irresponsible—something she never would have been at home. *Well, that's the point of a vacation without kids, right?* Plus, she'd talked to them at bedtime just shy of three a.m. local Scottish time this morning, half asleep, after rousing a few minutes prior to the call with the phantom cries of her children echoing in her ear. After the call, she'd lain in bed for another hour before finally falling back asleep for thirty minutes and then decided to run.

Trudging to the hotel through the dense rain and now muddy trail, she crossed her arms against her chest in an attempt to keep her core warm. She'd catch pneumonia. Not even twenty-four hours in Scotland, and she would be holed up in her hotel room with a fever. At home, when the weatherwoman's special report of *Southern California Storm Watch 2024* announced over her radio, she'd giggle at her hometown's hyperbolic view of rain, but she'd still layer her children with sweats, long sleeves, beanies, then raincoats, rainboots, and umbrellas, while she donned a jacket and grabbed her larger-than-life umbrella to watch them play in puddles.

Noah would be running in his booted feet, splashing water up his sweatpanted legs, laughing, while her little adventurer daughter would follow right behind him with her unicorn rain coat and matching boots. But that's what they're supposed to do at three and six. *Play.* Especially when they're dealing with a dad who misses planned visits, scheduled baseball games, and play dates.

Squishing her running shoes in the muddy path with thick rain piercing her to the bone, she longed for a warm embrace from her children. As much as she enjoyed her solitude thus far, out here in the cold, wet foreign environment, she longed for their sweet faces and warm snuggles.

Following the roadway back to Edinburgh, Brie felt her teeth rattle incessantly. They clinked in her head like a typewriter's keys hitting paper. Her body trembled and shook. So much for a relaxing run. Now she'd be in bed with soup. A swift flash of lights flickered on the road in front of her. Someone smarter was driving in a car, rather than trudging ahead in this God-awful rain. The swoosh of tires had her quickly turning her head.

A dark SUV slowed.

Brie inched closer to the grass edge and quickened her pace. Although it was early in the morning, the rain darkened the lush landscape. Even the scant glow of streetlights in the distance didn't aid her plight with the pouring rain blurring the yellow radiance.

"E'scuse me?" a voice said.

As her heart rapped in her ribcage, Brie pressed forward, sludging through the mud.

Tires squeaked to a halt.

Unease crept up her spine.

"Can I give *ye* a lift?" a voice bellowed.

Brie shook her head. The last thing she needed was to get into a car with a strange man with who knew what kind of intentions. "I-I'm f-fine," she choked out. Damn her chattering teeth for betraying her words.

"Are *ye* sure? 'Tis miserable out here."

She stopped for a moment to catch her breath and peered through the rain at the driver. He'd turned the interior light on. Bright-blue eyes shined from below a cobalt cap and red curls winged around his ears. He looked…strangely familiar.

A smile turned up on one end of his mouth and then the other. " 'Tis *ye*!"

Brie raked a hand over sopping wet hair. The long, braided tail snapped water across her already soaked shirt. *Great.* "Bryce, right?"

"Yeah, I'm all for a run, but the devil himself wouldna run in such weather." He laughed. "Can I give *ye* a lift?"

Brie glanced ahead. The lights of Edinburgh barely dotted her view like stars encased by a storm. She could either freeze for a few more miles or take a leap of faith. "I don't make a habit of getting into vehicles with men I've barely met."

"Aye." He bobbed his head. "I can understand that. My intentions are purely innocent."

She gazed through the spotty rain. The warm glimmer of the interior light set his face aglow and highlighted a golden cross that dangled and sparkled from the rearview mirror. Brie hadn't had much luck with men in the past, Ryan included. Yet, Bryce had a warm smile and kind eyes. "All right then."

"*Ye've* got to be freezin' all *drookit*."

She entered and adjusted the heater, directing warm air toward her. To prevent her teeth from chattering, she nodded numbly, but her lips still trembled. Suddenly, warmth seeped into her body as if she were wrapped in a cozy blanket fresh from the dryer. *Oh. My. God. Heated seats.*

When she noticed Bryce adjust, then reach an arm behind her, Brie stiffened. She hoped she hadn't made the worst decision of her life by getting into an SUV with a man she'd literally run into. She was a mom with responsibilities. She braced herself.

A moment later, he draped a jacket lined with soft cotton over her shoulders. "Here. This should help warm *ye* further."

"Oh." Brie released a breath and lifted a hand. "I'll ruin it."

"With water?" He chuckled. "*Yer* fine. My jacket is no' likely to get a cold, but *ye* are."

She smiled and snuggled into his jacket, which smelled subtly masculine and warm with a husky cologne. "Thank you."

"My pleasure."

"I should've grabbed my jacket before I headed out, but the sun had risen a bit, and this is a thermal." She pinched her soaked sleeve.

Bryce laughed. "*Ye* know *yer* in Scotland, right?"

"Yes." Brie grinned.

"The weather's *dreich* and changes rapidly. We

have a saying in Scotland—four seasons in a day, depending on where *ye* travel. 'Tis all about layering. Where are *ye* staying?"

"At the apartment hotel near Edinburgh Castle."

With a nod, he drove slowly, checking his rearview mirror. "I know it well. Have *ye* had a chance to see the castle then? Scotland's rich with history."

"It is! Practically a castle around every corner I hear, but we haven't visited one yet. We…my friend—the one who was chasing her Knight in Shining Kilt when we first met—and I are taking a tour of Edinburgh Castle today, then walking the Royal Mile. Tomorrow, we'll hop on a boat tour."

He adjusted his hands on the steering wheel. "Sounds like *ye've* got it all planned out."

"Yes. I'm excited for some more Scottish adventure, although Andrea isn't quite as excited for all the extra walking. She's more of the drink-at-a-bar, spa type, but she's up for it."

He chuckled. "That's grand. So, *yer* an adventurer then?"

"Yes, well, um not, uh," she began and told herself to stop jibber-jabbering. He was handsome, but she could still speak, for goodness sakes. "I am right now."

"I've a fondness for travel myself, though I haven't taken a vacation for pleasure in some time."

Brie smiled, yet at the same time, she spied two, tall coffees in the center cupholders. Although she'd rather swim in the hot, dark liquid right about now, she wondered if the second coffee was for his wife or girlfriend.

When Bryce stopped at a light, he followed her gaze to the coffees. "*Yer* welcome to one. It'd warm *ye* from the inside out."

"I wouldn't want"—she cleared her throat—"to take someone else's coffee."

"*Och*, 'tis for my colleague. She'll be fine. We've coffee on…in the, em, coffee room."

She shrugged and silently thanked him and his colleague. With the first lovely, hot sip, she sighed. "I hope I'm not making you late for work."

Bryce's eyes sparkled from the glow of the streetlights, igniting them like the ocean glistening in the first few rays of the morning light. "No," he said with a deep brogue. "I'm always early. Besides, what kind of gentleman would I be if I left a lass out in the cold?"

Quirking a brow, she stared at the surprising Scotsman. When was the last time she bantered with a handsome guy? She thought back to her college days before Ryan when one of her study partners joked from across the library table. He had sandy-brown hair, and he liked her—at least, that's what Brie's other study partner told her—but Brie hadn't believed her. Glancing at Bryce, she smiled. "Well, I suppose not one at all, although I was under the impression gentleman didn't exist anymore."

Pausing at another light, he glanced toward her, gaze set. "Not if I have anything to say about it."

A quick thrill traveled up her body. Were all Scotsmen like Bryce?

"Besides, what do *ye* call this?" He swept a hand around. "I very keenly rescued *ye* from the downpour in my trusty steed here."

Brie lifted a brow. "You could've been an ax murderer or a drive-by killer. You and your SUV."

"*Och*." He palmed a hand to his heart. "Now, all I'm good for in a four-by-four is murder, eh? I'll have to upgrade my vehicle."

She laughed and waved a hand. "No—no, that's not what I meant. It's just…I was in the rain, alone, and you pulled alongside me…"

With an upturn of his lips, Bryce's eyes shone. "I understand *ye* well, Brielle. 'Tis a plausible beginning for a movie." Arriving at the hotel, he swiveled toward her.

Brie was torn. She needed to slip into dry clothes, but she longed to stay in the car with Bryce. "Thank you again. I don't know how I can repay you." She removed his coat, whilst adjusting in her seat. A great wet spot appeared on the leather seat. "Oh! I've ruined your seat."

"It'll dry. Don't *ye* worry."

"Can I pay to have it cleaned? It's the least I can do after you helped me."

He tilted his head. "How about dinner?"

Gasping, she widened her eyes. "Dinner?"

"Sure, *yer* not leaving back to America today, are *ye*?"

"No," Brie said. "I have another week and a half."

"Might I have the pleasure of *yer* company this evening? Say six?"

"Yes, I'd love to." Catching herself in the mirror, although she expected herself to look worse for wear after getting caught in a downpour, the rain softened her French braid. Now, along with a few waves framing her face, her cheeks glowed, thanks in part to Bryce.

After exchanging numbers, Bryce strode around the SUV and opened her door with an umbrella in hand.

Her insides pooled like the water at her feet. "Thank you again." She lifted a hand to the wet doorframe, fingers gliding gently across his. Sparks ignited under her cool hands. "See you tonight."

"Tonight."

With one last glance at Bryce, she fled into the hotel. Once she was inside, she breathed, steadying her racing heart. She just gave her number to a man she met twice. Would he really call?

****

Bryce drove toward the studio in a lighter mood. He'd seen Brie on his drive to the gym around Queens Drive, and he'd appreciated the way she moved—focused, poised, and dressed in form-fitting, pink-striped runners and matching pink jumper, showing well-cut legs traveling in perfect cadence. Of course, he didn't know the bonnie figure was her. But he was glad he'd chosen that particular route. Sure, the course wasn't his typical one, but after visiting L.A., he needed to immerse himself in his home country. With dramatic hills, steep crags, and rugged landscape, the park gave him a feeling of the Highlands.

When he noticed a female runner propel forward around a bend, Bryce leaned over to catch one last glimpse and nearly ran into the back of a lorry. Slamming his brakes, Bryce felt the four-by-four lurch to a jolting stop. If he'd gotten in another accident, then Eleana would be in stitches yet again, especially after their last visit to Los Angeles and his incident driving downtown. What could he say? He didn't get his license until his mid-twenties, and he either had a driver in Scotland or took the train. But when in L.A…

Then, he'd caught Brie's slim form on her way

back. *Christ almighty.* He couldn't believe it. Alone in the pouring rain. He couldn't just leave her.

Bryce recalled rescuing his own sister a handful of times growing up, especially after one of her so-called "incidents." The lorry couldn't just fall into a ditch. Her albeit brilliant mind juxtaposed her poor driving skills. Luckily, he and his mates could push the lorry out most days to avoid a steep tow fee.

Och, his character even notoriously rescued Lady Charlotte on set, though Eleana would often burst into a fit of giggles after the daring rescue was finally accomplished. Of course, acting was different than real life. After discovering Brie beautifully drenched, he knew she couldn't be a fake. He'd taken a risk, and he was glad he did.

Arriving at Heather Studios, he swung the door wide and strolled in with one fewer coffee. He chuckled. Eleana would have his hide. He'd blame it on the lorry.

Chapter 5

Brie burst into the hotel room, cheeks warm, even as the cold dampness of her running outfit penetrated her bones.

Andrea paused, fork midway to her mouth with a golden waffle. "Whoa, the rain won, huh?"

Sighing, Brie strolled in, stopping at the small dining area. "I saw him."

"Who?"

To keep herself from smiling too big, Brie bit her lip.

"Wait?" Andrea dropped her fork with a *clatter*. "Not Sexy Scottish Mystery Man?"

"Yes!" She told Andrea about her short run, the downpour, and her knight in shining four-by-four. She still couldn't believe it.

"Oh, my God." She threw her hands up. "It's like a movie!"

Brie laughed and toweled her hair. "I told him the same, but my version didn't end with a romantic date in mind...more like a horror film."

"Ha, classic. Where are you going?"

"I'm not sure." She set the towel down. "He said he'd pick me up at six."

Andrea rubbed her hands together. "A surprise, huh? Kudos to the sexy, mysterious Scotsman. We'll need to get some pampering done, especially after that horrendous run."

"Definitely! And with that sentiment, I'm jumping into the shower." Brie stripped down to her sports bra and leggings, then tossed the wet clothes in the bathtub.

"So, what will you wear?" Andrea hollered.

Strolling to the closet where clothes hung in color coordination, she gazed at the soft, sage-green dress. "The green sweater dress you bought me for my birthday. It's perfect with the nude heels."

"For sure. And, of course, don't forget what goes underneath." Andrea popped a head in the closet and wiggled her brows. "Lacy underwear for later."

Heat filled her cheeks. "Oh, you!"

"Come on. You know you've thought about it."

Brie skimmed her fingers down the velvety fabric, her chest fluttering with nerves. Did Bryce see her like that—sexy and desirable? Sure, she was drenched when he picked her up, but he also asked her out. Still, she hadn't been intimate with a man in some time…she didn't even know if she'd actually go through with it if the invitation arose. Yet, she still wondered what he'd be like as a partner and lover. She laid a hand over her rapidly beating heart.

First things first: she was going on her first, first date as a single mother. But Bryce didn't know that yet.

****

After getting their nails done, Brie and Andrea lunched at a craft brewery with big-bite burgers and chips with a yeasty, fruity aroma in the air. Walking the Royal Mile later today, they'd burn off those calories easily. At least, Brie told herself so. "Edinburgh Castle and Royal Mile. Ready?" She slipped on her jacket.

"You bet." Andrea lugged her bottom-heavy purse

off the seat, then peered out the window. "Though I think it's going to rain again."

"Oh aye, it should," their server acknowledged. Swirls of red, black, and sage-green tattoos tangled from his arm to his hand. "Be sure to grab a brolly if ye don't have one."

"A brolly?" Brie asked.

He grinned. "An umbrella."

With a glance out the window, she noted the fluffy white clouds dotting her view. "Thanks. I guess we'll buy one, but it looks beautiful right now."

Andrea cocked a brow. "Didn't you just get caught in the rain?"

"Yes." Brie smiled wide. "And what a lovely time it was."

Andrea snorted.

They purchased compact umbrellas at a small tourist shop, then strode up a cobblestone road toward the castle. Yet, as Brie climbed, Edinburgh Castle grew grander and vaster with every step as the castle walls and other structures towered into view. Sure, she gazed at the large castle on the rock, known as Castle Rock from her hotel window, but the formidable structure was even more impressive as she hiked up the gray, cobbled road.

Striding up the wide, circular path, she noted multiple stone buildings comprised the exterior three-or-four stories high with small, crisscrossed windows and towers facing the city below. An arched entry with a sharp-toothed iron gate loomed overhead, while a fire engine's sirens carried up from the city, mixing with chatter from tourists. The juxtaposition was incredible. She was standing at the entry of a twelfth-century castle; yet tourists with selfie sticks stood beside her. She'd never set foot somewhere so full of history. She swallowed thickly.

After purchasing a ticket, they climbed up a steep flight of steps, boots smacking the concrete, toward the summit. At the top, a street post pointed toward destinations including *St Margaret's Chapel, David's Tower, Town Square*, and more. They meandered toward a large, black cannon pointing toward the colorful city.

"*Mons Meg*," Andrea read. "Wow, she's five-hundred years old!"

"Holy smoke." Brie peered at the inscription. "I love that they use a female pronoun. Meg was a strong, powerful lady! Imagine her defending the castle, keeping oncoming invaders at bay."

Since her divorce, Brie had grasped the strength of other women including Andrea, Mimi, and authors and memoirists. In particular, the strength of female memoirists stood out. By telling their stories they helped not only her, but other readers and inspired them to trust themselves again, as well as to live in the moment and be their best self as a mom and beyond. During her divorce, she grasped these stories like an anchor, while discovering her own voice. Like these women, like Meg, she discovered her own strength.

With one last glance at Meg, she strolled alongside Andrea toward a tiny, arched doorway formed by large stones into St. Margaret's Chapel—the oldest building in the castle—where bold, colorful stained glass lit the dark passageways with a kaleidoscope of colors. Farther inside, small sconces warmed creamy walls of the tunneled passage leading to an altar room. From the chapel, they hiked up dense, steep steps toward the battery sight where other large cannons protruded through holes in the castle wall. The stone—etched with hundreds of years of dirt—looked like a patchwork quilt of history with nooks and crannies of various shades of gray and black clay. But what was beyond the battery sight was worth stopping for—the views across the capitol city. From high above, she saw Edinburgh and the mix of historical and new architecture encircled by rows of forest-green and sage trees. Near the center, tiny people circled the mound of Arthur's Seat where she'd been running a few hours earlier. But Brie had seen more than the scenic landscape; she'd seen Bryce. And he was charming, sexy, and chivalrous.

As a light breeze ruffled her hair, she tucked her beanie over the light brown strands and snuggled into her coat. The breeze blew around her and snaked toward the castle like magic, while a brilliant-blue patch of sky appeared above. The sparkling cerulean reminded her of Bryce and his crystal-blue eyes. She wondered what he was doing at this very moment and if he was thinking about her, as well.

Climbing up a winding staircase, Brie viewed the Scottish Crown Jewels, passing a room with exquisite painting exhibitions and life-sized mannequins portraying the crowning of King James IV and more. Afterward, they toured the royal apartments, admiring the detail of the ceilings and antiques. Exiting, Brie heard her phone shrill and Mimi's name flashed across the screen with a Face request. "Hi, Mimi! Hi, kiddos!" Brie waved. "Guess where we are? A castle!"

"Really?" Noah asked.

Phoebe squished her face into the frame. "Is there a

princess?"

"I'm sure there is, sweet pea. A beautiful princess with a long, lovely gown and brown hair."

"Like me!" Phoebe danced in purple, princess-dress-style pajamas.

Brie giggled. "Yes, like you."

"What about a dragon?" Noah's gaze swept around her.

"Nope, haven't seen a dragon yet, but I'll keep my eyes peeled. We did see this ginormous cannon though and a knight's sword and crown jewels."

Noah's lips formed into a pout. "I wish we could come."

Brie slid her gaze toward Andrea who snapped pictures. Guilt settled in her stomach and tangled. Yet as she watched a family of four breeze past, she swallowed the guilt and flashed a smile. "We'll take a family vacation here one day, I promise." She'd work hard to ensure her children could experience other cultures and learn about the history of the world, including some of their own ancestral history. "What are your plans today?"

As her children told her about their plan to go to the beach, their voices heightened with excitement. They told her about the sandcastles they planned to build and how Phoebe wanted to search for mermaids, while Noah was eager to find a crab.

Brie smiled.

"Enjoy yourself sweetheart."

"Thanks, Mimi. You, too. Have fun, kiddos!" Continuing the tour, Brie and Andrea strolled toward the Royal Scots Museum. A statue of a Scottish piper in full garb stood in the entry, leading to the museum with armor, history, and miniature battle reenactments. She stared at the small soldiers. As she scanned the battle-ground with redcoats pointing bayonets at the Scottish across the field, and others sprawled on the ground, she thought of her dad. He never returned from the Gulf War, dying at the young age of nineteen.

Before Brie was born, he bravely enlisted to give her and her mom a better life, but then, he tragically died six months later. She never even got a chance to know him. War. Battles. Struggles between countries and people. Regardless of the time period, war altered families and separated loved ones.

Her parents' love story ended too early, and Brie's ended a little over a year ago. But her parents had love…

****

As they exited the Governor's house toward the Royal Mile, she felt a quick, cold wind swirl and stir the dark clouds above. Moments later, rain *drip-dropped* on Brie's head. She opened the umbrella, which helped at first, but as the rain dragged on, her socks squished in her cheap ankle boots. She should've known the knock-off, ten-dollar shoes weren't a good fit for Scotland, but she didn't realize the seams would allow water in. They were getting tossed in the hotel trash as soon as she returned. Tomorrow, she'd venture out with Andrea to purchase some real boots.

When her phone chimed, she retrieved the device from her purse. Bryce's name etched across the screen, sending tingles of excitement over her rain-soaked skin. "He texted me!"

—*How're ye enjoying Edinburgh Castle?*—

Beside her, Andrea gestured toward the phone.

"Well, text him back!"

Brie flew her fingers over the keypad, dashing a text.

—*Great! But you need to tell your country to stop soaking me.*—

Bumped in the back by another tourist, Brie lost her grip, and her phone flew. "Oh, no!" She lunged forward, dropping her purse, but caught the phone before it landed in a million pieces on the cobblestone.

With a growl, Andrea snatched Brie's purse. "Excuse you!"

The tourist, clad in a larger-than-life black trench coat, continued trudging ahead.

Brie glanced at her phone where the bubble icon reappeared.

—*A* dreich *day. Got stuck in the rain again, did* ye?—

—*Yes, but I'm having a great time. How are you?*—

She followed Andrea into a tourist shop and tucked inside behind a cluster of tourists in raincoats. A rainbow of postcards, magnets, and a variety of colorful and bold plaids greeted her. While waiting for a response from Bryce, she scanned the postcards. A magical snapshot of vivid green mountains arching over glistening lochs under a bright-blue sky caught her eye. Selecting the notecard, she noted the location: Quiraing, The Isle of Skye. When she heard the chime of her cell, she set the card down and seized the device.

—*Fantastic. My schedule changed. I hope* ye *don't mind pushing dinner, say 8?*—

—*Sounds great! See you then.*—

"Brie! Check this out." Andrea wrapped a plaid

around her. "Just like the show! Alexander Mackenzie wears a kilt this color, and Lady Charlotte has a matching shawl."

She brushed her fingertips across the soft fabric. "It's really beautiful." The bold-blue and forest-green threads wove together like a tight-knit family. She loved the plaid represented belonging, and a husband and wife could wear matching items. It was similar to color-coordinating for a wedding to show the world you belonged to one another and so romantic. She wondered what kind of plaid Bryce wore.

With the fabric wrapped around, Andrea angled her head. "How's the Scottish hunk?" she asked. "I can't believe you've seen him twice, and I don't even know what he looks like."

Brie laughed. "Good. He said *hi*, and that he needed to change our dinner date to eight."

Humming a response, Andrea headed toward a large, local jewelry selection with Brie close behind. Stone-and-glass necklaces and bracelets, as well as silver-and-gold dangles were displayed in a cascading waterfall display.

"His eyes are as blue as"—she gazed at the colorful variety and grasped a necklace—"this stone, but clearer like the ocean shining on a sunny day."

Andrea smiled. "Oh, oh really? And I suppose the rest of him is put together, as well?"

She thought back to his chiseled cheekbones, strong chin, and wide shoulders, and a little dancer twirled in her stomach "Yes."

"Ugh. I knew it!" With a chuckle, Andrea cupped Brie's elbow, pointing to a tri-leaf earring set of aquamarine, gold, and copper. "These are SO you. You should get them."

Lifting the set to her ears, she noted the way the emerald green complimented her eyes. When she flipped over the set to peek at the price tag, she sighed. "They are lovely, but a little pricey."

"Buy them, Brie. You never get anything for yourself. If you don't, I'll buy them for you."

She held the delicate earrings in her palm. They were exquisite. If she couldn't indulge now, when would she? Five minutes later, she left with the earrings, while Andrea purchased a *Swords of Scotland* scarf, a hat, and spring-green bangle. And much to her pleasant surprise, the rain had stopped. At least for now.

As they perused shops and buildings along the Royal Mile, Brie's stomach growled. The time was near four p.m., and they hadn't even snacked. At home, her kids lived for snacks, and so, she supposed did she as she usually joined them with sliced apples and peanut butter, smoothies, etc.

Spotting a pie shop, they popped in to taste more local food. Upon entering, she inhaled delicious notes of rich, buttery and savory aromas.

A throng of people stood in line to order, while others crowded around small bistro tables lining the inner edges of the quaint shop.

Spying a black-and-white menu with thick, block lettering, Brie perused the hearty list naming pie variations from classic sweet pies such as cherry, apple, and blackcurrant to *haggis*, steak and ale, chicken and vegetable, cheese and onion, and more. When the line thinned, she admired the shining glass cases filled with thick, circle pies. "There are so many choices."

"Are *ye* visiting?" A tall man stood behind the

counter with a white apron and dark curls.

"We are indeed," Andrea purred.

"Well then, welcome." He flashed a smile that highlighted a dimple on one cheek. "I highly recommend the traditional pasty."

"Okay," Brie replied. "I'll have the traditional pasty and the mushroom."

"Traditional and the cheese-and-onion pie, please." Andrea pointed to the pies. "Hell, we earned this feast! I'm wet, tired, and hungry."

A few minutes later, Brie bit into the savory, traditional pasty with a satisfying crunch. The rustic filling was a perfect end to their time jump back into history today. And in just a few, short hours, she would be jumping back into dating.

****

Bryce scrolled through products from a local shop on his phone. He searched and clicked open a few pages until he found the item in the color he sought. A grin spread, tugging his cheeks. Sure, flowers were standard for a date, but why be predictable?

"Bryce, how are *ye*?" the familiar store director greeted.

"Good, good, thanks. I need a favor, mate." Bryce filled him in on his request, noting the delivery location. Being a model for the line, he had a little pull.

After placing the order, he headed toward the meeting room, ready to dive into the script straight away. With one last thought of those piercing, glassy-green eyes and curled eyelashes dewy with rain, he opened the door.

A cacophony of voices muddled together with a variety of accents, and a pit formed in his gut.

Chapter 6

Later in the evening, Brie soaked in the warm, bubbly tub, basking in bubbles and trying to calm her pre-date nerves. After the bath, she lathered herself in the hotel-provided sea kelp lotion and snuggled into a soft, white cotton robe.

Knock-knock.

Brie peeked out of the bathroom. "Did you order dinner?"

"Nope." Andrea sprang from the bed and strode toward the door.

She tucked inside the doorframe out of eyesight, though she didn't recall giving Bryce her room number. "He better not be early."

"A delivery for Ms. Brielle from Los Angeles."

Intrigued, she tightened her robe and peeked around the door Andrea held half-open. "I'm Brielle."

A well-dressed man from the hotel stood in a black-and-white uniform holding a square package with plaid-and-gold ribbon.

She accepted the box and glanced at Andrea. "Did you send this?"

Andrea shook her head. "Don't look at me. Is there a note?"

Retrieving a small, white envelope, Brie opened the flap, and finding a hand-written note, she read.

Brie,

Proper wellies from Scotland to keep those American feet dry.

Bryce

Brie smirked. "Wellies?"

The hotel attendant smiled shyly.

Setting the box down, she untied the silky ribbon, while bubbles of excitement bounced around her insides. Lifting the lid, she squealed. "Oh!" Shiny, clover-green rain boots nestled in white tissue paper.

"He got you rain boots?" Andrea asked. "That's so cute!"

She grinned. The gesture was adorable, and her feet would stay dry. She slipped them on and wiggled her toes. They were a tad spacious, but thick socks might help.

The gentleman stood in the hallway.

"Oh, I'm sorry. You need a..." Brie pivoted to retrieve her wallet.

"Do they fit, Mum?" he asked.

Brie inclined her head. "Excuse me?"

"How's the fit?"

"They're a little roomy, but they'll fit once I put thicker socks on, I think." She tapped her heels, trying to convince him he wouldn't need to deliver bad news to Bryce.

Clearing his throat, he twisted and produced another box with a smaller size.

"The man thinks of everything," Andrea mused. With hands on hips, she peeked around the doorjamb. "Got another pair in eight-and-a-half?"

"No, em, sorry, miss."

Andrea harrumphed.

Brie quickly tugged the first pair off, grabbed a

pair of socks, and slipped the second pair on. Her feet fit snuggly inside. "Perfect."

"Enjoy, miss." He nodded briefly and rotated.

"Wait!" she called. "Your tip."

He turned with a warm smile. "There's no need, miss. I've been taken care of already."

As the door closed, she wondered who exactly she was going on a date with tonight. Fifteen minutes later, Brie smoothed her dress and peered at her reflection. "Why are you so nervous?"

Andrea appeared in the bathroom doorway. "Here." She extended a hand with the new green bangle.

"Really?"

"It matches the outfit perfectly." She grasped Brie's wrist lightly and slipped the piece on.

Brie exhaled. "Thank you. I don't know why I'm so nervous."

Andrea tilted her head. "Yes, you do."

"Okay, I do." Brie threw her hands up, jingling the bangle. "My last date was nearly a decade ago. Am I ready to go on a date? To get back out there?"

Andrea captured Brie's hands in hers and squeezed firmly. "Hell yes, you are! You deserve to have some fun and go out with a man you obviously find attractive."

"It's just been a long time."

"*Pshh* like riding a bike. If he doesn't fall head over heels, then he's crazy because you"—Andrea twirled her around—"are stunning."

Brie giggled. When her phone rang at seven-thirty p.m. with an unfamiliar number, she pressed a hand to the butterflies flittering in her stomach. "He's early," she said to Andrea, then answered. "Hello?"

"Brie, it's Bryce. My…em, meeting is running late. I'm sorry, but I have to cancel."

"Oh." She tugged her dress down with the sting of disappointment. She should've known better. "That's all—"

"Can I make it up to *ye* with breakfast?" he asked quickly.

Her lips curled. "I like breakfast."

"Great, text me the time that works best, and I'll be there."

Brie exhaled. "Okay, and Bryce?"

"Aye?"

Glancing at the shiny green boots perched by the entry, she smiled. "Thank you for the wellies. That was really sweet."

A brief pause ensued, while the sound of muffled voices carried over the phone. "My pleasure."

Still undeniably deflated, yet excited, Brie disconnected.

Andrea stood a foot away with hands on hips. "What's up?"

"He's…running late from work I guess." She shrugged, yet the disappointment still perched in her chest. "Who works at eight at night?"

Andrea gazed at her.

Their eyes met in silent answer.

"Do you think…?" she asked.

Slinging an arm around Brie, Andrea shook her head. "I don't know, but I don't know him, and neither do you."

Brie exhaled, though she couldn't rid her memory of the late sales calls from Ryan and the numerous work meetings he had to attend in the evenings. They were legitimate at first—calls with Australia and Singapore late at night for business, but then the evening work became more frequent. He returned home later and later, and traveled more and more. Deep in her heart, she knew something wasn't right. But she had wanted a family—a whole family—with a mom, dad, and kids, so she ignored her inner warning.

She'd married Ryan, Mr. Tall-Dark-and-Handsome who'd said all the right things and swept her off her feet, but he turned out to be Mr. Tall-Dark-and-Wrong. What about Bryce? Sure, he wasn't dark-haired, but he was tall and handsome. Perhaps, she should find someone soft, short, and sweet and protect her heart from further heartache. Brie unclasped the bracelet from her wrist. "I should probably cancel."

"What are you talking about?" Andrea tilted her head. "You were so excited this morning and a few minutes ago. You're definitely going."

With a heavy sigh, she plopped on the bed. "I didn't come here to meet a guy."

"Well, consider it an added bonus. But since you're free, now we can hit up the local scene and find me a sexy Scot!"

Brie straightened. "I suppose you're right."

"Damn right. A local recommended this pub named after a duck."

Brie laughed. "A duck?"

"Yup. Ready?"

She snatched her purse from the side table and stood. "Yes."

They danced under neon lights shoulder-to-shoulder with locals and tourists alike and the sharp musical notes of the band playing in the background. Yet, when the music slowed, she couldn't help but wonder, where was Bryce tonight?

Chapter 7

Brie savored a forkful of fried, creamy egg the following morning in a small café near the Royal Mile. She moaned, appreciating the velvety texture on her tongue. "Oh, my God."

Bryce stifled a laugh. "Do *ye* need a moment?"

Closing her eyes, Brie savored the first mouthful. "Just having an orgasmic experience with my breakfast."

He laughed, eyes dancing, watching her. "A Meg moment?"

Adrenaline rushed to her chest, and she curved her lips. "You know that movie?"

"I do. 'Tis a classic film."

A man and a chick-flick. It could've been a movie title. "I'm glad you've seen it. Her sandwich scene is award-winning. She's an amazing actress. One of my all-time favorites."

"I have to agree wit' *ye*." He grinned and dug his fork into a pile of potatoes. "And every man in his right mind."

She giggled, dipped her fork into her own breakfast with a happy hum, and then glanced at Bryce with a soft smile. The morning sun shone through the window behind him, highlighting his auburn curls with golden flecks as warm as the sunflower-yellow trim in the café.

"I'm glad *yer* enjoying it."

"My," she began but caught herself and paused. Andrea had told her not to mention her kids. She almost said, "my daughter." The truth was, she wanted to tell Bryce about Phoebe and Noah and share that part of her. Instead, she cleared her throat. "I, um, don't eat eggs normally. This is a luxury. I eat certain kinds of eggs…flax egg, applesauce, and banana."

With an uptick of his upper lip, he tilted his head. "A banana egg?"

"Yes, you can use a banana in place of an egg to make something…vegan," she added. *Egg-free and vegan were pretty similar.*

"So, *yer* a vegan who eats eggs?"

"No. I eat meat, sometimes. You know what I am?" She leaned forward.

Bryce cocked a brow and lifted his coffee cup. "*Ye've* piqued my interest."

"I am a flexitarian," she said with a horrible English accent.

Bryce half-choked, half-laughed on his coffee. "A British flexitarian?"

She snorted a laugh. "No, it just seemed right to adopt a British accent."

Once Bryce set the coffee mug aside, he grinned. "Accents aren't easy."

Brie leaned forward with a hand on her chin. "Oh, you have experience with accents?"

"Yes." He mirrored her tilting forward and disheveling an auburn wave, so the curl glided from above his ear across his temple. "Now, what exactly is a flexitarian?"

Oh boy, Brie licked her lips. *How could he get more good-looking?* "I heard this on a radio station. I'm not making it up." She felt giggles rising. "It's someone who has mostly a vegetarian diet, but who occasionally chooses to eat meat or fish, which is good because I love fish and seafood, especially sushi."

"I'm on a pretty strict regimen myself. Some might call me a bit of a health freak."

Studying his face, strong cheekbones, and square jaw, Brie could appreciate Bryce took pride in his health. Yet, when she noticed he popped his baseball cap on a few minutes later and tugged the bill lower as people slowed near their table, Brie couldn't figure out why. Apparently, they chose the best corner to sit or something. Everyone wanted to be near the bright, rare sunlight, but, upon realizing it was taken, strolled slowly by, talking.

"*Ye* said *ye* liked sushi?" he asked.

"Oh, love it. Tuna *tataki* sashimi with fresh radishes and Philly rolls are my absolute favorites."

He tilted his head. "I've had sashimi, but what exactly is a Philly roll?"

"Oh! It's a cut roll with salmon and cucumber, although I've sometimes had it with asparagus, as well, though not as tasty, and a specific brand of cream cheese, hence the name."

"Cream cheese in sushi?" Bryce's lips curved.

"Yes, and it's incredible." Still, she wondered if he'd agree with her roll choice. Ryan never understood her fascination for Philly rolls, and she never understood his fascination for roe and *tar-tar*. "The crunch from the fresh vegetables with the creaminess of the cream cheese and salty note from the salmon make the perfect bite."

He relaxed into the chair. "I'll have to try that one

day. I was actually going to take *ye* to a sushi restaurant last night I'm fond of, but work…ran a wee bit late."

At the mention of work, Ryan's face popped into Brie's mind, and her stomach turned. She inhaled, acknowledging the feeling and released a breath. She glanced back at Bryce. His blue eyes shone. They had many things in common, and he was a pleasure to share a meal with, but she wondered if he was telling the whole truth.

****

Bryce watched a wave of emotions dance across Brie's face. He mentally kicked himself for cancelling their date previously. But he was here now. "What's your favorite meal?"

"Right now?" She tilted her head, shuffling soft waves, then immediately pointed her fork at her plate. "This."

He grinned wide.

"Since I have the famous Scottish Breakfast, what's your favorite Scottish food?"

"Haggis with *neeps* and *tatties*." He explained haggis was the national dish of Scotland—a pudding comprised of sheep's liver, heart, and lungs mixed with beef, suet, oatmeal, and seasoned, then served alongside turnips aka *neeps* and potatoes *tatties*.

"That sounds…delicious," she said slowly.

Bryce laughed and picked up his coffee.

"Did you grow up nearby?"

He gazed over the coffee cup. He could give her the rehearsed answer he'd told the press time and time again, or he could give her an honest one. He took a nip of coffee, then set the mug down. "I'm from a little town outside of Stirling. 'Tis an artsy town with local

69

theater and festivals, some of which I partook in as a young lad. My *maw* worked in theater, as well, and I'd sneak in often to watch the performance from the right wing offstage, mimicking actors. We also lived near rural farmland and a castle—plenty of space to exercise our imaginations."

Brie paused with her fork mid-mouth. "Are you royalty?"

"Not even close." He laughed. "There are castles all over Scotland, including The Royal Palace in Stirling, but no. I'm not royalty." Though in the television industry, he was often thought of by that word. He didn't want to divulge that part of himself. Not yet. "And *ye*?"

Sitting tall, Brie lifted her hands and pretended to crown herself. "Oh, sure. Regular American princess." She giggled. "No, although I'm known to wear a tiara with…" She paused and shook her head. "Never mind, tell me more about where you grew up."

"It was a small town filled with opportunity. My imagination ran wild as I fancied myself to be William Wallace or Robert the Bruce with a stick in hand or a great Viking conquering new lands, which is probably why I got into theater at a young age."

"I can imagine. I also grew up with land around me at my grandparents' home. They had horse property that butted up against a nature reserve. I remember coming home from school, mucking stalls, riding horses, and being outside until sunset. My grandmother even bought an old-fashioned bell to call me in for dinner and homework." Brie smiled. "I'd stay out there for hours, playing and exploring as a fairy amongst the foxgloves or a forest warrior protecting the trees."

Bryce could imagine Brie as a young lass—wide green eyes devouring the world around her as she explored barefoot amongst the fragrant ferns and spongy moss. "Aye. We've some things in common then. Tell me one of *yer* bucket list items."

With an upturn of her lips, she leaned forward. "This is one. Taking a vacation. You?"

"Climbing a tall mountain."

"Like Everest?"

He nodded. "Maybe."

"I've climbed Mt. Whitney."

She's a climber? Brie was becoming more and more fascinating by the minute. He leaned forward again. "*Ye* have?"

"I have"—Brie wiggled her brows—"with my uncle and cousins. I was seventeen and didn't realize at the time that it was the tallest mountain in the U.S. I'd gone up to Mt. Whitney portal campgrounds for years with my uncle and cousins. My mom, you see, always worked and couldn't take vacations, so I looked forward to this camping trip every summer when a few of my relatives came to California."

"And now?"

She arched a caramel-colored brow. "Now?"

"Would *ye* hike the mountain now?"

"I haven't really thought about it. But my uncle would jump at the idea. Even at sixty, he still climbs the peaks every year with friends. He invited me and…" She paused again, pursing her lips.

Bryce nodded, inviting her to explain further.

"He invited me a few times…the last couple of years, and I've always said *no*, but maybe it's something to aspire to once again. Though I'd definitely need training."

The corners of Bryce's mouth tugged. When his mobile vibrated in his pocket, he retrieved the device, noting a text from Eleana and the time. He'd have to leave soon, or he'd be late to readings. Yet, he relished the time with the woman before him. Brie was beautiful, refreshing, and witty. He couldn't help but want to hear more. "So, *yer* an adventurous one then?"

She shrugged, yet the corners of her rosy lips curled. "Yes—"

"What are you doing?" a woman's voice interrupted.

Bryce dragged his gaze from Brie and stiffened. The tall young woman with piled, bleached-blonde hair and busting bosom seethed with anger, while her silent sidekick—a woman he'd had enough unfortunate meetings to understand her as the sister—pressed her lips in a thin line.

Not again.

Not here.

They'd found him. He'd gone two months without an episode, but eating locally was always a challenge. Although the risk was worth the time, Bryce should have picked a more private location.

Instant dread settled in his gut when Brie glanced from the two women, then to Bryce with a pinched expression, while worry etched her green eyes like a storm rolling through the evergreens. Why couldn't they leave him alone?

"I've waited for you to return," Miss Crazy said with trembling lips. "By the sword in the stone just like you promised."

"Christ," Bryce muttered. "I'm sorry, but like I've

told *ye* before and my lawyer prior, I am not who *ye* think I am. If *ye'll* excuse us—"

Slamming her hands on the table, she pressed forward with tears streaming down her cheeks. "How can you say that?"

Jesus, she could get an award.

"We're meant for each other. Just like your show tells the world. Alexander Mackenzie and Lady Charlotte will always reunite, no matter what befalls them. And who…who is this?" She pointed a sharply manicured black nail at Brie.

He ignored the question and retrieved his wallet. At Brie's pinched expression, he extended a hand to help her out of the booth. "Time to go."

Brie's brows jammed together, and her green eyes darkened. "Yes, it is."

She was fuming mad. Bryce didn't understand why. He was the one being stalked.

****

Following Bryce out the door of the café and down the cobblestone steps, Brie was filled with frustration. Once outside, she tore her hand from his. "What's going on, Bryce? Who are those women?"

He glanced around. "I'll tell *ye*, but not here. I promise I'll tell *ye* everything."

Worry skittered through her stomach like the lurch before getting seasick. *Can I trust him?* Her trust in men had diminished since Ryan, and she didn't even know Bryce. The thoughts spinning in her head— player, two-timer, etc.—were deafening, but the pleading in his eyes told her she should at least listen to what he had to say. "Fine."

Slipping his hand in hers, he sprinted down the

winding street toward an alleyway with Brie alongside. A few minutes later, Bryce slowed his pace and tugged her inside a dark and dank arched alcove.

Brie shivered. She tried not to think about what creepy crawlies were around them and, instead, directed her gaze toward Bryce. "Who were those women?"

He grimaced.

"Do you know them? And that woman…she was waiting for you?" she inquired. *Not again.*

"Unfortunately." Bryce sighed, then glanced over her shoulder.

The pit in Brie's stomach knotted. "You know what? I didn't come to Scotland to date. I came here for me. The last thing I need is to spend my time with someone who is taken. I don't need any more drama in my life. I should go—" Brie twisted.

Bryce stopped her with a gentle, yet firm, hand on her arm. His gaze held hers.

"Let go of me." Emotion bubbled up in Brie's chest and threatened to burst. She couldn't go through this again. She had finally begun to feel whole.

"Brie," Bryce whispered. "I'm not sure what *ye* think, but I'm not involved with that woman. I'm a man of standards."

She blinked, repressing glossy tears, while her heart thudded.

"I've had the displeasure of meeting her quite a few times now."

"So"—she searched his eyes—"who is she?"

"I have to tell *ye* something." He drew her farther inside the corridor, fitting his body against her curves.

Awareness hummed, even as anger simmered. She gazed into his clear, blue eyes.

"I'm an actor," Bryce said.

She widened her eyes. "You're an actor?" She couldn't believe this was his secret. What did acting have to do with some crazy woman?

He nodded briskly. "Yes."

"Are you a good one?"

He cracked a smile. "I'd like to think so." As he leaned against the rock wall behind, he relaxed.

"So, that's your secret? That's why we've been hiding?"

"Yes."

Brie blew out a breath. "You could've told me."

"I was enjoying just being Bryce for a moment and getting to know *ye* without my trade getting in the way." He shifted and placed a hand on the wall. "I'm a private person, as well. I don't air my relationships in public. And when I'm working on my show or doing interviews, I don't discuss family, friends, or significant others; I've learned to keep it strictly business. This industry has sculpted the way I live my life and who I trust, as well as who I see and date."

"I can respect that." Brie was also private about her life, although she had yet to trust another since Ryan, unless she counted breakfast with Bryce.

"Have *ye* heard of the show *Swords of Scotland*?" he asked. "I play the main character, Alexander James Mackenzie."

She tilted her head. "I have. My friend's a fan, but I've never seen it." *And oh boy, Andrea was going to flip!*

He stared unwaveringly.

"I'll watch it if you want me to." She smiled and rested a hand on his jacketed forearm. "So, who were those women, and why did we need to make a mad dash?"

With a glance down the alley, Bryce sighed. "Super fans."

Brie laughed. "I'm sorry. I'm, oh my gosh. I'm sorry. I'm not laughing." She covered her face with her hands, but giggles erupted, and she couldn't stop herself.

The corners of his lips curled. "Oh, *ye* think 'tis funny, do *ye*?"

She shook her head, biting her lip to keep the giggles from tumbling out.

"They're terrible. This woman—Miss Crazy herself—and her sister have followed me to different filming locations—New Zealand, Prague, and back. They even made an Alexander tracker to keep tabs on where I am. She wants me to marry her."

Chills pimpled her arms. "Stalker status."

"Exactly. We have some incredible fans and some enthusiastic ones, as well, but there are a few who make my ordinary life miserable at times. They really think I'm Alexander James Mackenzie."

"Well, I've seen *Braveheart* a couple of times. If your role's anything like his sexy character, I can understand why female fans follow you."

He shifted closer, and his gaze lowered to her lips. "I'd like to think I'm sexier."

And right there, pressed against Bryce heat to heat where she felt every hard curve of his body, she definitely agreed. Tingles of lust swirled in her stomach, and Brie licked her bottom lip.

When he dipped his head toward hers, he drew closer, breath caressing her skin.

Brie rose to meet him. A ringing sounded near, yet far away.

Bryce cursed and drew away, retrieving his phone. "That's the car." He directed her to a black sedan at the end of the street and stepped away.

A small twinge of disappointment settled within Brie. *Would he leave me now?*

Yet, quickly Bryce slid his hand into hers and led her along the street.

A large man in black strode toward them. "Let's move, sir." He inclined his head and matched them stride for stride until they arrived at the passenger door.

Seated in the pristine, black sedan, they rode the short distance back to the hotel. Her mind spun with the almost kiss. When she angled toward him, she gazed at his full lips. A knowing smile teased at his. She couldn't believe Bryce was some well-known movie star. He seemed so real—so normal. Thinking of normal, Brie thought back to Miss Crazy herself. "She really thinks you're the character?"

He sighed. "Truly. I didn't believe it, at first. Some Super Fans insist I wed my co-star, since we belong together according to the show, while others want to marry my character like Miss Crazy herself."

"Wow."

"Aye. I have to get to read-throughs, but"—he grasped her hand and directed those sparkling blue eyes at her—"I'd like to see *ye* again. Would *ye* have dinner with me tomorrow?"

She glanced down at their entangled hands, then back. "Yes. But you should know, tomorrow's my last day in Edinburgh before we travel to Glasgow."

He nodded. "I'll be returning to Glasgow myself in

two days' time to prepare for shooting."

Brie chewed her lip. If she dated him again, she couldn't hide the truth any longer, especially since he divulged his own secret. "There's one more thing I need to tell you since you're being honest." With an inhale, she attempted to suppress the rapid beating of her heart as she noted his eyes darkened like a looming storm. "I used to be married. And, I have two kids."

He furrowed his brows. "So, *yer* divorced?"

"I am." Although a weight lifted when she uttered the truth, she wondered if she'd ever see Bryce again.

Chapter 8

Opening the hotel door, she spied Andrea having breakfast in bed and strode toward her bedroom. One thing Brie could always count on was her best friend, and that being on vacation, Andrea was still in bed.

She glanced over. "Well, that was the quickest breakfast date ever. No fireworks, huh?"

Brie exhaled. "Not exactly."

Dabbing her mouth with a napkin, she cocked her head. "What do you mean? What happened?"

She trudged farther into the room and plopped onto Andrea's queen-sized bed. Yet, a familiar voice echoed from the television. And an even more familiar face was on the screen. "Is that…?"

"Yeah, my show. Apparently, they're streaming it since he and the cast are getting ready to film season five"—she paused the show with one hand, while the other held a forkful of square sausage—"Spill."

Gazing at Bryce's handsome face highlighted on the screen, she couldn't believe she dined with him. She bit her lip.

"Brie! Out with it already."

"I had breakfast with Bryce Fraser." She clapped a hand over her smile.

"What!" Andrea dropped the utensil, then shoved the plate aside and climbed over the forest-green comforter toward Brie. "You went on a date with Bryce

Fraser?"

Noticing Andrea's wide eyes, Brie straightened. "Yes."

"Hot damn. Mr. Mystery Man is Bryce Fraser? Scottish Heartthrob, AKA the Television King of Scotland, Bryce Fraser? What was he like?"

With a sigh, she fell back on the fluffy comforter. "Wonderful. He's charming, funny, and adventurous."

Andrea dropped down beside her. "Is he as hot as he is on the TV?"

Glancing at the television screen, Brie gazed at Bryce as he sat beside a stately woman in an ornate blue-and-white gown with a broached cloak. He appeared to be giving a speech to a company of kilted soldiers. "I dare say even more handsome."

"I knew it!" She threw her hands in the air. "So, can we visit him on set? You know I planned to take you there anyway in a couple days during the *Swords* tour." Rolling her eyes, she huffed. "Well, at least to the fan barricade, since they have a closed set."

"I don't know. We were having the most wonderful time, and then these strange women appeared, and we had to leave the restaurant. Apparently"—she pushed up to sitting—"he has stalker fans."

Andrea followed with a huff. "I've heard that in some of his interviews."

"Well, that's how I learned he was an actor. I couldn't figure out what those women were talking about…something about a sword in the stone."

Andrea laughed. "Oh! They're bat-shit-crazy fans? Frickin' awesome."

"Ha, not quite, but he told me the reason they were acting so weird is because he's a well-known actor. He couldn't believe I'd never heard of him or seen the show."

"Well, he doesn't know you have two beautiful babies who keep you busy."

Angling her head, she met Andrea's gaze. "Actually, he does."

Andrea's eyes widened. "Why would you tell him? Remember, this is vacation. You are on VA-CA-TION. You can be anyone you want to be. No strings. No attachments."

"It's a great theory, but I love being a mom. Noah and Phoebe are the best part of me. And I didn't come to Scotland to meet a man. I came for me. If he wants to see me again, I'd love it, but I want him to see me, not some single American chasing after him. If there's anything I've learned this past year since the divorce, is, I am happy being me."

"I know, Brie, but *God*." Andrea exhaled. "This is Bryce Fraser. Millions of women would pay to be in your lovely heeled feet right now."

She felt her stomach pitch and pressed a hand to the rolling wave. "You know what he told me?"

Andrea shook her head.

"He refrained from telling me he was an actor in a hit show, because he wanted to just be Bryce for a while. Just him."

Andrea smiled, dimples winking. "That's pretty cute."

"It was. Oh, and he's so cute!" She beamed. "He's got the best smile, and his eyes are incredible. I've never seen such blue eyes in my life—like crystal-blue gems."

Andrea snorted. "If you think those are incredible,

you should see him naked."

Brie blinked. "What?"

She wiggled her brows. "The show has some really juicy sex scenes. And I can tell you, as a fan of the show and Bryce Fraser, he's got a-mazing assets."

With a hum, Brie repressed the butterflies in her stomach. "I bet he does."

Andrea rolled over and snatched the remote. She lifted the device to the television. "Let's skip to the good scenes. You can see what you might be getting a taste of."

Brie glanced at Andrea, then back at the screen. She liked Bryce before she knew he was a famous actor. And maybe she wanted to see him naked. *Oh, my God. But I haven't seen a man naked in...*

Grasping Brie's shoulders, Andrea turned her. "What's going through that head of yours?"

"What if we have sex? What if I want to have sex? I haven't seen a man naked in two years...and I haven't been with a man since..." She stared wide-eyed.

"I know, so this will be the fun part. You get a little free show per se. Get your re-virgined feet wet."

Brie pressed a hand to her forehead. "You didn't just say re-virgined, did you?"

"Brie, you-know-who was your first and only, and you haven't slept with a guy since."

"Thanks for the reminder."

She patted her shoulder. "Well, it's not really normal these days. Most girls do it in high school or earlier."

"I know, okay?" She huffed. "I didn't want to get pregnant early like my parents. But I'm not in high school; I'm a thirty-one-year-old single mother with scars to prove it."

Andrea waved her hands in the air. "You can barely see your C-section scar anymore."

Dropping her gaze, Brie examined her petite chest. "And my boobs shrank."

"Excuse you?" Andrea plunked a hand on a hip. "Weren't you just talking about how you have accepted yourself for being you?"

Brie puffed out a breath. "You're right."

"Damn straight. Now, let's bring our tits to the show. Ready to watch some good TV?"

With a wistful glance at the television, Brie bobbed her head. "Okay, but I don't want to see him naked. There are some things I'd like to see in person if and when it happens."

"All right, the show doesn't show you his blood sausage anyway." Andrea winked. "However, it does show…everything else." As she punched the Play button, bagpipes and flutes mingled together in a delicate, yet powerful, tune, while the *Swords of Scotland*'s introduction appeared on the television screen.

Bryce emerged in a forest-green kilt, leather boots, and glistening sword and strode over the sharp-green grass toward a gathering.

Brie gripped Andrea's hand.

Addressing a group of grimy-looking soldiers with dirt and blood splattered across their faces, chests, and arms, Bryce aka Alexander James Mackenzie spoke, inspiring them with compelling words and a delivery suitable for a king.

Bryce was talented. She saw that easily. He was a great actor. But she had one question. "What is he doing with me?"

Andrea grinned. "He's got the hots for you, obviously."

"But I'm not a Hollywood A-lister."

"Maybe he's searching for someone more normal. The guy has barely been seen with celebrities except his co-stars. Trust me—I've followed him on social media for years. Brie, this might be the best thing that's ever happened to you."

Brie thought about her kids and then the women this morning. How could this be a great idea?

"Come on. I know your marriage broke you, but you deserve to have some fun."

Sucking in a breath, Brie stood on shaky legs. "I tried to make it work for Phoebe and Noah, but—"

"Exactly," Andrea agreed. "What have you got to lose? Think of this as an adventure."

"Why?"

"Because this is vacation, Brie! You have the chance to go out with a star. Who cares what happens? Just have fun and enjoy him for the next few days. Do this for you." Andrea pointed a finger.

"For me?" Brie stared out the window at the magnificent castle. Was this reality?

"Yes, just like this trip. You're always taking care of everyone else—the kids, your mom, all those sales people. This time is for *you*."

Brie leaned forward. "You mean us, right? I took this trip to travel, explore Scotland, and spend time with you, my best friend. It's our time, right?"

Fanning her hands, Andrea scrunched her nose. "We have plenty of time. Don't worry about me. Go out with the television King of Scotland!"

As the show continued, Brie watched the first episode with excitement racing through her veins. Though after a few minutes watching Bryce wield a sword and vanquish oncoming redcoats, she grew uncomfortable, and her heartbeat rapped steadily along with the thunder of hooves. She needed to write. She grabbed her notebook and a pen.

April 27

I went on a date this morning. A first date. In fact, my very first date since my divorce.

We had breakfast and talked, getting to know one another. Although Andrea told me not to mention Phoebe and Noah, I kept catching myself almost saying, "my kids" multiple times. I hated myself for hiding them—for hiding the best part of who I am—that person isn't me.

After our date was interrupted by some Super Fans as Bryce called them, he told me he was an actor in the show, Swords of Scotland. *But before then, when a gorgeous woman appeared at our table, she reminded me of the day Ryan showed up with Jasmine, the twenty-something, model-actress, and emotions hit me like whiplash. I hate how Ryan's actions continue to influence me. When will they not? A month from now? A year?*

But Bryce wasn't involved with the Super Fan...well not really, his character was, or so she believed. Bryce is a well-known actor. Who would have imagined I'd meet and go on a date with an actor and a famous one even? Still, worry creeps into my mind— will I be enough? I'm a single mom from America, not some Hollywood starlet.

I'm grateful I told him the truth. I don't want my

children to ever be a secret. Catching myself from mentioning them in our conversation felt like a betrayal, and I'd never betray my children. That was Ryan's role—the betrayer, the family divider, the man who hurt me to my very core. My children are the absolute best part of me. When I told Bryce I have kids and shock flashed across his eyes, I felt the weight in my chest lift. Since my divorce, I've slowly uncovered parts of myself I lost during my marriage. I'm still rediscovering who Brielle Finlay is. And I have to be true to who I am.

Bryce stirred something inside me—something that's been dormant for some time. If we see one another again, then I welcome his company, but I will enjoy the country, culture, food, and all Scotland has to offer. As me.

Chapter 9

Brie had kids.

That was a revelation. Bryce liked kids. He had a niece and nephew he was extremely fond of, but he'd never dated someone with kids. Hell, he'd never dated a tourist either, though he'd flirted harmlessly often enough.

Scrolling through the diary on his mobile, he perused the jam-packed schedule slated for today—a photoshoot with his brilliant co-star, Eleana, final script read throughs with the cast, directors, writers, and producer, as well as a video interview with ScotStars. Although the *Swords* production team typically met in Glasgow, they'd be shooting the video interview together in Edinburgh where a portion of the final scene of Season Four was filmed. With production beginning on Season Five in just a few days, the cast and team needed to gather.

His driver pulled to a stop outside Heather Studios where centuries-old brick juxtaposed the sleek, glass street-level entrance.

When Bryce swung out of the car, he braced himself as fans swarmed with phones high, and the press thrust cameras in his face.

"It's Alexander!" someone yelled.

"Bryce! Can *ye* tell us something about the upcoming season?" a member of the press with a full mustache and black scarf asked.

"No, I can't." He accepted a pen from a young lass with blonde braids and a unicorn beanie. "How are *ye*? Nice to see *ye*."

She blushed three shades of red. "You play my absolute favorite character on TV. I-I can't stop watching!"

"Thank *ye*." He signed a T-shirt she held, then posed with another fan. As an actor, he always made time for *Swords* fans—they were his livelihood—but some, including Ms. Crazy, made his job and hell, his life, challenging. He spent five more minutes signing autographs and taking pictures before offering a wave and retreating into the studio.

Moira, the makeup queen, stood ready beside a chair, red curls in full glory with matching red lips and a vibrant crimson-and-white tartan dress. "*Och*, if it isn't the King o' Scotland himself."

Chuckling, he strolled toward the chair under a bright beam of lights. "Morning to *ye*, as well, Queen Moira."

She picked up a few colorful tools. "How was the call?"

"Good." Bryce nodded. He'd returned from America after an audition for an American superhero movie. Although he'd yet to call back his agent, he was nearly certain he'd accept the role. "We'll see. What's new wit' *ye*?"

"*Och*, the usual. Kids driving me mad. Aaron just got his license, and I pray the lorry will be in one piece when I get home."

Bryce laughed loud and strong. "He'll do fine. Aaron is a good lad. Lucky he's not in America learning how to drive. Christ, the freeways they call them—seven lanes thick in some places. Glad I had a driver this time."

She sponged some color on his cheeks to make his complexion more copper-toned, then attended to his hair. "Ye best take heed and keep away from local spots. Miss Eleana told me a certain fan's been spotted around town."

As if a dagger had been driven into his side, he inhaled sharply. "Aye, I had the misfortune of seeing her while eating breakfast."

"*Tsk*. It's a sad day when a man can't eat his breakfast in peace, but I'd guess *ye'd* do that at home then?"

Clenching his jaw, he bobbed his head. Bryce sought a normal breakfast with a beautiful woman, and his alter-ego caught up with him. When he heard a text sound, he glanced over. A link from his agent popped up, informing him actress Kathryn Bailey would be on the *Regina Show*. Bryce exhaled through flared nostrils.

Fifteen years his junior. Was he mad? Sure, she had the looks and a bloody amazing body, but he wasn't twenty or thirty any longer. Eleana had even warned him. Kathryn and he dated for close to a year until his professional connections landed her a role opposite Hollywood A-lister, Thor Johansson. She hadn't returned his calls since. Yet that didn't dissuade her from splashing his name across headlines again with a tell-all of how he broke her heart.

Bryce knew his agent, Joanna, was already working on a response. She was like a bloodthirsty bloodhound, and he was grateful, but he was growing tired of the Hollywood drama. When a pair of mystical, green eyes came into his mind, he relaxed into the makeup chair as Moira worked her magic.

****

The following morning, Brie peeked over the bow of the tour boat at the dark, rippling water shadowed by a gray veil. Luckily, they'd snagged a spot on the covered deck to ensure they wouldn't get drenched again. Ahead, the intricate arches of the Forth Bridge appeared, while the cries of sea gulls pierced the air. Flying her gaze up, she followed the white-and-gray birds as they soared. "Who knew Scotland had seagulls?"

"Your unworldliness is showing," Andrea teased and earned an elbow from Brie. She inhaled, lifting her arms up like wings. "This is what I needed—to be chauffeured in a water bus versus stumbling my now-tired feet around this beautiful city."

Brie grinned. Although she hadn't traveled much, she knew Andrea had traveled around Europe and throughout Asia. Brie couldn't wait to fill her passport with more stamps one day.

A pop of fiery-orange in the dark water drew her attention. "Look! A puffin." Brie pointed toward a black-and-white bird bobbing in the water with a silver fish dangling from its bright-orange beak. "Now, that's a bird I've never seen except on a cereal box."

Andrea snorted and snapped pictures with her phone.

With the wind drifting through her hair, Brie breathed in the briny air, enjoying the change of pace. They approached Inchcolm Island where rocky cliffs and vibrant, green grass welcomed them to a medieval Abbey.

"In 1123, Alexander the First, King of Scotland, sailed the Firth of Forth when his ship veered off course during a storm. He landed on Inchcolm Island where he sheltered throughout the gale," the guide's voice carried over the loudspeaker. "Then, he vowed to build a monastery in gratitude for surviving. Unfortunately, the King passed before fulfilling his promise, and his brother David the First built what is now Inchcolm Abbey."

Brie scanned the ancient buildings, some crumbling near the sandy shores, showing interior walls, deep cavities, and hollow doors, while other portions appeared intact including a cone-shaped center with arched windows and entry. According to their guide, the island provided sanctuary for Alexander the First, but as far as she could tell, the only inhabitants now were sleek sea lions and seals lounging on the beach and rocks along the shoreline.

But she understood the need to seek refuge. She, herself, sought refuge from a broken heart. After seeing Ryan with Jasmine in front of their home of six years, Brie crumbled. She couldn't breathe in the home they once shared, not when the very act of opening her front door filled her with instant sorrow.

Mimi welcomed her and the kids into her small, one-bedroom apartment without any objection or explanation.

Pressing her eyelids closed, Brie attempted to push aside the memory that snaked into her mind, but not before the familiar images appeared like a movie reel.

The front door opened.

Ryan's red sports car parked in front of their house.

The sleek brunette in the front seat.

Ryan strolling in the house like a salesman, selecting suits from their shared closet and unimportant trinkets from their home.

Noah crying, reaching for his dad.

Phoebe hanging onto her legs, sobbing, because Noah was crying and because she didn't understand.

Brie begging him to stay.

The door closing…

"Aren't they cute?" Andrea poked Brie.

She jumped. "What?"

"The seals. Like little water pups lounging and playing…" Andrea gazed at Brie. "Are you okay? You look kind of pale."

"Sorry, my mind wandered…and it's cold out here, right?" She tugged her green jacket closer. She thought she was over the betrayal. She'd even written journal entries that noted she'd moved on; yet, sometimes, the memory snuck up like the tide when she was least expecting. She flicked her hair and breathed deeply.

"Uh, yeah, it's Scotland." Sliding her sunglasses down the bridge of her nose, Andrea scrutinized Brie for a moment, then, two. "You good?"

She inhaled the salty air. "I will be." When something splashed to her left, Brie spotted a dolphin leaping out of the water, then another. Their sleek bodies sliced through the water, while they leapt and glided along the gentle waves wafting from the tour boat.

Brie loved dolphins. They were a symbol of protection in the water, but also of joy. She was ready to find more happiness and progress past the sorrow Ryan left in his wake. Watching the spectacular mammals frolic in the foam, she leaned over the rail, smile blossoming.

After the boat tour and a quick lunch, they took the train across Edinburgh to Rosslyn Chapel where the sheer size and intricate stone carvings made the chapel appear more like a cathedral, then returned to the hotel to relax as the rain *pitter-pattered* once again.

Brie added notes to her memoir, summarizing the wanderings today and the heartache that surfaced, then tucked it away and grabbed her travel watercolor notepad and paints. She sketched the colorful puffin Andrea so beautifully captured with her phone.

Although she wasn't an artist by trade, she'd painted for as long as she could remember. Mimi's apartment still boasted paintings from when she was young with quick strokes and lots of water, then later, paintings as a teenager when her strokes became surer and truer. When they lived together after the betrayal, Mimi reminded Brie of her love of painting, pulling out new paint sets and crisp, white paper for the kids, then handing Brie her younger self's set. Now, Brie painted a few times a week by herself and with her children. Painting calmed her. Dipping a brush in the vibrant orange, she brushed the puffin's beak.

"Hey." Andrea popped her head into Brie's room. "So, the ghost tour starts at six p.m. sharp. Nothing like exploring creepy alleys in Old Towne, underground vaults, and a haunted graveyard for our last outing in Edinburgh."

"Nothing like it." Brie ignored the squeak in her voice.

She wandered into the room. "We can grab an early dinner, too, if you want."

She flashed a smile. "That sounds great." Although she didn't want to disappoint Andrea, she didn't like being scared, visiting creepy places, or even thinking about meandering in dark, mysterious caverns. But Andrea said the tour was highly rated and when in an old, Medieval city... She gulped and refocused on her happy painting, adding vermillion to accentuate the colors.

"Oh! It's so cute," Andrea commented. "Can I have it when you're done?"

"Of course! I can teach you some basic watercolor techniques, if you like."

"Nah, I know where my talents lie." Andrea winked.

Brie lifted a brow. "Word puzzles?"

"Of course. Puzzle Queen here, hello!"

With a whip of her paint brush, she pointed. "And of course, we can't forget, pasta goddess."

"True. You can't forget that! Pasta always sounds good, but it's been nice to let someone else cook for a while."

Brie grinned. "So true."

Ping!

Her text dinged, and Brie glanced at her phone

—*Hello, Brie. Can I take you to dinner?*—

"Oh..." Brie's heartbeat quickened. *He wants to see me again.* And she did, too. Chewing her lip, she glanced at Andrea.

"What's up?"

"Bryce asked me to dinner."

Andrea's perfectly penciled, dark brows jammed together. "Tonight?"

Nodding, she set down her brush. "Yes, and I know

we have plans, but you know anything with ghosts creeps me out. I've been preparing myself for the next few hours by painting this happy little puffin, but I'm kind of a nervous wreck."

"Why didn't you say something?" Andrea propped a hand on her hip.

"I didn't want to disappoint you." Rising, she faced her. "Would you mind if I skipped this one outing?"

"But it's already paid for."

"I'll pay you back, I promise. Like you said, this is a once-in-a-lifetime opportunity to date Bryce Fraser, right?"

Andrea flicked her hair, then pursed her red lips. "Fine. You better meet me for a drink after, so I can fill you in on all the gruesome tales."

"Deal." Brie picked up her phone.

—Sure, I'd love to. When and where?—

—Pick you up at six thirty?—

—Perfect. —

—And Brie? Wear your wellies.—

She stifled a laugh. With a quick glance at the shiny, green rainboots, she wondered, where was he taking her?

Chapter 10

Bryce arrived at the hotel ten minutes early and texted Brie. He considered himself a romantic and disliked the idea of waiting at the curb for a lass. Yet, strolling into a hotel full of tourists would bring a rapid end to his carefully laid plans.

A couple minutes later, one of the entry doors swung open followed by two young lassies in bold beanies and fur-covered jackets.

He tapped his fingers on the steering wheel. When he glanced back, he paused, watching Brie approach his four-by-four with a nervous smile, green coat, snug jeans, and new wellies. With a grin, he opened the door.

"Hi," she said.

Her voice edged with nerves. "Hello again, Brie. *Ye* look lovely."

"Thank you." She buckled and lifted her silky hair over the belt, then turned toward him. "Where're we going?"

"For a picnic." Bryce gazed at the wee scattering of rain dusting his windshield. "If the weather holds."

Brie laughed. "Well, rain or not, I'm happy to be going with you, since you unknowingly saved me from a ghost tour."

He arched a brow. "Oh, aye? *Yer* not a fan of ghosts?"

Brie shuddered. "No. Not at all."

Chuckling, he maneuvered onto the road. "Well, I'm happy to be *yer* rescuer."

They conversed easily during the fifteen-minute drive and arrived at Blackford Hill. Luck was on his side as the rain eased, though clouds still loomed above. He'd take his chances. Once he opened Brie's door, he proceeded to gather the hamper and tartan.

"You were serious about the picnic." She gazed at him with a soft smile gracing those rosy lips.

"Aye, I was. Blackford Hill is relatively quiet compared to other hills in Edinburgh, and that's what I'm after today...a little peace and good company." He'd been holed up in a room all day with nearly thirty people making last-minute script adjustments. Christ, they'd be filming the first show the day after next. He had lines to learn. Luckily, the first few days involved him escaping capture with minimal lines, whilst Eleana had the majority.

They strolled up the dirt path past colorful yellow-and-violet flora, amongst rich, grassland, and birdsong in the air. When they descended down wooden stairs, he cupped Brie's elbow and directed her toward the pond, cutting through grass, brush, and thistle as the tree line before them thickened. With Brie's quick intake of breath, he knew he'd had the right foresight to take her here.

Swans glided across the pond a few meters ahead.

Her face lit like the luminescent sunlight through the cloudy sky.

"Oh, they're gorgeous! And, oh my goodness, little, gray fuzzballs, too." Brie leaned closer, pressing her hands together. As she stared out toward the rippling water, the breeze ruffled her hair, while the clouds reflected off the pond. "This reminds me of *The Notebook* when Allie and Noah are out in the middle of the lake, and thousands of angelic swans circle them. It's probably movie magic, but I still remember how breathtaking it was"—she rotated toward him—"and how breathtaking this is."

"Aye." Bryce lifted a free hand to brush a strand from her cheek. Warmth radiated through his fingertips. " 'Tis breathtaking." The wind whipped through the trees and sent his cap sailing.

"Oh!" Brie sprinted after the flyaway hat.

Striding forward so as not to break the glass and spirits in the basket, he caught up and grinned when she snugged the old cap back on his head. "Thank *ye*. Better try a hand at this picnic before the weather changes our minds." He wove his fingers through hers, igniting an ember in his palm with the connection. Her soft hand felt comfortable and welcoming.

She paused, glancing down at their entwined hands, and then looked up. Her eyes softened like fresh moss.

With a gentle squeeze, he led her down a trail that bordered the dense woodland toward open grassland. When he found a bonnie spot, he laid out the tartan and motioned toward Brie. "Would *ye* like to sit?"

"I would, thank you." Brie tucked her legs beneath her and touched the soft fabric with an unadorned hand. "This is so beautiful. I realized since being in Scotland I don't wear enough plaid."

"We'll need to remedy that," Bryce agreed. "But it's not a plaid; 'tis a tartan."

Her lips curled. "Oh, really? What's the difference?"

"A tartan is a particular cross-stitch-patterned fabric worn by a specific clan. Historically, the colors were harvested from plants, roots, berries, and trees in a local area where a clan lived, so the colors were unique to that clan." He removed containers of colorful sushi, sparkling waters, and red wine. " 'Tis not just a fabric. 'Tis family."

As she set out silverware and napkins, she smiled. "Family is important to me, as well. Is this a Fraser tartan?"

"Aye." He nodded and poured a glass of wine. "This particular one is a hunting tartan." He handed her the glass, then directed her attention to the forest-green, pale-blue, and wee stripes of red. "See the way the colors are more muted and earthy? When hunting, they'd allow the clansman to blend in with the foliage. Every tartan has a purpose. And as clans grew or branched off through birth, death, or marriage, the new clans added an over-stripe onto the basic pattern of the parent clan, such as these red stripes here." He pointed. A smile curved on her lovely rose lips. He couldn't help but notice how the warm forest-green notes of the tartan made her eyes more fiercely green than before—like green glass, so clear and arresting he couldn't stop staring.

"I love that." Brie sipped her wine. "It's like a piece of art telling a story through the chosen colors and arrangement."

He cocked his head. "Are *ye* a fan of art, as well?"

"I am. I draw and paint a little watercolor. Art's a hobby, but it also helps me relax after a busy day. My kids love painting, too."

From under the brim of his hat, Bryce watched her.

He still couldn't believe she was a mother—she seemed so uninhibited when they'd met—yet he noted the joy on her face when she mentioned her children. At his age, he was bound to date someone with kids. He was even attending his friends' second marriages with their children, and that in itself left a bitter taste in his mouth. He wanted children. They just hadn't been a priority. He'd put his career first. Opening sushi containers, he lifted the colorful array toward Brie. "What do they like to draw?"

"Mmm"—she selected a few sushi rolls and added them to her plate—"Phoebe likes to draw mermaids and unicorns, though they aren't too realistic yet. She's grasped basic shapes like circles, squares, and triangles and blends those with her own creative flair, while Noah paints tractors and natural scenes."

"That's brilliant. I don't have the talent for art, but I appreciate it. I've been partnering with a brand I endorse for collaboration on a clothing line, which will reflect my Scottish heritage." He grasped a roll with chopsticks and popped it into his mouth.

Her eyes shone. "That's amazing! Will you be designing kilts?"

"Em"—he chewed—"Perhaps, as well as jackets, shirts, and vests."

"But you wear kilts, right?" Brie asked. "Besides on your show?"

He nodded. "Of course."

"Andrea and I have been fortunate to see people wearing them firsthand during our trip just out and about and on street performers, too."

"Oh, aye. I have a dozen or so myself. They're quite comfortable." He grinned.

"Really? I think kilts are so sexy, but don't worry, I've been warned not to ask a Scotsman what he wears underneath." Her face colored three shades of red.

Bryce's grin widened. Yet, behind Brie, he noted dark clouds converging above.

****

The familiar ring of a cell phone sang.

Although Brie didn't want to interrupt their date, her best friend was with a group of strangers exploring an underground ghost world. Friends check on friends. "Sorry, I should make sure Andrea's all right."

"No problem."

Glancing at her phone, she noticed Mimi was calling. If memory served, the children should be with Ryan today and the next few. Hoping nothing was amiss, she answered on the second ring, striding a few paces away. "Hi, Mom, everything okay?" Brie asked as she eyed the tinge of gray in the clouds gathering above.

"Absolutely. Phoebe wanted to talk to you."

Her chest warmed. "Of course."

"We're going to the zoo, Mommy! I'm going to pet the goats and see the monkeys, giraffes, and zebwas!" Phoebe gushed.

Biting her lip to contain a giggle, Brie strolled forward. All those animals weren't at the local zoo, but her daughter could dream. "That sounds wonderful. I want to hear all about your visit, okay? Take pictures! Is Noah there, too?"

"Hey, Mom," Noah's voice came on the line.

"Hey, big guy. Have fun today."

"We will," he said, then silence ensued. "You coming back soon?"

101

She couldn't prevent the quick jab in her gut. "Not yet, buddy. I love you." When she disconnected, she wandered toward Bryce who watched with a quiet expression. "Those were my kids." She folded her legs beneath her.

He nodded. "Aye, I gathered. Sounds like they have a big day planned."

"They do—a zoo adventure." Brie glanced at her phone. She had a device full of pictures of her children, probably too many, but she was a mom. Moms take pictures. She'd never shown another man her kids; yet, Bryce had shared a part of himself today. When she glanced at him, she noted his eyes crinkled with a soft smile. "Would you like to see pictures?"

"I would."

Opening the photo icon, she scrolled, selecting a picture of the two of them in the backyard. "This is Phoebe—she's three, and Noah—he's six."

A full smile stretched across his face. "She's a wee, bonnie thing and what a strong lad." Bryce gazed at Noah with a tool, hanging from a branch. " 'Tis that a hammer?"

"It is." She beamed. "He's really into construction and is always climbing something."

Bryce chuckled and asked more questions about her children.

The simple act of asking warmed her soul. Continuing their conversation, she talked about adventures with her children and then asked Bryce about his own likes, while they shared sashimi and finally, the Philadelphia roll.

"The sushi chef couldna believe when I asked him to make this, but he made two and decided to test it on the menu tonight."

"I'm glad." She bit into the roll, savoring the creamy, salty bite. "Yum. What do you think?"

Bryce tossed one into his mouth and chewed. A slow grin formed. " 'Tis grand."

"Told ya!" She flashed a smile.

Bryce's lips curved. "Does that ever go away?"

"What?"

"*Yer* smile. *Ye've* a bonny smile."

Brie couldn't help but beam brighter.

Before the last sushi roll was eaten, a roar rippled across the air. In an instant, rain poured down in thick, watery sheets.

"Ah!" Brie threw an arm up to protect from the freezing, thundering rain and sat up, tossing items into the picnic basket alongside Bryce. The thoughtful picnic now resembled an impressionist spring painting with blurred colors amongst the boggy backdrop.

A moment later, Bryce hoisted the basket up and tossed the tartan over them. They jogged down the hill carefully stepping around fast-moving, miniature rivers diving between them. Yet even in their swiftness, the soil glided past.

Brie kept stride with Bryce, while her left hand held the tartan above her like a tarp. But when she stepped onto a slick rock, her boot gave way, and she lost balance. As she pitched toward the uneven ground, fear pricked her chest, and her breath caught.

Bryce shot a strong arm out, steadying her. "Are *ye* all right, lass?"

With a nod, she gulped air.

Drawing her against his side, he moved carefully, yet swiftly, veering east and then tucked under a thick tree canopy. "We can wait for the rain to subside here." He snugged the thick, tartan around her shoulders, while narrowly keeping himself covered. "The tartan will keep *ye* warm."

Her heart beat so loudly it pulsed in her ears, and she gazed at him unwaveringly. Rain dripped from his cap and dotted his dark lashes, while his warm breath caressed hers and eyes deepened like the sea. Bryce was so much more than what she first believed.

"Brielle?"

Her name rolled off his tongue like music. As she looked into his bright-blue eyes framed with dewy lashes, time stood still while the rushing rain obscured the scene around them and perfumed the air with notes of sweet pine and rich earth. Her lids fluttered, and her lips met his. They were cold and wet and tart from the wine. She slid deeper, tasting and exploring as Bryce drew her closer, caressing her cheek, and wrapping an arm around her. A piece of her that lay tucked away deep ignited like a shimmering star after a storm. She was safe and wanted…and glorious. Her body simply melted like the soft puddle below the wick of a candle.

Snug in Bryce's strong arms under the sheltering canopy of evergreens, wrapped in the Fraser tartan, she drifted.

****

The hotel door slammed.

Brie rose with a start. The green-and-white interior of her room blurred with thick cobwebs of sleep as the sound of boots stomping toward her echoed through the hotel, and Andrea appeared in the open doorway.

"Geez, Brie! I thought something happened to you." Andrea glared.

Brie rubbed her eyes, and then reality set in as she sank back into the pillow. "Oh...I must've fallen asleep. I'm so sorry, Andrea."

Wrenching off her beret, Andrea stomped farther inside. "I texted and called you. Why the hell didn't you respond?"

"I'm sorry," Brie repeated. "We got caught in the rain. We had a picnic, and when the downpour roared through, we took cover under the trees. But it wasn't as awful as it sounds." A smile tugged at her lips, remembering the feel of Bryce and the tartan around her. "It was wonderful."

"Well, I'm glad you had a good time." With a toss of her bag on the side table, she strode to her bedroom.

"I said I was sorry, okay?" Brie yelled.

The white door *clicked*.

Regret tugged and pulled at her gut, dispelling the enchanting evening. She chose to see Bryce. Andrea even pushed her to date him. So, why did she feel so guilty?

Chapter 11

Brie woke the next morning with a pounding head and a case of the sniffles—perhaps penance for ditching her best friend and kissing in the woods during a rainstorm. But oh, how delicious the kisses were! She couldn't remember the last time she'd been kissed like that—slowly, deeply, thoroughly. Time didn't matter—just she and Bryce existed, while the storm raged around them. She snuggled back into her cozy cocoon and dreamed of the sweet Scotsman.

A shrill sounded in the distance at some point, and Brie slapped a hand at the alarm and rolled over, tugging the comforter.

Sometime later, the covers flew off. "Hey!"

"Brie! We slept in. We check out in less than an hour." Unruly curls sprung from Andrea's head.

"Oh." Brie rose, then slowly sank her head into the pillow again. "I'm not feeling so hot."

Andrea flicked her curls. "Should've come on the ghost tour. You would've been drier, that's for sure."

With effort, Brie sat up and guzzled water from a bottle beside the bed. "Are you still mad?"

Andrea lifted her chin. "No." She snatched clothes from atop the couch.

"Liar," Brie called. Ugh, she needed coffee, or tea, or bed…she needed to go back to bed. She followed Andrea's lead and tidied up the hotel room, then packed. Ten minutes later, she wheeled her luggage into the common room. "I showed Bryce pictures of the kids."

Andrea rose from the settee. "Oh, yeah?"

"Yeah. Mom called when we were on the picnic—I thought it was you—but instead, the kids wanted to tell me about their adventure yesterday. And Bryce wanted to see pictures of them."

"Maybe he'll be like Blake Shelton—a guy looking for the love of his life and a family."

Brie snorted. "Well, I'm no Gwen Stefani."

"True."

Brie softly punched Andrea's shoulder. "Hey."

"That's friend abuse!"

Brie grinned. "How about we check out and get a full Scottish breakfast in the lobby? My treat."

Andrea eyed her. "Extra bacon?"

"You got it."

After breakfast and a stop at the pharmacy, they rode the train to Glasgow, gliding through Edinburgh past pastures and housing communities as her senses filled with pungent grass. They arrived at Glasgow Queen Street an hour and fifteen minutes later with subtle notes of diesel in the air.

Once they scheduled a ride, Andrea requested a scenic drive to their hotel, since it was raining, yet again, and they had no agenda today.

"Happy to oblige *ye*. I'm Angus." The driver had a piercing through his brow and hair slicked back casually, ends brushing the tips of his ears and collar.

"Are you a local?" Brie asked.

"I em. True Glaswegian." He drove along George Street, while the sidewalks glistened with rain from the car's headlights.

"Awesome!" Andrea leaned forward. "I bet you know all the secrets."

"Aye, I do." Angus and Andrea chatted, amiably laughing and conversing like old friends.

Meanwhile, Brie gazed out the drizzly window, and her thoughts swayed to Bryce standing in the rain beside her the night before. He'd shared he had a home in Glasgow in addition to the flat he kept in Edinburgh. He wanted to see her again, too, though wasn't sure when he could due to the busy shooting schedule. When they drove past a Renaissance-style building with domed towers, clover-green lawns, and towering statues, she wondered *when*.

"This is George Center Square, the principal civic square in Glasgow, which boasts many statues of famous Scots like Sir Walter Scott and Robert Burns," he said. "Lucky *ye* have a good view of them today, since the rain washed the seagull poop off."

Brie laughed, gazing at the stately statues and magnificent architecture.

"I love how writers have such a special place in the hearts of Scots," Andrea commented.

"Me, too." She hadn't told Bryce yet that she was a writer penning a memoir about finding herself again. Perhaps, she was apprehensive about telling him everything. She told him she had kids, and she was divorced, but he didn't know Ryan left her or that she poured her heart and soul into her memoir when she couldn't fall apart in front of her children. If she divulged those details, she wondered what he'd think of her. Still, this was supposed to be casual. That's what Andrea kept telling her, and she kept telling herself, but

Bryce…something about Bryce existed that she couldn't deny.

"If shopping is what *yer* seeking, Buchanan Street will no' treat *ye* wrong. 'Tis an entire street of shops and eateries."

Brie nodded, while Andrea chatted to Angus about recommendations. With one last thought of Bryce, she glanced out the window. A drummer stood under an adjacent building awning smacking drumsticks on a drum, sending splashes of water into the air along with a rhythmic *boom-boom, boom-boom*, while a distant-sounding, upbeat piping tune carried through the glass window before she caught sight of a bagpiper on another corner. Even in the rain, the city was vibrant. As they turned onto Queen Street, she spied an orange accent atop a statue. Squinting, she peered closer. "Is that a traffic cone?"

Angus laughed. "'Tis! Arthur Wellesley, Duke of Wellington, resides outside the Gallery of Modern Art. There's often a cone on the horse's head, as well. It's iconic for we Glaswegians showing the city's character and a wee bit of humor."

Rolling the window down since the rain was now a fine mist, she snapped a picture and texted the snapshot to Bryce.

—Your city has some great personality!—

With the drizzling ambiance, they continued toward their hotel past tall, brick buildings with glass storefronts on the bottom. Suddenly, Brie spotted a vibrant, splash of green and white down the entire side of a building. As they neared, she saw a beautiful mural of a woman blowing a dandelion. *Make a wish.* She smooshed her face closer to the window, admiring the colorful artwork. "Look! It's gorgeous!"

"Aye, our street artists and some others created these brilliant murals all around City Center. New masterpieces crop up regularly, as well. *Ye* can even take a tour or walk the mural trail." Angus pointed to the mural. "For that piece, if *ye* peer closely, *ye* can see windmills springing from the flower, celebrating Glasgow's and Scotland's sustainable energy."

Brie was astounded by the artist's style and confidence—to display their artwork for Glaswegians and the world to see. She supposed she would be doing something similar with her memoir soon—getting her books into hands of readers. But was her story good enough? She'd read dozens of memoirs and self-help books over the last twelve months, but did that make her an expert? Would someone want to publish hers? A nagging voice that sounded like Andrea, whispered, *Of course*, in her ear; yet, she still had doubts.

With another glance at the mural, Brie thought about renewed energy. Wasn't that why she'd taken this trip? Yes, Andrea and Mimi surprised her with a ticket, but the trip gave her an opportunity to change her routine and rejuvenate herself. And even though her head pounded from an impending cold, she was embracing everything Scotland had to offer. Perhaps this trip would inspire the ending she needed to her memoir, as well.

Andrea swiveled. "Didn't you say Bryce lives in Glasgow?"

"I did."

Angus stared back from the rearview mirror.

Even though the rain slowed, Brie noted cars zipped past, while people strolled and sloshed on sidewalks with and without umbrellas.

"Well, I've seen like a dozen redheads so far," Andrea observed. "I'm sure he would be more inconspicuous here with that flaming red."

Brie laughed, then leaned forward. "You know, he's not really that red? He must dye his hair for the show or wear a wig, because he's more of an auburn right now, although his beard has a coppery tone."

With an eye roll, Andrea exhaled. "Don't spoil all the fun. Just because you're dating him doesn't mean my fantasy has to end."

Brie chewed her lip. Was she dating him? She'd spent time with him, yes, and almost the entire evening yesterday. And she'd kissed him with the world storming around them. The memory brought a flush to her cheeks and warmth through her body. "Fair enough."

Angus, their driver and not-so-amateur tour guide, continued through Glasgow, offering humorous tales and vibrant color to the city until they arrived at the hotel. "If *ye* ladies are looking for something to do tonight, pop in Ben Nevis' pub. They'll have live music and good conversation. *Ye* might even see me there! That is if *yer* not absolutely scunnered."

With thanks and a handsome tip, they exited the car and strode up concrete steps toward the Victorian-style hotel. Once inside, Brie widened her eyes as she flew her gaze around the pastel walls, arched wooden entries, and stained glass blended with modern pieces in a lovely combination. But she couldn't observe the decor long. The medicine she'd taken a couple hours earlier had worn off, and her head ached.

****

Brie dreamt she was walking along a wooded path with running water echoing in her ear and the smell of pine and foliage filling her nostrils.

In the distance, a highland soldier emerged with his sword drawn. As he approached, Bryce's face appeared.

But something was wrong. A ringing echoed. And then, the ringing grew louder. And louder. She sat up quickly, noticing her phone glowing in the dark. She hastily answered. "Mom?"

"Everything's all right. We're at the Emergency Room," Mimi said quickly.

Brie sucked in a breath, while her chest seared with a quick stab of fear. "What happened?"

"Phoebe ate a little bit of dessert with egg, and a rash spread across her face quickly, so they gave her an antihistamine and called the paramedics. On the way, she started coughing, so the medic had to give her an epi-pen dose."

"Who? What? How?" Brie choked out. It was Saturday, or rather Friday in America. Ryan's day. Her mind raced. "Where's Ryan?"

"He's with Noah and Jasmine. It was an accident, sweetheart, but she's okay."

Brie's eyes stung with unshed tears. "Can I talk to her?"

A moment later, Phoebe sniffled. "Mommy? I choked."

"I know, baby. The doctors are going to make sure everything is okay. Mimi will stay with you."

"I need Mommy," she cried.

Tears dashed down Brie's cheeks. "I know, sweetheart. Mommy's here. I'm here with you now. Everything will be all right."

"I want my mommy."

Pain pierced her chest, and she swiped a hand over her tear-laden face. She wished she could wrap her baby in her arms, but she was thousands of miles away. Blinking back tears, Brie felt frustration ripple through her and guilt flood her instantly like a downpour. Yet, she couldn't give in to her feelings, not while Phoebe needed her. With a few deep breaths, Brie calmed her own voice and told Phoebe a story about a magical unicorn.

A few minutes later, Mimi's voice carried across the phone. "She's resting now, sweetheart. The doctor says it was a mild reaction. She only had a small bite. She ate all the sherbet on top of the cone. Don't worry, okay?"

"Okay." Yet, fear clogged her throat. After she disconnected, Brie stared at the now-blank screen. All she could do was worry—worry if she'd made the wrong choice going on vacation and worry, she shouldn't have left her children. She raked her fingers through her hair as fresh tears sprang to her eyes. A moment later, she swiped the tears aside, marched over to the dresser, and yanked the first drawer open.

Andrea sat up in bed. "Brie?"

She bunched clothes into her hands. "I have to go home."

"What happened?"

As more tears dashed down her face, she threw the clothes onto her bed. "I'm her mother."

"I know, and you're a great mother, which is why you answered the phone in the middle of the night. But we have a week left. Mimi can handle it."

Brie shook her head, while her vision blurred.

"Phoebe had an allergic reaction. It…it could've been worse, and I wasn't there."

"Oh, Brie." Andrea tossed the covers off and wrapped Brie in a hug. "I know, *shh*. I know. It's okay."

With a sob, she let go, burying her face in Andrea's shoulder. Quickly, tears soaked Andrea's bed shirt and her own. After a few minutes, she sniffled and stepped away. "I-I need to go back. I need to leave now."

"Brie, it's the middle of the night." Andrea glanced at the clock. "Well kind of, but you can't just leave. You wouldn't even arrive home for almost another day. I'm sure Phoebe will be feeling fine by then, and to change the ticket on a Saturday will be pricey."

Sitting on the edge of the bed, she pressed her palms to her eyes. "I don't care. I'm her mother." But she knew Andrea was right, even though she would use every last cent in her bank account to make sure Phoebe was okay. Phoebe would be back to normal soon. But would she?

"Brie…"

She stood. "I need to find out what happened, so I can calm down. Ryan knows about her allergy. How could he let this happen?" Without waiting for an answer, she seized her phone and called. "Ryan? What happened? I just talked—"

"It was an accident. Jasmine took the kids out for ice cream, while I finished work. She didn't know waffle cones have egg."

Jasmine. Brie still couldn't stand to look at her. She wasn't jealous anymore, but she couldn't talk to a woman who dramatically changed her life. "Did she ask?"

114

"I don't know, Brie. She didn't get her ice cream, and she asked about the ingredients in the sherbet."

"Well, she should've asked about the cone," Brie snapped. "Anytime there's something pre-made, you have to ask. God, Ryan. Phoebe could have…could have…" She couldn't finish the sentence.

"I know. Jasmine feels terrible."

"Terrible?" She flung a hand in the air. "Terrible? Imagine how I feel helpless in Scotland! I don't want her taking my kids out to any restaurants by herself."

"They're my kids, too, and Jasmine's a part of their life now. Get used to it, Brie."

"Seriously? Don't you get it?"

Ryan sighed heavily over the phone. "Enjoy your vacation."

Seething, Brie grabbed a sweater and tossed it across the hotel room. "Are you serious? You're blaming me? This is your day."

Ryan cleared his throat. "I have to go."

After enduring Andrea's failed attempts to settle her down, Brie retrieved her notebook.

April 29

Phoebe could have died today. She was given a dessert with egg ingredients. I still haven't come to terms with what happened at the ice cream shop. Ryan knows what to do, what to ask, and what to avoid, but he sent Jasmine with the kids. How could he? Jasmine is a stranger to my kids and Phoebe's severe allergy.

I know it was an accident, but I still can't wrap my head around being here and away from Phoebe—away from my kids when they need me.

And Ryan, I can't stand talking to him. His voice puts me on edge from the first word uttered out of his mouth. How could someone I once loved be so appalling now?

Before we were married, Ryan and I knew one another for a year. We had fun. We dated, though the only date I can remember now is a concert at the Hollywood Bowl. And when we were married, we blended our lives fairly seamlessly as if the honeymoon continued after we returned.

I'm not painting a rosy picture that everything was perfect, but we had a good life together. In the beginning, we had very few arguments. I remember poignantly a question from my old grad school friend, Rachel F. How the hell can you have steamy make-up sex if you don't fight?

I laughed. But I didn't want to fight. I wanted to be happy, so sometimes, yes, I let things go to avoid an argument. And when the kids came, when we disagreed about sleep training, I took over the training. What was the point of arguing if I was the one getting up and losing sleep anyway?

I know we've both changed, and now Jasmine is a part of my life whether I want her to be or not. I don't know if I'll ever want to get to know her, but now she's spending time with my kids. My kids.

Ryan mentioned "his kids" on the phone. The kids he rarely sees and, more often than not, disappoints, leaving me to pick up the pieces. Sometimes, I wonder if the kids are just something to brag about versus something he wants in his life. He's typically off living the single life with Jasmine, choosing when he wants to see them, while I'm a mom, a title I couldn't be prouder to bear.

They used to be ours. But now more than ever, I've

become more possessive over Noah and Phoebe.

All I ever wanted was to have a happy family with a partner for life. My mom was robbed of her chance to spend a lifetime with my father, and although I had a wonderful childhood, something was always missing—Dad.

After our divorce, I pieced back together my broken family. I put every ounce of myself into being the best mother and making sure my children knew they were loved. I created a happy home life, even if that life meant being a single parent. And I know in my heart, I've succeeded.

Sometimes, I wonder if ours will ever be a term I use again. With two kids, I always imagined dating would be difficult. Then, the night before last, Bryce asked about them and commented when I showed him pictures, which meant so much to me—to share the best part of me.

Just three days ago, he was a stranger. Even though I know we're just getting to know one another and I only have a week left in Scotland, what Bryce has given me is hope—hope that one day a kind man will love my kids and me.

Chapter 12

In the morning, Brie blew her nose and assessed the puffs under her eyes. She'd finally fallen asleep around four-thirty a.m. and awoken twenty minutes later in a cold sweat, screaming for help and holding her arms close as if she held Phoebe. Her daughter's cries echoed in her ears.

Yet, she couldn't fall back asleep. *Why did she let Ryan do this to her?*

Phoebe had a reaction—a common occurrence a year and a half ago. But Brie knew what to watch for since the allergy diagnosis, and she rarely frequented restaurants that had uneducated servers or staff. She couldn't take that risk—not when her baby's life was on the line.

"Brie, you almost ready?" Andrea called through the bathroom door.

"I'll be out in a minute." She dabbed another layer of concealer over dark circles and puffy bags. Even though she hadn't gone back to sleep, she'd slept all day yesterday, and the head cold, somehow, was miraculously gone. She inhaled and heaved a breath out, then swung open the door.

Bending, Andrea stuffed her large brown purse with snacks. "I can squeeze one more bar in here and then, she's full."

Brie lifted her gaze toward Andrea, feeling the

118

sting still lingering.

"Let it go, Brie, okay? She's fine. They're back home, right?"

Brie bobbed her head. Mimi sent a text update they were home, and Phoebe would have twenty-four hours of steroids as a preventative measure, as well as allergy medication. Still, the guilt hadn't dissipated.

"Hey." Andrea stepped forward, squeezing Brie's shoulder gently. "Today, we're going to have fun."

She nodded, yet the last place she wanted to be was in a bus full of screaming fans on a tour of *Swords of Scotland* sites. She needed to breathe. She needed fresh air. Sitting on the edge of the bed, Brie pressed her fingers into her temple. "I don't think I can do this, Andrea."

Andrea tilted her head. "Why? It's going to be a blast."

"I know." She swiped a few strands of hair behind her right ear. "I know it's going to be a wonderful tour, but I just need some time to myself, okay?"

"So, you're not going now?" Andrea huffed. "You're letting him win, Brie."

Her brows jammed together. "I'm not. I just need some alone time. I'm dealing with a lot right now."

"Fine." She swung the giant bag onto her shoulder. "I'll take pictures."

Brie looked up. "Thanks. I'll make it up to you, I promise."

"Don't worry about it. But when I get back"—Andrea paused at the door—"I expect a reservation somewhere awesome."

"You got it." With the click of the door, Brie fell back on the bed. Sometime later, she woke up groggy with the sun piercing through the window. The hour was just after noon.

Brie ate one of Andrea's protein bars and guzzled water. She glanced at her phone, which showed messages from Andrea, Mimi, and Bryce. She clicked the message open from Mimi, smiling when a picture of Noah and Phoebe appeared with pajamas and huge smiles.

—*Everyone's doing great!*—

—*Thanks, Mom. Kiss my babies for me.*—

Exhaling, Brie massaged the sharp stab of guilt wedged in her breastbone. She checked Andrea's text next, laughing at her silly poses in front of a castle, hugging the infamous sword in the stone, and more. Finally, she clicked Bryce's message.

—*We Glaswegians do have a sense of humor! Enjoy your tour today!*—

—*Actually, I decided not to go…*—

Setting the device down, she was surprised when a follow-up notification chimed.

—*Up for a hike?*—

Wasn't he busy? She imagined his television shoot would be occupying his time, but here he was asking her to go for an afternoon hike. And perhaps, a hike was just what she needed.

—*Sure.*—

—*Can you meet me at the market? Getting the messages for the hike. I'll text ye the address.*—

—*Of course! See you shortly.*—

What the heck were messages? She freshened up, then tugged on her running shoes and scheduled a car. She would meet Bryce on the East End of Glasgow.

Grabbing her waterproof jacket because she'd been

stuck in the rain enough times to count, she prepared to swing out the door and paused. Andrea's red beret hung on the hook—bold amongst the cream-colored walls like a warning. Would Andrea be upset with her for leaving? Knots tangled in her stomach. Yet, she couldn't join the excursion mid-tour. They could be hours away. With a shake of her head, she glanced at the accessory, then slipped out the door with a *click*.

****

Inside the grocery store, Brie scanned the aisles for Bryce when a piercing cry carried through the air.

In the middle of the aisle beside a check stand, a little boy with curly, blond hair screamed, tears coating his pink cheeks.

The mother glanced around with a baby asleep on her shoulder. Talking in hushed tones, she tried to calm the little boy, while patting the sleeping baby.

But Brie noticed the panic in her eyes as she attempted to keep her little girl asleep and glanced at gawking shoppers. Brie's heart tugged. She strode over. "Hi, I'm Brie. Can I help you?"

The young mother's eyes widened. "He's tired. Em, I'm sorry."

"It's okay. I remember this stage. Can I talk to your son?"

She glanced from her son to Brie. "I dinnae ken if it'll do any good."

Smiling softly, Brie knelt to the toddler's level and pressed a finger to her lips. "*Shh*. You'll wake the dragon."

He stopped for a moment, then started crying once again.

"Dragons, you see, have tiny ears, and they hide

121

when it's noisy and become teeny tiny."

The boy slowly stopped crying and sniffled.

"My name is Brie, and I have a son named Noah. He loves dragons. What's your name?"

He rubbed a small fist in one eye. "Rowan."

"Hi, Rowan. How old are you?"

"Free," he said with a squeak.

Brie grinned. "My daughter is three."

"I ha' a baby sistaw." He pointed.

Glancing at Mom and baby, she smiled. "She's beautiful. Since your sister is asleep, how about we see if we can find the dragon, while your mom gets the groceries ready? Is that okay, Mom?"

"Aye, thank *ye*." She set items on the conveyer belt.

Brie peered between food items on the adjacent shelves and under the cart with Rowan in search of the mysterious dragon. They giggled and searched, while she told the tale of the tiny, shy dragon, and Rowan's mom checked groceries.

A few minutes later, she gathered Rowan in her arms, smelling his sweet, little boy smell, and thought of Phoebe and Noah at home. Her eyes glistened.

****

Stealing glances at the privy, Bryce paid for the messages. He wasn't sure what happened. One moment, he saw Brie holding a screaming, wee lad who she miraculously calmed with soothing tones and laugher, and the next, she excused herself.

Though he had to admit, turning a corner and finding Brie holding a young lad blindsided him. He couldn't deny it. He'd been watching for her. Then, he heard her sweet voice. For a moment, he considered perhaps her own children had traveled to visit, because what other option would there be for her holding a wee lad?

But after a quick observation, he realized the blond-headed boy belonged to the woman beside him with the same shade of hair, holding a fair-faced babe. He stood aside, watching. Why had Brie stepped in to help the mother? Was it due to her being a mother or a kind heart, or both? Still, the sight of her holding the wee lad struck something within him.

Of course, he wanted kids. Bryce hoped one day he'd be blessed with children and always wanted to be the young, adventurous Da. As his fortieth birthday passed, and his career sky-rocketed, he wasn't sure that was possible any longer...

Seeing Brie stroll toward him a few minutes later, he quickly assessed the redness in her cheeks and the way her wee smile didn't quite meet her eyes. "Everything all right?"

"Yes."

With the messages in hand, he led the way to his four-by-four. On the drive, though he mentioned a few sights, he only received a spare upturn of those rosy lips or acknowledgment from Brie. She was quiet and fidgeted. One thing with women, especially growing up with a sister, he knew not to pry too soon.

Arriving at the carpark at Balmaha near the entry of Queen Elizabeth Park where oakwoods soared toward the patchy sky, Bryce slid a glance toward Brie. In the near forty-minute drive, she relaxed, staring out the window or offering a small smile when he made observations. As he watched her take a long, quiet glance out the window, he wondered what was bothering her. As much as he didn't want to press, he keenly desired to see her smile bloom once again.

So, they'd walk. Being outdoors always helped clear his mind, and he hoped this would aid Brie. They strolled toward the entry. "This is the gateway to the east side of Loch Lomond and one of my favorite afternoon hikes when I can steal away for a few hours."

Brie scanned the entrance. "Sounds great. I just need to be back in Glasgow by six p.m., since Andrea should be back by seven. She wouldn't," Brie began, then trailed off.

He cocked a brow.

"She'd want to go out to eat by then."

"Understood."

Hiking up the well-maintained trail through lush, green forest with native oak sweeping around them and scents of rich earth and vibrant moss filling his nostrils, he kept the conversation easy. He led her higher and higher, pointing out wood sorrel vining amongst the fallen trees with their bright clover-like leaves and white, delicate flowers on fine stems and then red squirrels darting back and forth, climbing up large trunks, and chomping seeds.

When they reached the top of a hill, he spied a large narrow-winged bird soaring across the sky above Loch Lomond. He stretched an arm out. "Look. An osprey. She's fishing."

Brie raised a hand above her brows to shield herself from the spotty sun. Her lips parted.

The brown-and-white osprey glided above the water elegantly with long, narrow wings. With legs dangling and talons displayed, she plunged into the loch with a sharp splash until she disappeared completely under the dark water. A moment later, the osprey's wings shot out of the water retracting and flapping, fighting to get airborne.

As her gaze fixed on the bird, Brie's chest rose with an inhale.

Bryce leaned. "A big trout can match an osprey kilo for kilo for weight, especially since the trout's instinct is to swim to the bottom. 'Tis a fight of survival."

"Really? Then, how do they…?" she asked, yet her gaze didn't stray from the osprey.

The magnificent bird flapped her large wings, head above the foamy water, while the lower half of her body remained submerged.

"Watch her," Bryce whispered. "She'll fight tooth and nail to take care of her young."

The osprey smacked her wings on the water, lifting them up, then down until she rose into the air. A moment later, she soared down the loch toward her nest, past green, dotted islands, and into the tree-lined skyline.

"She's incredible," Brie whispered. "I understand the battle to take care of one's offspring." She inhaled and exhaled, yet she kept her gaze trained on the tree line. "Last night, my daughter had a medical emergency. She's allergic to eggs, and I wasn't there. I don't know if I could've done anything if I was home, but at least, I would've been there for her. I almost left."

An alarm coursed through him. "Left?"

Nodding, she shifted, facing him. "Yes. Left Scotland. I felt helpless and guilty about staying while she was in pain, but my mom assured me it was a mild case, and Phoebe's doing well today. Yet, I still feel the guilt...the guilt of not helping my own child." With a sniffle, she turned and folded her legs under her, glancing down the loch.

Bryce sat beside her. "I can imagine being a mother takes an enormous amount of strength"—he turned, wrapping an arm around her shoulders—"and I see that strength in *ye*." With a tilt of her head, she rested on his chest, golden-brown hair cascading down his left arm, while her scent—sweet like honey and undeniably her—enveloped him.

He wanted to take care of Brie and hold her until the sun set below the lofty evergreens. That revelation rocked him.

* * * *

Brie needed this. The fresh air calmed her, and much to her surprise, Bryce calmed her. He sat quietly beside her with a cap tucked over his crop of reddish-brown hair and told her about the ospreys' return to the Highlands every spring to escape the African summer heat.

"Ospreys mate for life, returning year after year to their beloved nest perched high in a pine or other sturdy, lofty tree," he noted.

Mate for life. Brie repeated in her head. She'd always dreamed of having a partner, a husband, a lover for life, but she knew better now. She didn't believe in permanency any longer—only the stability she created for herself and her kids.

" 'Tis mostly the males who hunt, especially when the chicks are small."

Surprised, she gaped, lips parted. He'd made her believe the osprey was a female, a mom, or maybe he'd just reinforced what she needed to hear. But Bryce had been right. Seeing the battling osprey, she was reminded how far she'd come.

With a quiet grin, he rose and strode toward the thick tree line behind them.

Brie skimmed her gaze over his tall, sturdy profile. Much like the trees, Bryce was solid and sure of himself. She wondered if she'd met him in L.A. if they would have dated and if… She blew out a breath. *No. There cannot be what ifs, only right now.*

He returned a moment later, holding something small between his clasped hands.

With a gasp, she widened her eyes. "Don't tell me you've caught a chick?"

Bryce chuckled. "No, Brie. I wouldna steal a wee babe from its nest." Lifting a hand, he revealed bright, red strawberries.

She smiled. "Strawberries?"

"Aye, they grow wild here and in many parts of the highlands. I have fond memories of strawberry picking as a wee lad." He joined her on the grass once again. "Would *ye* like to try one?"

"I would."

Bryce lifted a strawberry to her lips.

Opening her mouth, she bit into the wild berry, tasting the tart, sweet fruit and found Bryce staring, gaze focused. "Do I have something on my face?"

"No." Leaning forward, he kissed her softly, then drew back. "*Yer* so bonnie."

Flutters filled her chest. "Thank you."

"*Yer* eyes are emerald-green with a touch of blue like a jewel, and *yer* hair…" He paused and grasped her long tail, fingers feathering down the strands.

She felt her lips curve. "Yes?"

"Like Celtic honey with streaks of gold and amber intertwining."

With butterflies beating their delicate wings around her heart, Brie brushed at a strand that fell over her forehead. "I dyed it for a long time. He"—she swallowed when she realized what she was about to say—"my ex liked dark brown hair. After the divorce, I allowed my hair to return to its natural hue. I never realized how pretty the color was until I was admiring Phoebe's hair one day and realized we have the same shade. I suppose it was one of the first acts of finding myself again. I don't know. It probably sounds silly now."

Bryce shook his head. "No. It doesn't. I've dyed my hair for numerous roles—to get into character—including a fiery red for *Swords* every few weeks. I've grown it, cut it, and everything in between, but I'm what *ye'd* call auburn naturally."

"So, this is you?" she whispered and leaned forward, sliding his cap off to run a hand through his thick, reddish-brown curls bronzed in the sunlight.

He cupped her face with his wide hands. "Aye. And *ye*."

"Yes." Brie brushed her lips over his, which were warm and welcoming. They kissed while wind danced through her hair, and the sun parted the clouds above. Voices of other hikers carried on the breeze like whispers as if she were in a dream. She drew back, lips gloriously tingling.

A shout pierced through the trees.

She startled. "Oh, my God! What time is it?"

Bryce glanced at his watch. "Nearly four."

"Oh! We have to head back." Jumping up, she dusted off her pants. "Andrea should be returning around six, and I have to make dinner reservations. I promised."

"We can head back, but if it's a rare dinner *yer* after, I can make a call."

Her lips curved. "You can make a call?"

He nodded and weaved his fingers between hers. "Aye, as soon as we have cell service a bit farther down the trail."

As they descended, she heard the *ping-ping-ping* of text messages notifying her that service resumed. She scrolled through photos of Andrea posing beside other people and noted the guilt that settled in her stomach. She couldn't deny the hike with Bryce improved her state of mind, but she had abandoned Andrea. Her text chimed once again.

—*Make the dinner reservation for 4! I met two other Swords fans who are awesome!*—

"Oh." Brie stared at the message. Apparently, Andrea didn't miss her, but could she blame her? She glanced at Bryce. "Is it possible to reserve a table for four?"

"Absolutely." Bryce fished the phone from his side pocket and dialed.

Fifteen minutes later, tucked warmly inside Bryce's four-by-four, Brie leaned toward him. "I don't know how I can make this up to you. Today was incredible."

His gaze roamed her face as a hand cupped her cheek. " 'Twas my pleasure. Truly." Trailing his fingers down, he grasped her chin lightly and drew her forward, kissing her softly.

Sparkling fairies twirled inside her chest. Brie wanted to stay there and kiss Bryce until the park rangers kicked them out, but she had to get back.

When he eased away, he exhaled. "I'm on set the next ten days."

"I understand." Yet, she couldn't deny the deflating feeling within.

"No, 'tis not that. I was going to ask if *ye'd* like to visit."

"Visit you?" Brie tilted her head. "You mean visit you on set?"

He grinned. "Aye. And bring *yer* friend, too."

"Andrea's going to flip! We'd love to." Grasping her phone, she texted Andrea she had a surprise in store in addition to dinner. She prayed the surprise would be welcome, especially after she broke their plans, again.

****

Brie closed the hotel door at half-past six p.m.

"Where've you been?" Andrea marched around the corner from the bathroom, hair curled in ringlets and red, sweater dress showing all her ample curves.

Brie stripped off her jacket. "I went on a hike with Bryce."

Andrea gaped. "What? Is that why you didn't want to come today?"

Hanging her jacket, she faced Andrea. "You know why I couldn't go with you today. After all that happened with Phoebe and Ryan last night, I was a wreck. I passed out after you left, and when I woke up, Bryce messaged me and invited me on a hike. I needed to get out. I was suffocating with guilt."

Andrea blew out a breath. "I know, but you could've gone out with me and had fun, too. Remember me, your best friend?"

A heavy weight settled on Brie's chest, and she had the sudden urge to sit. "Yes."

"We are on this vacation together—you and I." She forked two fingers between her and Brie. "I planned, well, planned most of it, but I had ideas of what we would do here in Scotland, and now, you're spending so much time with Bryce."

Remorse crept into Brie's stomach. She should have called Andrea and asked where she was on the tour. But she didn't. Standing a few feet from her, she nodded for Andrea to continue.

"It's incredible—don't get me wrong. I mean, who wouldn't be excited their best friend is dating Bryce Fraser?" Andrea whirled. "We only have a week left. Am I finishing off this vacation by myself?"

Exhaling, she sat on the bed. "No, you're not." Why had she said *yes* earlier? Why had she gone with Bryce? "I knew this would happen. Remember when I said I shouldn't pursue him, and remember *you* telling me to have fun?"

"Ugh, yes, but I didn't realize—"

"It would continue?"

"Exactly." Andrea plopped beside her. "It's amazing you're seeing him. Incredible. But I'd like to see my best friend a bit more." She bumped Brie's shoulder with hers.

Brie slung an arm around Andrea. "You will. Let me change, and we'll head to dinner. Bryce actually made reservations for four at some popular place. The address is on my phone."

"He did?" Andrea twisted with dark brows high.

"He did. And he invited us to the set."

Andrea's mouth flopped open. "He…wow." She stomped a foot as a smile spread across her face. "Ugh, that's sneaky! You knew I wouldn't be mad now."

"No." Brie shook her head. "I thought you'd love to see the set because I know he works on your favorite show."

With a slow smile, Andrea softened. "Okay, okay. You're forgiven. For now."

Brie released a breath. She didn't like conflict, and she was determined to make things right.

****

They dined in one of Glasgow's finest restaurants eating whisky prawns, succulent scallops, and craft salads. The modern design with shiny gold-and-turquoise detailing blended with wooden accents and created a warm, inviting space. Gliding a hand across the shiny wooden table, Brie was transported to the wooded trail she hiked up a few hours earlier and the man beside her.

"So, Andrea told us you met a handsome Scot," Marta, one of the *Swords* fans from Poland who'd joined them along with Ivy from Australia, said.

Brie swiveled and lifted a brow. Although she was well aware Andrea was a huge *Swords* fan, Brie thought she understood she wanted to keep her relationship a secret.

Leaning forward on the table, Andrea smiled slowly. "She doesn't kiss and tell, ladies."

With white-blonde French braids twisted like a warrior princess, Ivy crinkled her nose. "What? That's no fun."

"Sorry," Brie said, though she wasn't the least bit. She understood Bryce's desire for normalcy. And even though he didn't directly ask her to keep their time together a secret, she valued his privacy. She also didn't want to jeopardize what was blooming between them. "But I can tell you that he's wonderful, and his accent makes me melt. It's so sexy."

Ivy flicked a piece of lint off her sweater and lifted a wine glass with the other hand. "Perhaps we'll meet a Scottish dreamboat of our own, though I can't believe we missed Bryce and Hugh. We got the tip and everything!"

A quiver shuddered in her stomach. "What do you mean? What tip?"

"There's a fan tip line whenever they spot Bryce Fraser or one of the main actors, so other fans can try to meet them, too! We received a tip at our second stop. Bryce and Hugh were at a local coffee spot in the West End this morning."

"Interesting." *And a little possessive, as well.* She was glad they'd gotten out unseen.

"All right. What do you think, ladies? Ready to head to the pub?" Andrea asked.

"Definitely," they agreed.

When Brie signaled for the check, she was surprised to discover the server informed her the check was already taken care of by a fan. She opened her mouth to inquire, but realization quickly hit as Bryce's face appeared in her mind. Her lips curled.

Chapter 13

The following morning, Brie and Andrea explored the West End. People sat and talked, lingered over breakfast and laughed, and relaxed with a paper in colorful chairs of sunflower-yellow and navy-blue, lining either side of the interior streets. Flower buckets graced white building walls, while black wrought iron railing and window frames accentuated the white canvas, and the strum of a guitar floated in the cool, morning air. Brie sighed. She felt as relaxed as the morning ambiance. She'd spoken to her children last night before heading to the pub, and all was well. She was ready for a bright, new day. "I love all the music here." Brie dropped a few banknotes into a busker's bucket.

"Ditto," Andrea noted, while two young women cut across them toward the red-brick and cement-striped pilasters ahead, invoking an annoyed growl. "Is everyone going to the Botanical Gardens?"

"Aye, the sun is out!" someone hollered.

"Yeah, stoater," another commented.

When she and Andrea followed them through the gateway, Brie was mesmerized. Lush green trees dotted her view, along with rich foliage, while park benches lined the natural path beside vibrant monochromatic flower beds of red, white, and yellow tucked between the vast, green lawn, and children raced and played tag in the center. "Look at the kids playing. Phoebe and Noah would love it here."

"They would," Andrea agreed, then pointed. "And check out all those park benches! It certainly lives up to the hype of being the 'finest garden' in Glasgow." She retrieved the travel book from her purse and flipped it open. "The Botanical Gardens date back to 1817. Oh! And, it was a pleasure house. Ooh lala. Can you imagine being here in the nineteenth century? I wonder if it was the same."

Brie flew her gaze over the gardens. "I bet it was." She visualized men and women in their best Victorian dress, lounging on the grass with lace parasols and dapper clothes, strolling arm-in-arm into the glass house. Less than twenty-four hours ago, she strode hand-in-hand with Bryce up a winding trail surrounded by natural foliage and flora. *Nature's garden*. Today, Bryce was on set. She texted him last night, thanking him for dinner, and felt her face light up when he replied with a kissy face emoji. Seeing couples saunter toward a glass dome a hundred feet before them shining like an orb in the center of a forest, Brie pressed a hand to her humming heart.

Walking through a metal archway, she strode through two double glass doors into a short hallway to Kibble Palace. Steamy heat curled the tiny hairs around her hairline, while a damp, earthy smell filled her nostrils. Palm trees and ferns filled a circular planter with iron accents, and long, rectangular tables were setup with small succulents for sale on one side of the walkway, while park benches lined the other.

"More park benches!" Andrea waved her hand "Park bench city!"

Brie snorted. "Yep."

They continued through the Palace's narrow walkway, until it opened into a smooth, curvilinear dome design, flowing gracefully above like the interior of a wave. In the center, she noted a gorgeous, marble statue of Eve surrounded by lush ferns, waxy palm trees, and sunny daffodils. Eve gazed off into the distance pensively, maybe even anxiously. Brie stepped closer, admiring the smooth marble and delicate artistry, but even more, she admired Eve—her poignant stare, slight furrowed brow, and solemn expression. She wondered what she was thinking.

When she heard Andrea say she was moving on, Brie nodded, but she remained planted. Something about Eve tugged her heartstrings. The fallen woman had changed mankind by eating the forbidden fruit and damning herself and Adam. She imagined Eve battled the rest of her life. Yet, here and now, Eve was by herself, and the fear was evident. Brie had felt fearful in her own life as a single mother and wondered time and time again if she'd made the right choice leaving Ryan. But in her heart of hearts, she knew she did. Ryan broke apart their family. And though she looked back with regret of what could have been, she also focused on the future with hope. She rested a hand on Eve's. "You're not alone."

Brie continued around the garden, caressed by soft ferns and silky leaves, breathing in the lush air. As she strolled around the glass house forest with an array of greens she'd recently re-discovered in her children's box of crayons—cerulean-green, yellow-green, sage-green, forest-green, muddy-green, and jungle-green—she smiled. A moment later, she happened upon Andrea admiring a statue of two women.

"Check out the sisters." Andrea gestured toward the marble sculpture of *The Sisters of Bethany*.

Admiring the sculpture, Brie wrapped an arm around her friend of one year. The sisters leaned into each other, foreheads touching, while one sister wrapped an arm around the other and held her sister's hand in comfort. Even though they hadn't known one another very long, Andrea had quickly become like a sister to Brie—coming over to spend time with her and her children as Auntie A, checking in, making homemade pizza with her and the kids, and being a shoulder for Brie—and she was grateful. Until she met Andrea, she didn't realize how much she needed a true friend. She provided Brie with solid support, never-ending humor, and surprise, delicious, homemade dinners. Although Andrea might have been scared away by her divorce baggage, Andrea simply told her it was okay.

"I don't know if I ever thanked you for helping me get through this last year..." Brie began.

Andrea shook her head. "You have—"

"I don't think so," Brie interrupted. "And you need to know how much I appreciate our friendship. When we met, we connected instantly like bosom friends, Anne Shirley and Diana Barry."

Andrea popped a hand on a hip. "Will you stop talking about my boobs?"

"Well, they're so stunning!"

Andrea snorted.

"But in all seriousness, Andrea, thank you." She leaned her head beside Andrea's and wove an arm around her.

"You don't need to thank me. I know you love me, and I love you, too." She squeezed an arm gently. "Plus, I really didn't do much. You were the strong one, wading through your old life and coming out anew. I was just there to give you an extra heave when you needed one. I couldn't imagine anyone stronger, Brie."

Brie's eyes stung. "I had to be for the kids."

"I know. And look where you are now." Andrea glided a hand through the thickly perfumed air.

Brie grinned. "Best birthday surprise ever."

After embracing, they continued touring the Main Range Glasshouse past large hedges shaped like giant gumdrops and statelier park benches, then ventured to the palm house and beyond. At one p.m., they popped into the tea room and ordered petite sandwiches on light rye and Struan filled with lemon-and-coriander chicken with chili mayonnaise, hummus, sundried tomato, and rocket sprouts, soup of the day, and fresh scones with preserves and butter.

A short time later, Brie bit into her first Scottish tea sandwich and smiled at the creamy, tangy bite. "Oh, my God. So good!"

"My turn." Andrea selected a triangular sandwich with vibrant red hummus and emerald sprouts from the three-tiered silver stand. She took a generous bite of the veggie triangle. "Yum. It's a good thing we're walking with all this rich, delicious food we're eating."

"You bet! But you have nothing to worry about." Brie polished off the sandwich point. "Your curves are envious."

"You're right." Andrea dabbed at the corners of her lips with a napkin, then leveled her gaze. "Plus, I hear Scots like something to hold onto."

Brie flashed a smile. "Yet another reason I love Scotland. And with that, I'm going in." She cut the scone in half, applied a generous smear of butter and a spoonful of raspberry preserve. Lifting the half to her lips, she paused when a gaggle of giggles echoed through the tea room.

A group of five twenty-something girls sauntered in and sat at the table directly across from them. One girl with purple hair had a picture of Alexander James Mackenzie leaning on a rock across her full breasts, while another had *Got Swords?* and a picture of Bryce in character wielding a sword across hers. Other girls had Mackenzie tartan scarves wrapped around them.

"It's so crazy what a phenomenon the show is," Brie observed.

Andrea craned her neck to spy on the new arrivals. "Yup."

"Seeing his face everywhere is so strange." She picked at the corner of the scone. "I'm still not used to it."

Shrugging a shoulder, Andrea sliced a scone in half. "He's a star."

Although Brie had been seeing Bryce for close to a week, she saw him as Bryce Fraser—the kind, funny man she met in the airport. Even with the minor run-in with the Super Fan, he seemed so normal, save for, well, the sexy accent, excellent manners, and oh, who was she kidding? He wasn't normal. Bryce was incredible. Yet, thinking about visiting him on set tomorrow produced prickles of nerves.

"Brie?" Andrea asked.

Blinking, she turned. "Yeah. Just thinking."

"Well, I'm thinking since a certain someone is

taken, perhaps tomorrow, I'll meet my own star. I hear Hugh Macrae is single." She wiggled her brows, then piled black currant jelly on a scone. "Fuckin' fantastic male specimen." She licked the spoon front to back.

Brie laughed. "Perhaps you will." Lifting her scone, she tapped Andrea's. "Cheers!"

"Cheers to hot Scots and hotter friends!"

With a laugh, she bit into the soft, fluffy, and buttery biscuit. "Oh, my God," she hummed. The lightness of the biscuit paired with the creamy butter and rich jam was the perfect combination. "These are like a hug."

"A hug?" Andrea laughed.

"Yep!"

"How is everything, ladies?" The server appeared at the side of their table.

"Wonderful. The scones are so light and buttery," Brie said. "*Tapadh leat*."

She beamed. "*Tha thu di-beathte*. We're so glad you're enjoying the scones, miss." The server topped their waters off, then checked another table.

Andrea leaned forward. "Props for trying Gaelic. I have no idea what she said in reply, but she pronounced scone like gone. I'm going to say that from now on."

"You do that." Brie winked and bit into the scone. Yet, as delicious as the scone was, she couldn't help but veer her gaze every so often to the *Swords* fans and the image of the man plastered across their chests.

After tea, they worked off their deliciously rich afternoon meal, strolling along a dirt path through the garden. As the foliage grew denser, an opening appeared, exposing an iron railing and staircase. Brie wiggled her brows. "Do you think there's a secret garden?"

"Maybe." Andrea glanced down the stairs with a heavy sigh and then tugged her jeans. "Though the only secret is how I ate all that and still managed to button my pants."

Brie giggled. "What's the point of being on vacation if you can't enjoy yourself?"

Andrea expelled a loud breath. "I'm going to need vacation pants!"

"HA!" With a laugh, she hiked down the concrete stairs. Ivy spiraled on either side of the stairway, while ferns softly caressed her hand on the banister. At the base, Brie breathed in the rich earthy fragrance.

"Okay, I'm ready for a break. We must've walked miles yesterday on the *Swords of Scotland* fan tour, plus all the promenading this morning. We need to save our energy for tomorrow. Where's a damn bench when you need one?"

Cheerfully, Brie looped an arm through Andrea's. "Come on, old girl." She trudged ahead.

Andrea grunted. "I'm a year younger, you know?"

She smiled. "I know. So, follow your elder."

Andrea poked her in the side.

In response, Brie bumped hips with Andrea, and they giggled like schoolgirls. *Ping.* Brie's text dinged in her coat pocket. She fished her phone out and squealed when Bryce's name shined across the black screen.

"Is that our favorite actor?" Andrea asked.

Her chest fluttered like the leaves around her. "Yes."

—*How're the gardens?*—

—*Gorgeous! They're so dreamy and lush.*—

—*They don't call it the green city for naught.*

Where are ye *right now?*—

She lifted her phone and nudged Andrea. "Andrea, say, 'Cheese.' "

"Oh, God." She groaned, then flashed a smile.

Brie snapped a picture of them with the river meandering in the background.

—*Here we are! We just walked down a staircase toward the River Kelvin.*—

As she continued strolling, she simultaneously peeked at her phone. Perhaps Bryce was shooting a scene and only had a quick minute to text?

Although she heard Andrea protest twice that she was ready to head back, Brie tugged her along, enjoying the calm of the lapping river and the way the sunlight shimmered dancing orbs through the foliage. Rounding a corner, she came face-to-face with a tall man in a baseball hat, dark sweater, wax jacket, washed jeans, and movie-star black sunglasses. She gasped, while her pulse rapped wildly. "Bryce!"

Andrea's steps faltered, knocking into Brie's back. "Holy shit."

"Thought I'd surprise *ye*." He wrapped Brie in a hug. "Some of the cast and I wandered over here after wrapping scenes today."

Brie glanced around. "Where are they?"

Leaning forward, he glanced to the right and left, then back. "Down a wee, secret path."

She giggled.

"And *ye* must be Brie's fierce travel companion, Andrea?" He extended a hand.

Andrea bobbed her head. "I am. And such a fan of your show, Bryce." She shook his hand exuberantly. "Bryce Fraser."

"I'm so glad *ye* enjoy it. 'Tis a pleasure being a part of the show."

They stood awkwardly for a moment before Andrea cleared her throat. "I think I'll go plop on the grass like all the other smart people after tea, instead of hiking through this forest."

"Are you sure?" Brie asked.

"Absolutely." Andrea winked. "See you in a bit, Brie, and Bryce, see you tomorrow. I still can't believe it."

"Aye. See *ye* then."

When Andrea pivoted toward the stairway, she practically danced down the concrete path. Her curly hair bounced, and she sashayed.

Brie smiled.

Bryce extended a hand. "Shall we?"

"Yes." Brie slid a hand into his, entwining her fingers like a fine basket weave. Pleasure coursed through her.

They strolled down the winding path with the bubbling river cascading over rocks and a light breeze ruffling the leaves. Bryce asked about her visit to the glass houses, and she asked about his day on set. Although she relaxed in his company, with every soft graze of his fingers over hers, a sharp thrill shot into her stomach.

When the path forked, he tugged her gently into an alcove surrounded by thick, grccn foliage. He brushed his lips over hers and pulled her close, fitting curve to curve.

Brie kissed him softly and lifted her hands to his shoulders, threading her fingers through the curls at the nape of his neck, while his hands explored her back, sides, and hips.

Oh, my God. To kiss him, in the middle of a secret garden with the pungent scent of foliage surrounding them and Bryce holding her, was thrilling. Glorious sensations streaked through her, while need throbbed.

A distant sound of boots smacking the path echoed in her ears and then grew closer and closer.

Turning them away from oncoming foot traffic, Bryce adjusted so his back faced the passerby.

Brie was nestled protectively in front of him, safe and warm. She didn't care who passed. At that moment, she wanted nothing more than to kiss his full lips.

"Bryce?" a rich, female voice asked.

Bryce jolted, separating him and Brie.

A tall, gorgeous, willowy woman stood a few feet away with wide, cobalt eyes, long dark locks, and tightly pressed lips.

Bryce cleared his throat. "Ah, Eleana."

Lifting a brow, she leaned around Bryce. "And who?" Eleana asked.

She sounds so proper with her English accent, and here I am, a kissed-brainless mess. Brie pressed her lips together and prayed she had an ounce of gloss on them, even as they tingled with Bryce's kiss. She stepped forward, offering a hand, but couldn't deny the flush consuming her face. "Brielle. It's so nice to meet you."

Extending a hand with long, tapered fingers and skin like porcelain, she shook Brie's. "And you." Her gaze scarcely left Brie's before she glanced at Bryce with a pitch of a perfect brow.

Bryce simply cocked a lip.

Watching the silent exchange, Brie straightened. "Do you often come to the Botanical Gardens?"

"I do. Well, we all do." She tossed her wavy locks over her shoulder. "It's a charming place to unwind after shooting. Plus, there are areas with relatively few people, and after filming with cast, crew, and extras, we need a little tranquility. Don't we, Bryce?"

"Aye," he replied.

"I can imagine. It's so peaceful. From the moment we first stepped through those gates, I felt as though we were in a sanctuary."

Eleana smiled. "Lettie and George are past the bridge. Will you be joining us?"

Grinning, Bryce glanced from Eleana to Brie. "I'll catch up to *ye*."

Eleana nodded curtly. "Pleasure to meet you, Brielle."

She flashed a smile. "You, too."

With the grace of a dancer, Eleana floated on heeled boots like a prima ballerina on stage in perfectly tailored pants and crisp, button-down.

Brie lifted a hand to her half-up hairdo, tucking the loose swatches of hair back into the clip, and found a leaf. Sighing, she unwound the leaf and then smoothed her sweater. She was a mess—a disheveled mess in front of Bryce's beautiful, longtime co-star. She could only imagine what Eleana was thinking. Glancing at Bryce, she found him staring with sparkling, blue eyes. "I'm glad I got to meet, Eleana."

"As am I." Bryce grinned and trailed a hand down her arm to her hand. "Would *ye* like to walk a bit more 'round River Kelvin? Eleana and I still need to run some lines before end of day, but I'd like to spend a wee bit more time together while I have *ye*."

Run lines with Eleana? She was his co-star. Purely

a platonic relationship, right? Yet, Eleana had gazed at Bryce in question and perhaps something more. Protective, maybe? Brie wasn't sure; yet, Bryce had stayed with her. She ignored the little questioning bird on her shoulder and squeezed Bryce's hand. "I'd love to." But the sound of boots clicking on the concrete echoed in her mind.

****

While the late afternoon sun glowed softly through the trees, Eleana sidled up alongside Bryce in the garden. She slid a sideways glance, once, twice.

"Out with it, will *ye*?" he muttered.

"Where did you meet her?"

"In Scotland." Bryce released a long breath. "I'm actually happy *ye* met Brie, so I could talk about her. We met at the airport and then later I ran into her in Edinburgh, and we've been seeing each other since."

Eleana pivoted, weaving around a passerby. "Does she live here, then?"

Bryce shook his head. "No, she's on holiday."

Lifting a perfectly arched brow, she hummed. "Mmmhmm."

"I know what *yer* thinking." He stepped aside, allowing Eleana to proceed through the gateway first toward the carpark.

She met his gaze. "Do you?"

"Aye, I do, but she's no' like the others. She'd never even heard of the show until we met."

Eleana halted beside her car and touched his hand. "Are you sure, Bryce?"

Staring at his co-star and friend of five years, Bryce recalled their history together. They'd gotten along brilliantly the first week on set, flirted casually, then fought like siblings, and finally came to a mutual friendship of respect. She'd even gone to bat for him a few times during recommended line changes or answered a question during an interview when she was aware he wouldn't want to respond to a personal question. Like him, she knew how fame and the press could be, but she also knew how to use both to her advantage.

"Can you trust her?" She crossed her arms. "I don't want your face smeared up and down the West End and back again."

"Aye, me neither, but she's different. She's"— Bryce lifted his hat and raked a hand through his hair, then set the hat firmly down—"normal and beautiful. She even has kids."

"Kids?"

"Aye, she was married before."

"Just watch yourself, all right?" Her voice lowered. "It was horrid what Kathryn put you through, and you don't need a replication."

Bryce clenched his jaw. "Brie isn't Kathryn."

"True. Kathryn was too young for you anyway."

He heaved a breath. "Next time, give me *yer* opinion before we break up."

"I recall mentioning my opinion rather strongly." She swung the car door open. "A few times."

"Aye, *ye* did." Bryce would never date another twenty-five year old.

With a hand on his arm, she gazed directly at him. "Be careful, okay?"

"Aye, she's only here for another week anyway." Bryce would be careful. Since ending his relationship with Kathryn, he'd approached dating with a healthy dose of skepticism, but he couldna stop thinking about Brie.

Chapter 14

As the setting sun illuminated the cloudy sky with tangerine and burnt-red tones, Brie smoothed her fingers across the soft, knit lavender sweater, trailing them down to her abdomen and released a breath. She tucked a strand of hair behind her ears where gold hoops hung and gazed in the bathroom mirror.

"Are you ready?" Andrea asked from the doorway.

She smiled, even though nerves skittered through her. "It's just a drink."

"It's not just a drink." Andrea wiggled her brows. "I won't wait up."

Brie's face burned. "I—do you think?"

"Uh, yeah." She bobbed her head, bouncing curls. "You two looked at each other earlier like you haven't eaten in days. Plus, I noticed you put on that lavender, lace lingerie set."

Feeling her stomach flutter, she pressed her fingertips to her middle. "It makes me feel sexy."

Andrea rested a hand on Brie's forearm. "It should. You should feel sexy, beautiful, and desired. It's time." Tugging her in for a hug, Andrea gave Brie a quick squeeze, then released her, holding her hands at arm's length. "Now, go have some fun."

Brie glanced at the two, queen beds side-by-side. Hers was made with the comforter drawn and pillows fluffed, while Andrea's was disheveled from watching television. "Are you sure? I don't want you to feel like you're on a solo trip again."

With a cock of her head, Andrea flashed a smile. "We're good, okay? I'm a big girl. I can snuggle up early tonight, especially since we're going to the set of *Swords of Scotland* tomorrow. That's because you're dating Bryce."

Nibbling her lower lip, she glanced at Andrea. "Am I dating him, though?" They hadn't talked formally about what they were doing together. They were seeing one another and texting regularly. A few hours earlier, Bryce had texted her as she and Andrea left the Botanical Gardens, asking if she'd like to join him for dinner at his home.

Brie promised Andrea she'd spend the day with her, which included dinner at a steakhouse and a visit to another pub.

Yet, after the long, fan tour yesterday, dinner and drinks the night before, and Botanical Garden today, Andrea stated she wanted nothing more than to have a nice dinner, then lounge in the bath.

So instead, Brie declined, telling Bryce she had dinner plans.

He replied a few minutes later, asking her to join him for a drink. *Or was it a drink and a nightcap? Did it matter?* She was a grown, mature, thirty-one-year-old woman. But she hadn't had sex in over a year-and-a-half. Would she be bad at the act? Would she freeze? Or worse, would she cry?

Lord, she hadn't been naked in front of a man since Ryan. She had C-section scars and a few stretch marks. She wasn't a perfect, female specimen. What would Bryce think?

Andrea shook Brie's arms once, twice. "Brie! Stop overthinking everything. Go. Have fun!"

Her phone pinged, notifying her the car had arrived, so she disappeared into the night with the stars and her nerves for company.

****

Twenty minutes later, Brie arrived at a black iron gate surrounded by rich, green shrubbery on one side, bordering another home, and farmland on the other.

The driver pushed the intercom button, and immediately, a buzzing sound pierced the air. The gates opened.

A two-story stone home with a white-and-cream exterior, canopied entrance, and charcoal accents greeted her. Beside the main house, a separate garage with doors below and windows above suggested it was probably a guest house. Bryce's home was large, but not huge by L.A. standards. What made it wondrous was that the house was Bryce's.

The driver opened her door.

She stepped onto the charming cobblestone and took a deep breath.

"Have a wonderful evening, miss," the driver said.

"Thank you. You, too." As she pivoted toward the front door, passing manicured hedges, rich roses, and other colorful flowers, she pressed a hand over the tickles of excitement tangling in her stomach. A few feet before she arrived at his doorstep, the front door opened. Brie's breath caught.

With the warm, interior light blazing, Bryce stood with a dark sweater, fitted jeans, and broad smile like a shining star in the night.

"Welcome, Brielle." He stepped down to meet her,

extending a hand.

Oh, how he says my name. With her chest fluttering and pulse zipping, she slid a hand into his. "Thank you. Your home is charming."

"Thank *ye*." A smile teased at his lips. He led her into his home and closed the door. As soon as the door *clicked*, Bryce closed the distance between them, alighting his mouth firmly on hers and cupping a hand to her cheek. He drew Brie closer, deepening the kiss and gliding his wide hand down the curve of her jaw, length of her neck, and slope of her shoulder to her waist. *I've never answered a booty call, but if this is what it is, I'm glad I shaved my legs.*

****

Good God. Bryce wanted her here and now. When he heard her utter a faint sigh, Bryce withdrew with effort. He gazed at her swollen lips and heavy lids with desire. He could've taken her then and there, but he wanted to show her care. And, he intended to do just that tonight.

He slipped a hand in hers and prepared to give Brie a tour of his home, partly to calm his own craving and partly to show her the care she deserved. He didn't invite anyone into his home. In fact, he welcomed very few into his private space, but something about Brie told him he could trust her. He'd told Eleana so much just a few hours prior.

Leading Brie casually through the first floor past the reception hallway, he drew her toward the large, contemporary kitchen, grinning when her bonnie eyes widened.

"Wow. Your kitchen is incredible." She skirted the large, gleaming island. "You can roll out a half dozen pie crusts easily. Did I tell you I like to bake? Baking is one of the things that relaxes me besides painting. I'm not a chef by any stretch of the imagination. Andrea's the cook in our duo."

With a grin, he listened. He'd been spot-on with the idea of a quick tour to calm her nerves, even if it tortured him.

"Oh!" Brie's smile shined. "A waterfall design."

He chuckled. "*Ye* like waterfall designs?"

"I do. I'm a fan of those DIY shows, but I've never seen one in person. This is very cool." Brie glided her right hand across the marble top, then trailed long, slim fingers down the seam of the waterfall.

Desire roused within him once again.

She glanced up. "And I'm talking too much. Your home is beautiful."

With a shake of his head, he leaned forward and met her gaze. "I enjoy hearing *ye* speak." Bryce was glad she was talking instead of exhibiting nerves for what they both knew would transpire later that night. Continuing down the hallway, he showed her his study and the living room, then drew her outside to the firepit and sitting area.

"Oh!" She flew her gaze across the backyard and evergreens beyond. "I love this. It's so cozy."

Pride swelled his chest. This was his first home. Sure, he owned a flat in Edinburgh, but this was truly a home where he could relax and get away from all the bright lights. During the day, peacefulness reigned with birdsong, and in the evening, the blissful notes of cricket melody were the only spare sounds. "Aye, 'tis." He led her to the couch. "Have a seat. Can I get *ye* a drink? Scotch? Wine?"

"Wine. No, Scotch." Brie perched on the corner of the blue rattan couch, fanning her hands toward the full fire.

Lifting a brow, he tilted his head.

"When in Scotland," she said. "But make it a small glass, please."

He smirked and retreated to get the drinks. A few minutes later, he stepped back through the French doors and paused on the landing.

Brie's head dipped over something. Her warm brown hair shone in the firelight like liquid gold, and she appeared to be writing.

He clenched his jaw. *Why would she be writing? Was she a secret journalist?* Apprehension prickled up his spine. He gripped the whisky glasses and strode forward.

When she saw him approaching, Brie quickly closed the notebook and tucked the small book into her bag. She straightened and flashed a smile.

Bryce's chest tightened, and the air rushed out. Fearing she'd been writing secretly about him, he advanced cautiously. "What were *ye* writing?"

"Oh, a note." She waved a hand. "The stars are incredible here. I wanted to remember them—how luminous they rest in the dark sky like a white water lily floating effortlessly atop deep, blue water. Before this trip, I couldn't tell you the last time I actually gazed at the stars, actually looked up, and stared at the incandescent beauty of the sky."

He relaxed his grip on the glasses and passed one to Brie. Yet, with a flick of his gaze over the closed notebook, the tightness in his chest returned. Was she truly who he believed she was? He'd been played enough to know who was authentic. And he'd been around his fair share of actors. Yet, even gazing at Brie and her refreshing beauty, a nagging voice taunted him—did she truly like him for himself, or was she using him like others before? A *hoot-hoot* from an owl in the distance interrupted his thoughts, and he faced her. "So, *ye* were taking notes about the stars?"

She nodded. "It probably seems silly."

"No." Bryce sat beside her and fought the urge to lift his free arm to rest casually over her shoulder. "I often sit out here and gaze at them myself. Even on set, when we work into the wee hours of the morning, I find myself staring at the radiant stars."

"They're striking, especially here." She brushed his shoulder with hers.

With her gentle touch, electricity shot through Bryce. Choosing to focus on the drink in his hand, he lifted his glass. "Slainte."

"Slainte." Brie sipped.

He angled toward her. "So, are *ye* an astrologer? I don't remember asking what *ye* did for a living."

"I'm a writer."

He stiffened. "A journalist?"

"No. I'm not a journalist. I've been working on a personal project…a memoir about my journey to finding myself through my divorce. But my day job is all about proposals. I write professional, business-style proposals for a tech company."

Nodding, he relaxed back into the sturdy couch. *Get over* yerself, *man. Not everyone is after* yer *celebrity status*. "Ah, I see. Tell me about *yer* project."

She smiled, yet nibbled the corner of her lower lip. "You really want to know?"

"Yes."

"It started with me just…needing to get everything out in the open. I had hit rock-bottom emotionally and financially. After the divorce, I received alimony to put a deposit on a rental home and had a thousand dollars to my name. Ryan would pay child support, but the stipend didn't cover all the cost, and I didn't want to depend on him, not when he'd left us. So, I got a job to make up the difference. I wanted to stand on my own two feet and be a beacon for my children." She blinked her eyes and focused.

"I stopped working once we had children to be a stay-at-home mom. And I loved that role. Spending time with Noah and Phoebe, going on adventures, and creating a warm home was what I loved, but slowly, things changed. Ryan began working more and more and spent less and less time with us. I just never expected him to cheat or leave the kids and me." She paused, taking a shaky breath. "I had all this in me that I needed to get out—anger, frustration, and self-doubt. I poured all of my thoughts into a diary of a sort, but what in the book world we'd call a memoir. One day, I realized what I was doing was finding myself again through the pages." When she met his gaze, her eyes glossed with emotion.

"That's truly honorable." Bryce rubbed calloused fingers over her smooth palm.

"Thank you."

"Would *ye* read me something *ye've* written?"

Brie's eyes widened.

As he waited for an answer, a knot settled in his stomach, churning and jabbing his intestines. He'd find the truth now, even if it was the worst.

****

Brie bit her lip. She'd only ever shared her writing with Andrea, knowing it was a safe exchange between two equals—two aspiring authors—working on their craft. But Bryce… "Oh, I…" She glanced down at her hands, then at Bryce. "Are you sure?"

He angled his head. "If *yer* comfortable."

Comfortable. Wasn't she writing to share her story with others? She was nervous, but comfortable? Sitting beside Bryce, snug against his warmth, while his kind, reassuring eyes stared back, how could she be anything but? She'd come tonight. And she trusted him. That much she knew. But sharing her writing was an entirely different beast. Her prose was personal. And as much as she didn't want to admit, she was scared. Here he was a famous actor, and she an aspiring author. Was her writing good enough? Was she?

Bryce touched her arm with a hand. "*Ye* don't have to," he said softly.

When she lifted her gaze, she noted how his eyes were as clear as the cloudless-sky above and patient. Then and there, Brie decided if she trusted him enough to potentially be physically intimate, she would trust another part of herself and share her writing.

She took a quick, excited breath and grasped her journal. "This is what I wrote." She cleared her throat. "Okay, here we go." She flipped pages and settled on her entry. "The stars here are unlike any I've seen, although I can't remember the last time I gazed at the stars. As I sit here beside the glowing fire flicking tiny, dancing sparkles into the air, it seems the sparks have landed in the sky. When I was a little girl, I was told stars are brilliant, tiny fires producing light. And now, looking up, I believe it.

"The stars are a range of shapes and sizes—some opaque like a pearl in the ocean, while others dot like small snowflakes drifting from the sky, and others blaze like the most brilliant light I've ever seen as if the sun has just burst through the clouds. Have the stars always been this beautiful? Has life?

"This trip has made me take a step back in the whirlwind of my life and stop, and look—look up and look forward." She closed her journal. "That's what I have so far."

Bryce stared. "*Ye* have a gift, Brie."

"Thank you." She smiled. "And thank you for asking. This memoir has been life-changing. While writing my story, I've rekindled my love of writing and discovered things about myself and the world I've missed. My children have been my everything, but I'd forgotten what made me happy. Just me. I thought wanting something for myself was selfish—that's what my ex made me feel—but having my own interest is important."

"I can understand wanting to find *yer* feet again, especially with the wee ones, and I'm glad *ye've* rediscovered *yer* passion. *Ye* should keep writing." Bryce leaned in with a quick kiss. "*Yer* good at it."

"Yes," she whispered.

"Seems like we both found our way." He gazed into her eyes, holding, saying nothing, but so much in the silence.

When his phone *beeped*, he ignored the device.

But Brie couldn't help but wonder who would text him at nine p.m. Was the texter a friend asking him to go to a pub? A reminder from a director? Or someone else?

Yesterday, Eleana stumbled upon them kissing in the park. Even though she was warm and introduced herself, Brie noticed the cool undertone in Eleana's voice and the way she eyed Bryce, watching and assessing. She loosened her hand from Bryce's grip.

She still remembered the way Ryan had told her he wanted her. Yet, he wouldn't stay with her or leave Jasmine. She did everything he asked to make him happy—to come back to her and the kids, but they were empty promises. He had her fooled. He still wanted his lover. "You can't have me and her. You have to choose," Brie had said.

Anger flashed in Ryan's eyes. "Damn it, Brie."

"We made vows to one another," she cried. "We created a home and family. We have children. Don't you want that? Want us?"

"People change. I still want you. And you know you want me, too." He grabbed her and kissed her.

But even as Brie's heart tore in two, she still loved him, somehow. He was her first love. She pulled away. "I can't do this. Either you stop seeing her, or I'm filing for divorce."

"It's your decision, Brie." He pointed a finger, focusing his laser-hard gaze. "Remember, you're the one who's breaking apart this family."

She'd shivered and fled to her room. Repressing the memory, she found Bryce staring. She couldn't go through that again. She wouldn't share another man. "I know I probably should've asked this from the start"— Brie angled, so she faced Bryce—"but I would like to ask you something."

He inclined his head. "What is it *ye* want to

know?"

"What are we doing?"

With a grin, he gestured toward the twinkling stars. "Having a dram under the starlight."

She licked her lips since he stared intensely under those sandy lashes. "You know what I mean."

"Can we just enjoy one another's company?"

"We can," Brie replied slowly. "But as long as we're talking about the company we keep…your co-star, Eleana Evans, seems nice."

Nodding, he swirled his drink. "Aye, she is."

In turn, Brie sipped her whisky, letting the fiery notes coat her throat. Whisky courage. She didn't know if she wanted to find the answer she was seeking, and if she did, would she leave, or would she stay? She didn't know the answers, but she still had to ask, regardless of his response. She blew out a breath. "I don't want to intrude on something between the two of you. I get it—we met in unusual circumstances and acted on our instincts, and you've been, well, wonderful, but I don't go around dating men who are already involved, even if I'm on vacation, and we might never see each other again."

Bryce frowned. "No, *ye* have it all wrong. I'm lucky to work with her, but we're not lovers. We're more like siblings. She's an amazing actress, knows just what to do to crack me, and so much fun, but there's nothing romantic between us—even if *ye* do see gossip about the on-screen sex scenes. Shooting a scene with near two dozen people in a room, wearing a privacy pouch, and being tested regularly, doesn't inspire romance."

She tilted her head. "A privacy pouch?"

With a chuckle, he scrunched his nose. "A, em, modesty garment to keep"—he gestured toward his lap—"everything inside and protected."

She giggled. "I see."

"Part of the unglamorous bits about being an actor." He cleared his throat. "Anyway, Eleana's quietly engaged to be married."

"Oh." Brie relaxed back into the couch. She hadn't expected to hear that piece of truth, though she hadn't glanced at Eleana's hands when they'd met, either.

"But *ye*." Bryce curled the last word with his lovely brogue, then rose, tugging her upright, so they stood a breath apart with the firelight glistening around them.

"Yes?" Brie splayed her hands across the hard lines of his chest.

"*Ye* have surprised me from the first moment we met, and I can't help but want to spend more and more time with *ye*."

Her heart soared like a bird gliding in the twinkling night sky. *He wants me.* "I feel the same way."

With a dip of his head, Bryce brushed his lips softly against hers, then gently explored her depths.

Gripping his sweater, she sank into the kiss, tasting the subtle, sweet, and sharp notes of whisky and utterly Bryce.

When he drew away, his eyes were dark like the sea, and his chest heaved.

"How are you single?" Brie whispered.

The corners of his lips tipped up. "I guess there hasn't been much time for dating. I've dated on and off, but I've put my career first. Working on *Swords* eight months out of the year and movie roles during the off season doesn't leave much room for relationships."

"So, you've been busy?" Brie inclined her head. Her hands still splayed across Bryce's firm pectorals, alighting them with zips of energy with the possibility of touching more. Yet, nerves also danced through her. Was she ready for what might happen between them?

"Aye." He leaned in with a slow smile. "Apparently, not so busy that *ye've* never heard of me."

She poked him. "Don't get too full of yourself, Bryce Fraser."

"I tell myself that all the time actually."

"Oh, I didn't mean…" Brie began.

Bryce shook his head. "I understand well what *ye* mean." Leaning down, he touched his lips to hers once again, quickly this time. When he drew away, he trailed calloused fingers down her arms and then entwined his long fingers with hers. "Will *ye* come to bed with me?"

Her palm ignited and insides fired with his touch, letting her know the fire between them still smoldered. "Yes."

Chapter 15

Bryce led her through the house and up the oak stairs, while his thumb traced her palm. When he opened the bedroom door, he released her hand.

Trailing her gaze on him in the dark, she wondered if he was as anxious as she. He squatted, turning a key and igniting the fireplace with a soft, blue glow as fire engulfed wooden logs, then crossed to light a white candle beside his bed—a large, sturdy bed with wooden headboard and navy comforter—and another opposite. As he grasped the second candle, he fumbled the wax light. He quickly extended his other hand, catching the candle like a hot potato. With an exhale, he lit the wick.

He's nervous. Something about that eased her own anxiousness.

When he faced her a moment later, his chest rose up and down.

Brie sighed. "It's beautiful."

"And so, are *ye*." Bryce lifted a hand to caress her cheek and leaned down, brushing his lips across hers, kissing her soft and slow.

His tenderness was a gentle promise of what was to come. She circled his strong back, feeling the tangle of muscles and smooth skin, while he slid his fingertips under her lavender sweater, drawing a gasp.

"May I?"

She nodded. Though her blood raced with

anticipation—every vessel humming—Brie was ready.

When he lifted her sweater over her head, he grinned. "Sexy," he said with a thickened brogue.

Brie smiled softly, then glided her hands to his hips, undressing him further. His skin shone like gold in the candlelight, while chiseled muscles flowed from the hard curves of his chest and strong shoulders to the *V* below his firm stomach. The fire *crackled*, yet, it seemed far away as her heart pounded deafeningly in her ears.

As they continued undressing one another, Brie's body scorched with every graze of his fingers over her skin. Yet, she couldn't deny the somersaults in her stomach. When she stood naked before him, she watched as Bryce stepped back and studied her—gaze roaming every curve. Brie couldn't remember the last time a man looked at her so thoroughly and so completely. She wrung her hands together as the nervous somersaults morphed into back handsprings.

"*Yer* so bonnie."

"Thank you. I-I haven't done this in a long time."

Bryce's gaze softened; yet, desire still churned like a wild storm brewing in a calm sea. He stepped forward and clasped her hand in his, while his other stroked her arm. "Are *ye* sure this is what *ye* want?"

She studied him—his handsome face, sexy freckles, full lips she'd just finished kissing, and reassuring eyes. Here she was with Mr. Scotland, and all she could see was Bryce. The wonderful man she met just a few days ago who had surprised her, made her laugh, and melted her. She placed a hand on his bare chest. "I want to be with you." Rising to her toes, she touched her lips to his, feeling the spark ignite within.

In one swift movement, Bryce lifted her into his arms and laid her on the bed.

As she scooted toward the pillow, she watched him tug his boxers down. She bit her bottom lip, while her insides jumped with joy. She definitely agreed he was Mr. Scotland.

When he joined her at the base of the bed, he lifted one leg at a time and kissed his way up from her toes. He squeezed her calf.

Brie moaned. "What are you doing?"

"*Yer* legs are amazing." Bryce sculpted them with his hands.

She laughed. "Really? I've been a runner since I was a kid and played soccer, as well. I suppose I have athletic legs, but I've always been envious of those long, model legs."

"No," he said, accent thickening, and swept his gaze over her body, then up to meet hers once again. "Athletic bodies are sexy, especially when they lead to a nice, round ass." His hand gripped her butt.

Brie giggled and glided her hands through his curls.

As Bryce dipped his head and kissed one kneecap, then the other, he smoothed a hand from foot to ankle, molding Brie's calf once more, then squeezed gently and slid his hands up toward her thigh. He kept going, kissing her warm center, stomach, and navel, then trailed his tongue over the swell of her breasts and rose to meet her lips. Yet, this kiss wasn't soft and slow; his tongue swiped hers in a delicious frenzy, asking for more.

Brie met him need for need. She raked her hands

over his skin, gripping firm muscles, wrapping her legs around him, and drawing him closer.

Pausing a moment, Bryce reached across and retrieved a condom from the side table, then rolled the contraceptive on, chest heaving.

"I'm on birth control, too—an IUD." She squeezed his strong thighs.

Nodding, he drew her against him once more, and they joined in one swift movement.

She moaned and closed her eyes, flying on the sensations within.

"Brielle."

She winged her eyes open and found Bryce, looking so intently and so completely, she saw herself reflected in his eyes like a glowing goddess in the firelight.

Capturing her lips once more, he kissed her soundly, thoroughly, then slowly began rocking. They moved together rhythmically body-to-body and heartbeat-to-heartbeat, until Brie cried out with tears in her eyes, and Bryce collapsed on top of her.

A few minutes later, Brie feathered her fingers through dark, coppery curls. "Mmm, you have the perfect amount of chest hair."

Bryce lay beside her, one arm tucked around her, while the other rested behind his head. "I'm happy to oblige *ye*."

She grinned.

He tilted his head. "Is there something more?"

"Some men shave their chest hair…Well, I'm sure they shave more, but at the beaches and such in L.A., men strut around hairless. Their chests are…shiny."

"Shiny, *ye* say?" he asked with a crook of a smile.

"Well, they canna truly be men then. Real men have chest hair."

Laughing, Brie shook. "Okay, that has got to be on a license plate sticker somewhere."

"Aye." Bryce planted a firm kiss on her lips, then rolled off the bed and strolled naked toward the bathroom.

At first, she admired the amazing view of his strong back and firm butt, but once he disappeared, a pit settled in her stomach. Was he getting dressed? Would he send her home? She only had Ryan to compare to, and he wasn't the snuggle kind. Once they made love, he'd wait no longer than a few seconds before separating to take a shower.

But a moment later, Bryce reappeared. "Be right back." He winked and strolled toward the hall. He quickly returned with two glasses of plum-colored wine.

She relaxed into the pillows, shoving aside past memories. Sometime later, she circled a finger along his bicep, trailing it down to his elbow where a deep scar was visible on his forearm. She lifted her gaze to his.

"A battle wound."

"Battle wound? Like from the set of your show?"

"Yes." He laughed softly. "My on-screen uncle and I were sword fighting, and he got a wee bit too close for comfort."

She raised a brow. "You do your own stunt work?"

"Aye." He grinned and shifted closer. "I like to embody my characters. Plus, it's a lot of fun."

"I hope it didn't hurt too much." She traced her fingers once more along the worm-like scar.

Running a hand down her hair, he kissed her forehead. "It's fine"—his eyes held a devilish look—"especially since I got to kill 'em last season."

Brie widened her eyes. "Really?"

"Aye, the perfect payback for that gent." He stroked her lower back.

Brie giggled. "I have a few scars, too, though they're more miracle scars than anything."

"I noticed *ye* had a cut below *yer* belly button."

She blushed and tugged the sheet up. Why did she mention her scars?

Bryce tucked a swag of hair behind her ear. "I didna mean to make *ye* self-conscious."

"I was told I couldn't have children." She lifted her gaze. "Something about the way my hips are shaped. But I got pregnant and everything was fine, I mean relatively—I still experienced morning sickness…do you really want to hear this?" *This has to be the most unromantic topic. Ugh, why did I say anything in the first place?*

He nodded. "Yes."

Gripping the sheet, she twisted the fabric. "But when I went into labor with Noah, my body didn't follow course naturally. I had to have a C-section. It was the same with Phoebe."

"Ah, I see. Miracle scars, *ye* say?" He leaned down, gently pushing the sheet aside, and brushed his lips across the line, then trailed kisses up to her lips.

Butterflies lit upon her, winging their vibrancy up her body. "Mmm, then there's the way you do that." She sighed.

Bryce chuckled and drew her in for another before settling beside her once again. When he craned his head toward the clock, he grimaced.

Brie stiffened. "Do you want me to…leave?"

"No." He leaned forward to capture her lips once again. "Stay with me?"

"Yes." She nestled in the crook of Bryce's shoulder with her hand on his heart. But she couldn't stay forever.

****

Ring-ring! Ring-ring!

Startled, Brie reached for her phone on the hotel nightstand before remembering she wasn't in her hotel; she was with Bryce. And her kids were calling on video chat at three in the morning. She muttered a curse, clicked the silence button, and slipped out of bed guided by the flickering fireplace light.

As she stepped forward, she kicked something, lost her footing, and face-planted on the carpet. "Oomph."

Bryce shot up—hair sticking straight up on one side and curled on the other, resembling a super hair hero versus a sex icon.

She giggled. "Sorry. Go back to sleep."

He mumbled and fell back on his pillow.

Brie quickly tugged on a sweater and underwear, then called Mimi under the soft glow of the hallway light.

"Mommy!"

Squeals of delight sounded from the phone, and her smiling babies' faces squished into the frame. "Hi, my sweeties. I'm sorry I didn't answer right away. It's late here."

"I put bubbles on my head!" Phoebe crinkled her nose, while her cheeks shined like rosy crab apples.

"You did?"

"We had a fun bath, didn't we?" Mimi asked.

"We did, but Mimi said it's time for bed." Phoebe pouted, while her eyes glossed. "I don't want to go to bed. I want Mommy to put me to bed."

Mimi made calming sounds and cradled Phoebe in her lap.

Phoebe, in turn, stuck her thumb in her mouth and sniffled.

"I know, sweetheart. Mommy loves you," Brie said, voice cracking.

Noah frowned. "She doesn't know the new story."

"I see." Brie drew a breath in and released it in an attempt to clear the tightness in her chest, as well as the three a.m. cobwebs. She could do this. Phoebe and Noah needed a story for bedtime…What was the story? She blinked. Outside the nearby window, the milky moon shone between puffy clouds and the outline of towering evergreens. "One day, fairy princess Phoebe and brave Noah ventured into a serene, green forest…" A few minutes later, she padded toward Bryce's room and crawled into bed and Bryce's warm center.

"*Ye've* quite the imagination," he whispered and wrapped an arm around her.

She snuggled in farther against the curve of his chest. "I'm sorry. I didn't mean to wake you."

Fanning his fingers through her hair the way he did, he tucked a wisp over her ear, fingers grazing her cheek. " 'Tis no' a problem. I'm sure *yer* missing them."

"Yes." Her bottom lip wobbled, feeling love and ache bursting within. She wished she could see Phoebe and Noah in a few hours, but they were thousands of miles away.

"What do you miss most?"

"Their sweet smell when I breathe them in before bed—lavender from their bath mixed with their own essence—and one more."

He inclined his head, drawing his forehead closer. "One more?"

"Yes." She smiled. "One more sweet kiss, one more hug, and one more time in the rocking chair. At times, all I want is to put them into bed, so I can climb into my own, but then, I feel Phoebe's angel-soft hair on my cheek, and I well up. Noah, too. He always wants one more giant hug and presses his tiny lips to my cheek before wrapping his arms tight around my neck."

"Ah, 'tis a grand feeling."

"It is." She missed her children, but being with Bryce and talking about them helped ease the longing.

"I've only a few instances to compare when my nephew stayed over, but when I finally got him to sleep, I couldn't help but stare."

Brie fit her right hand into his. "How old is he?"

"*Och*, somewhere around two then. I had both my nephew and wee niece stay over a few months ago, so my brother-in-law could take my sister out for their anniversary."

Intrigued, Brie propped a hand under her chin. "And how did that go?"

"One was easy. Two." He rolled his eyes in an exaggerated manner. "I needed a couple cups of coffee the next morning."

She laughed full and strong. She couldn't help but melt. Bryce was a family man, after all. She'd pegged him for a single guy, but that couldn't have been further from the truth.

Listening to him talk about his family, she followed along, enjoying the natural, effortless way he told stories until her eyelids fluttered. His voice grew softer and softer and then, she drifted.

Brie woke to a soft alarm a short time later. "Five-thirty a.m.?" She rubbed her eyes.

" 'Tis, I need to get a workout in." He stretched an arm across to click the alarm off, fitting perfectly against her backside.

Brie snugged her body against his. "We can have our own workout."

"Aye." He retrieved a condom, then rolled her on top of him.

Seeing desire smolder in Bryce's eyes, Brie felt a surge of confidence burst through her. With her gaze set on him, she moved.

An hour later, Brie meandered into the kitchen hand-in-hand with Bryce fresh from a hot shower and feeling quite sexy. She examined the large island and six-burner stove. "Hmm."

He inclined his head. "What are *ye* thinking about?"

"Pancakes." She placed her hands on her hips. "I haven't made them in a week."

The corners of Bryce's lips curled. "Do *ye* make them often?"

"Twice a week with special requests. Just last week, I made snowman and dinosaur pancakes. I can pretty much make pancakes from scratch by memory."

"Truly? *Yer* an artist in the kitchen, as well then?" Bryce nudged her against the counter to nuzzle her neck.

"No." She giggled. "Not in the slightest. I like to paint, but pancake art is an entirely different beast. My kids think they're great, and that's all that matters. And as much as I tire making them normally, I've been missing making the cakes with them. Plus, I love berry pancakes."

Leaning back on those well-defined arms, he gazed at her. "Shall we make some then? I've about thirty minutes until I need to head to set."

Brie smiled. "Really?"

"Absolutely." He planted a kiss smartly on her lips, then stepped back. "What do *ye* need?"

Brie rubbed her hands together. "This is going to be fun! We need a bowl, measuring cups and spoons, a whisk, flour, sugar, baking powder, salt, milk, oil, and an egg."

Bryce opened a cupboard and retrieved a glass bowl. "Bowl, and em"—he pivoted, turning right, then left—"I know I have a whisk. Ah, here 'tis." He drew a wire whisk from a caddy of utensils.

Selecting the coconut milk and an egg from the fridge, Brie began organizing wet ingredients, while Bryce arranged the dry.

"So, we need a cup of flour."

"A cup?" He raised a quizzical brow.

"Oh shit, metric system, right?" Brie stared at the instruments before her.

"So, *ye* swear then? That's the first I've heard."

Leveling her gaze, she hummed. "I know plenty of swear words. But I don't really cuss much because my kids repeat *everything*."

He chuckled. "Aye, I gathered that for myself."

"Um, how many grams in a cup?"

He grinned. "I'd leave that task to the web, but fortunate for us"—he dropped to his haunches and opened a few drawers, then rose with a collection of metal measuring cups—"these have both measures."

Brie peered at the metal handles. "You're right. Ml's and cups. Perfect." She measured and added the flour, then retrieved the measuring spoons and scooped baking powder, salt, and sugar. "Would you like to whisk?"

"Aye." Retrieving the metal whisk, he twirled the tool through the powdery mixture.

"And four ounces of oil." She glanced at Bryce who lifted a shoulder. Brie laughed as she lifted the measuring cups. "Don't worry about it. I'll eyeball it."

He leaned toward her with a grin. "Eyeball it, *ye* say?"

"Absolutely!" She selected the second largest cup and poured oil.

"So, 'tis a bit of a game, cooking with *ye*?"

She laughed. "It's really all about consistency." Brie added a cup of milk to the bowl. "I'm an efficient, makeshift cook, but Andrea's the gourmet. You should try her linguine pasta *alle vongole*—it's my favorite!"

"Well, whatever *ye* are in the kitchen"—he kissed her exposed neck—"I'm impressed."

With a giggle, she measured and mixed, but the batter clumped. "We need a splash more milk."

"A splash?" Bryce's eyes crinkled around the edges. "These are precise measurements. I didna know I was cooking with a kitchen magician."

Laughing, she snagged the coconut milk container. With a quick flick of the wrist, she added more milk to the mixture, then lifted a hand toward Bryce. "Whisk, please."

"Aye." Gripping the bowl, he turned the whisk in the creamy mixture.

Brie appreciated the way he spun the wire whisk in his hand and the way his forearm muscles and biceps bunched with movement. Witnessing him shirtless with a pair of running shorts on, she licked her lips. *God, he's sexy.*

Bryce glanced from Brie to his chest. "Have I mix on me?"

She hummed. "No, just admiring you."

"Oh, aye?" He grinned devilishly. "Happy to oblige, but *ye've* got to stop undressing me with those eyes. I've not enough time to take advantage of *ye* again."

With a quick squeeze of his bicep, she nearly skipped to the refrigerator. She scanned the shelves, but she didn't find what she was after. "Do you have syrup?"

"Em, no."

"We can whip up some berry syrup or serve it with yogurt."

He chuckled, then wrapped an arm snuggly around her. "Berry syrup, *ye* say? Let's do it."

They mashed and muddled raspberries with lemon juice and sugar, perfuming the air with citrus and sweetness, until the mixture boiled, turning the fruit into a thick, luscious sauce. When they sat, overlooking the garden with coconut flour pancakes topped with raspberry syrup, Brie sighed and took her first bite. Yet, as she ate, she couldn't help but glance at Bryce's phone glowing with messages. She didn't want to face the outside world yet.

****

April 30

Oh, my God. I had sex. Mind-blowing, toe-curling, delicious sex with a devilishly handsome Scotsman.

I don't even remember the last time I had sex, but I'd forgotten how wonderful the act could be.

Bryce took his time drawing out the foreplay until each of us writhed with desire and made me feel like the most beautiful woman in the world. To be wanted, to be desired, and looked at so completely, isn't that what all women want?

I'm not saying foreplay is always needed, but God, my ex never wanted much. He was always in a rush. I don't even remember the last time I orgasmed; I faked it so many times. Why do we as women fake it, anyway? Do we value our husband's or partner's desires and pleasure over our own?

I was probably one of the only twenty-three-year-old virgins left in L.A. when I met Ryan, but I wanted to make him happy. Perhaps my pleasing nature placed his satisfaction over my own, but sex is a mutual act that should be enjoyed equally.

Bryce took his time lengthening kisses and making me feel desired and desirable. He looked at me so completely and saw me so fully, I cried. And when we rose together, I glowed like the radiant candles in the night.

Last night was incredible. Yet, I can't help but wonder: why me?

Chapter 16

Later that morning, Brie and Andrea strolled through the Kelvingrove Art Gallery and Museum bursting with selections from the Avant Garde to Scottish Romanticism.

Brie observed the dangling white heads from ornate ceilings, a giant elephant bull with tusks and trunk projecting in the air, smooth sculptures, as well as traditional and playful architecture and whimsical interior design displays. But her favorite artwork was the selection of Scottish Romanticism paintings, which included scenes and myths depicted in oil of the famous Robert the Bruce, vibrant-green highlands, and proud, kilted warriors. She paused at a painting of a fierce warrior atop his mount, sword drawn, and features set.

In a few, short hours, she would see Bryce in costume as fictional hero, Alexander James Mackenzie. Although she'd watched the first episode of *Swords of Scotland*, she didn't know what to expect. She'd had an incredible night with Bryce, and now, she'd be entering his acting world. Nerves tangled in her stomach and danced up her chest. Would seeing him in his working environment change her perception of him and, possibly, his perception of her? She wasn't a movie star; she was simply Brie. With one last glance at the powerful warrior, she released a long breath.

****

"Last season on *Swords of Scotland*, Alexander and Lady Charlotte returned to one another after being separated for ten years," Andrea filled Brie in on what happened previously and what they could expect to see on the upcoming season, while they traveled to Doune Castle in a requested ride. In the last forty minutes, the landscape had transformed from stone buildings and community camps to lush green woodland.

"You see, Alexander was imprisoned for his involvement with the Jacobite Rebellion and having the foresight of his involvement in mind, he concocted a plan to smuggle her into France where his cousin resided before the big Battle of Culloden."

Brie adjusted to face Andrea in the backseat. "Really?"

Andrea leaned forward. "Yes, and against her will obviously. She would've stayed by his side until her last breath, but she was pregnant. Then, newspapers reported he'd been killed in prison, but nope, not Alexander James Mackenzie. He's hard to kill."

As they turned from the two-lane highway onto a single road lined with ferns and evergreens, Brie listened. Bryce's character seemed like an eighteenth-century super hero. *Is that why he's so appealing to fans?*

"After a decade, Lady Charlotte returned to Scotland with their daughter and found Alexander—" Tiny sprinkles speckled the windows, and Andrea stopped abruptly. "No, don't rain! We're almost there, according to the dot!" She tapped a finger on her phone screen.

Although the light drizzle peppered her view, what lay before Brie was mesmerizing. She peered closer, breath puffing soft clouds onto the glass as towering trees thick with glossy green foliage surrounded them on either side and rose up and over the car, creating a natural tunnel transporting them back into a loop-hole in time.

And, they were.

They were being transported back—back to the fourteenth-century when Doune Castle was constructed and, also, to the eighteenth-century set of *Swords of Scotland*. Tiny drums beat in her chest. What was on the other end? Would she see television magic or something more?

Gradually, the tree-lined drive opened, and Brie caught a glimpse of gray stone bordered by forest-green tents, white dividers, and large, black semi-trucks blocking the view of the castle. Yet, she couldn't see anything farther.

A man in a bold, orange safety vest directed the driver toward the barricade and away from the castle into the dense foliage once again.

After arranging a pickup time, Brie opened the door and squished a boot in the mud, while her senses filled with rich dirt, damp grass, and sweet pine. She hadn't expected Bryce to be filming near a wooded bend. Well, if she were honest, she didn't know what to expect. The one-hour *Swords of Scotland* episode she viewed showed panoramic Scottish landscapes, glimpses of a castle, and the introduction of beloved characters. From her current view, thick brush and towering trees created a natural privacy fence beside man-made tarps and screens, yet also prevented fans, press, and now Brie from catching a glimpse of the in-progress filming. The entrance of the fan barricade—a waist-high metal gate—already brimmed with close to a hundred fans on the far side of the historical site's property. Brie searched for Bryce.

"Damn, can't see anything." Andrea craned her head.

"Here they come!" someone yelled.

When Brie pivoted, she dropped her jaw.

A warrior with long, black hair trudged to the entrance in a belted kilt with a knife tucked on one side, pistol on the other, a loose-fitting, linen shirt, and leather boots.

A woman with a full petticoat, long-sleeved mocha dress, and obvious corset trudged through the mud alongside him with a travel coffee in hand. The woman's hem dragged in the mud, no doubt adding to the period charm.

Click! Click! Click! Numerous fans snapped pictures of cast members who generously waved. Yet, as the hum of excitement penetrated through the crowd, Brie was sardined between Andrea and other fans. Sharp and pungent perfumes assaulted her senses from the throng of females standing shoulder-to-shoulder behind the barricade.

"I've been here since midnight," a woman said to her right.

"I got here at three a.m.," another, with thick, powdery makeup and a gold beanie, declared. "We've already seen the primary cast, but the leads, Bryce and Eleana, have yet to return for afternoon filming. But don't worry, they always stop by for signatures and a chat."

"That's wonderful." Brie flashed a smile, though the butterflies returned. Would Bryce see her as a fan,

through the gated entrance, hand gliding on the cold metal, while her stomach flip-flopped.

Meanwhile, Andrea danced through.

"Where are they going?" someone screeched.

A throaty cry tore through the crowd. "Take me, too! I need to see Bryce. I'm going to marry him!"

Glancing back for a millisecond at the surprised, irate, and sorrowful faces of hundreds of women, Brie stumbled. Of course, Bryce was a television icon and had starred in a few hit movies, but she hadn't realized the depth of his fandom—even after a run-in with the Crazies on their first date. Regaining her stride, she smoothed her clammy hands on her green coat, then with a hesitant step in the mud walked through the fourth wall.

A woman with a choppy bob, matching bangs, and a wide smile approached. "Afternoon! I'm Bonnie." She extended a hand and grasped Brie's in a swift shake and repeated the gesture with Andrea. "I'll take *ye* on a quick tour, then to Bryce himself."

"Thank you." Brie followed Bonnie between dark, swamp-green tents lining either side of the walkway, set up between trees like visitors, rather than permanent guests of the majestic land. Delicious scents fanned from the first of spices and coffee, while another held a number of people, camera equipment, thick wires coiled like snakes, as well as various lights and shades. And in the distance, she spied rich, clover-green meadows peekabooing between pockets of dense wood.

"Where are *ye* ladies visiting us from?" Bonnie asked.

"The states, California," Andrea said.

"This *yer* first time in Scotland?"

"Yes," they said in unison.

"It's been an incredible trip so far, seeing the sights, experiencing the food and culture, and meeting new people," Brie added. *Though I won't mention Bryce.* "Your country is gorgeous."

Bonnie sidestepped a stray branch and flashed a smile. "Thank *ye* kindly. Scotland's a way of wrapping 'round *ye*."

Weaving through towering trees and brush on the four-foot-wide path, they stepped into the clearing. Thatched straw houses dotted Brie's view, while in the distance, across the sweeping, emerald-green grassland, a large, formidable medieval castle perched on the hill. "Wow!"

"I'll say!" Andrea gripped Brie's hand. "This is amazing!"

" 'Tis," Bonnie agreed. "We have incredible set designers and fabricators and are pleased to employ local craftsman and builders."

Brie scanned the scene as actors dressed in earth- and jewel-toned period wear strolled and congregated, while a man in a horse-drawn wagon wobbled down the road with the *cluck* of chickens. She glanced toward the castle. With the strong, stone face, lofty towers, and impressive architecture, as well as thatched roof structures surrounding the fortress, Brie felt as though she was transported back in time. A few hours prior, she perused paintings of the Scottish landscape and eighteenth-century portrayals, and now, she was there, boots planted mesmerized. Bonnie's lyrical voice drew her out of her stupor.

"Doune Castle was built around the fourteen hundreds and has a long history of fortification. There's even a Roman fort. It was most infamously known as the royal seat of Robert Stewart, the first Duke of Albany and Governor of Scotland. It inspires awe, does it not?"

As she flew her gaze over the incredible structure, Brie nodded.

"It's Castle Roderick in the show," Andrea piped in.

Continuing tales of Doune Castle and the role the structure played in *Swords*, Bonnie led them down a short dirt path. A moment later, she paused and pointed toward a far hill, butting against a natural green perimeter. "Over yonder is where they're currently shooting."

Brie lifted a hand to her brow to shield her eyes from the hazy sun. Groups of men in dark-hued kilts rode horseback down a dirt trail, while cameramen captured the scene from tall ladders, as well as behind wheeled devices with large mounted cameras. Dozens of crew members stood or sat in chairs with headsets on, while others strode in and out of white pop-up tents lining the dense forest edge. Even though she'd lived in L.A. her entire life, she was far from the bright lights of Hollywood. She'd never hiked up to the Hollywood sign or strolled down Hollywood Boulevard to see the stars on the Walk of Fame. The world of Hollywood was as foreign as the semi-historical scene playing out before her very eyes.

At the top of a ravine, kilted warriors on horseback circled as if preparing for another take.

Yet, Brie couldn't tell if any riders were Bryce. She wished she could see him.

"And this is where we house all the costumes."

Bonnie gestured toward a large, metal garage opposite.

Tearing her gaze away, Brie followed Bonnie, stepping through the entry and came face-to-face with a tall woman with dark, curly hair piled high, skin akin to porcelain, and startling blue eyes. A soft, blue dress with lace accents completed the costume.

"OMG, Eleana Evans," Andrea said.

"Hello." She smiled politely, observing Andrea and Brie from her three-inch advantage. "What brings you to the set?"

"Br—" Brie began.

"We're huge fans," Andrea interrupted and stuck a hand out. "I've watched your show since the very beginning. Love it!"

"Thank you so much."

Brie didn't know what to say. Bryce had told her he kept his private life private, but what exactly did he tell Eleana? She'd witnessed them kissing already, so she obviously figured out they were more than just acquaintances, but still, Brie wondered.

Admiring the delicate lace craftsmanship of Eleana's dress, Brie flashed a smile. "Great costume." She wasn't just being complimentary. If she lived in the eighteenth century, she would've believed Eleana to be a queen by her regal appearance and poise.

"Thank you. We have the most talented costume designers in the industry."

Another woman appeared by Eleana's side. "Your tartan." She handed Eleana a tartan similar to the one Andrea purchased in Edinburgh.

"Thank you so much, Lily," she said in her lyrical voice. "Lovely to meet you both." Inclining her head in a regal manner, she exited, discussing the upcoming scene and wardrobe change.

Although Bryce eased Brie's concerns regarding his and Eleana's relationship the night before, she still had questions. Did they date previously? How long? Was Eleana still in love with him? Brie might live far from Hollywood, but gossip was everywhere. And once Andrea told her about Bryce and Eleana's alleged love affair, she'd noticed magazine headlines sporting gossip of the two actors in local shops in Glasgow, not to mention the recent fan remark. But Bryce had told her the truth, hadn't he?

With an exhale, she glanced at the rows upon rows of organized clothing, then ventured toward an adjacent building of equal size and stature. Yet, Bryce didn't stray far from her thoughts. How would she react when she saw him? Would she be as excited as the night before? Extra nervous? So many questions raced through her mind.

"And this here's the armory," Bonnie continued, then paused at the entry.

A large figure approached.

Bonnie's cheeks flushed three shades of red.

"Afternoon." A tall, burly man, with a dark, auburn beard and black apron taut around his thick middle, opened the heavy door, forearm muscles bulging.

His forearm could've matched a strong man pound-for-pound. But he wasn't Bryce. Bryce was built like an all-around athlete with roped muscles, defined abs, and runner's calves softened only by a dusting of auburn hair and sexy freckles.

"Thank *ye*, Rory," Bonnie said.

"Pleasure. Need to sharpen a blade for Bryce."

Brie's ears pricked up. Bryce was here, but he was

like a ghost in the room. *Where is he?*

"Rory Cameron's *Swords of Scotland's* lead swordsmith," Bonnie noted.

Brie widened her eyes. "You actually made these?" She flew her gaze over the sprawling weapon wall where immense long knives with metal handles like something out of a King Arthur movie hung from hooks beside daggers, axes, pistols, muskets, and more.

"Aye. My team and I fashion authentic sword reproductions, but we also work with historical weapon suppliers, as well."

Smiling widely, Andrea leaned toward him. "I like a man that works with his hands."

Rory's lips curled, and he made his way toward a long, wooden bench with an anvil.

Bonnie laughed. "Don't we all, lass."

With a grin, Brie strode forward, admiring a large, elongated sword resting on a wooden table. The weapon was composed of a solid, shiny metal blade nearly four feet in length with an intricate leather handle at the grip. She could imagine how the sword and the man who carried the weapon would be a fearsome thing to behold.

"That's the claymore." Andrea gestured. "Big-ass sword."

"Aye, 'tis," Bonnie agreed.

Andrea reached a hand out, fingers splayed ready to grasp the weapon. "Can I hold it?"

Bonnie clucked. "No. They've just been re-polished for the actors. Plus, they're heavier and more dangerous than they appear. All the actors have been professionally trained by historical re-enactors on how to hold and carry the swords. Though these are steel for close-ups, Rory's team also creates aluminum for stunts and fighting and a rubber copy for riding and such."

Frowning, Andrea swung a hip around the sword table.

Brie bit her cheek to hide a giggle. She could see Andrea swirling the sword around like Joan of Arc or a princess knight, then injuring herself in the process.

With a quick raise of a forearm, Bonnie checked her watch. "Shall we see if we can catch Bryce himself? They should be on break soon."

"Yes, we'd love that." Brie pivoted. Though as she followed Bonnie, she felt a ripple of fluttering butterflies within, beating their wings against her ribs.

Exiting the armory, Bonnie led them along a well-trod pathway where grass swished against Brie's boots and lavender-and-blue wildflowers winked through the landscape.

A shout carried across the land.

Turning, Brie glanced toward the sound. Her steps faltered.

Bryce charged across the terrain, riding a giant, black draft horse with his bright-red curly hair flying in the wind, wielding a sword at an oncoming man in a decorative red-and-gold jacket on horseback.

Her lips parted and heart pounded. "Oh. My. God."

"Pinch me," Andrea murmured.

He wielded a sword and connected, striking metal-on-metal, then knocked the man off his horse, only to have more opponents emerge from the trees with swords drawn.

As she watched Bryce, Brie's pulse hammered in her throat, and excitement skittered through her.

A moment later, hooves thundered in the air, and

the ground shook. Kilt-clad warriors galloped toward Bryce, then disappeared into the dense forest beyond.

"Cut!" echoed a deep voice across the valley.

Bryce and four other actor-warriors wearing kilts, various jackets, and vests, reappeared and trotted back to where the scene began. Laughter danced in the dense air, while horses flicked their manes and pawed the ground.

She released a long breath.

"Exceptional, isn't it?" Bonnie asked.

Brie nodded; yet, her gaze stayed on Bryce. The heart-pumping scene, combined with Bryce's rugged costume and curled hair, added a sex factor she wasn't prepared for. She understood the throng of female fans now. Bryce was a star.

Chapter 17

Bryce noticed Brie—her glow of golden-brown hair and bright-clover jacket amongst the brown-and-earth-toned cast and extras—but he had to focus. The twelve-hour schedule was brutally jam-packed. And even though he was a wee bit sluggish, he didn't mind. 'Twas nothing a second cup of coffee couldn't cure, especially after a night with Brielle.

Still, he could admit, an extra fire surged through him as he wielded the claymore—even if he was using a stunt sword today. Hearing "Action!" Bryce dug his heels into the horse's sides and raised his sword once again. He tilted the blade toward the approaching redcoat and barked the Mackenzie War Cry. "*Tulach ard*!" As he swung the sword, he moved quickly, stealthily like his ancestors had done thousands of years ago and thought of the bonnie lass he'd return to after battle.

Fifteen minutes later, he galloped toward the stables, grinning wide when Brie approached with Andrea and the vivacious Bonnie. He swung a leg over the saddle and slid to the ground, handing his reins to the equine assistant, then turned toward Brie. "I'm glad *ye* made it."

"We did." Brie smiled, and her cheeks pinkened. "Thank you for inviting us."

"Yes, thank you, Bryce." Andrea danced in place,

curls flying. "This is incredible! You've made my dreams come true today."

Bryce chuckled. "I'm glad. 'Tis our pleasure."

"What's your favorite part about being Alexander James Mackenzie?" Andrea asked.

"Oh"—he expelled a breath—"immersing myself in my country's history and creating an amazing show for our fans year after year."

She nodded, yet quickly her mouth curved into a wide *O*. Gripping Brie's arm, she angled her head. "There's Hugh Macrae. Like a Scottish Hercules."

Raising a brow, he glanced at his braw mate, marching across the field toward the snack tent. Oh, how Hugh enjoyed his title and used it to his advantage with his brand endorsements and the ladies alike. Still, he'd rather be staring at Brie than his mate any day. He'd seen enough of Hugh with kilt and without.

Andrea sighed. "I think I'm going to swoon."

"*Och*, I've already been surmounted, have I?"

Andrea grinned. "You're the Television King of Scots, are you not?"

Bryce cocked a half-smile. "Aye." He was indeed. At least, according to fans of *Swords of Scotland*. He'd worked his hide off to land the role of Alexander James Mackenzie during a myriad of screen tests, and thanks to the show, he now had half a dozen movies to his name, as well. When interviewers asked how he'd gotten the beloved role, he'd answer with "blind luck." *Swords* fell right into his lap. And so, he realized had Brie. Although, he truthfully fell on her.

She watched him with those bewitching, sea-green eyes, while her friend chattered on about Hugh and his ferocious axe. One thing he knew: he wanted to get

Brie alone. Nearly eight hours had passed since he'd left her in the hands of his long-time, trusted driver, and he had a hunger for her lips.

"Can I meet him?" Andrea asked Bonnie.

"Of course." Bonnie glanced at her clipboard, then back. "Thank *ye* for your time, Bryce."

He stepped forward. "Actually, I'd like to show Brielle around for a few minutes, if *ye* don't mind."

"Aye." With a wave of a hand in the air, she twisted. "You know where to find us."

Bryce gazed at Brie, while need gathered in his belly.

"You look amazing," Brie cooed.

He smiled broadly. "Thank *ye*. So do *ye*."

"And your horse is so, um"—her hands fluttered in front of her—"so regal."

He cocked his head. "Do *ye* want to meet my horse?"

With a bob of hers, she smiled nervously. "Yes."

They strolled a short distance to where his horse was tethered.

Approaching, Brie gasped. "Oh, he's gorgeous."

"He is." Bryce patted his horse's withers. "Kingsley's his name."

Brie extended a hand toward the gentle giant who puffed breath across her hand. She brushed Kingsley's ebony cheek, then glided her hand under his mane. "You're very handsome, Kingsley." She sighed. "I don't know if I told you, but I grew up with horses. My grandparents had two, and after I mucked the stalls, I'd get to ride." She continued scratching his mane, while the other hand caressed the underside of his jawline.

Kingsley whinnied.

Bryce appreciated Brie's gentleness as Kingsley obviously did, too. Not that her tenderness was anything new—he'd perceived her to be kind to the core. Yet, many a lass would've been standoffish with a large, braw Friesian. Although Bryce had put in his CV he had experience with horses, that was far from the truth—his riding experience was minimal. Luckily, the director mandated a two-week riding and training schedule for the primary cast members prior to the first episode. He was by far a more experienced rider now, but he wouldn't mention that to Brie. He fancied she'd be a first-class rider. "Sounds like *ye've* plenty of experience. How about a quick ride?"

"Really?" Her green eyes shone. "Can we do that?"

A young man with curly, brown hair approached.

Bryce glanced back at set. He had thirty minutes. He'd use every, single, last one. "He needs a cooldown. All right with *ye*, Fergus?"

Fergus patted Kingsley's flank and untied the halter. "Aye. A wee one, Bryce."

With a nod, Bryce hoisted himself into the saddle. Once he adjusted, he stretched a hand toward Brie, who slid her soft hand into his.

"Now, place your wellie on mine, and"—he lifted her up—"there *ye* are."

She settled herself with her round ass snug against him. He bit back a groan. This would be a long ride.

****

A jolt of excitement raced up Brie's spine as she rode, nestled cozily in front of Bryce.

"Are *ye* comfortable?" He leaned in.

Notes of grass, sweet sweat, and Bryce's warm cologne wafted toward her. "Yes," she whispered as her heart smacked against her chest. *Too comfortable.*

They rode away from the stables down a dirt-and-gravel trail, surrounded by trees tall as giants and vining greenery. Although the cool wind nipped at her face, the heat from Bryce's body warmed her.

They rode leisurely, enjoying one another's company. Fitted against Bryce's strong chest and lulled by the rhythm of Kingsley's hoofs against the earth, Brie forgot all about the questions in her head. If she were an eighteenth-century woman, she'd let Bryce take her anywhere. Yet, here and now, she settled against his warmth, happy to be with him for a little while longer.

****

Five minutes later, Brie gazed into Bryce's bold blue eyes with rich, dark irises, back snugged against a giant oak, while Kingsley nibbled wild grass on the forest floor twenty feet away. "We're heading to Glencoe and the highlands tomorrow morning."

His brows furrowed. "Already?"

"Yes." Her chest pinched. "I know you're busy with the show, but maybe I can see you when we return to Glasgow before our flight?"

"Aye, *ye* can." He crushed his mouth down on hers.

A sound of surprise echoed in her throat before her arms wove instinctively around his neck and drew him closer. They kissed greedily, each hungry for more. When she felt Bryce slide a hand to her coat and unbutton one polished button at a time, she didn't protest.

He opened her jacket wide, then unzipped her jeans, while his tongue danced in a frenzy with hers.

Her breath came in eager gasps, and her body burned. Separating for a moment, he tugged her pants down, then hoisted her up against the tree, and plunged into her.

She cried out. She'd never let a man take her like this; yet, she'd never wanted anyone more. Meeting him need for need, she wrapped her legs around his kilted hips as they climbed the peak together.

A few minutes later, Bryce smacked a hand on the tree and buried his head in the curve of her shoulder.

Brie giggled. She was encased by Bryce's strong arms and warm body and felt completely uninhibited for once in her life. But as her heart rate stabilized, she heard the *neigh* of Kingsley and a shout from the distance. She flew her gaze around them, gripping Bryce. What was she thinking? Someone could've seen them—a stranger or the press, or worse, a fan. Yet, no one else existed. The evergreens surrounding them were a thick, fragrant privacy screen. She released a breath.

Bryce lifted his head. "Are *ye* okay?"

"Yes." She smiled, while her body sighed. "I liked it."

His mouth curved, and he learned forward, brushing his lips across hers. Yet, when he released her, he stared with those intense, blue eyes. "I don't know what came over me."

Brie smoothed a hand over his firm chest, which was still covered with a linen costume shirt. "I wasn't exactly an unwilling participant, Bryce. You're incredibly sexy and make me want to do things I've never done before."

A grin spread across his face. "Happy to oblige *ye*."

As she watched him tuck his shirt into the belt over his kilt, which she now knew covered nothing but Bryce, she beamed with pleasure. "So, it's true."

"Aye, I'm a true Scotsman." Bryce kissed her quickly before gasping her hand.

Weaving her fingers through his, Brie wished she could stay with him forever under the private, canopy of evergreens. Yet, they were out of time.

****

Andrea wiggled her eyebrows at their return. "Did you have a good ride?"

Brie's face heated. "We did."

Tapping a finger to an earbud, Bonnie lifted the other hand. "Five minutes, Bryce."

"Aye, thanks Bonnie." He swung off Kingsley, then lifted Brie off the steed with ease. "'Twas lovely to meet *ye*, Andrea, and *ye*, Brie."

"You, too." Beaming, Brie stared after her warrior as he pivoted with his kilt and red curly hair, whipping in the wind.

Then, he swung up on his mighty steed and rode away.

Brie longed to be seated alongside him again. A few moments weren't enough.

****

Returning to their hotel room, Andrea followed close on her heels. "Spill. You've had a dopy grin on your face since we left the set. I need details!"

Brie dropped onto the bed, allowing her head to fall back onto the pillowy comforter. "We had sex on set."

"I knew it!" Andrea plopped down. "Give me some juicy details."

Brie had told Andrea about her first night with Bryce earlier and how he took his time and made her feel beautiful, but this Bryce…was unexpected. "Being with Bryce on set was…was completely different, and oh, my God, so amazing."

"Details, Brie. Focus." Andrea leaned forward.

Brie nibbled her lip. She loved Andrea, but she didn't want to share every private detail. "We rode away from set toward the east side of Doune Castle and let Kingsley graze on the grass. We were just talking—me leaning against a tree with his arm relaxed above me, but there was something stirring between us—like some force drawing us together—zipping along our bodies like electricity. And then I told him we were leaving for Glencoe tomorrow and asked if I could see him before we left Scotland. He hauled me up on the tree—"

Andrea licked her lips. "Oh boy, oh boy."

"And we had hard, fast, incredible sex."

"Oh!" Andrea fell back on the bed beside her. "Did he leave his kilt on?"

Brie grinned. "Of course, he's a true Scot."

Andrea sighed.

Later, they ventured to one last pub in Glasgow and toasted *Swords of Scotland*, Bryce, and each other, then danced into the night. Yet, amidst the gaiety, Brie couldn't help but think of Bryce and the wonderful week they'd shared. In a few days, she'd return to L.A. A sharp twinge pierced her chest. Would she ever see him again?

Chapter 18

On their last morning in Glasgow, Brie strolled beside Andrea along the river Clyde where new, attractive construction bordered the water's edge.

"Such a dramatic change in landscape from yesterday," Andrea noted.

"Completely," Brie agreed. "Medieval castles one day, contemporary construction the next." Although she admired the massive Finnieston Crane soaring above the water, she remembered another Scottish tourist site she'd been wanting to visit since their first night in Scotland: the ancestral home of the Farquharsons. But one problem existed: timing. She fished her phone out to double check the distance and drive time.

"Oh, good! Ready for a selfie?" Andrea flashed a smile with full, voluminous curls. "I'm photo ready."

"Sure." Brie angled the phone toward them, so a shiny, armadillo-looking, titanium stadium across the river framed the background. Once she snapped the picture, she plugged in the destination details. She huffed. "So, I'm thinking we should probably scratch the idea of visiting the Invercauld Estate."

"What? No way." Andrea shook her head. "You've been wanting to go."

Brie weaved around couples and groups of young people who cut across the path to sit on the green grass bordering the walkway. "It would take us almost two-

and-a-half hours to get there from Glasgow and another two to Glencoe. I can't change our itinerary to see one castle, especially after I've already altered enough of our vacation to see Bryce."

Andrea quirked a brow. "Are you sure?"

Brie nodded. Although she'd love to see the Estate, she realized her experiences thus far, and detours along the way, including excursions with Bryce, had helped her open her eyes to the world around her again. And even, her heart. Perhaps one day, she'd return to visit the Invercauld Estate and see where she fit amongst her ancestors.

****

"Don't rain on us. It's bad enough your roads are flip-flopped." Brie squinted at the heavy, dark clouds out the driver's side window, while her hands white-knuckled the steering wheel.

Flipping through her ever-present guide book, Andrea snorted. "You tell them."

Brie considered the smooth, present drive a miracle in itself, especially after she'd almost turned onto oncoming traffic twice, while leaving the rental car shop. Now, they were on the open road, and she focused on the journey ahead. Relaxing her grip, she flew her gaze over the shiny, water-soaked A82 as it curved around the banks of Loch Lomond like a silvery ribbon. The glow from the car's headlights sent tiny fragments of light across the water, alighting the loch with sparkling jewel tones, while the towering earth-and-forest-green-toned mountains framed the lake. "It's majestic."

Andrea glanced. "Yup, fucking beautiful."

"When Bryce and I hiked the other day, I was so

upset about everything that happened with Phoebe, I was stuck in my head, you know?"

"I do," Andrea confirmed.

"But it really was the best escape—getting back into nature and hiking. He just kept talking about the birds and wild strawberries of all things… And with each step, I felt myself relaxing and letting go. Then we…we had this moment at the top of Loch Lomond."

Turning toward Brie, Andrea tilted her head. "Why didn't you tell me?"

She lifted a shoulder. "You were already mad. I didn't want to make the evening about me."

Andrea rested a hand atop Brie's.

With a swivel, she smiled.

HONK! A car headed straight toward them.

"On the left! Left!" Andrea yelled.

"Shit! Shit!" She quickly straightened to the sound of squealing tires.

"Holy crap, Brie," Andrea harumphed. "Do you want me to drive?"

"No, I'm good. The loch…distracted me." And it still did, though her heart continued to race as a result of her too-American-right-side-of-the-street-driving.

After a few minutes of deep breathing, she glanced at the glistening loch once again. Wind ruffled the surface cascading tiny waves over the glassy water, mirroring Brie's insides. As excited as she was to journey to Glencoe, she felt her stomach flutter with unease. What would happen between her and Bryce? Wasn't the point of a casual vacation fling that it was casual? She gripped the steering wheel tighter. Nothing about her was casual, as much as she liked to repeat Andrea's opinions of "just have fun" during vacation—

that wasn't her.

Bryce had awakened a part of her she hadn't felt in a long time, and she yearned to be with him. Late last night, he texted, telling her that he was thinking about her and made Brie laugh out loud when he noted Kingsley already missed her. Still, he had a busy day of shooting and expected a twelve-hour day today, as well as long days the rest of the week before filming in the highlands next week. But that was once she was back in L.A...

She blew out a breath. She needed to focus on the drive ahead and what she could control.

****

Andrea's phone chimed. She flipped over the travel guide and lifted the phone to eye level. "Those *Swords* fans you met the other night will be in Fort William tomorrow. Want to meet up with them?"

Brie shrugged. "Sure, why not?"

"Nothing like bar-hopping in the highlands, right? And speaking of which"—Andrea swiveled, set her phone down, then lifted her guide book—"we are officially in the highlands."

"Hello, highlands!" Brie greeted the rolling green hills and then squinted as a smudge of reddish-brown appeared in her view. "What's that?"

Throwing her hands up, Andrea dropped the guide book. "Stop!"

Brie swerved. "Andrea, what the heck? I can't just stop."

"It's a fucking coo!"

She veered the car onto the gravel side road, parallel to green fields with a few furry occupants.

"A heilan coo!" Andrea rolled down her window.

"Hi, coos!"

"Oh, they're so cute and shaggy." Brie gazed at the handful of long-haired cows meandering near the edge of the road.

"And *big*," Andrea said, then cleared her throat as one stepped onto the black pavement. "And where do you think you're going?"

The coo hoofed toward the car, *click-clicking* on the pavement.

"Uh, oh." Brie swiveled. "Are they friendly? Roll up your window!"

Smashing a finger on the automatic window button, Andrea quickly retreated farther into her seat.

Yet, the coo simply shook his head in front of the car, hair flying like a seventy's hair band member, blocking their advance.

"Do we have coo insurance?" Brie asked.

"I don't know. We're in Scotland!"

"Should I honk?"

"Brie," Andrea said, a bit more controlled and eyed the slow-moving coo. "I bet it's friendly. Tourists post pictures beside them all the time. Let's get out and pet it."

As a single mom, Brie couldn't afford to endanger her life, even if the coo was adorable. "It might be, but let's not take any chances."

The coo stared through the windshield, standing a few inches from the bumper.

A second passed.

Then two.

Then three.

The coo flicked his head once more, obviously bored by the two Americans in the strange rolling box, then sashayed past the car and across the street toward fields of fresh grass.

"See," Andrea remarked. "Friendly."

With a laugh, Brie rolled her window down to snap pictures. She'd definitely be painting the coo later.

After swapping seats, they drove north, following the natural curve of the road alongside Loch Lomond. Besides their car, the two-lane highway was relatively unoccupied, save for a random car or camper. Brie rode with ease alongside the rolling mountains splashed with brick-red, tangerine-orange, and vibrant-green, stopping with Andrea only to view cascading waterfalls down rock faces and tourist viewpoints.

"O.M.G." Andrea pointed out the driver's side window. "Check out the tiny cottage."

Brie followed Andrea's pointed finger where in the center of the rich, jade valley a quaint, white cottage nestled. "Do you think someone actually lives there?"

"Who knows? I sure wouldn't, not out in the middle of nowhere. No matter how beautiful it is."

Gazing at the cottage, Brie wondered if a family lived there or a single man or woman? The first few months after Ryan left, Brie couldn't sleep. She had to wrap her head around the idea she would be raising her children in a home by herself. Alone. Sure, Ryan would have them every other weekend, even though he still didn't keep that bargain either; she was a single parent. She slept in the center of the bed, made sure all the doors were locked, fed and clothed herself and her children, and slowly started taking care of herself.

Glancing back at the cottage once more, growing smaller and smaller as they drove farther and farther away, she wondered what their choice was.

Sometime later, Brie craned her head, squinting toward the mountains. In a small turnout a half mile ahead, something or rather someone, gathered the attention of a dozen or more people. Nearing, she spied a Scot, dressed in full Scottish garb with a red-and-black tartan kilt and sash, standing atop a rock wall with the infamous bagpipe in hand, while another man dressed like Bryce's character in a moss-and-cobalt kilt stood a few feet beside him, wielding a fake sword.

"A bagpiper and an Alexander impersonator. We're stopping!" Andrea turned into the carpark.

Prickles snuck up Brie's spine as she opened the car door. Women were taking selfies in front of the impersonator, while others cried because he wasn't the *real* Alexander James Mackenzie. Brie's chest tightened, and heart rate accelerated. *No wonder Bryce didn't tell me who he was at first. It's overwhelming.*

With an inhale and exhale, she focused on the talented piper, but a swoosh behind her had Brie turning to see a *Swords of Scotland* tour bus screech to a halt. *Great.* "There's really no escape from this show is there?"

"Nope!" Andrea bounded down the rocky road toward the piper and impersonator. "Come on. Let's get a picture!"

Two dozen screaming women from teenage to Mimi's age sprinted out of the bus with Bryce's face plastered across their chests, while she stood motionless with her hand cemented to the car door.

Bryce was famous. Something she was becoming more and more aware of, especially seeing him in his element the day before and the impersonator with screaming fans here and now. She had ignored his fame previously, wanting only to focus on the person who stood before her. Yet, he was more than the man who made her chest swell—he was a man of many fans' dreams—and she couldn't ignore that any longer. She'd be leaving for home in two days. She didn't want to invite any more complications into her children's lives, which was why she hadn't dated previously. She didn't want to rock the calm boat she'd finally steered out of danger. *But why did Bryce have to be so wonderful?*

His face appeared in her mind, and she heard him whisper her name with that lovely, full brogue—*Brielle*. She pressed her lids shut, telling herself to end things and not delay the inevitable. Bryce was hours away. They wouldn't see each other until she returned to Glasgow to hop on her return flight anyway. And that's only if she wanted to. *If.* Brie blew out a breath. She *wanted* to, but she shouldn't.

An ear-piercing scream rocketed toward her.

She snapped her lids open.

"It's Alexander!" a woman yelled.

She rolled her eyes. *The last thing I need is a bunch of screaming fans angry at me, or paparazzi chasing me, and flipping my children and my world upside down. I have to end it.* With a decision made, she marched to the front of the car and leaned against the bumper. But the tall piper's melancholy notes drifted toward her, and her thoughts returned to Bryce. A tear slid down her cheek.

Chapter 19

"Oh, my God. There's a car. What do I do?" Andrea swiveled her head as she drove down the single lane road in the quaint city of Glencoe sometime later.

Brie averted her eyes from the bright-red, two-story houses and traditional white-and-black cottages lining the streets. A silver car approached from the opposite direction. "Um." She glanced to the right where a small curbed sidewalk perched and to the left where cars parked. "Back up?"

"It's a flipping one-lane road! Back up? Back up she says," Andrea screeched. They were playing chicken, only at half speed. Andrea threw the gearshift in Reverse.

Trying to control the giggles, Brie craned her head and spied a small space. "There! An empty parking space." She flung an arm out the window, pointing toward the spot. "Pull in!"

Yet, there was no need to panic. The other driver—a gray haired man with a soft blue cap—slowed and waved as he passed.

Brie returned the wave with a full smile.

Andrea huffed. "Okay, Scotland. I know you drive on the left, but can you have a two-lane road, please?"

"You did great." She gazed at the towering mountains beyond. "It's charming."

"It'd be more charming with another lane."

Brie snorted. "Come on."

A few minutes later, they continued down the road, hugging the glistening Loch Leven, until they arrived at their destination. A sweet, one-story cottage with cream-colored paint and red-and-brown accents nestled into lush evergreens with the majestic mountains of Glencoe in the background.

Andrea made a sound of pure glee. "Now, this is glamping!"

As Brie stepped onto the gravel path, crunching pebbles, she breathed in sweet notes of pine. "It's perfect." Lugging her bags inside, she gazed at the cute cottage. Large picture windows invited the serene, natural woods inside, while open beams and wood accents with touches of rust-red made the cabin feel homey.

A handwritten note welcomed them and stated their grocery order service had been fulfilled with items stocked in the refrigerator and pantry, along with complimentary local honey, coffee, and oats. Brie opened the fridge and gasped at the colorful salmon, meats, local produce, and other items. After a three-hour drive, the last thing she wanted was to go traipsing to the grocery store. *Kudos to the owners.*

Andrea, meanwhile, clomped up the stairs, then down again, checking out the bedroom arrangements. "There are two bedrooms upstairs—one includes an en suite and one wee." She grinned. "And a master suite downstairs."

Brie peeked around the corner at the master bedroom with a fluffy, white bedspread, natural wood accents, and gold-and-red curtains. "Since you booked the cottage, why don't you take the master?"

Her grin spread to a full smile. "Really?"

Brie nodded. "Absolutely."

"You don't have to tell me twice!" She practically danced toward the master with bags in hand. "The tub is calling my name."

"Enjoy." Brie sighed and picked up her luggage. She hiked the short flight of stairs and stopped at the landing, pausing where a small room welcomed with two, single beds topped with forest-green quilts. She couldn't help but think of her children. They'd be asleep right now in America. *But they'd love it here. All this space to run and discover.*

With one more longing glance at the small beds, Brie pivoted and stepped into dreamland. Forest-green and pearl-white décor welcomed with light-brown and earth-toned furniture, while French doors with rectangular, picturesque windows framed the deep, blue loch, inviting the serene outdoors in. She dropped her bags, strolled across, and opened the door to the balcony where a quaint two-seat bistro set summoned. Leaning onto the railing, she breathed in the crisp, fragrant air perfumed with earth and pine. An eagle swooped toward the calm cobalt loch, while abundant, towering evergreens framed her view.

When Bryce weaved his way into her thoughts, she imagined setting him free like the eagle soaring away. Determined to live in the moment, she retrieved her travel watercolor set and set up her paints on the patio. She sketched the loch, the mountains rising into thick clouds, and the village below, then dipped her brush and began painting.

May 1

I just finished painting the mountains of Glencoe

capturing more than my camera would in one still shot with each stroke. The mountains are like natural guardians—protecting and watching from high above. "You can rest," they whisper.

Andrea fell asleep atop the fluffy, down comforter after a bath, not that I blame her. We've been on the go since arriving in Scotland, and now, it's time to relax. We'll have plenty of time to explore. In fact, I tell the same thing to Phoebe when I put her down and she protests.

"Five more minutes, Mommy!" she says.

"It's time for naptime, baby girl," I tell her and sing her one more song, alight one last kiss on one of her plump cheeks, then tuck her into bed with baby.

Noah, too, knows we have quiet time on the weekends, especially since his school doesn't have naps like his kindergarten class used to. Instead, he plays quietly, reads, or assembles puzzles for at least half an hour before he watches a show.

As an adult and mom of two, I've never valued naps more. And, don't worry, I will lie down here in this quaint cottage shortly.

I feel so at peace here. The lush green mountains and sparkling water have calmed me, similar to the day I hiked around Loch Lomond with Bryce. Nestled in the spongy grass, we sat watching the birds soar, while the natural world around us fed our souls. I'll treasure that day forever, especially since I've decided not to see him again. Whatever this is can't last, even as I feel myself falling for him. Perhaps this is for the best—ending the relationship before I fall deeper—before I really get hurt. I haven't figured out a way to tell him yet, but I will. He deserves my honesty.

Luckily, Glencoe is a welcome distraction. Sitting here, with the symphony of gentle cascading waterfalls, lyrical birdsong, and delicate breeze ruffling the leaves, I can see how this is termed one of the most beautiful places in Scotland.

Being here is a gentle reminder I need to take time to go out into nature more—to dig my feet into the soil and revitalize my soul. I've let my cup run empty for far too long, and being in Scotland has helped me realize I need to find time for myself. For just me.

****

In the mid-afternoon, Brie devoured fresh bread with cream and smoked salmon, then laced up her running shoes and strode out the backdoor alongside Andrea.

They followed a dirt trail, chatting about what they'd like to do the next two days, and before they realized, they'd reached the banks of the loch. Thick, gray-and-white, puffy clouds dotted across the baby-blue sky, while the sun bathed the mountains in rich brown-and-copper hues, and tall evergreens surrounded the shores. The water was still and calm and reflected the landscape above and around like a mirror image.

Brie breathed deeply, inhaling the marshy air accented with sweet pine, while Andrea snapped pictures. Eying vibrant pink-and-lavender flowers blooming below Douglas firs and sequoias, she knelt down, delighted with the happy-faced flowers, and picked one. Instinctively, she tucked the tiny bloom above an ear. "Channeling Phoebe."

"Totally!" Andrea squashed her face next to Brie's, snapping a quick picture. "The flower fairy princess and Noah the explorer would love this."

211

Giggles floated in the air as a young family rounded the path ahead, including a dad with sandy hair and a camera looped around his neck and an older gentleman with a walking stick.

Smiling, she feathered her fingers through the tips of soft ferns bordering the path and thought of her children. Every Saturday morning, they strolled around their neighborhood, Phoebe's light-up sparkle shoes skipping over concrete cracks, and Noah always one step ahead. She could see them running ahead now, zipping through the path, and chattering about the fuzzy ducks and fairy flowers. Longing struck her chest and swelled. "I worked so hard to make a home for us," Brie began and glanced toward the Loch, which darkened to navy-black from the clouds gathering above. "But they need more space to run and play, more nature, more earth, and more…green." She swirled a hand around. "More this."

Andrea stopped and grasped Brie's other hand. "You've created a safe, comfortable home with a hell of a lot of warmth. You're doing great."

A light wind picked up, ruffling her hair, whispering through the trees, and rippling soft waves on the water's edge. "I know. But one day, I'll find them a forever home like I always wanted where they can run, play, and explore."

Andrea squeezed Brie's hand. "You will."

Bobbing her head, she gazed at the water, watching ducks swim gracefully along the edges, while the breeze blew gently and the trail ahead awaited. "What about you? Do you like where you live?"

Andrea shrugged. "I don't *not* like it. It's L.A.! I'm close to amazing restaurants, theater, and the beach isn't too far. I imagine once I get promoted, I'll get some snazzy apartment in the city."

"I'm sorry." Brie glanced at Andrea. "I should've asked. Do you think they'll announce promotions soon?" She'd been so wrapped up in her own head, she'd neglected to ask Andrea about her climb up the corporate ladder to Chief Human Resources Officer. Their company's current CHRO had given her notice three weeks before they left for Scotland, and Andrea, Vice President of HR, had worked tooth and nail, taking over initiatives, as well as duties passed from the CHRO who was always too busy to finish tasks. But Andrea told her the late nights were worth it—she was climbing the ladder.

"It'll be a little while, but I'll keep you posted. I've been checking email every day."

Brie's jaw dropped. "Andrea! You shouldn't. You're on vacation."

She fanned a hand. "It's fine."

Slinging an arm around Andrea, Brie leaned toward her. "Just imagine, you'll be a CHRO and a best-selling author one day."

Andrea grinned, winking dimples. "One can dream! Though I haven't written this entire trip."

"We're on vacation."

Andrea bumped her shoulder with Brie's. "We are!"

As the delicate breeze caressed Brie's skin, she lifted her face to the gray-blue sky and inhaled. She imagined herself sitting in a big backyard with nature all around.

"Finlay Aileen!" a rich, deep voice shouted.

Brie whipped her head around as a toddler with

white-blonde hair and rosy cheeks dashed past, giggling with a large, black camera in hand.

The tall man she'd seen earlier flew down the dirt path with brows knitted and hair disheveled. "E'scuse me."

"I have one just like her at home," Brie called. Grinning wide, she observed the father-daughter chase.

The dad skirted after his squealing daughter, then swooped her into his arms. Plucking the camera from her tiny grasp, he leaned forward kissing his forehead to hers. "Finlay."

Brie's ears pricked up. *Finlay? Like my surname?* When she noticed them walking back, Brie flashed a smile. "Great job, Dad."

"Thank *ye*."

"Did you say her name was Finlay?"

He nodded. " 'Tis. Finlay Aileen. Named after her mother."

Tingling ran up Brie's arms. "Is her mother's last name Finlay?"

"Aye."

"Mine, too. I'm…well, I'm Brielle Finlay." She deliberately left out her married name. "I'm from the U.S., but I'd love to learn more about where my name comes from if she doesn't mind. I heard Finlay is an ancient Pictish clan." She glanced around. "Is she here?"

"*Ceud Mile Fàilte*." He extended a hand. "Daniel MacDonald. A hundred thousand welcomes. She's not here, but I'm sure she'd be pleased to talk to *ye*. We'll be at the pub tonight." With his daughter in his arms, he told her the details of where she could meet them.

Watching them disappear down the path, Andrea

lifted a brow. "What do you suppose you'll learn? That she's a distant cousin?"

Brie considered. "No. I just want to know more about…about me somehow. I don't know. It probably sounds stupid. I'm American, and I've lived in California my entire life, but being here has made me open my eyes again and remember who I am little by little. I know I'm not Scottish, but I want to learn more about me…about my roots." Sighing, she trudged down the trail and wondered what a conversation with another Finlay had in store.

****

Later that evening, Brie and Andrea strolled into a lounge bar with gray-and-red interior, artsy décor including what looked like a papier-mâché stag head, booths covered in cowhides as well as modern, open seating, and polished, wooden floors. At seven in the evening, the bar and booths were fairly full, and a band readied to play in the corner.

Brie spotted Daniel beside a young woman with white-blonde hair like the daughter on her hip and waved. Strolling toward the family, she smiled, even though she felt like her insides were vibrating along with the strum of the instruments. "Hi, Daniel. Finlay. It's so nice to see you again."

"And *ye*," he said and turned. "This is my wife, Holly."

With a warm smile, she held out a hand. "Holly Finlay-MacDonald. Pleasure to meet *ye*. I see *ye've* met my Daniel and Finlay."

Brie shook her hand. "I have. I've been missing my own daughter and son on this trip, and seeing your daughter playing today brought so much joy."

"I'm glad. She's a true blessing." She pressed her nose to Finlay's, then turned back.

Nervousness tangled in Brie's gut. What should she say next? *Do you know anything about the Finlay line? Are we related somehow?* Nibbling her lip, she glanced over at Daniel who scrolled through pictures and noted the high-quality, natural images. "I noticed you snapped pictures earlier, but I didn't realize you were so good! Are you a professional photographer?"

"I am."

Holly's features warmed. "Aye, he has a gift capturing nature's beauty and also some of Scotland's finest history. Has over fifty thousand followers on social media, as well."

"Really?" Andrea lifted her phone from the table. "What's your handle?"

He relayed his handle. "It's a hobby, but I've sold some pictures to a few Scottish travel sites."

Andrea tapped the screen. "Following!"

Brie chuckled, feeling the tension ease. "That's wonderful. I'd love to follow, as well, if that's all right with you."

"Of course!"

Tucking one leg over the other, she told herself to calm down and picked up her wine glass. "Tomorrow is our second to last day in Scotland. It'll be wonderful to visit your page and remember your beautiful country—the majestic mountains, unique cities, and striking castles."

Daniel angled his head. "Have ye seen Invercauld Castle? The historical seat of Clan Farquharson?"

Brie paused with the wine glass halfway to her lips. "No."

"Well, it's only open to the public at select times," Holly noted.

Fishing his phone out, Daniel scrolled, then handed over the device. "There 'tis."

Her lips parted. The clan seat was nestled in front of a forest of evergreens with emerald lawns, gothic-style architecture with a number of turrets, and blue-and-white Scottish flag flying above. Excitement skittered through her veins, but as she scrolled through a few more pictures, gazing at the castle from the center of a forest, then from a bird's-eye view from a mountaintop, cut off from the bustling world, the clan seat appeared private and unapproachable. She expected to feel something—some sort of connection—but how could she feel a connection to a picture on a phone and even more, to somewhere she's never been or even lived?

"Since you have a strong-willed daughter as well, *ye* should know the story of Anne Farquharson," Holly said.

With a nod, she glanced back and handed Daniel his phone.

"Anne married Angus MacIntosh—the Chief of Clan Chattan. During the Jacobite rising, Anne was a force to be reckoned with and even earned herself a wee nickname." She flashed a mischievous grin, displaying identical dimples. "She raised over three hundred troops in support of our Bonnie Prince Charlie, defying her husband. They called her Colonel Anne."

"Aye, Colonel Anne," Daniel concurred.

"I love that." Brie's chest warmed. "Strong women run in my family, as well. My mother raised me as a single mom."

"Oh, bless her." She pressed a hand to her heart. "I'm blessed with my Daniel." Flashing a smile, she patted Finlay's back, and soon the little angel was snoozing on her shoulder, while the bar brimmed with occupants. "What about *ye*? Is your man here, as well?"

When Bryce's face appeared in her mind, Brie felt her chest crack like a fissure on an iceberg. "No." She cleared her throat. She'd been trying not to think of Bryce all day, but he wasn't *her* man. He was a man she was seeing, right? She swallowed thickly. She wasn't seeing him anymore, but she still needed to tell him. Dread welled in her gut.

Noticing Brie's pause, Holly adjusted her daughter and changed the subject. "Do *ye* have questions about the Finlays?"

She nodded. "I do. I discovered my dad's side had roots in Scotland a few days ago, and I was wondering if you could tell me a little bit more about the Finlay side."

"Well, *ye* kin the Finlay clan has warriors, but also poets and artists—*ye* can see some of their work in Edinburgh. There are also famous Scottish International Rugby players and even a Viscount."

"Are you an artist, too?" Brie asked.

"*Och*, just for fun. I enjoy a wee painting now and again."

"I paint, too. Watercolor mostly, but my mother is an amazing artist." She lifted her phone and showed Holly some of Mimi's artwork she'd snapped at the last show.

"She's quite talented!"

Brie smiled. "I think so, too."

When a musician stood up with a single guitar, he

strummed lightly, imbuing the bar with a soft melody and then lifted his voice, singing a poignant ballad about Glencoe's history. The way the entire bar joined in, lifting their warm voices to the ancestral tune, sent tingles up Brie's arms. After she and Andrea hiked around the loch, they toured the visitor center and learned about the glen and how it was forged by ice age glaciers, the effects of Scottish weather, and the tragic Glencoe Massacre of 1692. Listening to the chorus around her, she realized Scots were as much a part of their history as the land around them, and the song connected them back to that history. *A story in a song.*

After a moment of applause, a musician beside the guitarist lifted a fiddle and picked up the tune.

Brie leaned forward. "Are many local songs about history?"

"Aye." Holly nodded. "Some are and some sing about ancient legends, as well."

"Are there any local legends of Clan Finlay?"

She considered for a moment. "There is an ancient tale my grandad used to tell—he was the storyteller of the family—about *Finlay and the Giants*, though I'm no' sure if Finlay is his first or surname." She paused and lifted the dark, foaming beer to her lips. "Finlay was a hunter in the highlands who lived with his sister, but unbeknownst to them, giants dwelled nearby who were descendants of Beira, a mighty mother goddess who was said to have built the mountains of Scotland with a giant hammer. She was also the god of winter. Beira and her giants were trying to slay Finlay, *ye* see, and a wise woman warned him. Finlay listened to the wise woman and overcame the attacks and was rewarded with a gold-hilted magic sword and even wed the wise woman's daughter. He went on to have three sons and prospered."

The story was one of magic and myth, and Holly told the tale well. Perhaps, Brie did have something similar to her ancestors: the gift of stories. She'd been telling her children stories since they were little and was currently writing her own story. Mimi told her for years her storytelling trait originated from her dad who was known for spinning tales of his journey across the sea, especially when he couldn't tell her what he was really doing or where he was stationed.

After sharing a meal and talking about their families, the Finlay-MacDonalds said goodnight, but not before exchanging emails to keep in touch.

Watching them exit, Brie couldn't help but smile. *I come from warriors, artists, and storytellers.* Her entire being hummed with energy, and she wanted to tell Bryce. But she couldn't—she couldn't be drawn back into the enchanting bubble they'd created; she still planned to end their relationship. Instead, she snatched her phone and texted Mimi.

—I met some Finlays today! A little girl and her family. I'll tell you all about our chance meeting and conversation when I get back.—

The familiar bubble icon didn't appear, and she realized Mimi must be busy with the kids. She relaxed into the sturdy, wooden bar chair, watching Andrea dance—or rather hop-hop—with an older gentleman who was as skinny as he was tall. With one last glance, she set the device aside. Yet, no sooner had she placed her phone down that the screen lit. Her breath hitched in her throat. *Bryce.*

—I caught a day off tomorrow, while Eleana

finishes an episode. Would ye *like to go for a drive?—*

As she stared at the text, her mind reeled. Laughter carried from the dance floor.

Andrea kicked her feet up, imitating some jig the locals were doing. Her booted feet struck in every other direction.

Brie inhaled and exhaled.

Ping! The device glowed once again.

Brie was torn. She wanted to see Bryce, but she'd convinced herself she needed to break this off. She was leaving. What was the point?

Andrea flopped back onto the stool. "That was so fun! I was doing it. Did you see me?"

With a nod, Brie lifted the wine glass, taking a long drink.

Andrea puffed a breath. "Shit, I'm out of shape. Haven't we been walking this entire trip? I should have stamina."

With a little laugh, Brie gave her a small smile. "I guess." She stared past Andrea, watching couples dancing. She wanted that happy reality—someone to dance with in a bar full of people, someone to share memories, someone to laugh with as the kids acted silly, and someone to love. But that reality wasn't possible; it was a dream.

Andrea leaned forward. "Hey, what's up?"

"Bryce wants to take me somewhere tomorrow."

She kicked a brow up. "He's coming here?"

"He's driving up, I guess." She crossed and uncrossed her legs, then rubbed her clammy hands on her pants. "Something about a filming day break."

Andrea flicked her curls. "Well, when the Television King of Scotland comes to you, I guess you go."

Brie released a breath. "I don't know…"

"What do you mean? I know I was mad the other day, but I also know how unhappy you've been the last year—personally, I mean," Andrea said.

"Andrea, I—"

"We've had a great, few days together." She held up a hand. "I can't be selfish, not when I see how happy he's making you."

"But…it'll end the day after tomorrow. I wasn't thinking. I was soaring with Bryce, but there's bound to be turbulence. Remember those fans yesterday? The tabloids? The super fans? I should just—"

Andrea grasped Brie's shoulders. "What you should do is enjoy. This is your time."

Time. Brie's time was rarely her own; yet she relished the busy and even chaotic times with her children. Here and now, she had time to spend with her best friend, and tomorrow, the opportunity to spend time with a man she genuinely adored for a little while longer. She could decline and try to forget the last week and a half, or she could stay in the present. Rarely living in the now, Brie always thought about what she needed to do for tomorrow—the laundry, grocery shopping, etc. Perhaps what Scotland had given her was time, though she knew too well her time was running out. Her heartbeat echoed in her head like a countdown clock.

"And while you're off with Mr. Wonderful, I'll explore with the *Swords* girls like we planned."

Shaking her head, she repressed the sting in her chest. "I can't, okay?"

Andrea leaned forward on her elbows. "What are

you so scared of?"

While laughter and gaiety surrounded them, Brie blinked back her frustration. "I…"

"Which of *ye* lassies wants to dance?" a lanky, young man appeared with an eager grin.

"She does!" Andrea shoved Brie off her barstool.

"Oh! Actually—"

"Come on!" The boy tugged her onto the dance floor.

Brie glared at Andrea before the young man spun her around. When she plopped onto the barstool out of breath sometime later, she noticed her phone was missing. She flipped napkins over and dug around the interior of her purse, but the device was gone. Panic gripped her. "Have you seen my phone?"

"Yep." Andrea lifted the dark beer to her lips.

"Where is it?"

"In a secret location."

"What?" Brie exclaimed. "Give it back. I have to text Bryce. I can't go tomorrow. I—"

"Nope. I'm saving you from yourself." She settled into the chair. "And, I texted Bryce. He'll pick you up in the morning. Eight sharp."

"Andrea!"

She flashed Brie an overly bright smile.

Leaning forward, Brie crossed her arms. "Why did you do that?"

"Because you deserve it."

Leveling a glare at Andrea, she downed her wine. This was not a good idea.

Chapter 20

The following morning, Brie stepped onto the tiny welcome mat and faltered. A gleaming black motorcycle parked at the base of the cottage walkway beside a man who looked as powerful as the machine. Her stomach flip-flopped with nerves and desire. *I have to tell him what's on my mind. I have to break this off.* Twisting her hands together, she gazed at the brawny motorcycle, which shone in the morning haze with a sleek design, intricate pipes, and muscular frame, giving the vehicle an edge of danger. Then, she dragged her gaze toward Bryce, and her heartbeat quickened.

With auburn waves drawn away from his face, gleaming helmet in hand, black sunglasses, and accompanying black boots, dark, washed jeans hugging his strong frame, and black leather jacket, he oozed sex appeal.

They stared at one another for a moment, then two, then three until the gravitational pull was too great. She stepped forward and breathed, willing her heart to steady, preparing for what she was about to do—for what she had to do. "Before we go anywhere, I have to tell you Andrea was the one who texted last night."

Bryce tipped his head.

"I don't know if this is a good idea, Bryce. I'm leaving tomorrow."

"Aye, I'm aware. I didna drive over an hour to just

look at *ye*." He strode forward, tearing off his glasses and captured her lips, sliding a hand through her hair.

Brie smelled leather and damp rain, while she tasted Bryce—a hint of mint mingled with his own intoxicating scent—then separated.

As he gazed longingly into her eyes, his chest heaved. "I've missed *ye*." He trailed a hand down her arm.

Electric current blazed where he touched, even though she wore a sweater and an undershirt beneath her jacket. "I missed you, too."

"Come on a ride with me."

And then and there, she knew as much as her head told her she should turn around and dash back into that cute little cabin, her heart said, *GO!* "All right."

After securing his helmet, Bryce unfastened a second that was attached to the back of the motorcycle. When he caught her staring, he eyed her through the open pane. "Brie, *yer* no' afraid of motorbikes, are *ye*?"

"No." Her pulse hummed with nerves and excitement. "I've just never been on the back of one."

He stroked her cheek. "Do *ye* trust me?"

She sighed into his touch. She could second-guess herself and her feelings, but she couldn't second-guess Bryce. "Yes."

"Good." He kissed her quickly and then popped a helmet with gold swirls on her head. "Ready?"

She cinched the strap. "As I'll ever be."

Chuckling, he swung a leg over the bike and started the engine. The powerful machine growled to life. He held out a hand.

She grasped his, then threw her heeled boot around the bike and snuggled behind. With her arms wrapped around his waist, she roared onto the road with Bryce. As they zigzagged around the glimmering loch, snaking past slow-moving cars and the casual morning stroller, her heart thudded nervously. She gripped Bryce tighter, ever-aware of the powerful motorcycle beneath her, while he maneuvered the bike expertly, navigating them through Ballachulish and onto the open road.

Living in L.A. all her life, Brie always considered motorcycles, and motorcycle riders for that matter, dangerous and a bit crazy. Heck, she'd seen them weave in and out of lanes on freeways like performers, nearly smashing into dividers or colliding with a car. Yet, as she glided down the vast road, her grip softened, and she relaxed into the seat. Miles and miles of scenic mountains lay before her, while Bryce maneuvered the bike, flying through the wind. She was free.

She lifted her head, welcoming the cool, caressing wind that grazed her cheeks and breathed the crisp air perfumed with grass, pine, and floral notes mingled with the strong, masculine leather Bryce wore. She couldn't deny he'd gotten even sexier on the bike, or how she enjoyed the feel of her arms around him, and the extra warm center where their bodies merged. Perhaps it was because she'd recently been intimate with him or perhaps it was the sexy Scotsman riding tandem, but riding a bike made her feel uninhibited. With one hand holding tight, she extended the other to dance upon the brisk wind.

They zipped under a bridge and continued weaving through the mountains where rocks towered beside dark, forest-green evergreens and the road wound ahead. She lost track of time. Yet, time didn't matter— just she, Bryce, and beautiful Scotland existed.

Sometime later, salty air filled her nostrils, and seagulls *flip-flapped* overhead. They stopped at a ferry crossing where numerous cars lined in anticipation. Luckily, they didn't have to wait long.

An attendant opened the entry gates and waved them forward.

Bryce drove the short distance onto the ferry and parked. After removing helmets, they climbed the neon-yellow, hazard-marked stairs.

Brie excused herself to use the bathroom and stared wide-eyed in the mirror. *Oh Lord*. Her hair plastered to her head, while mascara ran under her eyes from the cool wind. She retrieved her lip gloss, mascara, and a few other items from her bag and tidied her face and hair. In the end, she settled with a side fishtail, befitting a quick ride over the water.

Weaving between tourists and perhaps locals, Brie meandered to the ferry deck where a little girl with a fuzzy pink cap squealed in delight. Phoebe was Brie's pink princess. She could imagine her here giddy with excitement, while Noah pointed out marine life. Although the sting of missing them still welled in her chest when she least expected, being with Bryce helped. She smiled and waved, continuing toward the bow where Bryce waited.

He stared out at the water, strong arms resting on the white metal railing with the ocean and land framing him, cap low.

Her pulse skipped. She couldn't believe he was taking her on a surprise trip to the Isle of Skye and couldn't wait to see what he had in store. Joining him, she tucked an arm through his and leaned into his warmth, inhaling rich leather and foamy seawater. A few sail boats dotted her view, gliding over the sparkling water like white swans on a vast lake as the sun peeked through patchy clouds. "It's so beautiful."

" 'Tis, and look." He wrapped an arm around her side, drawing her more firmly to him, then pointed to the right where a colorful rainbow stretched over the mountains.

"Wow. Every time I think I've seen the most beautiful picture of Scotland, a new one appears. Your country is magical." She fished her phone out. "Would you mind if I took a picture?"

"Not a bit." He relaxed onto the rail.

Once she snapped a couple of pictures, Brie swiveled. Yet before she could put away her device, she felt Bryce's hand snake around her midsection, tugging her close once again.

With his free hand, he lifted the phone and directed the camera toward them. "There we are."

Looking at her and Bryce smiling before the lovely landscape behind them, she felt her insides sparkle like the blue cerulean in the background. *We look good together. Happy and carefree.*

Bryce snapped a few pictures, then leaned against the rail again. "Send it to me," he said. "We should also keep a close eye out for kelpies."

She lifted a brow. "What exactly is a kelpie?"

"A mythical water-horse said to have the power and endurance of a hundred horses. They mostly live in lochs and rivers."

"Like a unicorn?" She tilted her head. "Can you ride them?"

"No." His lips turned up in a devilish grin. "They're no' a friendly horse. 'Tis said if one mounts a kelpie, the fierce creature will drag *ye* under water."

She gawked. "Remind me not to tell my children that story."

He laughed heartily and squeezed her side, drawing a giggle from Brie.

Something jumped out of the water, glistening in the sun.

"A dolphin!" Brie pointed. "And another one!"

Bryce chuckled low. "Aye, a magnificent sight, aren't they?"

"They are." She leaned forward, watching them glide in the soft waves. Like magical sea nymphs, they appeared for a few minutes and then disappeared into the sparkling sea. "This has been a fun morning so far. I never thought I'd get on a motorcycle, but I did, and I enjoyed the ride, more than I ever imagined I would. And now we're on a ferry, which I haven't ridden since I was a little girl."

"I'm glad. Everyone deserves a wee ride now and again. And there's nothing quite like getting on a motorbike."

"You know, I've ridden just about everything on this trip with you..." She turned and found Bryce a breath away. Her face flamed and body followed.

Dipping his head, he kissed her—pressing his full lips against hers for one heartbeat, then two.

His kiss was like a speed boat creating ripples of current within her. She flew with him, while the salty wind whipped around them and her heart soared like the wings of a seabird.

When they separated, she rested her head on his shoulder. Today was incredible. Yet, she couldn't help but think about how this all was coming to an end tomorrow.

****

When the ferry approached the Isle of Skye, Bryce pointed to the skeleton ruins above the shore. "There you'll see Armadale Castle, the clan seat of the MacDonalds—the largest clan in Scotland."

She leaned farther onto the railing. "It's stunning." A second later, she straightened. "Wait, did you say the MacDonalds?"

He nodded. "I did."

"I met some MacDonalds yesterday and Finlays."

He angled his head. "Did *ye* now?"

"I did. They told me a few stories about some Farquharsons and a Finlay tale, which was amazing. Finlays are storytellers and artists…like me."

"Oh, aye?" He squeezed her side. "*Ye* can never get far from *yer* roots."

"I guess not." She glanced back at the castle. "And they showed me some pictures of Invercauld Castle. I guess it isn't really open to the public very often." She sighed. "I don't think I'll ever get over how many castles are in Scotland. Are we visiting Armadale?"

Bryce shook his head. "Not today. I've a bit of a surprise for *ye*."

"Really?" Brie's eyebrows arched above her sunglasses.

"Aye." He grinned. Bryce liked surprises, and he was fairly certain Brie would be thrilled with what he had in store.

In Armadale, they swung back onto the bike and drove past the boat yard, heading north. Peering up to the sky, he noted the darkening clouds. He cursed under his breath and gunned the engine, hoping the weather would hold for a wee bit longer.

Not a moment later, a peppering of rain shot across his vision. *Damn four seasons.*

Though when Brie tightened her grip around him, he relaxed. Regardless of how the day unfolded, he had a beautiful woman beside him. They'd make the most of their time. When he drove into the Broadford Aerodrome, he noted the sea plane awaited. He helped Brie from the bike and heard a quick inhale of breath.

"A plane?" Brie's eyes widened, and a smile bloomed. "Is this the surprise?"

"Aye. I didn't know how we'd fare with the weather, so thought I'd show ye some of the amazing sights of the Isle of Skye from a different view." With her hand still in his, he lifted it to his lips.

A few minutes later, they soared into the sky. Stretches of grassland and mountains lay before them outside the wide, clear windows.

Brie gripped Bryce's hand.

As he rubbed a thumb across her knuckles, Bryce grinned. He didn't know if she was a nervous flyer, but he wanted to make her feel as comfortable as possible on their adventure. Within minutes, the plane glided onto the water where the colorful town of Portree with pastel-colored houses dotted above cliffs.

"It's like a painting." She leaned closer to the window. "Even under the shroud of clouds, the city is so vibrant. And, oh! A pink house. I love it."

He laughed. "Aye, *ye* would."

She poked him in the side. "What does that mean, Bryce Fraser?"

He grunted. "Well, *yer* a lassie."

"I am." She gazed at him sternly.

Chuckling, Bryce stroked a hand down her hair. The guide's rich voice came over his headset, and Bryce tugged Brie close once again as he listened to the guide inform them about the popular tourist destination. Of course, he'd visited the Isle more times than he could count, but he enjoyed watching Brie experience parts of his country for the first time—the way she marveled at the natural harbor city bordered by high ground and slick cliffs with her bonnie eyes widening and wee gasps escaping parted lips with pleasure.

They continued north over glens and mountains, gliding past glistening lochs reflecting the sky above until they circled a new facet of the Isle. He grinned as Brie pressed closer to the window, hand gliding up the glass and watching the change in landscape.

He'd had a similar experience himself when he rediscovered his homeland after returning from Los Angeles near penniless with *Swords of Scotland* about to begin filming. Before shooting, Bryce packed a bag and headed north to the highlands, keen to get some insight into his new character—Alexander James Mackenzie—the beloved, highland warrior. But once he dug his feet into the rich earth, climbing his first *munro* in years, he realized he hadn't found his character, but himself. He was home.

Circling toward a black, rocky peak, the pilot's voice carried over the radio. "Up ahead, you'll see a rocky hill called the Storr, comprised of sharp pinnacles. Beneath the cliffs, 'tis the Old Man Storr himself full of magic and myth."

Light rain drizzled on the windows, while the plane circled the Old Man of Storr, making the location appear even more mysterious. " 'Tis a grand experience to hike up to the Old Man as well, though in better conditions."

Brie smiled. "The conditions make this place even more magical. But yes, I'd love to next time."

Next time. Bryce gazed at her bonnie face and rosy lips. Brie's vacation was coming to an end tomorrow. Yet, he couldn't deny he'd grown fond of her. More than fond if he were honest. He wondered if and when she would return.

"Some say giants used to roam the island, and one, grand giant is buried there with his thumb sticking out of the ground," the pilot noted.

"Wow." Her eyes sparkled. "Rocks and giants! It's like a fantasy."

Bryce chuckled. Yet, his gaze stayed on Brie. She'd brought excitement into his life and a rejuvenation to explore. The sun peeked through the clouds opening a small patch of blue and set Brie's golden-brown hair aglow. He twirled the end of her braid between his fingers. He felt like a young lad, and he couldn't keep his hands off her.

"On this sea cliff is a famous rock called Kilt Rock formed by basalt columns, and in the center, Mealt Falls..." the pilot informed.

Brie inched closer, peering at the glistening, cascading waterfall flowing into the cobalt ocean. "It's breathtaking," she cooed.

"Aye." He flew his gaze over Brie and inhaled her soft, floral scent. " 'Tis even more with *ye* beside me."

Brie's smile blossomed. "Thank you."

Tearing his gaze from her, he glanced at the cliff top where a wee dusting of purple heather accentuated the green foliage. The legendary flowers shined like gems in the sun, appearing like a violet cloud above the sharp pleats. If he could, Bryce would gather the glorious gems and present them to Brie. He didn't want this day to end.

A giggle escaped Brie.

Bryce angled his head, watching her lips curl and eyes shine.

"The rock does resemble a kilt! I wonder what's under that kilt." She glanced at Bryce and wiggled her brows.

With a quick hand at her side, he tickled Brie, igniting laughter. The warm, vibrant sound brought joy to his heart and a smile to his lips. Leaning down, he kissed her swiftly, muffling her giggles. A moment later, he drew away with a grin.

Brie settled beside him once again, snapping a few pictures as they flew to their next destination. They skimmed over the majestic Quiraing where patchy skies highlighted lofty cliffs, plateaus, and rocks, and then rounded toward the crystal, turquoise-blue water. In the sea plane, they soared high above the world with each other and the vast *munros* for company.

"The Red Cuillin mountain range was formed by sharp, volcanic peaks with numerous *munros* over three thousand feet. Plenty of *munros* to be bagged in these mountains for mountaineers, including the infamous In Pinn or Inaccessible Pinnacle with its huge drops and intimidating rock," the pilot noted.

"What's a *munro*?" she asked.

"A mountain."

"Ah." She gazed at the vast peaks. "I imagine you've climbed a few?"

"Aye. I've bagged more than a dozen and plan to

accomplish more once filming ends."

She nodded. "What's your favorite part about climbing?"

He considered for a minute, then shifted his sunglass-covered eyes toward her. " 'Tis an amazing feeling—driving your body to its breaking point—with mother nature beside ye, and then once you get to the top, all you feel is peace."

Slipping a hand in his, Brie rested her head on his shoulder.

High above the world beside Brie, Bryce was content. The woman had a way of calming and opening him up in a way he hadn't thought possible. Perhaps that's why—despite his own lingering skepticism—he'd driven to Glencoe with a wee five hours sleep. And he wasn't planning on remedying sleep tonight. As they soared above the island, following the curve of the coast toward Neist Point Lighthouse, he relaxed with her sweet scent wrapping around him.

Returning to the airport thirty minutes later, they rode a short distance to a local restaurant in Bradford known for fresh seafood. Tucked in a corner booth, he noted Brie's anxiousness returned as she swiveled her lovely neck back and forth, checking for Super Fans. He couldn't blame her, especially after their breakfast interruption. Yet, no one seemed to notice or care, and the server was a long-time acquaintance.

They discussed their adventures of the day with the musical conversations of a few tourists and locals around them. Laughing and teasing, they enjoyed the simple pleasure of sharing a meal together.

Sometime later, damp from the motorcycle ride, they rode the ferry back to the mainland. When Brie's shivers shook him, he peeled his own leather jacket off and warmed her, then snugged closer, resting his head atop hers. He should drive back to Glasgow tonight—shooting would resume at nine a.m., but he wanted more than a few extra hours of sleep; he wanted Brie.

Bryce parked at the cottage, drenched from the drive, and wrenched off his helmet, threw a leg over the bike, and lifted Brie off, while the rain pelted him like bullets. He followed close as she raced up the winding path. Once inside, he shoved off his jacket and pressed her against the door, seizing her mouth like a starving man. He needed more. He needed to touch her. Tugging her jumper free, he roamed his hands over her silky skin, smooth back, and round hips. When her head tipped back, giving him access to her long neck, he trailed kisses down skin that was as sweet as honey.

Brie arched, then pulled him back, fusing their lips once more, while her hands unbuckled his belt. A moment later, she whipped the leather belt off and smacked something.

Bonk! Hard metal bashed Bryce in the head, searing pain through his skull. "Ah, Christ." He shot a hand up in defense. "What the hell was that?"

Brie switched the light on. "The coatrack. Are you okay?"

Glaring at the coat holder that lay on the floor beside them, he rubbed his screaming scalp. "Damn lethal contraption." He shoved the rack back into place. "But it didna help that I've a feisty lass in—"

"Shut up and kiss me," she demanded.

He lunged forward. "I'll do more than kiss *ye*."

"Come and get me." She sprinted up the stairs.

Bryce raced after her. When he stepped into the

bedroom, his breath wedged in his chest.

Brie stood beside the bed in the soft, warm glow of a single light. She peeled the wet, green, floral top off inch-by-inch, gaze fixed and eyes dark.

His pulse quickened and body throbbed, chest thundering. "I ken what *yer* doing."

"Do you?" She continued unbuttoning her trousers, one button at a time, then shimmied out of them. Next, she reached an arm behind and unsnapped her bra, releasing those beautiful breasts tipped with rosebuds.

"Christ, Brie."

Last, she slid red lace down her long legs. "I want you, Bryce. Do you want me?"

"Oh God, yes." He strode to her in two, quick strides.

She wrapped her naked body against his hard, clothed one.

He feasted on her lips, tangling his tongue with hers in a seductive dance and groped her nice, round ass. Hearing his name catch on her lips, he sucked in a breath as his need swelled against his trousers. Lifting her up, he set Brie on the bed to shed his thermal and tugged trousers and briefs free. Remembering safety, he reached into his back pocket and retrieved a condom from his wallet. As he joined her, he drew his tongue around her navel, then up her smooth stomach toward her full breasts. He sucked and teased, while his fingers found her hot center. She writhed under him, arching with his movements. Her sounds of pleasure drove him mad. And even though his own desire burned, he wanted more. Yet, she surprised him by shifting and mounting him.

She captured his bottom lip in her teeth, then

kissed him soundly before stroking those incredible hands down his back. Releasing his lips, she nibbled his jaw, drawing a guttural moan before she bent down.

He sucked in a breath, then dropped his head back in surrender until he was ready to explode.

Slinging an arm around her slim waist, he rose and shifted, catching her eyes widen and lips part. He groped for the condom, fastened it, then slid her onto his lap, and firmly onto his cock. A burst of pleasure surged through him, and a sweet cry escaped Brie's mouth. He held fast for a moment, wanting the moment to last. With her lovely, long legs wrapped around him and arms holding his, he captured her lips, while his hands gripped her bottom and began a slow rhythm.

They climbed the Munro together until they peaked, and Brie shouted his name.

****

Bryce squatted naked, lighting the fire, muscles bunching as he struck a match.

"Mmm that's an incredible view."

Rotating, he grinned. "Glad to oblige *ye*." He rose and strolled toward her all bronze in the firelight. He tugged on jeans tossed on the floor.

"Oh, you don't have to…" she began.

He sauntered over with the top button of his jeans left undone. Leaning down, he kissed her softly. "Stay put," he ordered.

Brie sighed and stretched her naked arms dreamily atop the soft, feather pillows. "That's pretty much what I had in mind." The day was a dream. And Brie was on a dream trip. She lamented about the romantic adventure in the Isle of Skye as sounds of cooking carried upstairs. With a happy hum, she retrieved her journal from the side table and scribbled, *An Island Adventure* on the next blank page.

An hour later, they sat together in the cozy cabin, eating beef stew with the flickering fire behind them. The stew was flavorful, meaty, and rich with chunky vegetables and a hint of wine and herbs. Who knew Bryce would be handy in the kitchen? Cooking was such a simple, sweet gesture. Yet, she couldn't remember if Ryan had ever cooked for her. Definitely not anything besides eggs for breakfast when they were first dating, but she couldn't recall. She shook her head.

Bryce tilted his. "Everything all right?"

She dipped her spoon into the thick stew. "Absolutely. This is delicious. Where'd you learn to cook?"

"*Och, ye* can't live off takeaway all the time, and me ma taught me a few recipes when I was a young lad."

"And your dad?"

Casting his gaze toward his bowl, he cleared his throat. "He passed when I was a teenager."

Brie covered her mouth with a hand. "I'm so sorry…I didn't mean to…"

Shaking his head, he covered her free hand with his. "Shh, it's been some time now."

She nodded; yet, her eyes stung. "I never met my dad."

"No?" His brows jammed together.

"He passed in the Gulf War before I was born."

"I'm sorry, Brie." He rubbed his thumb over her knuckles in soothing circles.

"It's…okay. All he ever wanted was to take care of us—Mom and I. That's why he enlisted. And even though he passed away, his military pay helped us survive. But I still wonder what he was like, you know?"

"Aye, I can imagine." He laced his fingers between hers under the soft glow of the cottage lights. "There's a gaping hole within when *ye* lose a parent."

"I think that's partly why I was so excited to learn about the Finlay line. To discover more about my paternal heritage that I wasn't aware of before."

He nodded and brushed a hand down her hair. "I understand."

And in that moment, Brie realized Bryce had been taking care of her. From picking her up in Edinburgh in the rain, wrapping the tartan around her on their picnic, waiting for her to open up atop Loch Lomond, flying high above the Isle of Sky, so she wouldn't catch pneumonia sight-seeing, and lastly, here at the dinner table. She was so used to taking care of herself and her children, she didn't realize she'd allowed Bryce to care for her like a partner. But did he think of her as a partner or girlfriend? She wondered what he was thinking, and though she wanted to ask, the fear of rejection weighed on her.

Later that night, the familiar sound of a video chat echoed through the cabin.

Brie disentangled herself from Bryce on the couch and fetched her phone. A picture with Mimi's face and her two children appeared on the screen. "It's my kids. I can go—"

"No." Bryce shook his head, meeting her gaze above the script in hand. "Take the call."

Smiling softly, she sat again. "Hi, guys!"

Phoebe's face squished into the phone screen, so

one mermaid eye was visible. "I got wet, Mommy! It's raining, and I had my umbrella, and my boots, and now Mimi's drying me."

"Sounds like fun, big girl. Make sure you stay warm at school."

"Yes! I slide with baby!" Her grin spread across her face, flashing deep dimples on either cheek as she fitted her baby doll into the frame.

"I bet you will. Noah, did you get to play before school, too?"

The camera shook, and a scream pierced through the speaker. Noah appeared. "Yeah. I rode my bike through this *huge* puddle out front—splashed mud and water everywhere. It was awesome, Mom."

Bryce chuckled.

"Who's that?" he asked.

She froze. Slowly swiveling toward Bryce, she noticed how he stared quietly, an upturn of lips forming a soft smile. She'd never been put in this position before. When her children called her previously, she'd covertly called them back while Bryce slept. But he wasn't sleeping now. He was right beside her, staring with shining eyes. Should she introduce him? Would they ask more questions? But as she wondered about how her children would react, she also wanted them to meet him. She leaned over. "Would you like to say hello?"

With a nod, he set the pages down and peered at the phone. "I'm *yer* mom's friend, Bryce."

"Why do you talk funny?" Noah asked.

Brie chewed the inside of her cheek, concealing a giggle.

He chuckled. "Well, I'm from Scotland. We talk

different here."

Pressing his face closer to the screen, Noah's sky-blue eyes searched the small space visible through the phone. "Is it raining there, too?"

Bryce glanced out the large, front window. The sun had dipped below the mountains, highlighting peaks like golden nuggets and darkening storm clouds the color of clay. "Aye, it did and probably will be later if the thunder clouds have anything to say about it."

"Are there big, giant puddles there, too?" Phoebe appeared in the rectangular frame.

"There are. Grand puddles, and slow worms, and frogs, too."

Brie melted. Placing her hand on his upper thigh, she squeezed gently, while he teased the ends of her tumbled hair.

"I want to see!"

"You will!" Brie smiled. "One day. Have fun with Mimi and at school today, okay?"

After a chorus of good-byes, she disconnected, then snugged her head atop Bryce's shoulder. "You didn't have to do that."

Bryce wrapped an arm around her, drawing her closer. "Aye, I wanted to. They're adorable."

"Thank you. You're a natural."

He skimmed fingertips up and down the length of her hand, then paused. "Brie, what is a Mimi?"

She laughed. "One of the most popular terms for grandmother in the states."

"Ah, I had a feeling, but I wasn't completely sure."

When her text chimed, she glanced over to see a short message from Andrea, notifying her she'd be staying in Fort William tonight. Brie sent her a quick thumbs-up emoji and sighed, content to spend a little more time with the sweet Scot beside her. Dropping a kiss on his shoulder, she informed him, "We have the cottage to ourselves tonight."

"Oh, aye?" A smile spread across his face, and the flickering firelight danced in his eyes.

"Yep. What time do you have to be back on set tomorrow?"

"Nine. I'll leave here by seven."

Nodding, she twined her right hand in his. "It was quite a production when we visited. It must be something to be on such an amazing set every day."

"I still remember not so far in the past when I had less than a hundred pounds to my name," Bryce said quietly.

She widened her eyes. "Really?"

"Truly, but the casual *wanker* spat out the window helps ground me."

"What?" She gasped. "People really say that?"

Curling the end of the pages, he shrugged. "People are entitled to their opinions."

She shook her head. "But according to Andrea, you've busted your butt to get where you're at."

Bryce raked a hand through his hair, which had curled at the ends since drying. "The past seven years have been a whirlwind. The show transformed my life and gave me more opportunity than I could ever have imagined for myself."

She straightened and tucked her legs under her. "But I'm sure you dreamed about what success would look like, right?"

"Dreamed, yes. But I couldna imagine this kind of success. To see what's befallen me has been nothing short of a miracle. Of course, my dream was to be an actor, but I couldna have foreseen the blessings I've received as a result of *Swords*."

"You've earned it." Brie smiled, then remembered the excited fans on set and yesterday—the women, the screaming, and the real tears over Bryce's character. Agitation crackled inside her like the logs in the fire. "Do you ever get used to it, though? The attention? The fans?"

Bryce clenched his jaw. "No, I don't think I ever will. But I've been blessed with a career; I canna expect to ignore how I reached this point."

With a sigh, she settled against him. "I imagine you can't."

" 'Tis a lovely thing when people appreciate what *ye* do, although I'm getting older now. Not sure how long I'll be gracing the fronts of those magazines."

"What are you, mid-thirties?"

The corners of his mouth tipped up. "Em, forty actually."

"Well, think about George Clooney. That man is still sexy and making movies." *And mature and married now. Still, she didn't realize Bryce was nine years older, but she didn't care.*

He chuckled.

"Forty looks good on you." She bent down and picked up her wine glass, then raised the slim-hipped glass. "Cheers."

"Slainte." They touched rims and drank. "And what about *ye*? Will *ye* pursue *yer* writing?"

"Yes, I'd love to see my story published. Perhaps I'll be on the cover of something one day, as well. Brielle Finlay, Memoirist. It has a nice ring."

"It does, lass." Retrieving the stapled pages he'd set aside, Bryce flipped open the packet.

"Do you want me to read them with you? Would that help?" Brie asked.

"That would be brilliant." He handed her the pages.

Brie pointed to the page folded. "Here?"

"Aye."

She cleared her throat in preparation to read Lady Charlotte's line. "Alex, you must leave at once. The redcoats, they're near—they know you've returned from the Highlands and if they find you, they'll capture you...and kill you! You can't stay."

He leaned in with brows drawn. "No. I've only just found *ye* again, *mo ghràdh*."

"Please. Please, you must! You must go."

"No!"

"We will find each other again." Brie's voice thickened and heart thudded. When she glanced up, she found Bryce staring intently. "Trust in our love."

He lifted a hand and brushed a thumb softly along her cheekbone, gliding his fingers into her hair. "*Ye* have my promise."

At that moment, Brie wished Bryce could promise her more than tonight.

Chapter 21

An alarm sounded in the dark, pre-dawn hours of the morning.

"Mmm," Brie murmured amongst the sleepy cobwebs. "It's early."

"Morning, I did warn *ye*." He placed a quick kiss on her lips, then rolled out of bed.

"You did." She stretched under the pile of quilts, sliding her legs down the cozy warmth, and watched Bryce tug on a pair of pants. She loved how he was built—all muscled and manly. "Are you sure you want to go for a morning hike? You wouldn't rather have a workout here instead?" She sat up and allowed the flannel sheet to fall.

His eyes darkened like the early morning light. "Aye, I would, but there's something I want to show *ye*."

A half hour into their hike, Brie stepped into a small, woodland clearing. Her senses filled with damp earth, sweet pine, and subtle floral notes. Though the morning mist blanketed the mountains, bluebells carpeted the floor like bursts of jewels as far as her eyes could see, and beyond, a green valley sparkled like emeralds from the glowing, hazy sun. "It's a dream."

"Shhh." He placed a finger on her lips, drawing her astride a tree.

A stag stared from twenty feet away, ears and

antlers high. Even in the shroud of the dawn, the deer's coat had a reddish hue, while a white band circled the muzzle and black nose.

Brie inhaled, though she didn't feel afraid. Instead, she was in awe of the magnificent creature.

The stag flicked its ears, then hiked up the hill, disappearing into the lush woods.

"Is that what you wanted to show me?" she asked as her breath created cloudy puffs.

"Aye." He turned, eyes swimming with desire. "And this." Dipping his head, he captured her mouth, drawing her up to her toes. He drew away briefly and trailed kisses along her jaw, while he unfastened her coat. "Do *ye* want me? Want this?"

"Yes," she responded with heavy breath as his caressed her. Her skin blazed with each whisper of Bryce's lips over her skin, down her neck, and across her collarbone. He paused, sliding his tongue along the expanse. She moaned. "Oh, my God." She greedily lifted his thick sweater from his belt and scraped her nails up roped muscles, then tossed it aside.

Bryce stepped back and laid his jacket on the spongy grass. Grasping her hand, he lowered her to the forest floor. "I want *ye* here under the canopy of trees with the sun sparkling through your hair and mountains surrounding us." He captured her lips once more.

Although the air held a chill, her body burned. Brie arched beneath him, asking and yearning.

He tugged up her sweater and kissed the swells of her breasts exposed by a plum bra, while unfastening her jeans and tugging down her panties.

She gasped when Bryce dipped low. "Bryce!" His mouth covered and consumed, giving and demanding more and more until she raptured and let go. She felt like a fairy goddess glowing in the woods, floating on the spongy earth and held by the magnificent mountains. How could she have known he could make her feel like this? Or want him like that?

Bryce rose halfway, gaze fixed on hers. He tugged off the remaining remnants of his clothes and fastened a condom. They joined and moved together until that wonderful throbbing burst inside, and her entire body shimmered like the most magnificent sunrise.

After, she lay in the grass entwined with Bryce, caressing his back in slow, lazy circles.

An eagle *eered* in the distance.

"To be with *ye* here in my favorite part of Scotland is incredible. Watching *yer* eyes light along with the scenery around us." He kissed her nose, then brushed a hand down her hair. "And see *yer* hair shining like silk in the grass."

"You're incredible." She kissed his chest and breathed in his masculine aroma mingled with rich earth and morning mist. Yet, she couldn't help but notice the damp ground beneath. "I've never done this…in the grass. I liked it, but"—she leaned forward—"are there any bugs on me?"

His lips curved into a smile. "No, Los Angeles, the midges won't be out for a wee bit longer. But I'm sure a wee bug or two would be glad to crawl on us, if not already."

She hastily rose, rubbing her hands down her naked arms and body.

"Brie, wait a moment."

She froze. "What?"

Leaning forward, he smacked her butt. "Got it."

"Bryce!"

He roared with laughter, then silenced her wasted threats with his mouth. When they separated, Bryce stood naked in the glow of the morning sun. His curled hair shone like freshly minted copper and the outline of his powerful body sparkled.

Her breath caught, and Brie knew when she returned to L.A., the image of Bryce, here and now, would forever be fixed in her memories. Yet, at that same moment, a sudden heaviness settled deep in her core. All they would have after tomorrow would be memories.

****

As Bryce's motorcycle engine echoed through the hills, Brie closed the cabin door.

"How was the hike?" Andrea stood at the tiny stove. She flicked her wrist, and an omelet flipped a few inches above the pan, then returned with a sizzle.

"Wonderful." She plopped into one of the wooden, dining chairs. "We made love in the grass. I've never made love anywhere except the bedroom, well"—she blushed and continued—"except the other day on set. Have you?"

Andrea laughed. "Uh, yeah. I'm glad your sex drive has been reawakened because you're glowing, and it's barely eight a.m."

"Is it eight?" Brie craned her head toward the clock. "Shoot, Bryce will be late to set."

With a snort, Andrea tossed a scone.

Laughing, Brie caught it.

"I'm sure he's feeling really guilty right now," Andrea added.

Brie smiled and slid the knife into the fluffy center,

lathered on butter and jelly, and ate happily. "How was your night? Did you get lucky bar-hopping?"

"*Psh.*" She slid a giant, golden omelet flecked with bright peppers onto a plate. "Met a sexy-as-hell, jet-black-haired ruffian in a bar."

Brie quirked a brow. "What happened?"

Andrea sliced the omelet in half. "He got so drunk he forgot my name." She nestled half onto Brie's plate, then dropped beside her with the other. "The *Swords* girls also had too much to drink, and I left them in the first hotel room, while I settled into the second with chocolate cake and a hot tub."

"A girl's got to have standards."

Andrea toasted with tea. "Amen, sister." She drank. "Has Bryce said anything about what happens when you return to L.A.?"

Brie shook her head and felt the sting of tears swell. "No. And I haven't, either. What's the point? A cross-Atlantic relationship? That would never work."

Andrea settled a hand on Brie's and squeezed gently.

Brie gripped Andrea's in turn. Outside, dark clouds loomed and blurred the picturesque landscape.

****

An hour later, Bryce strode across the set entry, boots digging into the grass toward the makeup trailer.

A melee of extras and crew readied near the base of the castle, while the director's assistant relayed directions via a megaphone.

Cursing, he shook his head at his own tardiness. Being with Brie was worth the consequences, but he didn't make a habit of being late. When he caught sight of Eleana, Hugh, and Moira gathered below the steps of the trailer, he prepared for the onslaught by his cast mates.

Waving, Moira's features brightened. "*Och*, here he is now." She fisted the other hand on a full hip. "*Ye* all right?"

"Aye."

With her long, curled hair drawn away from her face, Eleana leveled a haughty look. "Bryce, really? You'd delay taping after a full day off? We're supposed to be professionals."

Bryce expelled a quick breath. "I'm sorry. I ran into some…traffic."

"Ah, get off him, Eleana. Ye know Bryce has never been late save for the morn we were all pissed." Hugh slapped a hand on Bryce's shoulder. "Get a lassie stuck under you, did *ye*?" He wiggled his brows.

Eleana rolled her eyes and stalked off.

"What?" Hugh glanced at Eleana's retreating backside.

"Leave off it, mate."

With a long look at Eleana, Hugh strode in the opposite direction.

Bryce followed Moira into the makeup trailer. After extra praise for his makeup artist, Bryce was ready in less than an hour. He put on his kilt and wardrobe, then squared his shoulders. *Time to grovel.*

****

"I said I'm sorry, and I meant it," Bryce apologized between takes, standing in the great hall of Castle Roderick.

Lifting her chin, she stared coolly. "It's fine."

"As fine as when Hugh pranked *ye* in the moor?" He grinned, recalling the time Hugh concealed a fake snake near her shooting spot. "That was a brilliant joke."

She glared, cobalt eyes blackening like the dark sea. "What is it with you two? Don't you take anything seriously?" She pivoted.

He extended a hand, pausing her movement. Eleana was near one of his closest friends. "I ken Hugh can be a vauntie lad, and I was late, but something else is amiss, isn't it?" When he didn't receive an answer, he squeezed her arm gently. "Are *ye* all right?"

"Fine." She tossed her hair, sending waves ruffling. "It was a long day yesterday—fourteen hours. I'm tired and don't appreciate having to wait on my co-star."

"I'm sorry. I was with Brie," he whispered.

Gazing into the distance where kilt-clad musicians readied to resume the eighteenth-century-style concert, she shook her head.

The gaiety of the setting with swags of pungent pine garlands and glowing, ivory candles contrasted sharply to her disposition. "Eleana, I had a day off. We both get them now and again, but I'm truly sorry I'm late, all right?"

"I know." She blew a long breath of frustration. "Gemma's in the hospital. Complications."

Understanding hit Bryce like a three-hundred-kilo cannon ball. When his sister was pregnant, he remembered the scare with his nephew, the prayers, and gathering of family. He rested a hand on her shoulder. "Everything will be all right. Your sister is strong. Perhaps I can talk to Daniel? Start earlier tomorrow to make up for it, so you can fly to London tonight?"

Eleana's eyes glossed. "Brie's a lucky woman, Bryce."

He nodded. But unlike luck, time wasn't on his side. He'd let down his guard, and he could admit he was falling for Brie. Yet, could he trust himself, trust her, with anything further than tomorrow?

Chapter 22

May 4

I've fallen for Bryce Fraser. I told myself to sever our relationship and stop seeing him, but Andrea, the stinker, stole my phone and changed my plans.

Now, how can I say good-bye? To look at him and leave him one last time seems incomprehensible.

I know I have to leave. Our flight takes off in less than eight hours. My bags are packed, and quilt and bedding folded. There's no denying the truth—my life and my children are in L.A.—that's where I have to be.

This morning, Andrea and I joined a paddleboard tour on Loch Leven, wearing borrowed wetsuits, booties, and boards. The loch was so peaceful with the water softly lapping onto the board as I dug the oar into the pristine water—like a meditation. Well, except the "Oh, no!" and "Shit!" shot from Andrea a few feet behind me. Yet, when I gazed into the lush, evergreen forest beyond, I thought of Bryce, this morning, and the past ten days...I'm still thinking about him.

How can I say good-bye?

****

The drive to Glasgow was quiet, not like before when anticipation and excitement loomed. The sky, too, was dark and heavy, threatening their easy drive as Brie stared out the window awaiting the downpour.

Andrea elbowed her softly from behind the wheel.

"You should go."

"I know, but it's going to be so hard," she said, voice thickening.

"If you don't, you'll regret it."

Tears fell, dampening her cheeks, and she palmed them away. "I've been running our possible good-bye conversation in my head, but nothing sounds right. 'Hope to see you again one day,' or how about, 'I had a great time?' "

Andrea slid her gaze sideways.

"See! Lame."

"The words will come."

Rain streaked down her window like a flood of tears. *I have to say good-bye, no matter how hard it's going to be.* "Okay." Brie puffed a breath and sniffled. "I'll figure out what to say when I get there, but what will you do?"

"I'll check in early, grab a drink, some *tatties*, and relax. Don't worry about me, okay? Go see the man of our dreams." She punched the radio dial, and a rock song blasted.

Brie nodded. With courage, she grasped her phone and texted Bryce they'd be arriving in Glasgow in the evening and boarding the plane at eight p.m. Then, she waited with the music mirroring her pounding heart.

****

A black four-by-four picked Brie up outside the rental car drop-off.

Arriving at Bryce's home thirty minutes later, she stepped onto the cobblestones one last time.

The front door opened, and Bryce stood tall inside the doorway.

Her pulse skittered as she stepped forward. He

drew her inside and kissed her slowly, achingly slow, that sorrow grasped her heart, and tears tumbled down her cheeks.

Bryce rubbed a thumb across her cheekbone. "Don't cry, fair Brielle."

She sniffled. "I'm sorry."

Drawing her into the living room, he gestured toward the coffee table. "I have something for *ye*." He picked up a blue, velvet jewelry box.

She tilted her head.

He smiled. "Open it."

While her heart skipped, she lifted the lid and gasped, pressing a hand to her mouth. A radiant, emerald pendant on a delicate, gold necklace snugged between blue velvet. "Bryce…this is gorgeous."

"Something to remind *ye* of Scotland." He carefully removed the necklace and stepped behind her.

His fingers grazed her neck as he secured the clasp, searing her skin with every touch. "Thank you." She turned. "I have something for you, as well." She picked up her bag and removed the handmade gift.

Accepting the present, he unwrapped the package. Quickly, a smile spread across his face, crinkling the corners by his eyes. "Glencoe?" He stared at the clear, blue loch, surrounding mountains, and birds gliding on the breeze.

"The first day Andrea and I arrived in Glencoe, I was thinking of you and painted this piece. Then, as I was packing, I thought you might like it, since it's…our special place."

Bryce arched a brow. "*Ye* painted it?"

"I did. I know I'm not a professional by any means, but—"

"Brie, 'tis fantastic." He tilted his head to touch his lips to her brow, then stared at the painting once more. When he set the painting down, he turned toward Brie.

Her heart hammered in her chest, while she watched his eyes deepen like a stormy sea.

Without taking his gaze off her, he lifted her into his arms, brushed a soft kiss across her temple, and carried her upstairs.

They made love like the first time, savoring one another. After, she snuggled close, feathering her fingers through his soft thatch of chest hair, brushing her cheek against his copper stubble, and touching her lips to his. She wanted to remember everything about him.

When he walked her to the door, Bryce paused, grasping the handle. He tugged her gently back, so her hands splayed across his firm chest. "Stay." He kissed his forehead to hers, hands cupping her face. "Stay another day."

She swayed, yearned, while the burn of fresh tears stung. She wanted so much to stay. She covered his hands with hers. "I wish I could. I-I can't. I'll never forget you." But in her heart, she meant, *I love you.*

"Nor I, *ye.*"

She kissed him once more, then tore away and ran into the pouring rain. Batting back tears, Brie texted Andrea in the private town car.

—*I said good-bye.*—

—*I'm sorry, Brie. I've got a drink waiting for you and a shoulder.*—

—*Thank you.*—

At the airport, she stripped off her jacket, placed her phone in her purse, and set everything in the dull-gray bin, preparing to go through security.

A roar of voices instantly filled the airport entry.

"Brielle!"

Her name rocketed through the air. She stilled. Pivoting, Brie's breath caught.

Bryce stood at the entrance gate with fans and press surrounding him, craning his head and searching the crowd.

People held cell phones high, taking pictures, while the press shouted questions.

Stepping slightly out of line, she gazed at him across the sea of people.

His movements stopped and lips curled. He lifted his large hand in farewell.

She smiled back.

Click! Flash! Click!

Brie closed her eyes, muting the sharp, bright camera flashes, and twisted toward security. Time to go home. Time to get back to her life.

But there's something about time—the master of moments and inescapable thief. A few weeks ago, I was a busy mom, balancing work, children, and an unsupportive ex, and gasping for air. But then I met Bryce, and time stood still for one blissfully, incandescent moment.

But a moment can't last forever…

Brie glanced back once more, gazing upon the man she'd known for just ten days, but in her heart, she'd love for the rest of her life. She'd never forget her time under the sparkling stars, in the highlands surrounded by pinewood and bluebells, and galloping through fields of vibrant green with his arms wrapped around her. As her gaze traced his strong cheekbones, copper stubble, and shining eyes, she sucked in a breath, chest stinging.

"Flight 137, London, United Kingdom, boarding," someone announced over the loudspeakers.

Her first flight was boarding. Brie couldn't delay. Her children would be waiting eighteen hours from now. She always told herself she'd do anything for happiness, but this was agony.

Chapter 23

The airplane circled Los Angeles International Airport, while gray concrete, skyscrapers, and cars invaded her sight. Brie already missed the miles of green, the fragrant air of heather, and one incredible person. Yet, she was home and would soon be reunited with her beautiful children. She couldn't wait to embrace them and breathe in their sweet scents.

But as she stepped off the plane, she couldn't help but think about Bryce and his longing look in the airport. She felt their connection and the powerful gravitational pull between them, and she knew he did, too. If things were different, she could have…she would have…yet, they couldn't be. Bryce was in another country, across the Atlantic, for goodness sakes, and she was a mother with responsibilities.

"Home! I can't wait to get back to the city life." Andrea power-walked through the terminal, tugging luggage.

Jogging alongside her enthusiastic friend, Brie nodded. But just like on the return flight home, she was numb. Her mind kept replaying the wonderful two weeks she'd had and the man she said good-bye to. She tried to watch movies; yet, she barely paid attention and instead, allowed the static to numb her.

Arriving home, she stepped out of the car as the front door flew open and happy squeals pierced the air.

Joyful tears filled her eyes.

"Mommy!" Phoebe ran down the short walk and flung herself onto Brie.

"Mom!" Noah wrapped his arms around her, squeezing in between Phoebe.

She kissed their hair, hugging them close, and breathed them in. A feeling of calm settled over her, and happiness flooded her soul. *Everything is all right now. I'm home.* "Hi, my sweethearts."

"Welcome home," Mimi said from the entry.

"Thank you so much for everything," Brie told her.

"Of course!" Mimi flashed a big-hearted smile. "We had a great time."

After a tostada dinner and bedtime, Brie busied herself in her routine. She started laundry, cleaned dishes, and when her eyes fluttered, she flipped off the lights. As her mind drifted, she heard the unmistakable *ding* of her cell phone and opened an eye. Seeing the notification was from Bryce, she quickly tapped the text.

—Hope you made it home safely! Keep in touch.—

With a throaty cry, she slumped into her pillow. What did she expect? She had come home. She didn't expect him to follow her. How could he? He was filming a show. And she had a home and children. They kept things casual, never discussing what the future held, but the truth of the matter was that she let herself fall. She fell whole-heartedly for Bryce Fraser. And now, she'd never see him again. Her chest cracked.

—Thanks! Safe and sound. You, too.—

Brie waited for a reply. When bubbles appeared, then disappeared just as quickly, she set her phone down and fell back into her pillow, while salty tears tumbled down her cheeks. Heaving a rough breath, she gave in, allowing the heartbreak to wrap her up in a sorrowful cloud.

Hours later, she stared into the inky void of the night. When she couldn't stand the silence any longer, she grabbed her journal.

May 6

I fell in love. All it took was ten days.

Two weeks ago, I left for Scotland, ready to take some time for myself and have fun with Andrea, and I did, but something happened—I met Bryce. He was funny, charming, sexy, and everything I wasn't looking for, but isn't that what a vacation is for? To meet someone unexpected? To have an affair? At least, that's what Andrea told me. And, I did.

I never expected to fall for him, and now he's in Scotland working on his show in his sexy kilt, and I'm here, missing him so much I can scarcely breathe.

My chest aches for him, my throat's raw from crying, and my eyes burn. Yet, every time I close my eyes and try to suppress the pain, all I can see is Bryce.

Why couldn't we have lasted more than ten days?

****

Keep in touch? What was he in grammar school? The truth was, Bryce hadn't wanted to see Brie depart. He'd asked her to stay, but she declined. And if she'd said yes, what would that have done? Extended the inevitable?

Bryce raked a hand through his hair and snagged a finger on a curl. Shaking his hand free, he exhaled. They couldn't extend something that was never meant to last, but he couldn't keep himself from seeing her one last time. He'd driven to the airport on instinct, not preparing for what might ensue. Sure, the press had a grand time snapping pictures of him and the airport crowd before them, which placed him in headlines this morning. But they didn't know who Brielle was, nor did they capture her bonnie face in the crowd.

The makeup trailer's door snapped open, jarring Bryce.

Popping his head in, the young production assistant inclined his head. "Five minutes, Bryce."

"Aye. Thank *ye*." He stared at his reflection in the mirror—the red movie blood dripping down his cheekbone and black-and-blue makeup bruises matched his insides. He was sore to see Brie go.

"Just one last…there we are," Moira added, adjusting his wig.

He blew a quick breath out. Back to work. The show would keep him busy, and Eleana would keep him entertained, albeit with a wee bit of digs.

As he walked down the steps of the trailer, the magnificent, emerald mountains of Glencoe surrounded him, and his mind wandered back to a pair of brilliant, haunting green eyes.

Chapter 24

Stepping onto the boardwalk in Santa Monica two days later, Brie inhaled the briny air, while the sun bathed her shoulders and exposed arms, and the breeze ruffled her hair. Holding tight to the beach cart's handle, she kicked her sandals off and sunk her bare feet into the warm sand.

In the distance, the sharp sounds of a bagpipe drifted on the wind.

She whipped her head around, scanning the boardwalk and skipping over bicyclists in bathing suits, beachgoers jogging with dogs, and roller skaters weaving in and out of foot traffic. And then, her eyes widened: a long-haired musician in black, torn shorts pranced on the boardwalk, piping away with an upbeat tune as he circled an open bucket.

Beachgoers stopped briefly to drop a few bills, while others paused a moment, and others still craned their necks and continued with their afternoon stroll.

Yet, Brie's heart raced so fast that the drumming of her heart rang in her ears and mingled with the pipes' notes.

Noah tugged her hand. "Mom, come on."

"Sorry, buddy, I'm coming." She stole one last glance at the musician. The song wrapped around her heart and transported her back to Scotland—back to Bryce. Breathing deeply, she strode toward the berm with her eager children. "So, what do you guys want to do first?" Since returning, guilt was her constant companion after Mimi mentioned Phoebe hadn't slept through the night in two weeks. And when Noah crawled into her bed shortly after she'd fallen asleep last night, she didn't protest; she simply lifted the comforter.

Now, they were at the beach, having a fun filled family day, but also to help remove some of the guilt that settled in her belly.

"I'm going to find sand crabs and make a habitat in my bucket." Noah skipped, swinging his large, red bucket full of beach tools.

Brie grinned. "Nice, buddy. And what about you, Phoebe?"

"I'm gonna splash in the water!" she shouted.

With a laugh, she kissed her plump cheek. "That sounds perfect. And then after a few hours, we'll have lunch and go on a few rides on the pier."

"Yeah!" they said in unison.

Brie trudged through the warm, golden sand, tugging the beach cart with her pint-sized mermaid sitting atop a mound of towels, and Noah blazing a trail in front. When they arrived at the berm, she snapped Phoebe's safety vest on with a quick warning to wait for her before venturing to the water. She set out beach chairs, towels, an umbrella, and mentally gave herself a high-five for putting sunblock on she and the kids before they left the house. "Okay, let's go play!" She slipped her hand in one of Phoebe's and padded to the water's edge.

With his bucket in one hand and the other deep in sand, Noah searched eagerly for sand crabs. Sand caked his legs and feet, while he determinedly dug deeper and deeper. When the water rose up to his knees, he didn't budge.

"Need some help, buddy?" Brie asked.

"No, I can find them."

"All right." She stepped into the lukewarm Pacific Ocean, allowing the ocean to ground her.

"Wee!" Phoebe danced and splashed happily, cascading droplets of water across Brie's cover-up.

With a laugh, she joined her daughter, kicking her feet in the water, then dipped her arms and splashed some more.

Giggles erupted as Phoebe danced.

"Look, Mom!" Noah lifted a hand toward her.

Pivoting, she held fast to Phoebe. "Find a crab?"

"Nope, a shell." He opened his hand, displaying a white, ruffled shell. "Check it out. It looks like a heart." Noah placed the shell in her palm.

Brie peered closer. The seashell appeared to be half a clamshell with a smooth interior and rippled surface. Yet, what was most beautiful was the shape—like her son had said—a heart. The shell wasn't perfect by any means, but the imperfection made it beautiful. Rubbing her thumb along the smooth surface and the tiny cracks around the heart's edges, Brie felt her heart ripple like the gentle Pacific waves.

Long notes from the bagpipe drifted from the boardwalk. Although Brie was happiest when she was with her children and glad to be home, part of her still longed for Bryce. Like the marks on the seashell, Bryce would always have a place in her heart. "It's beautiful." Her voice cracked.

Noah curved her fingers over the shell. "You can

have it, Mom, because I love you."

"Thanks, buddy. I'll keep it forever." Brie rubbed a thumb softly over the shell once more, then slipped it into her shorts pocket.

After half an hour of splashing in the foamy surf, she settled into a beach chair, watching Noah build a home for sand crabs and Phoebe play in a large water bucket with her baby and shells. For a moment, she closed her eyes, relishing the natural breeze, and breathing in the fresh, ocean air. A memory flashed in her mind—she holding fast to Bryce on the back of his roaring motorbike, feeling safe, secure, and free. Notes of leather and Bryce whirled and mingled with the briny air. She smiled.

"Lemme hold it, Noah!" Phoebe shouted.

Brie snapped her lids open. She had to stop lamenting over the past few weeks. She was here with her children, and they deserved one hundred percent of her attention.

****

After returning beach gear to the car, Brie strolled hand-in-hand with Phoebe and Noah toward the pier where a giant purple octopus' large, swirly tentacles welcomed them. Being mid-day, people huddled by the entrance, outside and inside food outlets, while sweet and salty carnival aromas filled the hot air.

She bought them pizza and cotton candy, rode the Ferris wheel, sat in the mouth of a tiger shark, swirled around a roller coaster, jumped on waves, and played games.

Two hours later, Phoebe rubbed a fist in an eye, and Noah whined about riding the twirling coaster again.

She grasped their hands. "It's time to go home, kiddos."

"But, Mom." Noah kicked a pebble.

"We'll come back another day, okay?" She steered them down the pier toward the boardwalk, strolling past a bright-blue column when a poster caught her eye. Her breath lodged in her throat. Before her on an eighteen-by-twelve poster was Bryce Fraser, or rather Bryce as Alexander James Mackenzie, staring off into the wild land beyond with *For Love* printed across the center in a delicate, white scroll font.

He was like a ghost, an apparition who haunted her with posters of him pasted around town, his face on the cover of magazines, and announcements of interviews on channels.

How could she ever forget him?

****

Once her sand-and cotton-candy-free children were tucked into bed, Brie plopped onto the couch. A slow, steady pulsation battered her forehead as fatigue set in. Jet lag was catching up.

Gazing at the clock on the wall, she huffed. "Eight p.m." She lifted a hand and counted, "Nine, ten, eleven, twelve, one, two, three, four a.m. No wonder I'm half asleep." Yet, she couldn't go to sleep, not yet. She needed a moment to sit. To be. On her journey to Scotland, her goal was to take her life back, and she did—she witnessed incredible art, strolled in the countryside, hiked through lush glens, flew on a seaplane, beheld historical castles, met interesting people, and fell for a movie star. But she had a life here—and her life began and ended with her children.

Andrea had texted earlier, asking how she was

doing. Her message displayed the *read* signal. Yet, Brie hadn't responded. She picked up her phone.

—I'm okay. The kids and I had fun at the beach today, but jet lag is killing me.—

—I hear ya! I'm drinking and eating my jet lag away on the couch right now with wine and a big-ass bowl of baked ziti.—

Brie snorted when a picture of a giant wine glass covering Andrea's entire face popped up on the text. She sent a thumbs-up emoji in response.

—Have you heard from him?—

—When we landed, but not since...I miss him.—

—Of course, you do! Put on Swords of Scotland*. You'll feel better.—*

—Maybe.—

—Watch it. Love you!—

—Love you, too.—

Although she deliberated for five minutes straight, while scrolling through available television shows, she noticed the advertisement for *Swords of Scotland* with the new season's announcement each time she returned to the main menu. With an exhale, she clicked the icon.

Episode One opened into a vast, green valley with the camera swooping over the natural landscape and up toward the hilltop, where a gorgeous, wooden-and-brick homestead appeared with smoke puffing out of two chimneys. Next, the screen focused in on a woman she recognized as Eleana in the front garden, picking vegetables, then expanded to include a young man and woman promenading in eighteenth-century attire, and finally, the view shifted to the side of the house where a silhouette of a man on a horse appeared.

Brie lifted a hand to her mouth.

Alexander James Mackenzie sat atop a dapple-gray horse with a towheaded toddler tucked before him, talking in calm tones. While the little boy stroked the horse's mane, Alexander leaned close, lifting his own hand to glide down the glossy locks while saying something in Gaelic. Giggles filled the air.

For a moment, she pictured Noah sitting astride Bryce as she stood beside them with Phoebe in her arms.

A shout carried in the distance. Bryce straightened in the saddle and called to Eleana. With a strong arm around the boy and the other clasping the reins, he spurred the horse forward, bellowing orders.

Redcoats rode into view up the dirt path and drew their swords.

The slice of metal being unsheathed pierced her ears.

Bryce deposited the boy in Eleana's arms, then rode toward the oncoming soldiers with other kilted men appearing on horseback beside him. His voice roared over the thunder of hooves.

As Brie leaned forward watching and waiting for the conflict to escalate, she couldn't help but notice he sounded different. Rather than Bryce's warm, rounded accent, Alexander's brogue was laced with heavy embellishments, and his voice had a slightly deeper tone.

She clicked off the television. She couldn't watch anymore. She wasn't watching Bryce, not really; she was watching his character. Sinking her head back into the cushion, she exhaled. What was she hoping to feel? Some relief in seeing him again? Alexander wasn't Bryce. Hadn't he told her that himself?

Our time together is over. Really over.

Even still, she couldn't deny how quickly she'd fallen for him or the unmistakable connection from the very first moment they'd collided in the airport. What was it? She still couldn't say.

Sometimes, she imagined she was in a movie, waiting for the handsome heartthrob to return. She snugged farther into the couch and glanced at the ceiling where the dining room light cascaded streaks like shooting stars. *I'm not a star, not even close. I'm as normal as anyone can be, but for a little while, I sparkled like the striking Scottish stars.*

Tapping her phone, she opened photos. She swiped to the day they took the ferry from Mallaig to the Isle of Skye. With the crystal-blue water behind them and sheen of the sun, they glowed beside one another.

She'd never forget her trip to Scotland or Bryce, but how long would she look back? Like her memoir stated, she needed to keep moving forward with her life. Glancing one last time at the photo, she inhaled and exhaled. She should delete the image, so she couldn't revisit or languish over something that would never be, but as she hovered her forefinger, she froze. Her own blissful expression stared back. Gently, she glided a fingertip across the screen, alighting on Bryce's handsome face. With an exhale, she set the phone down. She needed to find her own happiness now.

Chapter 25

Three weeks later, Bryce tucked the last piece of the Mackenzie kilt into his belt and shoved his socked feet into highlander boots. He was beginning to feel like Alexander James Mackenzie.

Boom! Boom! Canons fired with test shots outside.

Knock-knock. "Five minutes, Bryce," a voice sounded through the door.

"Thank *ye*." He snatched the sporran from the chair and strode to the entry of the battlefield where Kingsley awaited, inhaling thick dew and boggy earth.

Once extras were placed, the director shouted instructions and repeated them via a megaphone.

Bryce stood ready, awaiting the charge atop his trusty steed, broadsword in one hand and reins in the other. When the horn blew, he spurred Kingsley. "For Scotland!" He propelled into the moor and battle awaiting them.

Hundreds of extras rode and ran alongside, thundering and screaming, while redcoats across the field waited at the ready with stern expressions, holding fast.

Bryce's heart thudded in rhythm with the powerful cadence of Kingsley's canter.

"And cut!" someone bellowed from a blowhorn. "Let's do it again, lads, but have Bryce begin a second before *ye*."

Bryce halted and then, with a gentle nudge, trotted Kingsley back toward the mark.

Kingsley flicked his head and puffed clouds of breath into the thick air.

Patting his flank, Bryce leaned forward. "I know, mate. Just a few more I promise, then *ye'll* have *yer* mints."

Kingsley whinnied.

Re-arranging a couple hundred actors and extras took time. Once at his mark, Bryce swung off his mount, patted Kingsley, and thanked the waiting equine assistant.

Moira stood ready with her makeup brushes in hand to touch up the movie dirt. "Stand still," she ordered.

He straightened. "Aye." Christ, she coulda been a captain of her own militia. Bryce accepted the hot coffee from another set assistant and took a quick nip before Moira lifted a makeup brush once again. He scanned the droves of crew arranging extras, while more readied cameras and lighting on the sidelines. But when he caught a flash of a green-hooded coat, he snapped his head around.

"*Och*, Bryce. What the devil?" Moira wiped her fingers across his cheek, then quickly dabbed the hollow with a sponge.

"Em, can *ye* give me a moment, Moira? I need to…"

Tucking the sponge and brush into her case, she snapped the container closed. "Aye, hurry up. Greg will have my head if *yer* not ready before the next take."

With a brisk nod, he strode toward the set-up area, boots digging firmly into the moor. If he had Kingsley, he would've been quicker, but he'd left him on his mark.

People stirred, reconfiguring and resetting, keen to get underway.

Yet, he snaked through, searching.

"Bryce, can I get *ye* something?" someone asked.

"No, em, thanks." *Had she returned?* Near two fortnights had passed since Brielle left for America, and she was scarcely far from his mind. Yet, he had dug into his work like normal. They'd finished Episodes 501 and 502 and were deep into 503. He was keen to begin, but now, his attention was drawn away. He marched through a gathering of people and stood at the edge of the tree line.

Around the bend, throngs of fans waited for photos and selfies.

Where had she gone? Bryce lifted a hand to smooth his wig. Perhaps he was seeing things. Six long days of twelve-hour-plus work would play tricks on even the most seasoned actors' minds. Digging his boots into the soft earth, he trudged back toward his mark. They couldn't have any more delays today. Already a few injuries occurred, and they hadn't even shot the battle scene.

On his return to the battlefield, people stopped him and offered compliments, while others asked questions.

Christ, it was like a circus, but he loved the show— the action, history, and creativity, and the people he worked with day in and day out. He didn't know how many seasons he had left on *Swords of Scotland*—only the network was privy, but just like the first episode, he'd give every day his best effort. Bryce sidestepped around a light shade and stopped.

A woman stood a few feet away in a moss-green coat, hood drawn.

His breath whooshed out of him and heart beat like a Viking drum. He reached out and grasped her shoulder. "Brielle."

The hooded figure spun. A woman with coal-colored hair and clear-rimmed glasses stared.

"Sorry." He cleared his throat. "Thought *ye* were someone else."

" 'Tis not a problem, Mr. Fraser. Have a good shoot."

"Thank *ye*."

He trudged back to the battlefield, hope sinking like his boots in the muddy moor. Brie truly was gone.

****

With the summer heat in full force, the next month flew by like the clouds in the midsummer breeze. Brie busied herself in routine with drop-offs at care or Mimi's, then busied herself with work during the week. On the weekends, she explored river trails and hiked up to Signal Hill with her children. She colored their adventures with stories from her travels and told the kids about Finlay with the gold-hilted sword and pretended hidden, gorgeous mountains were covered with California poppies, rather than the concrete skyline.

On one Sunday, she visited a local garden center with her kids to add more natural elements to their quaint backyard. A myriad of colors and aromas filled her sight. She breathed in.

"This smells like basil!" Noah buried his nose in a small, potted plant with deep-green leaves.

Brie laughed. Noticing the name tag and the

familiar, sweet scent, she smiled. "You're right. Why don't you grab one for our garden?"

Noah hopped around, searching for the best basil.

She couldn't contain her grin when she caught Phoebe copying her brother, sniffing everything around her.

"Yum! These smell dewicious."

"They do." Brie squatted to near Phoebe's level. "See this one? This is cilantro, and over there is parsley. Auntie A would be so excited we're planting herbs. Let's grab one of each."

Phoebe squealed and held fast to a potted parsley, while Brie carefully added other herbs to the cart.

A salesman recommended they plant the herbs in a circular container with aerating holes.

So, she added the large container to their cart, then asked for assistance with the heavy soil.

"Strawberries!" Phoebe shouted.

Brie angled her head and squinted through the sun's rays. Above, ruby-red strawberries dangled happily from a woven basket between velvety, forest-colored leaves. "Great eye, sweetie. Let's grab two, since we love strawberries."

When she noticed Phoebe and Noah's exuberance grow as they began grabbing pot after pot, Brie chewed her lip. She wanted to start a garden, but she needed to start small, especially with her track record of forgetting to water plants and a tight budget. Squaring her shoulders, she peered at her children. "Great choices, kiddos, but let's stick to the ones in our cart, okay? You can each pick out a snack at checkout."

Fifteen minutes later, Brie dug gloved hands into the rich soil beside her children and sighed. She might only have a two-foot by four-foot planter, but she'd make every inch count. She was creating her own life from the ground up.

****

The following Monday morning, while Brie added information to a proposal, she noticed dirt outlining her cuticles. She'd worn gloves, then removed them, but with kids, she could never keep clean. Yet, she didn't mind. She stretched her fingers atop the keyboard and smiled.

"Brielle." Her manager, Rochelle, appeared at the threshold to her cubicle with Andrea. "With your return from your lovely vacation, we neglected to review your goals in the system."

"That's right! Do you want me to put something on your calendar?"

"Yes, if you don't mind." Rochelle pushed her black-rimmed glasses up the bridge of her nose. "I know we drafted your goals for the fiscal year a few months ago, but it would be good to review. Also, I'd like you to think about your five-year career plan. TechCo has a lot to offer."

"And remember, we have the Career Path page for ideas for future development opportunities." Andrea grinned wide. "Make sure you save your goals and plan in the system by the end of the week. Otherwise, I will come and find you." She winked.

"Will do!" Brie confirmed, then waved good-bye when they pivoted toward a meeting room. She opened a new document. "My five-year plan." She tapped the mouse. "Five years…" She stared at the blinking cursor on the empty page. Out of desperation, she'd gotten the job a little over a year ago. She needed a job and a paycheck, but would she still be here in five years? TechCo had a good culture, decent benefits, ample vacation time, and friendly employees, but this was just a plug. A job to fill the hole in her bank account and stock groceries in the fridge. Brie hadn't considered she'd still be there four more years down the road.

Maybe six months ago, she might have considered a longer future, but not now—not after glimpsing what life could be outside the corporate bubble, writing under lush green trees, editing below the sparkling starlight, and painting where the history of the past collided with the present. Brie wanted more for herself and for her children.

Her mini-notepad rested next to the cordless mouse. Since her return, she'd been jotting down notes, expanding entries she wrote in Scotland, and adding ideas for her final chapter. She was almost done with her memoir, and the idea of typing *the end* soon sent happy tingles dancing up her body.

She and Andrea frequently joked about being *NY Times* Best Selling authors. Brie even decorated a mug at the Paint-Me-Pretty store that rested on her desk with the words, *Best Seller*, swirled across the front. But, here and now, with a memoir almost finished and numerous children's books saved on her laptop, the dream of being a paid author didn't sound unobtainable. She could do it. She had the work ethic, drive, and motivation.

Glancing once more at the five-year plan, she crinkled her nose. She grabbed the mug from her desk and strode to the break room to fill a cup of inspiration. While she tore open a peppermint tea bag, she heard the *click-click* of heels.

"Brielle, right?" the new VP of Marketing asked with her dark crop cut perfectly at her chin.

With a smile, Brie nodded and filled her mug. "Brie's fine."

"That's an interesting cup." She gazed at the swirl of colors around the letters.

Pride swelled her chest. "Thank you! I painted it. It's an inspiration cup for my writing."

Nodding, she scooted past Brie to fill her own coffee mug. "I commend you for your dedication to your job." She glanced back. "How long have you worked here?"

"Just over a year, but in addition to proposals, I also write children's books for my kids and am finishing my first memoir."

Raising a perfectly penciled brow, she hummed. "Aren't you a little young to be writing a memoir?"

Brie's smile faltered. In five seconds flat, her happy mood soured like the neon-colored orange juice left on the far counter. Sure, she hadn't started out writing a memoir, but her journaling helped her heal. She documented her journey from broken, divorced, single mom of two to who she was today. Yes, with age comes wisdom, but at her age, she was going through something that other women were experiencing, too. At least, that's what Andrea told her when she insisted Brie keep going. And after joining the social community for memoirists, she discovered many other women in a similar position, and many had already asked to read her story. Plus, after returning from Scotland, she'd purchased nearly a dozen memoirs from memoirists ranging from eighteen to eighty. All had value—just like hers.

"No, I'm not. In fact"—Brie leveled her gaze at the new VP—"I just read an amazing memoir about a twenty-year-old woman's journey through the Alaskan wilderness. I'm happy to recommend the title if you'd like."

"Really?" She pursed her lips. "I might have to read it. I enjoy the outdoors."

Brie shared the author and title. "I'd definitely consider reading it. Thrilling read." She picked up her cup. "Anyway, I've got to get back to work. Busy, busy you know. Have a lovely rest of your day."

Striding back to her desk, she felt the fire of determination burning within.

****

Later that night, Brie sat in front of her laptop, formulating the final entry for her memoir.

A notification sounded from social media. Daniel MacDonald posted something new.

She opened his page and sighed at the gorgeous waterfall between foliage aglow in copper-and-rosy hues from the sun's rays. The video was only three seconds, but the reel was like a breath of fresh air. Since returning home, she frequented his account, devouring pictures and short clips of Scotland finding a brief escape. When the video replayed, she noticed a woman waving at the camera on the bridge. The woman was small compared to the frame, but her hair was light-brown like soft tree bark bathed in sunshine, and she appeared to be smiling. *I know how she feels*. A thought popped into Brie's mind. Powering up her laptop, she wiggled her fingers and let the words flow.

August 30

When I first received the ticket to Scotland, I

imagined I'd learn about my ancestral roots, rest, and maybe write. Of course, Andrea teased about meeting a hot Scot, and I did. I met a wonderful, extraordinary Scotsman, but what I have come to realize is in those ten, short days, I also rediscovered myself.

In Edinburgh amongst the history and traditions and diverse architecture, I revived my passion for adventure. I was attracted to the historical landmarks, enamored by the beauty of the people and country, and tasted wonderful food, while being immersed in a new culture. I also realized I could be attracted to someone again and that feeling could be reciprocated. After being cheated on and left for another woman, I felt unworthy, but Bryce made me feel desirable and cherished.

I discovered I can and should choose what I want to do with my life. I don't need to stand by and be self-sacrificial all the time. I'm a good mom, scratch that— an excellent mom—but I need to give myself permission to do more things for myself, including refilling my cup and rejuvenating myself more often. I need to use the time I'm given when Ryan or Mimi has the kids to do something I want—not just laundry and housecleaning, which while needed, can wait. I learned to make time for myself. And sitting here finishing my memoir is a perfect example.

In Glasgow, I discovered passion—deep, delicious passion. I am a woman, and I have needs. I don't need to be ashamed or embarrassed. To be with a partner who treats you with care and respect and gives you pleasure isn't just a gift, but a right.

In Glencoe, I rested. I allowed myself to nap, paint, rejuvenate myself in nature, and be. So often, I feel like

I have to go-go-go to baseball practice or take Phoebe to gymnastics or go to the grocery store, but I also need to take a step back and rest.

In the heart of Glencoe, I discovered ties to my ancestral roots, while meeting little Finlay, Holly Finlay MacDonald, and her sweet husband. But what's more, I discovered stories and tales of my heritage. Knowing that I am a storyteller from a history of storytellers, I feel more self-assured as I embark on the next phase of my writing journey.

What's more, I found love. A deep, soaring love I didn't think I was capable of after Ryan. Bryce gave me that gift, and I am forever grateful, even as I'll always wonder what if.

I don't know what this next chapter holds, but I know I'm ready.

I'm ready to live again—to discover, find joy, and to love.

As Brie re-read her final entry, she smiled, her eyes stinging with pride. She thrust her hands in the air. "I'm done!" She dialed Andrea and told her the good news.

"What? You're done? We need margaritas!"

Brie giggled. "I will definitely take you up on that."

"How do you feel?"

Brie exhaled a full breath. "Good. I'm really happy with the finished product. I hope an agent will feel the same way."

"Heck yes, an agent will! Are you sending me the whole enchilada?"

"You really want to re-read it?" Andrea had read the majority of her memoir in bits and pieces, but not the whole product.

She made an annoyed sound. "Of course, I do!"

"Okay, I'll email the manuscript now, but I want your honest opinion. I wrote this for me, but my story has to be relatable to readers."

"You got it!"

When she disconnected, Brie emailed her memoir to Andrea and then began researching, composing a list of agents who represented similar memoirs with success, as well as what she needed to put together to submit her memoir to agents: a book proposal. She created proposals daily. She could do this. She drafted a document with an overview summary, then began outlining one chapter at a time. Five pages in, Brie wound her arms over her head, stretching.

How could she have known that the worst year of her life would've inspired her to write a memoir? Writing helped. Just like that journal she used to keep in her top drawer as a child when feelings and thoughts overwhelmed, her memoir helped her breathe and find peace.

Shoving away from the desk, she spied the white, seventies-style bathtub through the quaint en suite's opening. Sure, a mountain of laundry waited to be folded—the task never ended, but she deserved a soak. She filled up the bath with steaming water, added lavender bubble bath, slipped in, and imagined what could be.

****

The next morning, Sunday, Brie returned to her desk and continued with her book proposal. She'd pick up the kids from Ryan's in an hour, though she was still surprised he showed up nearly on time to take them for the majority of the weekend. *Ding*! Her text chimed.

Andrea was up.

—I stayed up last night and read your entire memoir. I cried. It's so good!—

—OMG. Thank you!—

—Will you show Bryce?—

Stilling her fingers on the keyboard, she paused. Although he was in her memoir, she changed his name and the show's title, giving him the anonymity and respect he deserved.

—I don't know—

—Have you talked?—

—Not for over a month. I still think about him.—

—How could you not? You had an incredible affair in Scotland! We should go see his new movie.—

—It's not him. And, it's absolute torture watching him on screen.—

Chapter 26

Packing a suitcase, Bryce prepared to return to Glasgow. They'd wrapped up shooting for *Swords* in the Highlands. What perfect timing as the miserable midges were out in full force. The bloodthirsty savages left their marks on his legs, arms, and scalp. But he had enjoyed working in the Highlands again, revisiting Glencoe and Inverness, and taking a few days to hike and clear his head. Though he couldn't deny, he often found Brie popping into his mind every now and again. When his phone shrilled, he wrenched the device from his pocket.

"Good day, Bryce. I've *yer* final designs ready if *ye'd* like to pop by the studio one day this week," Fiona Taylor greeted.

"Thanks, Fiona." The collaboration pieces reflected Bryce's beloved home, land, and Fraser heritage. He was proud of what he'd helped create and how collaborating with a well-known brand also kept his mind busy.

"Or, I'm happy to meet *ye* somewhere to show them to *ye*…personally," Fiona said.

Bryce winced at her suggestion. He never mixed business with pleasure. He'd learned that early on, especially last year with Kathryn. But Fiona had hinted not so subtly recently she favored him, especially after he had one too many whiskies celebrating their new partnership. Still, he couldn't afford to be careless. "We're tidying up the show as we speak. Can *ye* email me the final designs? I'll have a look before I come in."

A brief pause ensued. "Of course. Don't *ye* be a stranger."

"Thank *ye*." Setting the phone down, he noticed the tinge of red and brown in his cuticles and across his knuckles—remnants of movie makeup. Although the show would be on break for a month, he would miss seeing his work family day in and day out. Yet, he longed to spend time with his own blood.

A few hours later, he parked behind the lorry at his sister and brother-in-law's house where horses grazed in the sizeable pasture and the white-and-brown, classic farmhouse stood. He no sooner closed the door when his legs were taken out from under him. He landed in soft, pungent grass.

"Uncle Bryce!" Archie peered down, grinning.

"*Och*, fine tackle, lad." He wrapped an arm around his nephew, scrubbing a hand through his mop of rich-brown hair, then shifted his gaze toward his sister who ambled into the yard. "What have *ye* been feeding him?"

"Good Scottish food." Rose Fitzgibbons grinned, round with babe. "It's good to see *ye*."

"And *ye*." He pushed to standing, then strode over and embraced her. "How's the wee one?"

She rubbed her belly, wincing. "Fine when he's not bouncing on my bladder or tangling in my intestines. He'll be braw like his brother."

"Aye, he'll be that and more," Ian Fitzgibbons added, rugby ball in hand, fiery-red beard trimmed above a dark sweater. "Evening to *ye*, Bryce."

"Ian, good to see *ye*." He slung an arm around him in a brotherly embrace.

"And, *ye*. 'Tis been too long."

"It has." He patted him on the back, then strolled up the path through the entry beside Rose.

Ma sat double podding broad beans with an apron over a floral jumper and his niece beside her at the vintage butcher-block island in the kitchen.

A savory aroma drifted from the large oven. Tipping his nose in the air, he inhaled buttery notes. "Do I smell shortbread?"

"Oh, Bryce, so you've returned. Give us a kiss." Ma lifted her face, fluff of rose-blonde hair curled just so.

"Hello, Ma." Bryce bent and kissed her soft, paper-thin cheek, then swung his wee niece up into his arms. "Lucy girl, how goes *yer* dancing?"

"Wonderful, Uncle Bryce. I'm competing in the Braemar games with my friend, Freya," she piped, with red curls spiraling around her face and a gathering of freckles across her nose.

"Are *ye* now?" He kicked a brow toward Rose.

"I think she's too young, but she twisted Ian's ear to entering, so now we're going." She gazed at her husband with contempt.

"I couldna disappoint my only daughter now, could I? Besides, she's a bonnie dancer." Ian leaned toward Rose and kissed her forehead.

Rose's lips curled.

Watching the quiet exchange, Bryce adjusted his cap. His sister and brother-in-law had been married for near a decade and dated a few years prior. He'd never been jealous of what was between them, until now.

"Aye, she is, there's no arguing that point, but—" Rose added.

"What are *ye* now, Lucy, ten?" Bryce interjected and winked at Rose.

She scowled, though wee smile lines appeared by her eyes.

Lucy giggled. "No! I'm four."

"*Och*, four!" He settled himself beside her.

Ma glanced from the broad beans. "Where were *ye* shooting this time, son?"

"Inverness recently. We returned to Culloden." A silence fell over the room for respect for their ancestors and brave warriors who met their maker on that fateful day. " 'Twas a grand last shoot with extras, cast mates, crew, and of course, Eleana and Hugh."

Rose wiped the counter with a striped towel. "Oh, how is Eleana?"

"Fine. Getting married soon, I hear."

"About time. Surprised you never tied her down the way *ye* used to look at her," Ma surmised.

Clearing his throat, he caught a quick smirk from his sister before she bent to remove the tray of shortbreads. When he first joined the cast of *Swords*, he had a wee crush on Eleana. How could he not? She was beautiful, intelligent, and an incredible actress. But a show is no place for a romance when saying someone else's words and acting like a character from a beloved book.

Sure, they kissed and shot some steamy scenes, but at the end of the day, they were friends. And Eleana was the only one he'd confided in about Brie. She'd warned him to be careful, and he was, but not careful enough to guard his heart, since he still longed for the bonnie, green-eyed lass. He grasped a warm shortbread and bit into the sweet, buttery biscuit.

"So, have *ye* been seeing anyone? Lord, I couldna stand that young woman and how she discredited your name."

Bryce winced. "That's been over for a while." He polished the rest of the biscuit in one bite.

"Well, it's due time *ye* slow down and meet someone." She shook a broad bean. "*Yer* not getting any younger, son."

"Ma, leave him alone." Rose nudged Bryce in the side. "But she's right, brother."

"Aye, well, I hear Archie calling me for an in." He shoved away from the table and retreated to the yard where he wrestled with his nephew, then threw passes to Ian, pushing aside thoughts of lassies.

****

Brie drove up the 605 freeway at six-thirty a.m. with the golden sun splashing sparkly shimmers across the San Gabriel Mountains. The normal smog hadn't yet surrounded the mountains, and for a moment, she was transported back to Glencoe. Slowly, Bryce's face appeared, gazing from under a canopy of pine and oak, with a smirk at his full lips. She changed the station to lively country music. She couldn't keep thinking about him.

She enjoyed a wonderful summer with her children, including beach days with Mimi, as well as movie dates and cooking with the kids and Andrea. She'd even sent queries out to agents with dreams of more. Her life *was* full.

At work, Andrea popped by her cubicle, leaning braceleted arms on the top glass. "Did you see the new

Product Manager?"

Brie glanced. "Can't say I have. I'm sure we'll cross paths."

"Well, you should." Andrea wiggled her brows. "He's cute. A little dorky, but cute. I think you'd like him."

Shuffling papers, Brie crinkled her nose. "I'm not ready to date again, and I don't need to meet someone at work—too complicated."

She twirled a stray curl, then tossed it behind her ear. "Well, at least we have some eye candy around here."

"Mmmhmm. So, how's it going with hot airplane guy?" Andrea met a Brit on their first flight back from Scotland and exchanged numbers. Since then, they'd been texting on-and-off for a few months.

Andrea leaned closer. "I spoke to him last night actually. We had phone sex."

Brie felt her mouth flop open. Once she recovered, she fanned her hands in front of her. "Shh! Aren't you the head of HR?"

With a laugh, Andrea smiled devilishly. "Not yet. But I'm a person, too, and a woman first and foremost."

"So, are you guys dating?"

"How could we be dating? He lives thousands of miles away. We're just having fun." She winked. "Any news from agents?"

Brie shook her head. "Not since I received those dozen rejections the first couple weeks. Still waiting on the partial and full requests, but those should be another month to two, according to their timelines." She spent an entire weekend editing her memoir six weeks ago, researching agents, and then sending queries to near three dozen agents who represented memoirs. Surprise hit her like an avalanche when two agents requested her full manuscript a month later and another agent, a partial soon after.

"Ugh, the waiting is killing me! I'm so excited for you."

"I know! Waiting is definitely the hardest part." Brie exhaled. "You'll find out soon enough when you get ready to query your own manuscript."

"*If* I ever finish it." She sighed. "But I did make this incredible homemade fettuccini the other day with spicy shrimp and snap peas. It was SO good."

Ding! Brie's meeting reminder flashed on her screen for their bi-weekly page exchange. Nerves rattled in her stomach. She didn't have any pages to share. "Are we still meeting today?"

Andrea glanced at her watch. "Shit. Can't. I've got a call soon—C-suite city. Catch up later?"

"You bet." As Brie lifted the curser to close out the reminder, she paused. *What if I write something new? I could sit for half an hour and brainstorm.* Excitement fluttered in her chest like butterflies set free. Something new. Something magical. Something, she could create.

Five minutes later, she strode to the café. Only two people sat in the courtyard on high-back bistro chairs with laptops. She quickly marched into line to purchase a mocha when a mid-height brunet with salt-and-pepper spiked hair sidled beside her. She shifted and noted the familiar face of Chad, the Technical Support Manager.

"Fancy meeting you here." He quirked a brow. "You rarely stray from your desk."

"Well, there's always so much to do, but today, I'm treating myself."

His lips curled.

Placing her order, she retrieved a few bills from her pocket.

Chad leaned forward and placed a hand on hers. "I've got it." He grinned, then pivoted toward the barista. "Iced Americano, and I'll pay for both."

Brie snatched her hand away. "You don't have to—"

He flashed a full, white-toothed smile. "It's my pleasure." A moment later, he handed her the piping, hot coffee. "So, Brie, where've you been hiding?"

"Hiding?"

"Yeah, I've barely seen you since you returned from that vacation." He inched closer.

Brie had forgotten she'd told him, since she rarely spoke to him. "Oh, I've been…"

The shrill of bagpipes blared from the television overhead mingling with flutes. She glanced up, eyes widening as a commercial advertising the new season of *Swords of Scotland* began. Images flashed of Bryce and Eleana riding through a deep-green valley, then clinging to one another and a young girl in a cave, while a blazing storm raged outside, and finally a great battle in a foreign land. Her chest warmed when Bryce stood valiantly, wind whipping through his red hair.

"So, you're a fan of *Swords,* too?" Chad gestured with his coffee.

She blinked and Bryce disappeared from the screen. "I am."

"Alexander Mackenzie's pretty kick-ass. What's your favorite season?"

She shifted her feet. "I haven't watched much of it actually."

"I don't believe that for a second." He leaned forward, so a strand of black, gelled hair fell over his forehead.

A soapy cologne wafted toward her. She crinkled her nose. "Well, I," she began, then shook her head. She didn't have time to waste. Her writing was waiting. "Sorry, I only have a few more minutes left on my break, and I need to finish some paperwork."

He straightened. "Sure, I've got a meeting with the CISO anyway. Don't be a stranger." He winked, then pivoted on a polished black dress shoe.

Strolling toward the bistro sitting area, she tugged a chair out, set her phone down, and opened her notebook. Closing her eyes, she waited for inspiration to strike. A memory weaved into her mind—she and Bryce galloping through a serene green glen on Kingsley, holding tight to one another with the thrill of complete abandon. This time, the memory wasn't sad; instead, the memory inspired. An idea sparked and blazed like a fiery star across the night sky. She immediately jotted notes—a Scottish solider, a fair maiden turned warrior, a secret past, and a love that would overcome even the most powerful forces from the Scottish Goddess, Beira. While she wrote, melodic highland music flowed through her mind, and her thoughts drifted to the MacDonalds and their daughter, Finlay. She wrote their names down, then circled Finlay—the fair hero—and decided then and there what her main character's name would be. Finlay would be her own hero, but she'd meet a warrior on her journey. Brie drew a heart beside the text along with a gold-hilted sword and unicorn.

Buzz-buzz. Her phone vibrated on the table.

She glanced, and her pen fell from her fingertips.

Bryce–1 text message.

Brie's heart clogged in her throat. She slowly tapped the message open.

—*Hey, Brie. How are you? I'm flying to L.A. for a quick trip tomorrow. May I visit you?*—

With pulse racing, she inhaled and exhaled, trying to steady her rapidly beating heart. Bryce Fraser was coming to L.A.

He.

Was.

Coming.

She glanced at businesspeople sipping giant coffees and talking on cell phones. Everything was normal, except the buzzing of excitement in her veins.

—*Hi! Yes. When?*—

—*Sunday afternoon?*—

—*I'll text my address. Would you like to come for dinner?*—

—*Dinner sounds fantastic.*—

Feeling her smile grow, she imagined Bryce sitting beside the crackling fire, texting under the starlight. Yet, immediately after the screen went black, her mind raced. What did his visit mean? Was he just stopping by to say, *hi* or another reason?

She bit her lower lip. Sunday afternoon was kid time. Just a day before Phoebe and Noah started back to school after Monday's staff development day. Bryce would be visiting her and meeting Phoebe and Noah in person. *Oh boy.*

Memories she'd filed away flooded her mind—his eyes smoldering midnight-blue as he leaned in for a kiss, the glow of his body in the glimmering firelight, and the way he held her so preciously.

Her heartbeat quickened, and she pressed a hand to her chest. Was this really happening?

Chapter 27

Brie touched up her lip gloss and checked her makeup again. Bryce would arrive in five minutes. Although excited butterflies filled her insides when she received his text an hour ago saying he was on his way, the butterflies quickly morphed into nervous, buzzing bumblebees.

"I want some, too, Mommy." Phoebe pointed to Brie's lip gloss.

"Of course, sweet pea." She bent down and dabbed tiny touches of gloss on her daughter's rosebud lips.

Smiling as Phoebe bounded away to show Noah, Brie stole a quick glance outside. So many questions raced through her mind. She wondered what Bryce would think of her quaint, simple home. Her single story was scrubbed clean, and toys were put away…for now. God knew in five minutes, her kids would pull everything back out. But he had a niece and nephew, didn't he?

Ding-dong. Brie jumped. Swiping a hand across her forehead, she tucked a strand of hair behind her ear, then strode to the front entry. She opened the door.

Bryce stood with a broad smile, bouquet of colorful wildflowers, and black sunglasses. "Brielle."

"Bryce," she breathed. She stood for a moment gazing at the way his curls skimmed his temple and tips of his ears, the way he wore the gray T-shirt so well, and how his lips curved just right.

"Noah! That's my yellow fwower!" Phoebe yelled from the living room.

Brie jolted out of her trance. *Get yourself together*! "It's so nice to see you. Won't you come in?" And Lord, didn't she sound formal? What was wrong with her? She stepped back to give him room to enter.

Ducking, he removed his glasses and entered the quaint 1950s bungalow, towering over her.

Was he always this tall? Bryce seemed to take up the entire entry. Her pulse jumped and skittered. As she closed the door, she clasped her hands.

He handed her the flowers with a slow smile. "These are for *ye*."

"Thank you." She buried her nose in the sweet wildflowers and sighed, allowing the fragrant blooms to calm her jittery pulse. "They're beautiful."

"My pleasure." He nodded, then scanned the entry, while a grin played at the corners of his mouth. "*Yer* home is lovely."

She beamed, feeling her stomach flutter. "Thank you. How was the interview?"

"*Och*, grand. Thanks." He bobbed his head. "The new season of *Swords* is highly anticipated, hence the interview across the pond."

"I'm glad. Would you like to—"

The door opened, and in strode Ryan with a blue polo shirt paired with a scowl. "Whose car's outside?" He wrenched his sunglasses off.

"Mine," Bryce said.

She narrowed her eyes. "Ryan, what are you doing here?" She didn't know why his boxers were in a bunch. An unplanned meeting of the two men in her life wasn't what she expected after dreaming about seeing Bryce again. Yet, Bryce wasn't in her life. He was just there, wasn't he?

Ryan eyed the mysterious red-haired visitor, hands on hips. "Who are you?"

He cocked a grin and extended a hand. "Bryce. Pleasure."

"Interesting accent." He shook his hand.

"I could say the same for *ye*." Bryce stared Ryan down, continuing the handshake.

Brie bit her lip. In two minutes, she'd gone from air-jumping joy to stomach-tangling discomfort. Yet, as she witnessed the two men's exchange, she noted how Bryce's large hand swallowed Ryan's and his tall frame towered over her ex by a couple of inches. Something about that made her happy inside. Bryce's self-confident grin told her he seemed pleased about those facts, as well. When she spotted a swatch of pink in Ryan's opposite hand, she stepped forward, hand out. "Thanks for dropping by Pinky."

Ryan lifted a brow. "Pinky?"

"Phoebe's baby." She gestured toward the doll.

He handed her the doll.

"Anyway, I'm sure you have plans tonight. I'll talk to you soon."

He stood for a moment. "I might as well say *hi* to the kids while I'm here."

Brie lifted the hand with flowers. "Actually, now's not a good time."

He sidestepped, striding past her. "Awfully quiet in here. Watching television, are they?"

"Building," she hissed. Fisting her hands together, she watched Ryan march through the house like he owned the place. Glancing at Bryce, she noted the way his brows drew together like a question mark. She prayed he wouldn't leave.

****

Brie's gaze danced between Bryce and her ex like evergreens tossing in a storm.

Bryce clenched his jaw. He didn't care for the way her ex acted, nor for the way Brie's radiance dimmed when he'd spoken. Impeccable timing on Ryan's part. If he had the choice, Bryce would've already strong-armed him outside. He glanced at Brie who smiled nervously. All she had to do was say the word, and he'd handle Ryan. "Are *ye* all right?"

"Yes." She released a breath and sandwiched the baby and flowers in her hands. "I'm good. Sorry about the...interruption. He'll be gone in a minute, I'm sure. Would you like to come inside?"

"Aye, I would." Brie's house invited. Calm blue paint and earth-toned furniture welcomed, while vibrant pictures of the children and her decorated the entry walls. He followed her through the wee entry to the kitchen where lively drawings caught his attention on the refrigerator. Swirls of bold-green, deep-blue, and light-pink decorated one picture, while another was more linear with lines and a crayon-red dragon. He leaned forward. "These are fantastic."

"The kids drew them," Brie smiled as she retrieved a vase. "Phoebe's flowers and Noah's castle."

He smirked. " 'Tis a grand castle. Have *ye* showed him pictures of Scotland, then?"

"I have." She blushed and busied her hands filling the vase with water, then placed the bouquet inside. Turning, she curved her lips. "He asked where the knights slept.'"

"Truly?"

"Yes."

She directed those incredible green, mystical eyes toward him. The color reminded him of the glorious mountains of Glencoe in the spring. Yet, the summer sun had made her even more radiant. Her skin glowed, and golden highlights streaked her hair. God, all he wanted was to wrap his arms around her, but *ach*, he couldn't. Not now.

The wee kitchen led to a living room where stacks of books were neatly arranged atop a coffee table and boxes of puzzles were visible underneath. An array of jewel-toned boxes opposite held toys that spilled out in every direction. And in the center, a young lass with hair the same lovely golden-brown as Brie's assembled a vibrant garden in a variety of colors, and a sandy-haired boy stacked wooden blocks.

Standing off to the side, Ryan busied himself with his phone. *Wanker.*

"Hi, sweetie. Come meet Bryce. Noah, you too, buddy."

Phoebe stood and shyly clung to her mother's leg. Yet, a small smile played at her wee lips.

"Bryce, this is Phoebe.'"

"Hi," she squeaked.

"Hi to *ye*, as well." He knelt, admiring her work. "What have we here?"

"A faiwy garden."

" 'Tis indeed," he surmised. "Many fairies would be pleased to live in such grandeur. I've known some fairies myself. Did *ye* know they love pink flowers?"

Her eyes grew wide. "I wuv pink! Pink. Pink!" She

danced around, then plopped down and re-arranged flowers.

Awareness prickled his neck. When he glanced across the room, he noted the heat of Ryan's gaze boring into his from the short distance. Bryce cocked a grin. He imagined Brie hadn't mentioned him to her ex. That fact alone gave him satisfaction, but also pride that she kept their short time together private.

"And this is Noah," Brie said.

Bryce nodded toward the boy. "Hello, lad."

"I remember you." He tipped his head to the side, then rose. "You're tall."

"I em. And so will *ye* be."

"I eat all my vegetables," he stated matter-of-factly.

Brie pressed her lips together as her smile grew.

Clearing his throat to suppress a chuckle, he nodded. "That's grand. Vegetables will help *ye* grow braw."

Ding!

Brie jumped. "Oh, that's my timer! I'll be right back. Can I get you something? Water or…juice?"

"I'm fine right now. Thank *ye*. Can I help *ye* build, master Noah?"

"Yeah!"

Stepping around Noah, he folded his long legs, centering himself between Brie and her ex. He wouldn't allow Ryan to upset Brie further.

Chapter 28

In the kitchen, nerves tangled in Brie's gut. Bryce and Ryan were *here*—so much for all of her careful planning. She opened the fridge and caught Ryan staring at Bryce. Glancing his way, she inclined her head, asking him to silently join her.

"Who is this guy?" he asked upon entering.

Removing the marinating carne asada and shrimp from the fridge, she placed the meats on the counter, then took her time selecting a trio of avocadoes from the fruit bowl. "A friend."

He snorted a response, flaring his nostrils.

"Thank you for bringing Phoebe's baby back. I'll talk to you later." She pivoted and selected a knife to slice the avocados.

Yet, Ryan didn't budge.

She could feel his scrutinizing gaze on her back like a laser beam as she sliced, then scooped out the green flesh in preparation for guacamole. But she wouldn't give him the satisfaction of acknowledging him further.

"Jasmine's waiting in the car, anyway," he quipped.

When she heard the front door open and close, she blew out a breath. Lord, the man got under her nerves, but she wouldn't let Ryan's appearance ruin today. She'd waited nearly three months to see Bryce again.

Tearing cilantro from her tiny herb garden atop the kitchen windowsill, she inhaled the crisp, herbaceous notes. Time for some fresh energy in her house. She chopped cilantro, minced onion and garlic, and diced half a tomato, then combined all the ingredients into a bowl with a squeeze of lime and finally a pinch of salt and pepper. As she finished the guacamole, she heard Noah call they were going out back. She peered around the corner to see Bryce's cute backside disappear through the screen door behind the kids.

Humming happily, she checked the rice and finding the grain fluffy and void of excess water, popped the cover on, then prepped a pan for the carne asada. A quick one-hour marinade was better than nothing. She'd cooked for Bryce before in Scotland, but that was before…

Somersaults returned. She wished she knew why he decided to visit. Even though she shied away from gossip magazines, every so often, she'd catch a picture of him with a salacious title, while checking out at the grocery store. She tried not to read, but the bold article titles were nearly impossible to ignore.

"Arg!" a loud captain's growl echoed through her home.

Peering around the kitchen entry, she felt a smile blossom.

Bryce stood in the tiny backyard with a stick in one hand and a small box on his head, while Noah sat atop the ladder, swishing another stick, squealing.

Below, Phoebe giggled in a bigger carton in the shape of a boat.

As Brie stepped closer, she felt her entire being warm as if the sun had just washed over her. Noah and

Phoebe had met Bryce just ten minutes prior and already he'd made a difference. Did he know?

When Bryce swiveled, stick in hand like a pirate, and caught Brie staring through the window, his lips curved into an easy smile.

The icy worry hovering over her heart thawed. For weeks, she imagined what seeing him again would be like, but she couldn't have dreamt of what the experience actually had in store. How could she? She pressed a hand to her chest where tingles of joy danced.

"Mommy!" Phoebe pointed. "Look, a strawberry!"

Brie slid the screen door open. "I see it, sweetie."

Bryce stepped to the side, swinging the stick gently toward Noah, ducking to and fro, then gently tapped Noah when he neared.

Little did Noah know, he was sword-fighting with a well-known actor. "You look very handsome," she told Bryce.

"Well, thank *ye*, my lady." He bowed.

Brie tucked her tongue in her cheek.

Noah paused play-fighting to search for a ripe strawberry. Plucking two large red fruits off the plant, he turned. "Want to try one?" Noah asked Bryce.

"Aye, thank *ye*." He popped an offered strawberry into his mouth.

"I got one, too." Phoebe held up a half-yellow strawberry.

Brie angled her head. "I'm not sure that's ripe, sweet pea."

Phoebe bit into the fruit, and immediately, her little features scrunched up. "It's good!"

A chorus of laughter followed.

When Brie's gaze met Bryce's, she felt her smile

blossom. Sharing this moment was wonderful, but she couldn't quiet the nagging question circling her head: why had he come?

Twenty minutes later, they ate together around the circular dining table with Bryce squished between Noah and Phoebe.

He lifted a stuffed taco in his giant hand. "These tacos are grand."

"I'm glad you're enjoying them. We love tacos, don't we, kiddos?" Brie asked.

"Yep!" Phoebe squealed.

"Yeah! And Bryce, guess what? The cilantro is from our garden." Noah bit into a taco.

"Is it now?"

"Yup," he answered around a mouthful. "We planted some herbs a couple of months ago. Got the organic dirt and everything. You should've seen Mom hauling the giant bag from the car." Noah swelled his arms wide to imitate Brie carrying the soil.

She giggled. "It was heavy, right, buddy? But you fixed that."

Nodding fast, he scootched forward. "I had the idea to use my skateboard. We rolled the bag over and over until we got it on my skateboard. I couldn't believe we did it! Then, we wheeled the bag into the backyard and dumped it in the dirt."

"Did *ye*, now? That's some quick thinking." Bryce grinned. "We had a garden when I was a lad, as well. We had massive kale and a horde of potatoes."

Noah tipped his head. "You did?"

"Aye. I grew up on the outskirts of the city, and there was a lot of land to plant."

"I've always wanted to have a vegetable garden.

This past spring, we finally planted our own little garden, didn't we, kids?" Brie flashed a smile.

"Yep. We have potatoes, and tomatoes, and more tomatoes! And the strawberries are dewicous," Phoebe added.

Bryce's grin grew, and a full-bodied chuckle escaped, while his blue eyes shone.

Having him in her home was surreal, and Brie's heart and head still couldn't comprehend why he'd come. But whatever the reason, she couldn't deny having Bryce here was wonderful. When she noticed him staring, she felt little zips of energy dancing along her skin. Rising, she quickly grabbed plates to busy her not-so-steady hands. "Speaking of strawberries, who's ready for dessert?"

After a few, private gulps of air in the kitchen, she re-entered the dining room with four bowls of mixed berries topped with fluffy, homemade, lime-zested whipped cream. She served the kids first, then pivoted to set Bryce's bowl down. When he lifted a hand to help, his fingers grazed hers. Heat sparked, and she nearly dropped the ceramic bowl.

Lifting her gaze, she felt the room go quiet. And for a moment, she was sitting on a hilltop above Loch Lomond beside Bryce with the breeze dancing through her hair, tasting her very first Scottish strawberry. Blinking, she stared at her children and Bryce. Was she torturing herself by seeing Bryce again?

****

As the evening light grew hazy through the windows, Brie swung Phoebe into her arms and shuffled a hand through Noah's hair. "Bedtime. Say good night to Bryce."

"When will you be back?" Noah asked.

Bryce dropped to a knee. "I'm not sure."

Noah frowned, then leaned and wove his arms around. "Good night, Bryce."

Bryce hugged him tight. Noah smelled of lavender—a far cry from the dirt-ridden wee lad from a few hours ago. But as the lad snuggled his face into the crook of Bryce's neck, something flickered within and spread. "Good night, Noah."

"Ni-Night, Bwyce." Phoebe leaned away from Brie and kissed his cheek with rosebud lips.

"Good night. 'Twas the most fun I've had in a long while."

Watching Brie amble down the hall with a slumberous Phoebe snug against her chest and Noah grasping her hand, he couldn't tear his gaze away. The flicker inside swelled and grew, pressing against his ribcage.

When he heard the creak of a bed, he swiveled. They were a bonnie picture—and *och*, something inside him responded to that picture, but he was an outsider, interrupting a family. He wasn't all together sure what he was doing. When he found out he'd be flying to L.A., he only thought of Brielle.

"I know it's a quick trip," Joanna, his agent, had said. "But the producer would like you to make it work. It's the first promotional interview for the show."

Settled with a dram after a long day on set, he swirled the amber liquid. "Aye, where am I jetting off to?"

"L.A."

He sat up, gaze alighting on the watercolor above his fireplace. "L.A.?"

"You can pop on the red-eye and be back Monday morning."

"I'll be there. Book the flight, please." The decision had been simple. As a dedicated actor, he needed to promote his show. But at that moment, the show wasn't on his mind, only a bonnie, golden-brown haired lass with calming green eyes. How could she not be? Brie was an incredible woman—honest, beautiful, and real.

Although three months prior, they had a fling with no attachments and no pressure, here and now, children were involved. He could admit they'd ignited a spark inside—one of playfulness and joy—but what was he doing? He had a movie coming out and more episodes of *Swords* to film in a few weeks.

He strode to the wall where pictures of Brie and the children displayed. Gazing at a doe-eyed Noah, angel-faced Phoebe, and young Brielle blooming with maternal bliss, he swallowed thickly, heart squeezing. Other pictures of Noah with a lizard on his arm and Phoebe holding a ladybug delicately in her palm graced the walls and drew a grin. Yet, adjacent to the wee wall, the kitchen held stacks of dishes. He shoved away and strode forward—then, he heard her—Brie singing a lovely lullaby. Bryce stilled. Listening to her soft voice, he felt warmth spread across his chest.

Beep-beep! Beep-beep! A neighbor unlocked their car outside.

Dragging a hand through his hair, he glanced once more down the hallway. He was due to return to Scotland in less than twenty-four hours. *What are ye doin'?* But he knew why he'd come: to see Brie. Damned if he knew what he'd do now. He marched into the kitchen and got to work.

A few minutes later, a small gasp sounded behind him. He pivoted.

Brie stood in the living room, a silhouette against the blue background like a sea goddess. "The kids are in bed," she whispered, but her gaze centered on Bryce's hands where a kitchen towel gathered. "Did you…do the dishes?"

"I might've called in some help from wee fairies." He winked.

She giggled. "Thank you so much. Send them over anytime." She joined him in the kitchen. "Sometimes, I wish I could sing a sweet song, inviting blue birds in to do my dishes."

"Oh, ye sing, too, do ye? I'm discovering another facet of Brielle."

"No, I…no." Her eyes widened, and she fanned her hands. "I can't sing at all. Just forget I mentioned that."

But he'd heard her singing to the children—a sweet, soft caressing voice he imagined fluttered the children's lashes and eased them into delightful dreams—and a song that would haunt him when he returned to Scotland.

"Do you sing?" she asked.

"Aye. When no one's listening."

She laughed. "All right. Would you like a drink?"

He grinned, "I would."

"I'm sorry I don't have whisky. How about some wine?"

"That'll be grand."

She selected a bottle of Sauvignon Blanc and poured two glasses, then passed one to Bryce.

He lifted his. "Slainte."

"Slainte." She touched her glass to his.

Taking a slow drink, he stared over the rim. He was drawing the evening out, but he couldn't leave yet.

Chapter 29

As the crisp, cool wine touched her lips, Brie glanced at Bryce. Her heartbeat quickened. They were alone again. Although they acted like nervous kids on a double-date at first, they'd had a wonderful afternoon. But now with Phoebe and Noah in bed, she grew anxious, even as desire etched and pulled in the space between them. Still, she wasn't sure what he wanted. Was he visiting as a friend or something more?

"It's a lovely night. Would *ye* like to go out?" He extended his free hand.

Before she could overthink, she slipped her hand in his. Heat blazed in her palm and spread up her arm, while her chest fluttered. "Yes."

They sat in her quaint backyard with the delicate glow of patio overhead lights and gentle tune from summer crickets, talking about the kids and laughing under the tiny flecks of Southern California stars. Before long, the small talk dissipated.

His eyes were deep like the ocean at dusk, and his shadowy beard glinted like copper, and his full lips...she remembered those lips. Hers tingled at the memory, and she pressed a thumb along her bottom lip.

Bryce stilled and followed her movements with his gaze.

She'd fallen in love with him three months ago. Two months later, she convinced herself she was over him. But sitting an arm's length away, she couldn't deny the desire in her heart. "It's incredible to see you."

"And *ye*." Bryce's lips curved. "How's *yer* writing going?"

She set the glass down. "I finished my memoir."

His smile spread. "*Ye* did? That's fantastic."

"Thank you. When I started, I didn't know what I was doing, but after Scotland, the words flowed."

"Do *ye* need help finding an agent? I could ask around and pull a few strings."

Toying with the stem of the glass, she considered. She imagined having his own agent and being a star would offer advantages, but the book was about taking her life back. If she allowed him to give her a leg up, what would that prove? Plus, she didn't want him to feel like she was using him. The book was hers, so intimately personal and connected to her, she felt as though she'd birthed another child. "I want to do this myself, but thank you."

He nodded. "I can appreciate that."

Her pulse hummed, and she rose, focusing on adjusting a light. "You'll be returning to Scotland tomorrow, then?"

"I em."

"I know I shouldn't, but I need to ask." Brie turned toward Bryce once again, tangling her hands as her nerves raced. "Why did you come?"

Setting his glass down, he hoisted himself easily from the chair, biceps bunching in his T-shirt, then sauntered the few paces to her. "To see *ye*."

"But why?"

Bryce lifted a hand and swept a strand from her cheek. "Because I couldna stay away." Slowly, he leaned forward and brushed warm lips over hers, once, twice, like a whisper.

She sighed, yearned, and her world shifted. Twining her arms around his neck, she sank into the kiss, while he drew her deeper and deeper, splaying his hands across her lower back. All the worry and apprehension dissolved, and Brie soared with Bryce.

When he adjusted, he stumbled.

Brie jerked to the right, and then, she felt weightless. She landed atop Bryce, safely in his arms.

"Fuck!" He rolled to the side.

"Are you okay?"

"What the devil?" He sat up with effort.

Brie swished an arm around and connected with a metal tractor. "Noah's dump truck."

Rubbing a hand on his lower back, he grimaced. "I'll have to remember to scan my surroundings before making a move."

She laughed softly. As they rose, standing an arm's length apart, the magic of the night faded and nerves returned.

Bryce dragged a hand through his hair. "I should go."

She bobbed her head and released a breath. "You don't want to miss your plane." Leading him to the front door, she found each step heavier than the previous. What else could she say? And how could she let him go?

They stood awkwardly under the soft glow of the porchlight before Bryce cleared his throat. "Thank *ye* for dinner."

"You're welcome." She fought to keep her voice steady. As she gazed at him—the man she fell in love with, the man she still loved, and the man she must now part from a second time—her eyes stung and chest quaked.

She reached for him.

He reached for her.

As they embraced, love, turmoil, and pain all bloomed within Brie. His heartbeat pounded strongly against her cheek, and his arms held her so fully. She didn't want him to leave.

With a soft kiss on her hair, he stepped into the night.

"Bryce—" she cried.

He turned, lips parting.

She opened her mouth, but the words wouldn't come. *Don't go. I'm still in love with you. I love you...* Finally, she released a shaky breath. "Good-bye."

He held her gaze, saying nothing and so much at the same time. "Farewell, Brielle." And then, he was gone.

Chapter 30

A water balloon smashed onto Brie's lap, splashing water onto her notebook. "Whoa." She snatched a beach towel and dried the pad.

Hysterical giggles from Noah ensued as he ran the short distance to the fence of the yard.

"Mommy got wet!" Phoebe held a soaking wet baby in one hand, standing in the small kiddy pool with a red-and-white polka dot bathing suit.

She laughed softly. "I did. Though I thought we were all done with water balloons, buddy?" She propped her hands on her hips.

Noah grinned wide in blue crocodile board shorts. "I found one beside the hose nozzle."

Sneaking around the lawn chair, she inched toward the hose. "Oh yeah?" With one quick swipe, she cranked the hose and sprayed Noah.

"Ahh!" He ran away. "You can't get me!"

"Eeee!" Phoebe skipped with her baby. "Get me!"

She sprayed Noah, sprinkled Phoebe, and made rainbows with the hose water, until they were all sun-soaked and tired. What better way to spend a staff development day than a day in the yard? Plus, Brie needed a diversion. Earlier, Noah had picked up a stick and Phoebe had hopped into the little cardboard boat and began playing like they had with Bryce the night before.

"You can be Bryce, Mom!" Noah told her.

She'd picked up the stick, which felt like a fifty-pound weight and instantly felt a splinter stab her forefinger.

A few minutes after, the kids played with each other.

She was grateful, for the prick of a stick was nothing in comparison to the pierce of longing in her heart. Maybe one day, Bryce would stroll into a bookstore and catch her name on a book cover. Intrigued, he'd pick up her memoir. Even though she changed his name, characteristics, and the title of the show, he'd know who had captured her heart. Perhaps that's why she hadn't told him she included him in her memoir—she didn't want him to feel sorry for her. They'd parted in Scotland, and he hadn't come after her, until a short visit yesterday. Still, he didn't say he wanted her...

"Can we have a popsicle?" Noah yelled.

When she opened the back door, she heard the shrill of her cell phone. Choosing to ignore the device, she ducked and opened the freezer. "What color popsicle, kiddos?"

"Can I have an orange?" Noah asked.

"Strawbewy, please," Phoebe said.

"You got it." She handed them popsicles.

With a pink popsicle in hand, Phoebe pointed to the box. "Mommy wants one, too."

Brie laughed and swiped a hand over her damp forehead. "You know what? Mommy does." Popping the pastel popsicle through the plastic film, Brie heard her phone *ding* again and again. Striding to the side counter littered with mail, drawings, and paintings, she noticed a plethora of missed calls from random numbers, her voicemail full, texts from Andrea, and social media notifications. "What the...?" She opened Andrea's text. An urgent, two-word message preceded a single picture.

—*CALL ME!*—

The popsicle fell from her fingertips. On her phone, two side-by-side pictures of she and Bryce—one, smiling in Scotland, and then a second, kissing in her backyard the night before appeared to be snipped from an online article. And the headline: *Secret Girlfriend in the States?*

"Mommy?" Noah asked.

"One." She gulped. "One second. Take your sister out back to eat your popsicles."

He shrugged and grasped Phoebe's hand. "Come on, sissy."

Bryce was the only other person who had the first photo. He was as protective of his privacy as she, so how could the photo have been leaked? And the one in her backyard...she had no idea. They were alone... A chill crept up her spine, and she shivered. Was someone spying on her? The paparazzi? A superfan? Raking her head, she couldn't stop her mind from whirling with possibilities. Besides herself, Andrea was the only other person who knew Bryce was in town. And Andrea was sworn to secrecy, wasn't she?

Yes, Bryce was Andrea's favorite actor; she belonged to the Brycers—the fan group—but she never would have considered Andrea to be jealous. She scrolled through Andrea's texts. More headlines. More gossip. *Oh, dear Lord.*

As she read more headlines aloud, she gasped.

WHO IS BRIEELLE HUNTER?
STALKER OR LOVER?
BRYCE'S SECRET
BABBY DADDY, BRYCE FRASER?

Another text from Andrea interrupted her scrolling.

—Call me!—

Brie shook herself from her stupor and dialed.

"I got a notification from the fan site! People are freaking out!" Andrea said upon answering.

"How? Who?" Brie stuttered.

"I don't know, Brie. I, God, I'm so sorry."

Panic clogged her throat. "You didn't tell anybody, did you?"

"No one, I promise. I'd never betray your trust or Bryce's." Andrea exhaled. "Do you think Bryce has seen the headlines?"

"I'm not sure. He might still be on the plane. Oh, my God." She pressed a hand to her mouth. The news would be all over Scotland by now. He'd be ambushed when he exited the plane by media from television and magazines, and then paparazzi outside the airport with no warning. He'd told the interviewer yesterday he was jumping on a plane back to Glasgow. They knew exactly where he'd be.

She didn't know how this could have happened. She was so careful. Nausea rose up her throat.

"Brie? Are you there?" Andrea asked.

"I'm here."

"Do you want me to come over? I'll bring pizza."

She gulped air. "Yes. I need my best friend right now."

Thirty minutes later, Andrea arrived with food and open arms. "I muscled through those papz like an

Italian momma at the grocery store."

Brie laughed and embraced her.

After hugs and serving the kids, Andrea sat across from Brie, shaking parmesan onto her slice. "Think about the last couple of days. Maybe someone got ahold of your phone?"

Brie considered. She only grocery shopped with the kids on Saturday morning, then they were home the rest of the day. Bryce arrived a few minutes before five p.m., and Ryan barged in shortly after. She told Andrea the same.

"Did he seem weird about Bryce?" She leaned forward. "Think he recognized him?"

Wracking her brain, she shook her head. "He didn't seem to. He just made a comment about Bryce's accent. I highly doubt he watches the show. He's always been more into reality TV."

"Well, was he by your phone?"

She lifted a shoulder.

"What's wrong with your phone?" Noah glanced up, pizza grease on his cheeks.

"Nothing baby. A picture's…missing."

Noah crinkled his brows. "Phoebe was playing with your phone when Dad was here. He said he wanted to check to make sure she didn't mess it up."

Brie glanced at Andrea. She mouthed, OMG. Snatching her phone, she opened her text messages, ignoring the pile up, but no message thread to or from Ryan existed. She didn't have a habit of keeping his messages anyway. He could've air dropped the photo, but she didn't know how to track that kind of technology transaction. She wasn't techy in the slightest, which seemed completely ridiculous right now, since she worked for TechCo.

Grasping her phone, she called Ryan, while her body shook. Ringing echoed in her ear and then his voicemail greeting began. She disconnected.

Mimi arrived a few minutes later. "What's going on, Brie? There are people outside your house."

"I know, Mom." She pressed her eyelids closed, then opened them with an exhale. "Remember when I told you I met a nice guy in Scotland?"

"Yes." She set her purse down and angled toward Brie.

"He's an actor. And somehow, the press got a hold of pictures of us."

She planted her hands on her hips. "Well, that's an invasion of privacy."

"It is." Brie tilted her head. "You're not interested to know who the actor is?"

She wrapped Brie in a hug. "I doubt I know him. I'm more concerned about you and the kids right now."

"We're okay." With a few taps into her phone, Brie showed Mimi their Scotland picture.

Mimi smiled softly. "He's handsome, for sure, but I don't recognize him." She turned toward the kids. "Hey, sweeties. Let's play out back."

Thanking her, Brie rose; yet, fury bubbled inside her again. She paced the length of the living room. All the time and energy she'd spent creating a safe, stable home was crushed in less than twenty-four hours. She'd invited Bryce for dinner, and she'd prepared herself for the explanation with her kids for his presence, but not this. Why would Ryan do such a thing? He might be an absent father, but she couldn't imagine he'd want to disrupt his children's lives.

While a pop culture show hummed low in the background, an announcement had her craning her head.

"Our partners across the pond caught up with the actor in Glasgow."

"Bryce! Bryce!" a voice yelled.

His name echoed across her living room for a few seconds, and then he appeared, baseball cap on, weaving past a throng of reporters.

Queasiness struck her stomach. She clapped a hand to her mouth and watched.

"Bryce. Welcome home! Can you comment on your relationship with the American, Brielle Hunter?"

With a quick snap of his head, he slowed his gait. Then just as quickly, he flexed his jaw. "No."

"Bryce! Bryce!"

He kept moving, pushing forward until a man in a suit joined him.

Bryce's face was set. She'd seen him this way once when Ms. Crazy appeared at their breakfast table. She hated she was the reason for Bryce's discomfort. What would he think of her now?

****

Ring-ring! Turning over in bed, Brie blinked and saw Bryce's name in bright, white lights across her phone screen. She hadn't wanted to turn her phone off, in case he called.

"I've woken *ye*," he said with a voice more gravelly than normal.

Shoving her hair out of her eyes, she switched the pink bedside lamp on. "It's all right." She rubbed the cobwebs out of her eyes and glanced at the clock. Based on the time, she'd barely slept an hour. Still, her pulse quickened as the unspoken words hung in the air like a bad dream.

He cleared his throat.

"I—" She didn't know what to say.

"Did *ye*?"

"I saw them."

He sighed heavily. "How are *ye*?"

"I'm more all right now than I was a few hours ago." She stared at the dark ceiling where a halo of light glowed from her lamp. "Andrea sent me the photos and showed me the stories." Brie waited for Bryce to respond, but his voice fell silent. "Bryce?"

"Only two of us have the photo, Brie, and the other—"

"Do you think I'd do this, Bryce?" She rose.

"Well, no, but I—"

"It was Ryan," she interrupted. "At least that's what I'm assuming after talking to Noah. He saw Ryan holding my phone while we were talking in the kitchen. Maybe he recognized you."

He cursed under his breath.

Brie fiddled with the tangled ends of her hair. "What should we do? Should I hire someone?"

"No, I'll take care of it."

"You're not responsible for me. I can handle myself."

"If *ye* did maybe this wouldn't have happened."

She sucked in a breath.

"I didna mean. Christ, I—"

"It's fine. I'm sorry this happened. Really, I am. It's late. If you need me to make a statement or do anything to help fix…this…just let me know." She pressed her eyes closed, while tears streaked down her cheeks.

"I'm sorry, Brie."

She sniffled. "Me, too." Upon disconnecting, she heard the familiar *ding* of a new email. She clicked open a query response for her memoir.

Thank you for sharing your project. I appreciate the opportunity and am grateful for the chance to consider what you have poured your time and heart into creating.

Unfortunately, after careful review, I'm passing on this project. I wish you the best of luck in your writing.

Another rejection. Brie flipped the phone over and buried her face in the pillow.

****

Bryce seized the Scotch. Yet, the neat glass wouldn't do tonight. He wasn't in the mood to savor the complexity and sniff the fine notes. He wrenched a tumbler from the cabinet and filled the glass to the brim. With a flick of his wrist, he downed half.

Dropping into the leather chair, he grasped his phone and opened photos. Scrolling, he thumbed past pictures until he paused at the image he sought—the picture he'd taken of Brie and he months ago. He remembered the day so acutely and how a day away with Brie became one of the most memorable days he'd experienced in years. And Christ, the way the sun shone off her golden-brown hair, while the ferry glided over the crystal-blue water.

But he hadn't meant for their relationship to continue. Yet, he'd taken that step as well, hadn't he? And now the press haunted him, again.

The press was the press. Their job was to report. Actors and the press had a delicate relationship that worked both ways. But Bryce had been in charge of what information he shared with the press about his life, what interviews he wanted to give, and photos he allowed to be distributed. *So much for privacy.* Then, he'd gone and doubted Brie. He expelled a rough breath. He could still hear the catch in her voice when he'd asked her if she was responsible and the way her tone sharpened when she told him the truth.

He downed the rest of the Scotch.

Chapter 31

A black SUV parked across from Phoebe's preschool Tuesday afternoon. In the window, a man peered out with a long-range camera.

"Let's go, sweetheart." With his hand tucked in hers, Brie walked briskly with Noah toward the adjacent preschool. Since walking through the mob of paparazzi before school, her momma-bear instincts were on full guard. She wanted to march across the street and tell them to leave her family alone, but she didn't want to make a scene.

Five minutes later, stepping out of the gated preschool closure holding onto Noah's and Phoebe's hands, she glanced up and down the street. The black SUV was gone. She exhaled. "Okay, kids. Let's head home."

"I painted a birdhouse today!" Noah sang.

She smiled. "You did?"

He skipped happily, blond hair flopping. "Yep. Going to hang it in the backyard later."

"That sounds great."

"I want to paint!" Phoebe joined Noah with a *bounce-bounce*.

She smiled and squeezed Phoebe's hand. "You can paint when we get home, sweetie." A few feet from her car, she saw a man step onto the sidewalk. She kept one eye on him and hands tucked into her children's.

Although she first suspected he had ulterior motives, when he strode past, she relaxed. *Stop freaking out. Not everyone wants a photo.*

Brie unlocked the car with a *beep* and then opened Phoebe's door.

Click!

She swiveled.

Click! Flash! Click!

She threw a hand up. "Hey! What do you think you're doing?"

Dark hair hung over the black camera lens as the press member clicked away, getting in her personal space. "How long have you been seeing Bryce Fraser? Did you know he was an actor?"

"That's none of your business." She buckled Phoebe.

"Can you tell us more? Where did you meet? When will you see him again?"

"Hi!" Phoebe squealed.

Click!

Slamming the door, Brie pivoted, seething. "Get away from my car."

"The public just wants answers." The man snapped another picture an inch from her face.

"Move!" Brie shouted.

But he barely budged.

She tugged Noah around to the other side of the car.

"Who is that, Mom?" Noah asked.

"No one." She lifted all forty-five pounds of him and set Noah in the booster. "Buckle yourself, now!"

"Okay!" he yelled.

Sliding behind the wheel, Brie cranked the engine,

checked the mirror, and roared out of the parking space, only to stop a few feet down the road behind a parked, white SUV in the middle of the street.

A passenger door flew open, and a child ran across the street, then jumped inside.

Brie gripped the steering wheel. "Really? That is NOT safe!" She honked the horn. Once. Twice.

The SUV inched forward.

Brie changed lanes, accelerated, and car-dialed Mimi. "The paparazzo was outside the kids' school!" she yelled. "What can we do?"

"I'm so sorry, honey. Are you all okay?" Mimi asked.

"Yes. Just rattled." She gripped the steering wheel at ten and two. "The nerve of those people."

"What's going on, Mom?" Noah asked.

"Some people want to take our pictures, but they aren't being nice, buddy."

"It'll slow down," Mimi's calm voice carried over the car speakers. "Can you take a few days off and get away? Stay with me?"

Mimi's one-bedroom condo wouldn't help. They'd filled that space too quickly over a year ago. But she'd made that work back then. She *had* to. "No, that won't work, Mom. We'll come visit for a little while, but we can't stay. Thank you, anyway."

Bickering arose from the backseat, then squeals.

She glanced in the rearview to see her kids flailing their legs about, trying to kick one another. "Stop, you two."

"Hey, poopyhead," Noah said.

"Peepeehead."

"Diarrhea face."

"Poop face!"

"Ahhhh," Noah said in his best monster voice. "It's Phoebe, the poop monster!"

"Eeeek," Phoebe screamed. "I get you!"

"Crap."

"Poop."

"Diarrhea."

Brie's hands tightened on the steering wheel. "That's enough." Yet, they continued incessantly. She gripped the steering wheel tighter. "Stop it! Just stop! Stop!"

Phoebe sniffled, then Noah.

"Waaaa!" Phoebe cried.

Noah sniffed. "Mooooooooomy."

"Mommy." Brie turned briefly, then snapped back, noticing the bright-red light. She smashed the brake. Backpacks flew forward, and the car lurched to a stop.

"Ah!" Noah yelled.

"You scared me," Phoebe wailed.

"Mommy's sorry. Mommy is so, so sorry." Even as the guilt pinched her chest, she knew this wasn't her fault—the paparazzi, the chaos, and the instability. She stared at the crimson-red light ahead, blinking back tears, while her children sniffled behind her. She had to confront the cause.

****

After dropping the kids at Mimi's, Brie arrived at Ryan's house. Manicured hedges, palm trees, a semi-circle driveway, and two-story mansion greeted her. She stepped out, hiked her purse onto a shoulder, marched to the door, and rang the doorbell.

The door swung open halfway.

Jasmine appeared with stick-straight hair and a

skin-tight, sunflower-yellow dress, clinging to every curve. "Brielle." She pursed her lips. "What are you doing here?"

"I need to talk to Ryan."

"He's on a call…"

"I really could care less." She shoved the half-open door wide and marched inside, her steps echoing off the gray, tiled floors. "Ryan!" She continued to shout until he appeared.

"Brie? What the hell are you doing?" Narrowing his gaze from the top of the stairs, he descended.

She advanced. "What am I doing? Oh, funny you should ask. I just spent the last hour calming Noah and Phoebe after paparazzo showed up at their school. And do you know why he showed up?"

"Brie—"

"No!" Pointing a finger, she stuck her chin out. "You don't get to talk. You *caused* this. You violated my privacy, Bryce's, and put our children at risk. You did this! How could you?"

Ryan glanced toward the front door where Jasmine toyed with her bracelet.

"Did you hear me?" Brie demanded.

Ryan snapped to attention. "Yes."

"Why did you do it?"

He stared. "Do what? Tell the world about you and that actor? Oh, I would have, gladly, but I didn't know who he was at least, initially, but I did wonder. I actually had to jump on a call with the Singapore office when I returned from your house."

"So, you…didn't?" She croaked.

"No."

Pressing a hand to her spinning temple, she shook

her head. "Then, who?"

"Me." Jasmine stepped forward with her nose high.

Brie glared. "You—"

"That's right. He showed me your little picture after he left your tiny house and wouldn't stop talking about you and the tall Scotsman." She rolled her eyes.

Ryan shuffled his feet, while his head whipped between Jasmine and Brie.

"I recognized Bryce. You see, I auditioned for a small, but essential role in the Nova Villains movie he's starring in. I met him. And it's a good thing he got that role in *Swords of Scotland* because besides his accent, he's boring—nothing like his character, Alexander James Mackenzie. Shame." She glanced at her nails. "I couldn't figure out how the two of you had gotten together."

"That's none of your business," Brie snapped. "Who I choose to date and see is my business, not yours or Ryan's. It's my life."

"Well, your life affects my life—our life." Jasmine twirled her fingers from her to Ryan.

Anger pulsed through Brie's veins and boiled her blood. She strode forward.

Ryan stuck an arm out, pausing her momentum. "She was just protecting the kids, Brie. She loves them, too. Surely you can see how strange it must've been for me to show up and find some stranger with Phoebe and Noah."

Shaking, Brie clenched and unclenched her fists. All Bryce had ever done was make sure she was safe, and she knew, in the depths of her soul, he'd do the same for her children. "You don't need to protect them from Bryce. He's," she began, then shook her head.

"You don't know him."

"Exactly, we don't." Ryan propped his arm up, gazing at his smart watch. "He called me, you know."

She narrowed her eyes. "He did?"

Ryan smirked. "But where's he now?"

Her eyes burned for the second time today. "In Scotland."

Chapter 32

As Bryce reviewed lines in bed, attempting to ignore the media with not one telly on, he was interrupted by the shrill of his mobile.

"I'm sending you a video," Joanna declared.

He swung his legs off the bed and scrubbed his face. "What's going on?" When an alert announced a new text, he clicked on the video message. Instantly, he tightened his jaw. Brie and her children paced down the sidewalk followed by paparazzo. He leapt up and punched his headboard. Once, twice, three times.

"What was that?" Joanna asked.

"Nothing." Gazing at the indent in the center of his headboard, he imagined Ryan's face and fisted a hand once again.

"I know you've always been very private, but if you give the press something, anything, they'd slow down. I know this is difficult, Bryce. But we have to respond."

"No, I won't add any more fuel to the fire," he growled. "I'll talk to *ye* later." He slammed the phone down, which had been going mad with social network notifications, and paced the room. He needed to talk to someone. Seizing the device once again, he texted his brother-in-law.

—*Can you pop over?*—
—*You all right?*—

—Oh, aye. Pure crabbit.—

Forty-five minutes later, Ian strode through Bryce's front door, fiery-red beard trimmed tight in dark jeans and leather boots.

"How're the kids and Rose?" Bryce asked.

"Fine." Ian nodded. "Archie has been looking for *ye* to come play rugby. The games will be starting up soon, as well, and Lucy will perform at Braemar in a week's time. She wanted me to remind *ye*."

"Aye, tell them I'll play soon enough and send me the schedule." Inhaling, he breathed deeply, then released a heavy breath. "Have a dram, will *ye*?"

"Sure." Ian settled himself in a leather chair opposite and met Bryce's gaze. "Is this about the American lass?"

With a nod, he poured the whisky, inhaling the sharp notes. He should've known Ian would have foreknowledge. He'd imagined he'd been privy to the news, as well. The paparazzi were like crows scrabbling for any scraps they could get their claws on. " 'Tis."

"All right."

"We met by chance at the airport of all places." He handed Ian a dram. "And again, later in Edinburgh. We enjoyed one another's company, but she was here for less than a fortnight, so we kept things casual."

Ian took a nip. "She has kids, no?"

Bryce bobbed his head. "She told me the truth of them early on. And after a run-in with Ms. Crazy herself, I told her about *Swords*. Can *ye* believe she'd never heard of me?"

Ian's lips curled. "Never heard of the Telly King of Scots, *ye* say? Oh, how *yer* ego must've been crushed, mate."

"Shut *yer* gob." He chuckled. "Anyway, we had ourselves a time and said good-bye three months ago, but I texted her now and again."

Shaking his head, he settled into the chair. "*Ye* and *yer* mad texts."

"What? *Ye* text, too, mate."

He slapped a hand on the armrest. "Not as much as *ye*!"

"When I flew to Los Angeles for the talk show and an interview with *Celebrity*, I saw her again. Brielle." Her name rolled off his tongue like a song. "Met her *bairns*, too." He swirled the whisky.

"You've always had a soft spot for children. Surprised *ye* haven't found a lass and settled down with a brood of *yer* own by now."

Bryce took another nip. He thought about Noah atop the play area and his eagerness as Bryce showed him how to wield the wooden sword, while fair Phoebe picked strawberries. He wished he could've spent more time with them.

"Where'd *ye* go, mate?"

He shook his head, clearing recent memories. "Anyway, I met the ex. Although he didn't seem to recognize me, he must've been wondering about Brie and I and got a hold of her cell. Now, the paparazzi are hounding her and the children." He stood, dragging a hand through his hair. "I should've stayed away. I've protected my family from the spotlight, but I wasn't careful enough with her."

Setting his dram down, Ian rose. "Don't chide *yerself*." He clapped a hand on Bryce's shoulder. "The paparazzi have their ways. *Ye* and I both know that for certain, but 'tis a surprise about her ex."

"Aye. I called and gave him an earful, though I wish I could challenge him." He gripped an imaginary hilt of a sword.

"But all *ye* do is poncy fight! Remember when *ye* invited me to that weapons training session with the re-enactors?"

With a smirk, Bryce leaned forward. "I seem to remember keeping up. I learned better than *ye*! *Ye* dropped the halberd near my boot!"

They laughed and shared stories.

Sometime later, Ian stared at Bryce. "So, what're *ye* doing next?"

Bryce considered, thinking of Brie, Noah, and Phoebe in their home in California—the sunny-yellow door, inviting interior, and tiny garden. He then recalled Brie's wondrous expression when they'd hiked up the East End of Loch Lomond and later explored Glencoe. She mentioned Noah and Phoebe would be in play heaven here. *Aye. Just as I was as a young lad.* "Bring them to Scotland."

Ian kicked up a brow. "Don't do anything rash, man."

"Just for a wee holiday."

He gazed at Bryce over his whisky glass, eyes set. "Rose will have plenty to say."

"Aye, I imagine she will."

****

Brie scrubbed cotton-candy-pink, lime-green, and sunflower-yellow paint off the kitchen table. Yet, the colors smeared across the soft, golden pine. She flipped the towel over and cleaned.

"Can I help?" Noah asked.

"No, I've got it. Go play." With the paparazzi

camped outside her house, she needed to focus. They were annoying, disruptive, and determined. But worse were the Direct Messages on her social accounts and letters in her mailbox from angry fans. They were either fiercely protective of Bryce calling her a gold digger and every other name under the sun, or jealous, angry women who told her she didn't have the right to be associated with him. She stopped opening mail—all her bills were electronic, anyway—and ceased scrolling through social media, but the constant barrage of opinions was becoming overwhelming.

Mimi invited her to stay at her condo again, but Brie would go stir crazy cooped up in a tiny condo, shuffling her children back and forth. She'd done it before, but she couldn't go backward. She needed to push forward and find her footing once again. When she glanced toward the living room, she uttered a silent *thank you* as her children built blocks quietly together.

A soft *ding* notified her of an email. She set the towel down and snatched her phone, hoping the email was a memoir query response, then paused when she noticed the sender. *Holly Finlay-MacDonald.* Opening the email, she scanned the message.

Brielle,

We saw the news on the television about ye *and Bryce Fraser. I can't imagine what strain* ye *and* yer *family are under, but know that we are wishing* ye *well and that peace and happiness will find* ye *once again.*

All the best,

Holly Finlay-MacDonald

Brie re-read the email. Her heart seared with gratitude at Holly's thoughtfulness, and her eyes stung with unshed tears. She'd only spoken to Holly once nearly three months ago. Sure, she had her email address saved, but she hadn't emailed her, not wanting to alter the tiny bond they'd formed in Scotland. She also liked Daniel's gorgeous photos and reels, but that was the extent of their connection. And now, Holly made the time to re-connect. Brie smiled and replied, thanking Holly for her kindness. Once she sent the email, she closed her eyes and imagined being back at the pub with Andrea and the MacDonalds and laughter all around. She even envisioned her own children dancing with little Finlay and let the imagined memory soothe her.

Ring-ring! The shrill of her cell phone snapped her back to reality. When she flipped the device over, she stilled her hand. *Bryce*.

"Come to Scotland."

She sucked in a breath. "What? I can't just pick up and go on another vacation. I have Phoebe and Noah to think about and responsibilities here."

"Bring 'em. We'll vacation in Aberdeen or Banff, go hiking, fishing, explore the outdoors, and get away from the paparazzi circus."

Strolling to the counter, she released a breath. Things were still awry. The press hadn't slowed, even though three days had passed since her face splashed across online and print media. Yet, Bryce wanted all three of them to come to Scotland. He'd only spent a few hours with them. Would they get along on an entire trip? So many unknowns existed. "Are you sure? I love my kids, but they can be a handful."

He chuckled softly. " 'Twill be grand."

"How would this work, Bryce? Where would we stay?" She seized a glass from the cabinet.

"Leave that to me."

With a shake of her head, she filled the glass with water. The delicate stream reminded her of Scotland's peaceful lochs and calming rain. Taking a slow drink, she let the cool water settle her.

"Can *ye* fly out tomorrow?"

She choked. "Tomorrow? That's so soon. I'd have to talk to my boss, pack, find the kids' passports…" *Empty passports*. Passports they'd secured two years ago when Ryan promised they'd go on their first family vacation, but like all the other promises, the vacation never happened.

"Come to Scotland," Bryce repeated. "The press isn't as crazy as L.A., and I can take care of *ye* here."

Brie steeled herself. He wanted to take care of her? She'd been on her own for a while now, and they weren't even together. She knew how to look after herself and her family, well, at least when things were normal. Now, she had a flock of press camped outside her house like noisy geese in the springtime. This new normal threw her off balance. "I don't think I could afford that, Bryce, and I wouldn't expect you to pay, either."

"Nonsense. I'd be happy to. Plus, I start shooting again for *Swords* in a few weeks. It's an ideal time."

Biting her lip, she considered saying *yes* to his wonderful invitation, but she wondered why Bryce wanted to fly them to Scotland. Was he only protecting them from the paparazzi? Did he feel bad about the way he'd reacted? Or scariest of all, did he feel the spark reignite like she had? Brie felt her heart rate increase— the palpitations rapping like a countdown clock. *This is crazy!* She heard Noah grumble about the paparazzi from the living room. A trip away might be the best for all of them *if* she could guard her heart.

****

On Thursday afternoon, Brie sat in first class with Phoebe and Noah, gazing out the window onto the tarmac. She couldn't believe Bryce purchased first-class tickets. Well, she could, but he never stopped surprising her. She gently touched the green pendant resting on her chest.

Save for Bryce, the only people she informed they'd be traveling were Andrea, Mimi, Ryan, and the MacDonalds. Although she didn't tell Ryan where she was staying in Scotland—he didn't deserve that specificity. Brie trusted her gut and that included the trust she felt with Holly and her family. After emailing Holly about their travels, she was surprised to find the almost immediate reply the MacDonalds would be at the Braemar Games at the end of the week, which wasn't too far from Aberdeen. She hoped they could reconnect.

"Check out the forklift!" Noah pressed his hands on either side of the porthole.

Outside, forklifts circled with luggage toward the airplane.

The window distracted her children for the first fifteen minutes. Once they were airborne, Phoebe and Noah settled into their lounge seats with drawing boards.

"Mommy." Phoebe tugged her sweater. "Draw."

"Oh, thank you." She picked up the attached pen and drew a flower and fairy.

"A faiwy!"

Brie smiled. "Yes, sweet pea. Where we're going,

we'll see so many flowers, and if we're lucky, we'll even spot a fairy or two."

With a happy squeal, Phoebe added circles and swirls to her drawing, while Noah retrieved playing cards. But the quiet play didn't last. Her children slowly grew restless, swinging their feet, making loud noises, and more. If her first excursion to Scotland was relaxing, her flight from LAX to London was the polar opposite.

When they changed planes in London to Aberdeen International Airport, her children sleepily followed as she steadfastly held their hands and led them to a shop for some fruit, oatmeal bars, and shortbreads, then through the terminal to the departure gates.

"Are we there yet?" Noah asked with a yawn.

Brie smiled. "Almost."

The plane from London to Aberdeen flew them over the bustling city and towering skyline to rolling moss-and olive-green. Descending a short time later, she saw a grand, stone structure jut up through the morning fog.

"A castle!" Noah squished his nose against the window and crunched a buttery shortbread cookie. "Is that real?"

Brie giggled. She'd experienced the same surprise the first time around. "It is." She huddled close with her children—Phoebe on her lap and Noah snugged at her side—gazing out the small window at the vast Scottish beauty below. Excitement fluttered in her chest. She was back.

Chapter 33

She was here. Bryce received a text from Brie a
few minutes before. Tucking his mobile in his pocket,
he scanned the cottage—Brie and the children's home
for the next five days—and gripped the keys. He'd
hand-selected the stone cottage after his assistant paid a
premium fee for the rental just a few blocks from his
rented flat.

All his specifications were met—two bedrooms, a
wee yard, full refrigerator, and bouquets of wildflowers
on the main floor and bedroom. If he couldn't stay with
Brie, he at least wanted her to know he was thinking of
her. Food lined the shelves in the fridge, and of course,
eggs were nowhere to be found inside or out. He'd even
painstakingly picked up the messages himself, checking
every prepared food item for egg ingredients. Hell, he'd
invited them. He wanted Brie and the children to feel
like they were at home or as close as they could be,
though he feared something was bound to go wrong.

Hearing a door slam, he strode outside and nearly
lost his footing. Brie stood, looking as gorgeous as ever
in tan trousers, a cream blouse, and his gifted necklace
at her throat. She was like fresh air filling his lungs.
"Welcome." He stared into her mesmerizing eyes
transfixed as the children began talking all at once from
inside the car.

A smile spread, while her eyes danced like clovers

in the breeze. She quickly pivoted and unbuckled Phoebe.

Noah bounded around the opposite side. "Bryce! Hi!" He launched himself into Bryce's arms.

Bryce caught him with a chuckle. "Hello, lad. Welcome to Scotland." As he embraced Noah, he couldn't contain his grin, and his heart swelled with warmth, flooding his entire being. At that moment, he knew he'd made the right decision. Setting Noah down, he beamed at Brie who stood with Phoebe tucked in her arms. "Well, hello. I thought for a moment I was seeing a wee fairy before my very eyes."

She giggled.

"And Brie"—he smiled wide—"welcome back." Extending a hand, he clasped her smooth one in his. He could protect her now.

****

Bryce held Brie's hand firmly, yet gently—his touch telling her everything would be all right. Lifting her gaze to his and seeing the sheen of happiness in his blue eyes, she felt her insides flutter like a hundred butterflies taking flight. Returning to Scotland was a risk, especially a risk for her heart, but she couldn't say *no*. She faced numerous challenges this week—stress, pain, and the press. Yet, she welcomed the result: traveling back to Scotland. Back to Bryce.

"Would *ye* like to see *yer* home for the week?" He swept a hand toward the cottage.

"I would." As she set Phoebe down, she admired the brick cottage with large, glistening glass windows hugged by a tall privacy hedge on the right and yard on the left. Nobody pointed a camera in her face or shouted her name. Peace flowed through her. She squeezed Bryce's hand.

"Come on, Phoebe!" Noah ran inside with Phoebe close behind.

As Brie stepped through the entry, she gasped. Soft, cream furniture and natural wood accents welcomed, along with colorful vases of wildflowers, thistle, and heather. "Oh, my goodness. Did you do all of this?"

Bryce glanced around with a grin. "I did. Well, a friend and I. 'Tis the least I could do if I couldna pick *ye* up from the airport."

"It's beautiful." She strolled slowly through the living area toward the kitchen and trailed a hand down the wooden island and over the smooth, white countertops lined with baking goods and floral vases. Bending, she buried her nose in a bouquet of fragrant blooms.

"There're toys in here!" Noah said.

Brie lifted her head, lips parting.

Bryce smiled softly. "I could only find a two-bedroom due to the summer season. Aberdeen is a fashionable location, but the city isn't overly busy either with the many coastal villages. And, *ye* rarely find paparazzi here."

Padding toward him, eyes stinging with grateful tears, she embraced him. Happy squeals from the kids in the next room had her retreating a step. "It's perfect. I don't know how to thank you. You've thought of everything." Now that they stood alone in the center of the flat, she wove her fingers through his, sending tingles up her arm.

He gripped hers. "I was keen to get *ye* away from it all. I couldna have foreseen this would happen."

Shaking her head, she squeezed his hand tighter. "It's not your fault."

He exhaled. "Are *ye* hungry? I thought perhaps the kids would enjoy a chippy."

With a nod, Brie smiled. "Starved."

Fifteen minutes later, they strolled along the streets of Aberdeen and stopped at a fish and chip shop for supper. Staring at the cardboard takeout box and the golden, flaky fried fish, alongside thick cut chips, she salivated.

Noah examined a golden potato wedge. "It's a French fry."

"It is," Brie said.

"I wuv French fries." Phoebe dunked a chip in ketchup.

As he eyed the chips, Noah furrowed his brows. "But you said it was a chip." He glanced at Bryce.

"Aye, lad, *yer* spot-on. We call them chips here."

Noah lifted a short fry and took a bite. "They taste like French fries." He popped the rest of the steaming chip into his mouth.

"Well, they are. We just call them something different. And crisps are what *ye* would typically call a chip in America."

Noah shrugged and dug into his food, but his gaze strayed. "What's that?" He inclined his head toward a large wheel jutting into the blue sky.

Brie glanced in the same direction. "It's a Ferris Wheel, sweetie, and an amusement park."

He straightened. "Can we go?"

Brie glanced at Bryce.

With a smirk, he casually placed an arm over the back of Brie's chair. "How about tomorrow? We can make a morning at the park, then settle on a different beach in the afternoon and build sand castles, if *ye* like."

"Yes!"

In the early afternoon, they strolled along Aberdeen Esplanade with the salty air and warm sun on their shoulders and then dipped their toes in the cool North Atlantic.

Though this trip seemed too good to be true, Brie didn't care. She wiggled her toes as the foamy waves lapped her ankles and calves. She'd worry about the paparazzi later.

****

"They're out." Brie padded back into the living room where Bryce lounged on the far end of the couch. Between the flight, introduction to Scotland, tour of Aberdeen, and the beach, the kids fell asleep at three p.m. side-by-side on Noah's twin bed—Noah with a book about a young knight in his hand and Phoebe with her ever-present Pinky doll.

He grinned. "Aye, I can imagine. It's been a day."

"It has." Brie settled beside him.

"I thought *ye* could use this." He handed her a glass of wine.

"Thank you." She tapped her glass to his and tucked her legs beneath her.

Bryce flipped on the television and began talking about a new show he was hooked on.

Brie mumbled her agreement, but the wine added a layer of fog to her already tired mind. Plus, snugged next to Bryce was like resting beside a human heater. Her lids fluttered, and sometime later, she felt herself being lifted and the familiar scent of Bryce wrapping around her.

Chapter 34

Splash-splash! The log ride plunged into the crisp water, splashing Bryce across the face and chest.

Laughter and squeals erupted in the seats ahead.

"Let's do it again!" Noah shouted.

They'd been at the amusement park nearly two hours, and Bryce couldn't contain his grin. Watching wee Phoebe bounce, beaming at the sight of a caterpillar roller coaster, he packed himself into the seat beside her, per her request, with Brie and Noah in front.

"I ready!" she yelled. "Ready, Bwyce?"

"Aye, lass."

Her angel gaze alighted on the coaster ahead with pure joy, and she patted his arm.

He felt his smile spread. *Och*, he was cold, but he would've done anything she asked with her big eyes and sweet hugs. Five minutes later, striding down the exit hand-in-hand with Phoebe, he felt his phone vibrate on his hip. He fished it out.

Joanna—Brit Agents. Missed Calls-3.

Releasing a breath, he shoved the device back into his pocket. She wanted a statement. Matched since before *Swords*, he and Joanna got along well, but they didn't see eye-to-eye on this subject. He valued his privacy. Yet, the whole Scottish-heartthrob-meets-American-Single-Mother subject line hadn't faded easily.

Brielle sidled next to him, hand on his arm. "Everything okay?"

"I need to make a call. Will *ye* be all right for a few minutes?"

She smiled. "Of course. Take your time. I think we'll order some pizza. What do you say, kiddos?"

"Pizza!" They squealed.

She looped each of her hands in Noah's and Phoebe's and strolled toward the food stand.

Turning, he noticed a group of teens and a woman near his age staring from across the path. He tugged his cap lower and pivoted. Finding himself alone a few minutes later, he dialed Jo. "I canna give them what they want."

"We've evaded the press for some time, Bryce, but they have information. And what's more, someone leaked Brielle is in Scotland with her children."

Gritting his teeth, he muttered a curse, while anger boiled within. *Damn, meddling ex.*

Jo cleared her throat. "I neither acknowledged nor denied the information, since I am not privy to that myself, but we need to provide a statement."

"I understand, but I'm not talking about Brie or her family."

"Well, you need to show your face for one thing. The Braemar games are happening this weekend. Would you do a charity throw?"

"I don't wish to take away from the athletes. It's one thing throwing during the off season for a dram and another during the festival."

"Think about it. This would give your fans something. I need an answer by end of day, so I can process the paperwork."

"Aye," he muttered. Striding back toward Brie, he noted the mother of the teens eying him suspiciously. He held the phone close to his ear and breezed in the direction opposite of Brie and the kids before backtracking once the way was clear. After lunch, more rides, including three consecutive trips around the carousel, and treats, they ambled to his four-by-four.

"Why do we have to go?" Noah whined and dragged his feet. "We could stay longer. You don't have to work, Mom."

"I want to ride more, too." Phoebe rubbed a fist in her eye.

Glancing at Brie, he noted she wore a fixed smile. He imagined she was wondering how he'd get along with the children's irritability. Although he had a niece and nephew, he hadn't seen much tears and rows lately, but he'd experienced some firsthand. And, he understood jetlag well. Even the wee youngsters on set had squabbles. Arriving at the cottage, he cut the engine. But when he rotated toward Brie, he halted.

A finger rested on her rosy lips. She gestured toward the backseat.

Phoebe and Noah were sound asleep.

"Brilliant fun," Bryce whispered.

Brie giggled, though dark rings smudged under her eyes. "They should nap well."

He nodded.

After a quick yawn, she shifted those mystical green eyes toward him. "I forgot to tell you little Finlay and the MacDonalds—the nice family I met in Glencoe—will be at the Braemar Games on Saturday. Holly"—she yawned again—"emailed me about the games after I told her we were visiting. Is that nearby?"

"A wee bit over an hour's drive. My agent asked if I'd make an appearance. *Ye* keen on going?"

Instantly, a shadow fell across her face. "Do you think it's safe? For the kids and I? For you?"

He skimmed a hand over hers and cupped it. "Plenty of people will attend. No one would expect *ye* to be there. And my agent will inform the games director to keep the appearance a surprise."

She smiled softly, then glanced at the children. "I better get them to bed."

Exiting, he circled to the backdoor on his side.

Brie unbuckled Phoebe, then picked her up and rotated. "I'll be right back."

With a nod, Bryce unfastened Noah's seatbelt and hoisted him into his arms. He stepped through the bedroom door a moment later as Brie placed Phoebe in bed. The wood floor creaked beneath his boots.

Turning, her gaze met his and held.

Something churned within him, and his chest expanded. Feeling Noah shift in his arms, he strode forward and lowered him into the soft bed, then smoothed a hand over his sand-colored hair. A smile played at the lad's lips, and Bryce's own grew. He had a grand time today and felt like a wee lad himself—spry and cheerful.

When Brie slipped her hand in his and tilted her head toward the door, they strolled quietly out of the room, padding to the living area.

Bryce drew her toward him, wrapping his arms around her, relaxing into the way she fit just so and how her floral scent enveloped. Although he should be rehearsing lines, he wanted to spend every moment he could with her and the children. As the afternoon sun breached through the clouds and flooded the living room with embers of sparks all around them, he held Brie close. What was happening to him?

****

A few hours later, Bryce lay on his rented flat's couch desperately trying to watch the Scottish National team's forward kick a penalty, while his sister berated him over the phone.

"I want to meet her," Rose persisted.

"Rose—"

"I don't wanna hear another word. I deserve to know who my brother's tangled up with. Ian told me plenty."

Rolling his eyes to the ceiling, he sighed. "It's not like that, Rose."

" 'Tisn't? *Ye* mean to tell me *ye* brought a woman all the way across the Atlantic and *yer* not sharing the sheets?"

He scrubbed his face with a hand. "Christ, Rose. She's here with her children."

"Aye, I'd like to meet them, too."

He wouldn't win this argument. Plus, he was spent after a day out. What would be so terrible about his family meeting Brie and the wee ones, anyway? They were here and so were his family. Plus, the sooner he agreed, the sooner he could get back to the game. "Fine, we're off to Forvie Sands tomorrow. *Ye* can meet us."

Chapter 35

At Forvie Sands, the wind whipped up the golden beach, ruffling Brie's blouse and tousling her hair, while salty notes drifted toward her. The swirling breeze mirrored her nerves. She'd be meeting Bryce's family for the first time today. His sister wanted to meet her, he'd said. Her two children would accompany her, which would be fun for Noah and Phoebe, but what would they think of her? Were they suspicious about the news scandal? And even more, would they be wondering what she was doing with Bryce? They hadn't spent more than a few moments alone since she and the kids arrived. And although she was enjoying herself, a little voice in her head nagged, what were she and Bryce now? After all she'd been through the last year-and-a-half, she desired permanency. Yet, she didn't know how this would end. Anxiousness overshadowed her like the numerous clouds gathering above.

" 'Tis common for seals to be found along the beach here," Bryce said to Noah. "Keep your eyes peeled, lad."

Brie shook her head and focused on Phoebe skipping beside her, while listening to Bryce educate Noah on Scottish sea life.

All of a sudden, a number of gray-and-white lumps appeared on the sand. Besides the mammals, the beach was nearly empty of visitors.

"Seals!" Noah shot like a rocket toward the sleeping sea mammals.

"Noah!" Brie hoisted Phoebe on her hip, preparing to run.

"I've got him." Bryce sprinted after Noah.

Phoebe kicked her feet. "I running, too." As soon as her feet touched the sand, Phoebe ran a few feet before she slowed her pace and grasped Brie's hand once again.

Brie squeezed Phoebe's hand gently, while Bryce and Noah disappeared over the dunes. Having someone else help with her children was abnormal. She was so used to tag-teaming the kids, hoisting Phoebe up on her hip or shoulders and racing after Noah, or chasing Phoebe with Noah alongside her. Yet, strolling with her daughter, swinging her hand happily, she embraced this change and lifted her face to the breeze, enjoying this new dynamic.

Hiking over a dune, she stopped, stilled by the sight before her. Bryce squatted beside Noah fifty feet from the seals speaking in a calm tone. As she approached, she listened to their conversation.

"They're a sight, for sure, but ye don't want to anger them. The bulls will protect the others sure enough. Better to keep your distance."

Noah kicked the sand. "I just wanted to see them."

"I know, lad." Bryce nodded. "*Ye* can see them fine from here."

"You don't have to tell me what to do."

He cracked a smile. "Aye, I don't, but I don't want to see *ye* hurt, especially with *yer* mother and sister watching. We're their protectors, *ye* see."

Noah gazed at Bryce, then bobbed his head.

Glancing over his shoulder, Bryce winked at Brie.

Her heart burst like the crashing waves on the shore. Did he know she longed for this? Longed for him? And could he see he was incredible with her children? That her children adored him?

Faint laughter carried across the dunes.

Brie swiveled. A brunette with a round belly, tall red-headed man, and two children, who appeared to be miniatures of their parents, ran from the opposite direction.

" 'Tis Rose, Ian, and the children." Bryce lifted a hand.

Her pulse immediately sprinted.

"Friends!" Phoebe tugged Brie's hand.

"I see them, sweetie." Descending the dunes where blue water rippled and foamed, she padded in the soft sand, giving herself a moment to prepare herself, while Bryce and Noah raced ahead.

A moment later, a woman puffed air and extended a hand. "You must be Brielle." She placed the other hand on her stomach. "I'm Rose."

"Brie. It's so nice to meet you." She shook her hand. "I see you've already met Noah. This is Phoebe." She grinned at her daughter.

"I'm three!" Phoebe's infectious smile lit up her entire face.

"Oh, *ye* are? My Lucy girl just turned four. She's over there with her brother and uncle."

Phoebe looked up with bright eyes. "Can I play, Mommy?"

"Of course. Have fun."

After a quick kiss, Phoebe ran lightly across the

sand as if she were a ballerina leaping across the stage.

Bryce returned and stood beside Brie, slipping a hand in hers. He squeezed hers gently.

She squeezed back.

"So, Brie, how are *ye* enjoying *yer* visit?"

"We're enjoying it immensely. Phoebe and Noah love exploring the countryside and beaches."

"I'm glad." Rose rubbed her belly.

"Would you like to sit?" Brie gestured. "We can walk closer to the children and sit near the shore." She swiveled, keeping an eye on her daughter near the water's edge.

"Aye, I would." She ambled over and slowly, dropped into the soft sand.

No sooner had Brie joined her when she spotted Phoebe getting closer to the water. "I'm sorry, I—"

Bryce stilled Brie with a hand. "I've got wee Phoebe. Why don't *ye* have a rest with Rose?"

"Oh, but I—"

Bryce already started jogging toward Phoebe. He arrived swiftly, lifting her in his strong arms, making her giggle and squirm, then repeated the action with his niece.

"He's a wonder with the children, isn't he?" Rose asked.

"He is." Brie sighed. "Not everyone is…Well, not everyone is so natural."

"Aye, I'd have to agree with *ye*. My Ian had never seen a wee bairn before, but once Archie arrived, he stepped up readily to the task and continues to amaze me." She circled a hand over her belly. "It must be hard raising them primarily by *yerself*."

Brie opened her mouth, then closed it. She hadn't

thought to even ask Bryce what he'd told his sister, but somehow, she didn't mind. "Sometimes, it is hard, but we've figured out a routine and made it work."

Rose nodded.

"How far along are you?"

"*Och*, thirty weeks or thereabouts."

As she watched Rose's stomach lift and settle, then lift again, she smiled. "Pregnancy is such a miracle. I loved being pregnant."

"Oh?" Rose tilted her head.

"Not the nausea, swollen feet, and achy back"— she laughed softly—"but feeling the miracle inside you, you know? And then once they arrive, every dream you've ever had is in this little bundle in your hands. Your entire life revolves around them, and you worry all the time. And then they grow older, and it's the same; yet, different somehow. You worry whether you're doing things right or you're doing things wrong, and you hope you've made the right choices."

Caressing her belly, Rose smiled. "Aye, I ken what *ye* mean. I can tell bringing them here was the right choice, even though I didn't rightly understand Bryce's decision at the time."

Brie opened her mouth. "I, well…he…"

Rose patted Brie's hand. "Let's go put our feet in the water, shall we? See if it helps these swollen ankles?"

"Yes." Brie grinned, clasping a hand to help her up.

When Ian strolled over with his daughter on his back beside Bryce with Phoebe, he smiled wide. "Ian Fitzgibbons, and this here monkey on my back is Lucy."

"Hi, Ian. Hi, Lucy."

"And I'm Phoebe!" she said.

Everyone laughed.

They spent the afternoon playing in the sand, dipping their feet in the water, watching birds and wildlife, and enjoying one another's company, then headed back to the cottage for takeout.

Yet on the return to Aberdeen, Brie couldn't help but wonder why Bryce invited his sister and family to join them. Yes, they'd had a wonderful time, and she genuinely enjoyed Rose and Ian's company, but was it because they were in town or for another reason?

As the road stretched before them, questions peppered Brie's mind once again.

****

On their second-to-last day in Scotland, Brie strolled hand-in-hand with Bryce through tall grass that perfumed the air and tickled her ankles, while Noah and Phoebe ran and danced through the swaying blades. A few other families also enjoyed the fresh, summer air and near-cloudless sky. Boys searched under rocks, while the soft wind feathered their hair, and girls picked wildflowers. Today was a day for families.

Families. Family. She glanced at Bryce as he watched her children play with a quiet smile teasing his lips. She'd wanted to talk to him since his family joined them yesterday, but when they returned to the cottage, the Fitzgibbons arrived behind with an armful of pies. A couple hours later, they left together. Now watching Bryce gaze fondly at her children, she wondered what he was thinking. They'd been in Scotland for three days, and he hadn't mentioned the future. Simply, he wanted to get them somewhere safe and away from the press and tabloids. She was grateful, but she couldn't deny the longing in her own heart.

"There's a wee brook over here. Who's up for skipping rocks?" Bryce asked.

"Me!" Noah tugged Bryce's hand.

"Me, too!" Phoebe followed eagerly, waves tossing to and fro as she ran to Bryce's side. When she wedged a little hand in Bryce's free one, she smiled wide.

Bryce peered down with a full-lipped grin, then wrapped his large hand around hers. He strolled hand-in-hand with her children, while the wind whirled around them, lightly toying with corners of clothing and twirling hair, as if nature too recognized the moment.

As the picture unfolded before her, Brie's heart filled with love like a bursting, bright-red balloon. The snapshot was a postcard photo, a photo for her walls, and for her to store in her memory forever. She grabbed her phone and snapped a picture of the tall, gentle Scot with her children, while an ache stirred in her chest. She couldn't remember a time when Ryan held their children's hands. The fact they might not remember the fatherly gesture was heartbreaking, but that's what made this particular moment so dear.

Watching Bryce kick his head up and laugh at something her children piped, she felt a yearning form in her soul. She wanted this; she wanted endless moments with Bryce and her children, days filled with laughter, and a whole family of her own. Following them to a bubbling brook where glistening water slid over smooth stones like trout swimming down river, she prayed he wanted them, too.

Noah stepped on a large, oval rock, balancing, then a millisecond later, hop-stepped onto another. His blue shoes slid on the rocks, hands flailing to gain balance.

"Careful!" Brie shouted.

He laughed.

Bryce joined in with a hearty, full one.

"Flowers!" Phoebe bent and, with her small fingers, picked a few, tiny, purple flowers.

Settling beside her, Brie gazed. "What shall we do with them, sweet pea?"

She glanced up with big, serious eyes. "I'm making a faiwy bouquet."

"Okay, Mommy will help you."

"*Och*, lad!" Bryce shouted, then laughed full and strong.

She swiveled.

Noah stood near the center of the two foot or so wide brook, kicking a foot about, splashing water. "It's cold!"

" 'Tis! Best be sure with *yer* footing, or *ye'll* be walking the rest of the way sloshing in *yer* shoes," Bryce warned.

Giving Bryce a mischievous grin, Noah stretched his arms out and stepped on one, two, three, and four stones, then arrived on the other side. He shot his hands into the air.

When she spied Bryce placing a booted foot onto one of the smooth stones and Noah cheering, she couldn't tear her gaze away. The ache returned.

✦✦✦✦

Bryce ambled his way over the rocks, teetering, gaining his balance once again, then moved swiftly across.

"Yeah!" Noah high-fived him. "Let's go back!" He leapt across the wee bank onto a rock, one foot still soaked from his first trial and made his way sure-footedly across.

Pride swelled within him. "Fine job."

When Noah stepped off the last rock, he stooped down to investigate the undercarriage of a log, hair flopping over, keen to discover something else about the land.

Noah reminded Bryce of himself a few years ago— new to the land after being gone for several years, discovering the facets of Scotland. Yet, Scotland was Bryce's home and as much a part of him as his brogue, which had also thickened after he returned. Swiveling his head, he scanned the glen in search of Brie.

She sat cross-legged next to Phoebe with an array of flowers in her lap—two fairies in their natural habitat. Her hair shined angelically. She'd brought radiance to his life once again, and wee Phoebe and Noah created joy he could've never imagined.

They had one more full day in Scotland together. The week had flown by quickly, and he'd savored every moment. Yet, he didn't want their time together to end. He was more alive than ever. His soul had grown, and he'd have to make some decisions. Still, he couldn't follow them back to LA. He had another three months of filming for *Swords*, and Brie couldn't stay in Scotland. She had a job and the children needed to return to school. Yet, she didn't need to work. Christ, he worked enough to support a family.

A high-pitched scream pierced the air.

He shook his head. *Bryce, what are ye thinking? Brie just came back into your life. You're not ready to make a rash decision.*

Glancing up, he found himself studying the three of

them once again. Could he be a part of their future? He'd jumped at every acting opportunity, every occasion to grow his career and brand as an actor. Hell, he'd worked nonstop the last ten years, hadn't he? And he had more than enough to show for his tenacity. So, why was it difficult to jump into his personal life?

He knew how to act. Yet, he didn't feel the need to be someone else around Brie. Since they'd met, he'd been free to be himself, not who she wanted him to be like so many others. Still, he wondered if this was all too good to be true. Even in the loveliest of moments, something agitated him—like he was waiting for the screen to be removed and the truth unveiled.

But gazing at Brie and the wee ones, warmth simmered within, and he shoved aside biases, even as he wondered what the hell he'd do. Stepping into a starring role of father and husband were two entirely new roles...

Chapter 36

As the late afternoon sun splashed amber-and-gold flecks across the living room, Brie curled up on the soft couch with a warm cup of tea. After a wonderful, exhausting day out, she relished the quiet. Her children played quietly, while Bryce returned to his flat for a shower and change. He had been with them from dusk to dawn and appeared to be enjoying himself. She couldn't have imagined movie star Bryce Fraser would blend seamlessly with her small family. Of course, they had their moments—Noah's quick remark or Phoebe screaming when she didn't get her way, but Bryce took it all in stride.

Her phone vibrated on the quaint coffee table.

She peered at the non-familiar number and tapped the answer icon. "Hello?"

"Brielle, this is Camille Copeland with Book Sense Agency."

Sitting up, she sloshed tea. "How are you today, Camille?" She swiped at her tea-soaked blouse and set the teacup down.

"I'm well, thank you. I've just finished reviewing your manuscript, which is the reason I'm calling. I received an out-of-office notification on your email, but I wanted to inform you I've come to a decision."

Brie nibbled her lower lip. Out of the queries she'd sent the past few months, she'd received twelve near-immediate rejections, one rejection six weeks later, and one partial and two full requests. The day the world discovered her and Bryce's relationship, she'd also received another devastating blow—a full manuscript rejection with a general reply. Yet, two remained. Although Brie hoped she'd hear something soon, she never expected a phone call. Excitement danced in her belly, tickling and tingling as she awaited the agent's decision.

"I loved your memoir. It's honest, romantic, and powerful. It's also utterly unique. I haven't read something quite like this. We'd like to sign you."

Jumping off the couch, Brie threw her hands in the air and waved them like she held invisible pompoms, but she quickly told herself to relax and respond. "Thank you so much." They spoke about the agency's vision for Brie's memoir and recommended alterations. Writing was a process, and she understood edits would be required. She also agreed with the minor changes the agent recommended, though pushed back on providing more details about Bryce. The book was about her. And although Bryce became part of her story, she didn't want to expose him further. She'd stick to the honest truth and maintain the name changes in the book.

At the end of the call, Camille agreed and affirmed she'd be sending a contract for review via email shortly.

Disconnecting, Brie flopped on the couch as joy and disbelief swirled in her chest "Holy shit." She dialed Andrea and told her the good news. Luckily, it was nine a.m. in California, and Andrea was awake.

"Amazing!" Andrea said. "The best news EVER. My best friend is going to be a published author!"

"It's incredible, right?" Yet when the sound of

rough chopping echoed through the phone, she straightened. "Everything okay over there?"

"Just smashing away my work frustrations with breakfast Carbonara and Pancetta."

"No decision yet, huh?"

"No." Andrea blew a long breath into the phone. "More work and more promises with the onset of this acquisition, but no word yet on promotions."

"I'm sorry. You'll get some good news soon! I know it."

"It's fine. Tell me about Scotland. How're the kids and my favorite actor?"

Relaxing into the couch, she twirled the pendant on her necklace. "Scotland is as breathtaking as ever, and Bryce is amazing. He's so good with the kids, Andrea. I couldn't have ever imagined."

"That's great."

"But we're leaving in two days."

"Have you guys talked about…staying in touch?" Andrea prodded.

Brie sighed. "No. We're going to dinner tonight— just the two of us. We've only spent a few minutes alone since the kids and I've been in Scotland. And if I'm being honest, I'm kind of nervous to go out on a date, while his sister and brother-in-law watch the kids."

Andrea laughed. "Brie! I know there're a million thoughts going on in that head of yours, and you'll get them out when it's time, but for tonight, just enjoy. Have fun with Bryce."

But Brie wanted more than fun.

****

A few hours later, Brie and Bryce arrived at a

classic stone-faced building surrounded by a charming park with lush green trees, expansive grassy areas, and rustic wooden benches that welcomed visitors to sit awhile. Stepping through the restaurant entry, Brie tipped her head and stared. Elegant tapestries, gold chandeliers, and gilded walls accentuated tables set with white rose centerpieces and fine silver.

"Good evening." A greeter politely led them through the dining area to a private room with a large window overlooking the park and soft candlelight. A four-course dinner menu awaited them, along with champagne.

Watching the door close softly behind the hostess, Bryce lifted his glass to Brie's.

She touched glasses, then sipped, keeping her gaze on him and feeling the thrill of anticipation like the wine's zesty bubbles.

"Is it to *yer* liking?"

His eyes were like brilliant, blue orbs in the candlelight. She curled her lips as the crisp and fruity champagne tingled on her tongue. "It's wonderful. Thank you for inviting me. We haven't even eaten, and I'm enjoying the quiet already."

He grinned. "Aye, privacy."

"Yes. I'm not used to this…dining without my kids. In fact, the last time I enjoyed a quiet meal was"—Brie paused, thinking—"with you last spring. And that was unforgettable."

A grin spread across Bryce's face. "I'm honored. Although the last few days with the children have been delightful, I couldna wait to have some time alone with *ye*." Reaching across, he laced his long fingers with hers.

"Me, too." She'd dressed in a deep-turquoise, silky halter dress that brushed the floor, which Andrea insisted she buy for the trip, and fussed and curled her hair in loose waves. To complete the outfit, she wore the emerald necklace Bryce gifted her with gold drop earrings. She wanted tonight to be special. When she saw Bryce take one look at her and grin when he arrived in a crisp suit, white, collared shirt, black tie, and pants, movie-star ready, she silently thanked Andrea for the nudge.

After selecting her courses, she relaxed with her champagne. "I can't believe Rose and Ian are watching the kids tonight."

He cocked his head. "Why?"

"It's unexpected, and they…they just met us. I've had trouble trusting people with my kids, especially after everything that's happened." They hadn't talked about the press or the situation a few days ago, which were still so fresh and ripe in her mind, yet also seemed so long ago. Still, she didn't want to finish her sentence; she didn't want to ruin the enchanting night.

Bryce nodded. "They're family. The kids will have a blast, if they're not asleep yet."

She laughed softly. "I don't know if I thanked you properly, but this week has been incredible. My kids are so happy, and I feel refreshed. I don't know how to thank you."

He grinned, eyes crinkling at the corners. "It's been my pleasure."

When the first course arrived, they savored the start of their meal, eating slowly and enjoying the food and each other.

"What are your plans for the next few weeks?" she

asked.

"I've a few interviews scheduled, but I've another week off before *Swords* begins filming once again. I'll be running lines, going to set for fittings, and such. I've received the script, and"—he leaned forward—"I'll be producing a few episodes this season with Eleana. 'Tis a step I've wanted to take for a long time."

Gripping his hand, she flashed a smile. "That's wonderful. I'm so happy for you."

"Thank *ye*. I'm looking forward to the challenge and having more say in our show. 'Twill be an amazing season. We're shooting in a few different locations and introducing new characters I know the fans will embrace."

Excitement danced within her at the mention of different locations. *Will he be coming to L.A.?* "Will you be filming in Scotland?"

"Oh, aye. We've found many locations in Scotland that resemble the book descriptions with a wee bit of television magic, of course." He winked.

She giggled. "I love how you say wee."

"Do *ye*, now?" His eyes warmed.

"I do. It's adorable."

"*Och*, and here I am trying to impress *ye*."

"You've already done that."

With his gaze on hers, he lifted her hand to his lips.

The gentle kiss sent butterflies fluttering in her stomach. She leaned forward and pressed her lips softly to his, while Bryce drew her in further, deepening the kiss and swirling desire within her.

A swift knock separated them. The server entered and placed plates of venison and roasted chicken before them, filling the room with rich, savory aromas.

"Good thing the course arrived or I'd have to take another bite out of *ye*." Bryce grinned.

Brie giggled, though the slow, simmering burn remained.

Slicing his venison, he smiled wide. "Have *ye* also fit some writing in?"

"Some"—Brie speared an asparagus with her fork—"I've added a couple chapters to a new story idea I'm working on, inspired by my visit to Glencoe last spring. And, I actually spoke with an agent earlier this evening about my memoir. She wants to represent me. Can you believe it?"

He stilled a hand above mashed potatoes, while his body visibly stiffened. "Her offer doesn't have anything to do with what happened with the press, does it?"

She froze mid-bite. "No," she said quickly, then set her fork down. "I sent the manuscript and query a few months ago. Her decision was based on my story, not recent headlines."

He gazed at her quietly, blue eyes sharpening. "Am I in it?"

"You are—"

"Brie." He scowled and dropped his fork, leaning away, while his features altered quickly from anger to betrayal.

Panic gripped her and squeezed her chest. "You're right to be upset, but it's not what you think." She grasped his retreating hand with a shaky one. "I included you in the last portion of my memoir, because I wrote my story chronologically and that included Scotland, and when I returned home, but I didn't use your name. I promise, Bryce."

He gripped her hand; yet, he clenched his jaw.

Blinking back tears, she drew courage from within. "Remember I told you my memoir is about my divorce and the journey to finding myself again?"

He nodded swiftly.

"It is. It was. But my memoir took a completely different turn after I came to Scotland because"—she swallowed—"because part of my self-discovery was because of you."

"Truly, Brie?"

"Yes." She bobbed her head as her pulse raced. "Would you like to read it?"

"No." He exhaled. "I trust *ye*." He released her hand and picked up the wine glass, settling back into the chair.

Yet, the playful air that once was dissipated. Inhaling, Brie steadied herself. She remembered when Bryce offered to make some introductions and connect her to a few people in the industry, but she'd declined. Placing her hand on the table palm open, she breathed, willing him to touch her once again. Her entire body sighed when he gripped her hand.

For the next ten minutes, they talked about the highland games over vanilla *panna cotta* and fresh berries, and the tension in the air simmered. She couldn't believe her memoir almost fractured their relationship—she'd been so careful.

On the drive back to Aberdeen, the quiet between them sparked like invisible, electric current, while the radio hummed softly in the background. As the car slowed, she noted the intricate, rustic brick of an upscale apartment building. "Is this your place?"

Bryce turned, eyes darkening in the night. " 'Tis. Would *ye* come inside?"

She felt her heart flip-flop. "Yes."

Once inside, Bryce switched a single light on and tugged Brie toward him, brushing his lips along the side of her neck, over the curve of her jaw, and then captured her lips.

His kisses were like a dream—clearing her mind and urging her to another space. Brie slipped her arms up, encircling his neck and slid the jacket off his muscular frame.

Caressing her shoulder, he skimmed a wide, calloused palm up her bare back and then unfastened the single clasp at her neck. The dress floated to the floor in an emerald-green cloud.

She watched as Bryce's gaze roamed her body, and then gasped when he hoisted her, fastening her legs around his waist. Desire deepened Bryce's eyes, making them dark and moody like the sky before a storm, and he seized her mouth greedily once again, carrying her to the bedroom.

She didn't protest the urgency. She'd waited for months and met him need for need, unfastening his tie and fisting her hands in his curls. She fell with him on the bed, and quickly, not a single item of clothing remained. Bryce's hands roamed and claimed, while his lips were hot and urgent on hers. With each graze, Brie flew, ignited by his touch and the warmth of his body against hers, and her lashes fluttered. She floated as if she traveled to another dimension, another galaxy where stars sparkled and time didn't exist.

When they joined, fitting perfectly together as one, she soared. Winging her eyes open, she stared at his handsome face—the way his hair curled over his temple and the depth in his eyes when he looked at her. Love burst inside her. Did he know? Did he know how utterly and completely in love she was? That what was between them hadn't left, but burned even brighter? "Bryce…" Emotion filled her chest and clogged her throat. She drew his head closer and kissed him deeply, giving him all of her.

Chapter 37

"Ready for your first Highland games, kiddos?" Brie asked.

"Yes!" the kids sang.

Phoebe twirled in her new Scottish dancing dress complete with a green tartan and puffed sleeves, while Noah stood like a mini-warrior in a kilt—both courtesy of Bryce.

With an inhale, Brie smoothed the green-and-blue tartan skirt with interlocking stripes of brick-red and gold, feeling the soft fabric under her clammy hands. She was still nervous about going to the games. With so many people in attendance, she hoped she, Bryce, and her children would slip in undetected. Perhaps, the gifted apparel was made to help them fit in. Yet, she wondered about the tartan. "Is this a specific family tartan?"

"Aye." Bryce smiled. "Clan Finlay."

"Clan Finlay," she repeated in awe and gazed at the fabric. *Her* family's ancient clan. He'd taken the time to consider her family's past along with her presence in Scotland. As she stroked the fabric, she felt the tension within her ease and strength flow through her veins like the bold crisscross design of the Finlay tartan. "Thank you so much. I still want to take the kids to Invercauld Estate and Braemar Castle."

He wove his hand through hers. "We can visit

Braemar Castle later this afternoon. It's near the games."

She flashed a smile. "I'd like that."

"Bryce, you said this was a kilt, right?" Noah frowned.

"Aye, I did." He released Brie's hand and squatted to Noah's level. "Is something the matter?"

He crinkled his little nose. "It looks like a skirt."

Brie grinned. " 'Tis actually an ancient style of dress, lad. The fiercest, strongest warriors wore them and still do."

"Really?" Noah eyed the kilt suspiciously, then glanced back at Bryce.

"Aye, 'tis the truth."

"You're wearing one, too."

"I am. And *ye'll* see many fine competitors and athletes wearing them today, as well."

The answer seemed to pacify Noah who squared his shoulders before grabbing a tractor to take on the drive.

Picking up her baby, Phoebe followed Noah.

"Wait for us, kids." She slid a look at Bryce. "I know I was excited to go to the Highland Games and see you toss the caber and visit with the MacDonalds, but are you sure this is a good idea?"

He touched her shoulder. "All will be well, Brie."

Although they'd visited local areas that were sparsely populated this week, save for the amusement park, they had enjoyed this trip undisturbed. But the Braemar Gathering was a large gathering of people. How could they know who all was in attendance? When she glanced back at Bryce as he tied his boots, she couldn't help but notice the way his brows jammed together.

She smoothed the tartan skirt and strode forward, ignoring the prickling in her gut.

****

They arrived at The Princess Royal and Duke of Fife Memorial Park in Braemar, following a line of cars into a parking lot surrounded by a dense line of forest-green pines and golden-tipped evergreens. Anxiousness scurried along Brie's nerves.

People strolled and dashed toward the entrance dressed in kilts, traditional Scottish garb, as well as plain and athletic clothes, while the sound of bagpipes pierced the air.

She strode forward through the open gates, holding Phoebe's hand and breathed. *Everything will be fine.* Glancing at Bryce, she noted he adjusted his cap, drawing the bill lower.

Bleachers curved around the mossy-green field already swelling with people, while athletes stretched and circled the field. Tiny dancers in bold-red and fierce-blue leapt and skipped. Behind the field, sage mountains stood reverently bathed in the brilliant sun's rays, while white-and-gray clouds dotted the sky.

When the announcer's thick voice carried across the loudspeakers, he asked for everyone to take their seats. Music drifted toward them, dancing on the cool air and then grew louder with the drumming and piping of a marching band.

Finding their seats in the second row to the front, Brie glanced right and left. Photographers speckled around the field. She nibbled her lip as a large pipe band entered the stadium with a Chief leading the way with a staff and feathered bonnet, diced red-and-black hose and staff, marching in perfect cadence to the lively music.

"Look, Mommy!" Phoebe pointed toward the decorated band.

"Drums!" Noah squealed.

"I see, sweeties." She nodded, though her heart thudded.

"Aye, 'tis a grand sight," Bryce acknowledged. "The local Chieftain and marching band are welcoming *ye* to the games."

The mechanical sound of pictures being taken clicked in Brie's ears. She whirled, only to realize a member of the press stood a few feet away with his automatic camera, snapping pictures of the procession. She relaxed.

Following the band, the royal family entered, and the games commenced. Athletes raced around the circular track, while large men in kilts threw hammers on one side of the infield, and vibrant dancers followed a tall man with a hat toward the stage at the opposite end.

Bryce leaned over. "I need to check in. If *ye* walk around with the children, let me know, so I can come find *ye*."

She smiled. "I will."

Although the games were entertaining, the kids grew antsy quickly, getting up and down, leaning into other people, and bouncing in their seats.

Brie sent a quick text to Bryce, then tucked one of Noah's and Phoebe's hands in each of hers and strolled toward the beautiful female performers with bold-red, deep-blue, and rich-maroon costumes complete with tartan skirts of a similar colored pattern. Approaching,

Brie realized the current dancers were around Phoebe's age.

They leapt in the air, feet moving to and fro, delicately toeing their routines, while their hands fisted on their hips for a moment. With the quickening of a bagpipe behind them, they jutted their hands in the air and hopped back and forth.

At first, Phoebe stood mesmerized, then she began happily skipping below the stage.

"Aren't *ye* a bonnie, wee dancer!" a woman acknowledged with a pile of dark curls. "Perhaps next year, *ye* can join, as well?"

"Yes!" Phoebe spun.

Brie nodded, though her gaze darted from person to person as the crowd swelled around them. Family members and onlookers cheered the little dancers on, shouting encouragement in English and Gaelic, and brushed against her. She didn't know what next year held and surrounded by all the Scots and tourists, she wondered just where she belonged. Yes, she wore a Finlay tartan, but she wasn't Scottish. She took a deliberate step back and collided with a full-figured woman in a blue dress. "Oh, I'm sorry!"

"Not a problem," she said in an American accent, then eyed Brie. "Are one of the dancers yours? You look familiar."

Brie shook her head as her pulse *tap-tapped*. "No. I don't think so."

"Finlay?" a familiar voice said.

Brie angled her head.

A fair-haired woman holding a white-blonde haired girl with a joyous grin approached.

"Holly?" Relief flooded her. "What are you doing

here?"

"We've come to watch the games, of course." She wrapped her in a light hug and leaned close. "I can't imagine what *yer* going through. How are *ye*?"

As they separated, Brie sighed. She was glad to see a familiar, friendly face. "Better since seeing you. There're so many people here."

"Aye." Holly glanced around Brie and flashed a smile. "Are these *yer* wee ones?"

"They are—Phoebe and Noah," Brie introduced. "Can you say hello to Miss Holly, Finlay, and Daniel?"

Noah greeted them, while Phoebe grinned coyly and spun back around, mesmerized by the dancers.

Holly leaned forward. "And where is Fraser?"

"Getting ready to throw the caber for charity."

She nodded.

When the music halted, applause and cheers rang out for the tiny dancers. A moment later, an announcer welcomed the next age group to the stage, and the music commenced once again.

Little Finlay clapped and cheered, then joined Phoebe dancing and hopping.

Holly smiled. "They're quite the pair."

"They are." Brie grinned, watching their pint-sized fairies, then leaned closer. "I wanted to tell you I started writing a new book—a fantasy with some historical fiction, and I'm naming the main character, Finlay. She's a maiden turned warrior who grasps ancient strength to wield the gold-hilted sword, in order to save her family from the goddess, Beira."

Her smile widened. "That sounds brilliant."

"Phoebe!" a tiny voice bellowed.

Lucy charged toward them in a green-and-red

tartan skirt, white blouse, and green vest followed closely by Archie, Rose, and Ian.

"Lucy!" Phoebe squealed and flung her arms around her. "I wuv your dress."

"Oh, so they've found *ye*." Rose huffed a breath, then lifted a brow toward the MacDonalds.

"Rose and Ian Fitzgibbons, and Archie and Lucy."

"Pleasure." Holly introduced herself.

"We met last spring in Glencoe," Brie explained.

With a wink, Holly smiled warmly. "Aye, we're old acquaintances."

"That's wonderful. How are *ye* enjoying the games?" Rose asked.

"I saw this huge guy throw a big rock!" Noah mimicked launching a boulder. "It flew."

Brie laughed softly, while everyone chuckled.

They stayed to watch Lucy dance and then grabbed food, talking and laughing.

But soon the MacDonalds left to find their own seats on the opposite side.

Next, Ian, Rose, their kids, and Noah disappeared for treats.

Brie held fast to Phoebe's hand and wove around crowds of fans and onlookers in search of a restroom. Without the familiar faces around her, the question that had been on her mind the last few days returned. Did she belong here?

****

Seated in the stands, Brie was grateful Rose and Ian were snugged beside them, and she knew Bryce was to thank. Thousands of people were in attendance; yet, she still worried someone would spot them.

Watching an athlete hoist a large telephone pole

aka caber in his thick hands, she felt her mouth flop open. She'd seen a brief clip of the highland games on television, but that didn't compare to watching in real life.

The gigantic athlete lunged forward and then ran across the field, balancing the tall caber between his hands and shoulder. With a mighty roar, he tossed the giant pole.

" 'Tis something, isn't it?" Rose asked.

"It sure is," Brie replied.

Another man followed with a thick middle and bald head. He strode forward, then stumbled back. With a loud curse, he angled himself and jogged forward once again, holding the larger-than-life caber.

"Wow! Did you see that guy?" Noah asked. "He's huge!"

"Aye, he is, but he doesna have a good grip." Ian pointed. "Their goal is to get the caber the farthest, and his caber came back toward him, which won't offer much momentum. *Ye* want to flip the caber end-over-end, ye see. Right now, they're getting ready for the event with a few practice tosses."

"Have ye done it, Da?" Archie asked.

With a snort, Rose slid a smirk toward Ian.

He puffed his chest. "Aye, I've tried it."

Rose rolled with laughter.

Grinning, Brie scanned the field for Bryce just as the announcer returned to the microphone.

"Please welcome our athletes from around the world and a very special guest, Scotland's own Bryce Fraser to start us off."

Entering the field clad in a soft-blue and earthy-brown Fraser hunting kilt and fitted white sleeves beside other athletes, Bryce drew her attention and the crowd's. Cheers filled the stadium. He waved and inclined his head toward the fans, while Brie's chest warmed. He looked as impressive as the athletes, but was he seriously picking up the caber? She didn't doubt his strength, but those cabers were huge. She chewed her lip, while he strode toward the caber and rubbed his hands together.

With two hands, he gripped the base of the caber, lifted the beam slightly with his fingers woven together, and lurched forward down the green. Slowly, he ran, gathering speed, then lifted his arms and threw the caber, which flipped on end in the grass and landed horizontally at three o'clock.

"Yeah, Bryce!" Brie yelled.

"Yay, Bryce!" the kids shouted.

"Yeah, Uncle!"

"Good job, brother!" Rose shouted.

Slowly, Brie noticed rubbernecking around her. As whispers drifted, her stomach knotted and tangled.

"It's them!" someone shouted.

"Brielle Hunter," another voice remarked.

Swiveling, she found audience members staring, while others lifted phones for pictures.

Click! Flash! Click! The press snapped photos from the side.

She froze.

"Are *ye* okay, Brie?" Rose asked.

Brie hugged Phoebe close and grabbed Noah's hand. "I…what should we do? I don't want to take away from the athletes."

Cameras continued to click, and people gathered. Brie's pulse pounded wildly in her ears. She pressed her eyes close for a millisecond, and when she opened them, she saw Bryce marching toward her, red curls flying.

"Brielle!" he roared. "Get away from her!"

"Bryce!" people shouted.

He shoved press members aside and climbed through the mob with fury etched in his features. Stopping before them, his brows jammed together and chest heaved. "Are *ye* all right?"

She bobbed her head, but her stomach squeezed.

"Do *ye* want to stay or go?"

"I think we should go."

He nodded and seized her hand, while Brie told the children they were leaving.

They whined and dragged their feet as she snaked through the bleachers with Bryce; yet, a few people stood and took pictures, hindering their exit.

"Get out of the way!" someone yelled.

"Go with them, Ian," Rose urged.

With a strong hand, Ian weaved through the crowd with Bryce and shepherded Brie and the children to the car.

And although the press snapped a few pictures, only two trailed after them.

"Why do we have to go?" Noah pouted. "Archie said there would be sack races, and we could run."

"I know, honey." She didn't know what else to say. She didn't want to take away from the competition, but she also didn't want to remain under scrutiny. As they drove away, she watched Ian amble back toward the games' entry. Bryce's family had surrounded her and her children, while he protected them. She felt the support of a family and siblings she never had; yet, had only just met. But now more than ever, she wondered where they fit. She rubbed her fingers on the Finlay tartan, which now felt stiff and brittle.

Arriving at Braemar Castle, Brie stepped out of the SUV and gulped fresh air. She unbuckled the kids, and they hiked toward the castle. With tall towers stretching toward the sky and gray stone encircling the base, the castle picturesquely resembled one she'd find in one of Phoebe's fairytale books. But she wasn't in a fairytale.

"It's like a giant sand castle!" Noah said.

Bryce laughed softly.

Brie tugged her sweater up and swiped a hand through her hair. She was glad her children could quickly push past the uncomfortable few minutes before they left the gathering, but she had yet to find her bearing. When she blinked, she saw a camera pointing.

Resting a hand on her forearm, Bryce drew her attention. "Brie?"

She shook her head. "I just don't understand why, I mean, I know you're a TV star, but we're just us. Why are people so interested?"

Bryce drew a breath. "Because *yer* with me. People will always be interested who I date."

She peered, brows drawing together. "So, we're dating?"

"Well, I don't know if *ye'd* exactly call this last week dating." His eyes shone.

"But what are we, Bryce?" She continued walking up the path toward the castle. The magnificent structure had stood for hundreds of years and symbolized a sense of permanency for the clan Farquharson, but what about her and her children? Sure, she had ancestral roots in

Scotland and made a few wonderful connections, but she'd created a stable homelife in Lakewood. Was that something she was willing to give up?

"I don't know, Brie." He tucked a hand in hers. "I'm figuring that out myself, but I'm here with *ye*."

She gazed at Bryce. To simply be with him wasn't enough any longer. She needed to decide what she wanted for her future.

Chapter 38

After tucking her exhausted children into bed for a quick nap, Brie found Bryce standing in the doorway, gazing at Noah and Phoebe with a loving, soft smile. Bryce remained by their side from the moment the press swarmed and put their welfare before his own. He was protective, kind, and genuinely cared for her and her children. He was everything she'd ever hoped for in a partner, but never imagined in her wildest dreams was attainable after Ryan shattered her heart. Bryce was incredible. No other word described him, but she needed more.

With misty eyes, she excused herself. In her room, she sat on the edge of the bed, peering at the closed whitewashed wooden door. She, Phoebe, and Noah were leaving in less than twenty-four hours, and she still didn't know where she and Bryce stood. Would they continue what they'd rekindled here with a cross-Atlantic relationship? Even thinking about a long-distance relationship sounded difficult. She didn't know how it would work, or even if one could. Raking her hands through her hair, she slipped strands behind her ears.

She'd almost said *I love you* last night, but she held back, keeping those three precious words tucked protectively inside. But she knew how she felt just like when she was pregnant with Noah and Phoebe before the tests displayed those wonderful positive signs. She felt the love of another deep within her soul, blazing brightly. She didn't know what tomorrow held, but she had to tell him. She would forever regret if she kept her feelings a secret and forwent a future of happiness with Bryce. Remembering a line from one of the memoirs she'd read, she closed her eyes and inhaled. *Do what makes you happy and be with someone who makes you happy.* The advice was simple. All she needed to do was grasp happiness.

The pieces of her life were falling into place—her children were healthy and thriving, her memoir would be represented by a wonderful agent, then pitched to publishers, and one day, Brie would be a career author. She could visualize a future where she wrote books for a living, had more time for her children, and did something she loved. And, she could imagine a full life with Bryce. He made her happy. Her entire being glowed when she was around him, and her heart soared. She had to take the next step. Changing out of the tartan skirt, she slipped into a pink-and-green floral summer dress with shiny pearl buttons, then ran a brush through her hair and touched up her lip gloss. She wasn't scared or nervous, but giddy with the knowledge she'd found love.

A few minutes later, she strolled into the main living area, walking toward Bryce who sat on the couch, back turned. "Thank you for helping with the kids." She attempted to keep her voice from pitching with excitement. "I—"

"I need to ask *ye* something." He swung around, and his features darkened like the late afternoon shadows—a deep frown wedged between his brows, while his jaw tightened.

Unease fluttered in her chest. "Of course."

He shoved up to standing and paced through the small kitchen. "Why did *ye* write about me?" Anger and hurt laced his tongue.

"What do you…" She began and then noticed her notebook wide open on the coffee table. She strode forward. "Bryce, it's not what you think."

He whirled. "Explain it, then because *ye* just told me last night an agent was interested in seeing your pages—*yer* story, but what I just read had my name all over it. Am I to be paraded around the gossip columns again, Brie? I trusted *ye*."

"No." She shook her head. *Oh, my God.* "Bryce, my memoir isn't about you. I mean, yes, you're in the book, but the book is about me."

"Is that why *ye* returned to Scotland? To finish *yer* book?"

She flinched as hurt tore through her. "You know why I came back."

He clenched his jaw, while anger stormed in his eyes.

"Bryce, I'd never hurt you intentionally. I told you I was writing a book about me, a memoir."

"Aye. A book about *yer* divorce."

"It was…at first." She released a breath. "But the memoir became more…more about rediscovering who I was as a person and a woman—who I am—and what makes me happy. Part of that discovery happened when I journeyed across the Atlantic to Scotland and explored and…met you. You became part of my story, and I had to include you. I promise, I changed your name and the show's title, but I had to include our story."

He tilted his head. "Our story?"

Brie tried not to focus on the croak when the two words escaped his lips. "Yes."

With a quick swivel of his head, Bryce glanced at the coffee table, then toward the stairwell, and finally, back at Brie. His nostrils flared and full lips thinned into a line. "I have to go." He strode out of the cottage.

The patchy sunlight pierced the kitchen for a moment, then quickly disappeared when the door closed firmly behind him. She lifted a hand to her mouth. "What have I done?"

****

The following morning, rain blurred the view from her bedroom window. Brie hadn't slept all night. She lay awake, agonizing about the night before when their incredible week in Scotland came to a startling halt because of something in her notebook. After hearing the door close, she'd strode over to the coffee table and picked up her journal, which held a portion of her first memoir draft and her heart tucked between the floral bookends. And yet, somehow, she hadn't been careful enough.

When she opened the journal to where the pink ribbon split the pages, she narrowed her gaze. The pages were near the midpoint and highlighted her first visit to the set of *Swords of Scotland*.

April 29

I stood in a crowd of women hoping to catch sight of Bryce as Alexander James Mackenzie. His face appeared on more than one T-shirted bosom, while his name floated in every conversation around me. Most fans were eager to catch a glimpse of him, others wanted a selfie for their social accounts, and others, to my surprise—hadn't Bryce told me?—awaited him as their destined, true love. Even Ms. Crazy herself was there. Although I'm not sure she recognized me from our brief meeting.

They all wanted him, but I was dating him. Me. Brielle Finlay Hunter, just a mom from Lakewood, California, dating the television King of Scotland. I still can't believe this is happening. I should ask Andrea to pinch me!

Watching Bryce ride up the glen on a majestic, black Friesian with his sword wielding in the air, curly red hair flying, I realized: I am dating Alexander James Mackenzie.

Brie snapped the journal closed. The sound of her heart echoed in her ears, while her children giggled in the background. The final draft of her memoir was so much different from her journal—what Bryce found—but he only saw what was in front of him. She waited for him to return for dinner like almost every night that week and even texted, asking if they could speak further, but he never returned.

She made spaghetti and meat sauce—one of her favorite comfort foods—allowing the meaty aroma to fill the cottage. Yet, the meal didn't comfort her. Her children devoured the pasta, but they, too, noticed Bryce's absence. She made an excuse for him, and she hated making excuses. She used to excuse Ryan for all of his tardiness, and now she was doing the same for Bryce. But she knew Bryce was processing. She'd seen the contemplation in his eyes—the way the clear blue swirled and clouded like a storm ready to rage. But in just a few hours, she'd return to L.A. She wished desperately that she could talk to him, but she didn't want to push him away further. So, she did the only thing she could—she tidied up the cottage and began packing, preparing to leave Bryce once again, fighting tears and breathing through the nausea twisting her stomach.

Chapter 39

Bryce parked in front of the cottage. After a five-mile run at dawn didn't do anything more to aid his situation than the Scotch last night, he drove and found himself here. He studied the wee cottage and thought of Brie and the children. They deserved a good-bye. Although he almost stayed away, he couldn't, not even with the fresh craig in his heart.

Hadn't he told Brie about the Super Fans? Hadn't she met Ms. Crazy? Perhaps she was the actress. Yet, even as the concept crossed his mind, his heart told him otherwise. He *knew* Brie. But the doubt still lingered like the morning mist.

He'd planned the conversation—what he would say and how. He was ready. With a swift crank of the door handle, he stepped out, runners crunching in the gravel. A warm, yellow hue radiated from the cottage interior. He knocked quietly, even as rage simmered in his tight fists.

Brie opened the door in a green shift and bare feet, hair framing her face in soft waves and falling down her shoulders.

The sight of her sent lust through his loins; yet, the sting in his chest was stronger. "Can I come inside?"

With a quiet nod, she opened the door.

The counters shone, floors looked spotless, and a few bags rested near the entry. He'd told her not to clean; yet, she did so anyway. Annoyance prickled up his spine. "Why did ye clean?"

"Why...?" Brie's brows pitched. "You're asking why I cleaned?"

"Aye."

"Because I believe in cleaning up after myself and my children, especially when someone takes care of everything else. Besides, I couldn't sleep." Turning on a bare heel, she strode away and picked up the journal on the coffee table. Spinning around, she held up the diary, eyes darkening like a dense, forest wall. "Is this what you wanted to talk about, or do you want to continue talking about my housecleaning skills?"

Bryce noted her voice rose an octave; yet, she still spoke in hushed tones. He glanced toward the stairwell. Darkness enveloped save for a wisp of light from the kitchen where they stood and not another sound could be heard. He tore his cap off and raked a hand through his hair. "Why did *ye* write it?"

"I told you I've been writing a memoir about me, and then I came to Scotland and I continued writing. Your home enveloped, welcomed, and rejuvenated me, and I had to write it down. All of it."

"And what of the part about me?"

"You ended up in my book because you...you were a part of my life." Her bottom lip wobbled.

He leaned down. "But why?"

"Why?"

He nodded.

Lifting her chin, Brie trained those majestic green eyes on him. "Because I love you, okay?"

The air whooshed out. He'd been sucker punched in the gut, again. "If that were true, *ye* would never have written about me. *Ye* know I value my privacy. I've told *ye* about Kathryn Bailey and the press, and *ye* refused to listen."

"How can you stand there and say that? I know you value your privacy. I'd never jeopardize that, Bryce. I never said one word to the press about us, even when they arrived on my doorstep. I kept silent, tucking away what we had in my heart, and I've already apologized for Jasmine and Ryan. Even with my memoir, I changed names and your show's title and excluded portions"—she flapped the memoir, shuffling pages as tears shone in her eyes—"that would jeopardize your privacy. But no, you wouldn't wait for me to explain. Oh, and you know what else? I'm using a pen name, as well, so you're not…connected to me anymore."

"That's not what—"

"Not what you want?" She crossed her arms across her chest, tucking the book tight. "Well then tell me, Bryce, what do you want? I would really like to know."

He noted the way her eyes clouded with anger like a storm raging over a glen. Clenching his jaw, he gazed around the quaint cottage. Almost every trace of Brie and the children was gone, save for wee shoes by the door and the toys he'd purchased in a box beside the television. With a puff of breath, he pivoted to face her once again. " 'Tis not that easy."

"It is." Her voice cracked. "What do you want, Bryce?"

He exhaled. The very same question roamed his own mind during his morning run and when he knocked on the door. "Brielle…"

"What do you want?"

He opened his mouth; yet, the words wouldn't

come.

She shook her head, waves tossing like a torrent of wind in the sand. "I'm such an idiot. I thought this last week meant something to you—that we meant something to you, but I was wrong."

"*Ye* do." He raked a hand through his hair. "Christ, Brie, I need time."

"Time? Our time has run out. We're leaving shortly, and don't worry, I'll get over you just like I did before. Because you know what? I'm done fantasizing. I need something real, something permanent, and someone who is proud to say he's with me and my kids." She pressed a fingertip to her chest, while tears glossed, then streaked down her pale cheeks. "I need a warrior who's willing to fight for me and fight for love. I won't settle for anything less."

He wished he could pause for a moment to gather his bearings and replay what happened the last few minutes. He'd rehearsed the conversation in his head, but the result was nothing like he planned. He didn't want to hurt her. Reaching out, he grasped her arms. "Brie, if *ye'd* just give me a damn minute."

She pressed her eyelids closed, tumbling another tear. "I can't. I have nothing more to give you, Bryce." And with that statement, she tore past and disappeared up the stairwell.

Chapter 40

Hearing the squeak of the front door handle, Brie kept climbing. At the top of the stairs, she slid to the floor and let the tears flow. He didn't want her. She'd fallen in love with Bryce once and left. Leaving him was one of the hardest things she ever had to do, and in just a few short hours, she'd leave again. And yet, he'd just stood there. He didn't fight for her; he didn't even try. As a cry tore through her, she dropped her head into her knees. She knew how to take care of herself and her children. She'd been a mother for years. She didn't need a man who didn't want her. Swiping a hand over damp cheeks, she sniffled. She could do it again.

Two hours later, the press stood ready with cameras in hand when they arrived at Aberdeen International Airport. But this time, a car followed them with bodyguards—Bryce's doing, of course—and she was grateful, even while her heart bled from the fresh break. She unbuckled her children, then stepped out of the vehicle where paparazzi shouted questions a few feet away.

A tall, sandy-haired man sidled up beside the car dressed in black, while another man with an impressive beard and tattoos stood opposite like a human barrier.

She gripped Phoebe's and Noah's hands, ready to start their journey home.

"How was your time with Bryce, Ms. Hunter?" a

reporter shouted in her face.

"Step aside, please." The tall bodyguard guided them through the throng of journalists.

The unmistakable *Click! Flash Click*! of cameras blinked in their faces.

"Brielle! Can ye share any news?" A reporter stuck a wide-mouthed lens near her face.

She pivoted and kept striding forward.

"Where's Bryce?"

"Did you break up?"

"Are you still together?"

"Can you tell us what's in your future?"

Noah glanced at a paparazzo, then tugged her hand. "Why are they asking questions about Bryce?"

"We'll talk about it on the plane." Brie strode forward and circled toward check-in. *Time to go home*.

They arrived at LAX in the sunny, yet smoggy midafternoon the following day.

A patrol car waited outside their house—courtesy of the home owners' association she imagined—to keep reporters at bay. But other than the patrol and a few neighbors' cars, she recognized, her street seemed normal. Perhaps they found a better story.

Phoebe and Noah greeted the officer sleepily and shuffled up the walkway.

After baths, she tucked them into bed, then dropped straight onto her own comforter. She awoke at midnight in a fog of jet lag and sorrow. Tears soaked her pillow. "Bryce," she cried. Memories flooded her mind—him smiling up at Noah crossing the rocky brook, holding a slow worm for Phoebe to touch, riding a rollercoaster with Noah, twirling Phoebe with flowers in her hair, holding her hand as natural as breathing, and making love until her heart burst.

Why did she say *yes*? Why had she returned to Scotland? Was she a glutton for pain? As sorrow raked through her, she blew a heavy breath. But she knew deep down in her heart, she knew why she returned. She might have desired to escape the paparazzi, but she yearned for Bryce—to see him once more and see if they could work. And they had, for a short while, until reality caught up. *But unlike television, we can't just cut and do another take*. What was between them was over. Truly over.

By the time lunch rolled around the next day, Noah and Phoebe rubbed their eyes.

Brie made grilled cheeses and tucked them in for a nap.

Noah barely complained.

Although Brie attempted to nap, as well, she knew Ryan was stopping by to see the kids before dinner, so she started laundry and waited.

He arrived at three p.m. "They're asleep?"

"Yes," Brie acknowledged. "It's the middle of the night in Scotland. They're not used to our time zone yet. I'm giving them a few hours, then I'll wake them."

He nodded.

Brie studied him. Ryan wore a collared shirt like normal and pleated shorts; yet, he also wore a pensive expression and was quieter than normal. He was different.

Stepping forward, he cleared his throat. "There's something I wanted to talk to you about. Something we need to talk about."

"What is it, Ryan? Because like the kids, I'm tired." Brie crossed her arms.

"I'm leaving Jasmine."

Brie widened her eyes. "What? Why?"

"Because we belong together." He extended a hand and caressed her arm. "We always have."

Recoiling, she unfolded her arms and stepped back. She couldn't believe what she was hearing. "No, Ryan, we don't. We're divorced. We had our chance. That's over now."

He smoothed a hand over his slicked hair. "Don't you see I want to make things right? I want to be a family again, Brie. You, me, and the kids."

She lifted her chin. "Why?"

His brows pinched together. "Why?"

"Yes, why now? Why the sudden change, Ryan? Almost two years ago, you didn't want me. You left the kids and me behind. I would've done anything to keep our family together, but you tore us apart."

He reached for her again. "I wanted you. I've always wanted you. You just couldn't accept me for who I was, but we can be a family again."

She shook her head. She was looking forward. She'd finally found herself and realized what real love was, even if she couldn't have it. The only feeling she had for Ryan was annoyance, and she was too tired to discuss further. Pivoting toward the door, she swiped a hand through the air. "Ryan, I think you should go. I'll call you when the kids wake up."

He bowed his head.

"Ryan?"

"Jasmine's pregnant."

"What?" She squeaked.

He lifted his head and swallowed, Adam's apple bobbing. "She's pregnant."

Brie gasped.

"I'll be a dad again. Maybe this time, I won't screw it up."

Once the initial shock wore off, she gazed at Ryan. Instead of his normal air of arrogance, he appeared sincere. Perhaps like finding her own happiness again, this would be his second chance. She lifted a hand and touched his arm. "Noah and Phoebe will always be a part of your life. They love you. Now's your chance to be a better father for them and your new child."

He bobbed his head, then straightened and adjusted his shirt. "Anyway, let me know when the kids are up. It's Sunday. Maybe Jasmine and I can take them miniature golfing or something."

"I'm sure they'd love that."

"Great. I'll, uh, see you later." He strode out.

Releasing a breath, she closed the door and padded to her bedroom, pausing for a moment to touch her fingertips to a picture of her, Noah, and Phoebe on the wall from a year ago. They'd all grown. A new season of happiness would soon begin for her children and Ryan; yet, she felt a tug of jealousy. She wished she was the one with happy news. Drawing herself a bath, she sat in the hot water, still raw with emotion from the ache of saying good-bye to Bryce and confusion with Ryan's revelation. The hot, bubbled lavender water should've calmed her—that's what the bottle noted. *Calming bath bubbles*. She put a few dollops in the bath water each night for her children. The bubbles worked. *For them.*

A few minutes later, she stepped out of the tub, toweled off, and wrapped herself in a robe. Her floral journal and pen rested on her small, bedside desk. She tugged the chair out and grasped the pen. She didn't have to think. The words flowed like the ink from the black gel pen.

I love Bryce, but sometimes, love isn't enough—not when the world is tearing you apart. We couldn't find a way to make this work. Not an easy way, at least.

I've always been told love was supposed to be easy. Mom said falling for Dad was the easiest thing she ever did—like breathing. But then again, they'd met as high schoolers, still kids themselves without the complicated bits of adulthood thrust in between their relationship. Well, at least until the war came along.

My first love broke me, and I thought falling in love again would be impossible. Yet, I fell. I fell incredibly, deeply, and passionately in love with Bryce Fraser. Then, we parted, and I thought we said good-bye forever, until our lives collided once again. I hoped we could work, and we did—the kids and I and Bryce blended together seamlessly for a while. Now, I know that a life with him isn't possible. I'm grateful for the love he gave me, even if he couldn't find the words in his heart. And, I'm grateful for loving him

I know I am worthy of love. And, I'm okay. I realized this long before I met Bryce: I am strong.

I can be me.

I can be a mom.

I know I can depend on myself and what to expect when it's just me.

I am strong. Even as my heart aches, I am strong.

****

The following afternoon, Andrea strolled into Brie's house with steaming, salty Chinese food and wine. "Have I mentioned how much I like Labor Day?

An extra day to the weekend to do whatever the hell I want."

Brie snorted. "You did. Thanks for coming over."

"Of course." She plopped the takeout bag on the coffee table and embraced Brie.

Brie held on, feeling the stress and sadness of the last few days seep from her body. Hugging Andrea was like wrapping herself in a cozy blanket. Her hugs said *I'm here for you* without uttering a word. When she finally released her, Brie invited Andrea to sit and tucked her legs beneath her. "The kids are with Ryan and Jasmine."

"You told me." Andrea rested a hand on Brie's arm. "Now, how are you, bestie?"

"I've been better." Yet, her lip trembled.

"Oh, Brie…"

"He didn't want me," she cried.

Andrea let her cry on her shoulder—one big, snotty, sobby cry after another. Brie thought she'd cried all her tears the night before, but she was wrong. They poured out like a torrential rain. She cried until her eyes burned and the sobs subsided.

As she dug a fork into the vegetable chow mein, she told Andrea about Bryce and then about Ryan and Jasmine and the new baby.

When they arrived to pick up Noah and Phoebe earlier that morning, they told the kids the news—they were getting married and having a baby.

Phoebe was excited about the baby, being the baby lover.

Noah quietly accepted the information.

Brie was sure both would have more questions when they returned home, especially Noah—her brave, sensitive, and protective boy—and she'd readily answer them. They deserved all the explanation she could give them, and support, during this change. Yet, she couldn't deny the stab of jealousy for Ryan moving on with his life.

Blowing out a breath, Andrea speared a sweet and sour chicken. "Wow."

"Yeah." She leaned her head on the couch. Her lids were heavy.

"I never thought…geez, Brie. I never thought Ryan would marry her."

"I know. Especially after he said he still wanted me, but I think he was afraid, you know? Afraid of messing up another family." She sat up. "He cares about her, and I really hope they're happy."

"Wow," Andrea repeated, then gulped her wine and faced Brie. "And you're sure things between you and Bryce are…over?"

Brie's chest pinched. "It's over. I emailed him a copy of the memoir while on the plane."

"Why?"

She shrugged. "So, he has some peace of mind, I guess?

"And, he responded?" Andrea prodded.

"No. I don't expect him to reply, either."

With a nod, Andrea poured Brie more wine.

She lifted the cool glass to her lips, but she didn't drink. Words weighed on her heart. After a moment, she released a breath. "I told him I loved him."

Andrea's eyes widened. "What did he say?"

She sniffled. "He didn't."

Chapter 41

Rose angled her head, searching past Bryce into the darkness when he marched through the front door. "Have Brie and the children gone back to America, then?"

"Aye, did *ye* not see the tabloids?" Bryce dragged his cap off and strode to the fireplace. Lifting a sweatered arm, he leaned on the mantle.

"No. I have more important things to do than listen to gossip," she snapped and returned to the basket of laundry. "So, what're *ye* doing here, brother?"

Gazing at the fire—the flicks of orange and red, and the darker, smoldering center where the flames engulfed the log and blazed—he clenched his jaw. "She wrote about me."

Rose's eyes narrowed.

Ian strolled in with Lucy in his arms and Archie trailing behind. "Bryce, wasn't expecting *ye*."

"I know. Thought I'd drop by." He raked a hand through his hair, which had gotten longer since filming. A fact his makeup artist, Moira, enjoyed.

"Oh, aye." He clapped a hand on his shoulder, then settled beside Rose with Lucy in his lap.

"When will Noah and Phoebe be back?" Archie asked.

Bryce cleared his throat. "I don't know that they will, lad."

"Why?" he asked.

"Because they live far away."

His face scrunched up. "Why?"

Ian cleared his throat, settling a hand on Archie's head.

"I miss Phoebe. She's my friend," Lucy added.

Guilt tangled and twisted Bryce's intestines.

With the announcement of bath time, Rose steered the wee ones toward the hall.

Later, he sat across from Rose and Ian. "Brie"—her name caught in his throat—"she's been writing a memoir, a book about the last year of her life as a single mom."

"*Och*, that's wonderful. I didn't know she was a writer." Rose bobbed her head, then clucked. "And how strong is she being the primary caregiver for her children?"

He ground his teeth. "But she included me, Rose. I opened her journal to a page when she visited the set, and she wrote all about Alexander James Mackenzie. How's she's dating the fantasy. I still canna believe it."

"Brother, I might have been quick to judge, but I didna see any fakeness with Brie. She liked *ye* 'twas clear enough, and she was a good mother, 'twas easy to see, as well."

"It doesn't matter. 'Tis over."

Ian leaned back in the chair. "Sounds like there's more to this story."

He glanced at his boots. "I thought she was different."

"Bryce Fraser." Rose rounded forward, curls tossing. "If *yer* going to sit there on *yer* pompous ass and tell me 'tis no' another side to this story, then *yer* a bigger fool than I thought."

"Careful, Rose," Bryce said quietly.

"I saw what was between *ye* with my own eyes. *Ye* were happy. *Ye* have to decide what *ye* want and trust *yer* heart. Trust what *ye* feel is right, not what other people have planted there like that actress. Brie's not like them. I discovered that true enough myself, and so did *ye*."

He rose and paced. "I canna wrap my head around why she wrote about me. She knows I value my privacy."

"Did *ye* ask her?" Rose questioned.

"Aye, she said she included me because I came into her life…and because she loved me. She sent me her memoir, as well."

Rising, Rose fisted her hands at her hips. "So, what are *ye* going to do?"

With a puff of breath, he gazed out the window into the darkness. "I don't know."

Rose threw her hands in the air. "Well, for a start, read the bloody thing. And secondly, do *ye* love her?"

He pivoted to face his sister. "She's already back in America."

"Well, she traveled here twice." She pointed a finger. "That doesna seem like she's no' fond of our country, brother."

"I canna expect her to pick up everything and move, Rose. I don't even know if that's what I want."

She stuck her nose in the air. "Ian did for me."

Ian cleared his throat. "*Ye* strode over after university graduation and told me we were getting married, and I'd be coming home with *ye*. 'Twas no' much of a choice."

Lifting a hand to Ian's face, Rose kissed him square on the mouth. "Was there ever a choice, love?"

"No." He brushed a hand along the curve of her cheek. " 'Twas always *ye* from the start."

Bryce stared at his sister and brother-in-law and the way quick-tempered Rose softened with her husband of eight years. A tug jerked in his gut.

"See what I'm saying?" she asked.

" 'Tis not that easy. She has kids and a life."

"*Ye* have a life, as well. *Ye* get to decide what *ye* make of it."

He scowled and glanced out the dark window once again and the blurred stars beyond. If the stars could speak, what would they tell him?

****

Three days later, under intense fluorescents, Bryce sat beside Eleana doing press in New York City. Cars raced by, throngs of people meandered and strolled down streets, fans squished against the glass, eager to get a glimpse of them, and lights flashed.

"Season four of *Stars of Scotland* was so strong." The interviewer angled in a tailored blue pantsuit. "What can we expect this upcoming season, Bryce?"

" 'Tis all about family. In the first few seasons, fans were introduced to Alexander and Charlotte, but now, they have children. This season depicts the family coming together and being"—Bryce paused, staring into the camera—"torn apart." He cleared his throat and settled in his chair.

"And were you able to lean on your own experience with children for this season?"

He bobbed his head. "Aye." Picturing Noah and Phoebe running across the grass and Brie's hair blowing in the wind beside him, he felt warmth spreading through him like the autumn sun, streaming through the window.

"I think we can both lean on family experiences," Eleana added. "I, myself, have near a half dozen nieces and nephews and can draw on my time with them."

"Thank you." The interviewer gestured toward Eleana's hand. "And, Eleana, congratulations on your recent engagement. What a fantastic surprise for your fans!"

She smiled and crossed one leg over the other. "Thank you."

"And what about you, Bryce? Do you see a family in your future?"

Bryce shot up. "Em, what was the question?"

She smiled slowly. "Do you see a—"

"We love you, Bryce!" a fan shouted.

He flashed a full smile and waved, happy for the distraction. "Thank *ye*. We love *ye*, too."

Laughing softly, the interviewer shuffled papers. "I think we have time for one last question."

"While you're in New York, what are you excited to see?" a fan asked.

Glancing at Eleana as she answered, Bryce drifted to the interviewer's last question. He'd heard her. In fact, he'd spent the last week thinking about his future. After he returned from Rose and Ian's, he packed a bag and headed to Fort William to clear his mind. With necessities in his pack and a quick call to his agent, he hiked and scrambled up the *Carn Mor Dearg Arete* toward the summit of Ben Nevis. Although he was physically-fit, the demanding route challenged him, and he embraced the task, driving past pain and fatigue. Ten hours later, he summited and was rewarded with the fine views of the mountain's north face along with a snapshot of the serene glen and glistening loch below. As he sat, drawing breath under the cloudy sky, while the cool wind whipped and nipped, he was brought back to a time when he flew high above the Isle of Skye in a helicopter with Brie, slicing through thick clouds with the world below.

Then, he reflected back to almost a week ago—the way braw Noah sidled up and followed him around, how Phoebe pressed a squishy, soft kiss to his cheek, and the fire in Brie's eyes when she asked him what he wanted—his future wasn't decided yet.

Je Suis Prest.

****

In the evening, Brie tucked the last dinner plate into the dishwasher rack.

Knock-knock-knock. A brisk rap sounded from her front door.

She jolted, *clanging* plates together. She rolled the rack in and snapped the dishwasher latch tight, then glanced at the clock atop the oven. Cherry-red numbers informed her it was just after eight p.m. With unease in her chest, she tiptoed to the door and peered out the peephole.

Bryce stood on the doorstep highlighted by the glow of the porchlight.

Her breath caught. *What is he doing here?* Brie glanced in the small, hall mirror. Her hair was piled high in a messy mom bun, and she wore a pink, tie-dyed T-shirt and yoga pants.

He knocked again.

Tugging her shirt down, she opened the door.

Bryce stood there with a deep-blue sweater that matched his eyes, flanked by dark rings and stubble.

They stared at one another for what seemed like minutes.

"Brie…" he whispered.

Her heart beat so fast the raps pounded in her ears. "What are you doing here?"

"I've just flown across the country to talk to *ye*."

"Why?"

"We make sense—*ye*, me, Phoebe, and Noah. After *ye* left, I went mad with wanting *ye* and missing them. When I invited *ye* and the kids to Scotland, I didn't know this would happen. I hadn't planned it."

Brie understood what he meant. She'd witnessed the way Noah and Bryce bonded and the unbridled joy in her daughter's eyes when he'd thrown her in the air, and she'd felt the tug herself—the wanting—yearning for more. And now, the wanting deep in her chest stirred again. "What are you saying?"

He stepped forward. "I want to be with *ye*. Do *ye* want me?"

"Do I want you?" Her heart blazed, burning with longing, and every molecule in her body vibrated. "I went to Scotland to see you. I flew hours upon hours across the North Atlantic with my irritable, beautiful children and risked being eaten by itty-bitty midges to see you."

With a shake of his head, he gazed earnestly. "But do *ye* want me?"

"I, do I…?" She inched toward him, yearning and aching. "Do you not know?"

"Not Alexander James Mackenzie."

She tilted her head. "Your character?"

"Aye."

"That's kind of impossible..." Then, realization hit, and she gasped. "Oh, my God, Bryce." She gripped his hands. "Bryce, I care about *you*. Not your character or your sword, not some fantastical person someone else wrote or your fame, just you."

The corners of his mouth tipped into a smile that warmed his face and sparkled his blue eyes. " 'Tis very good news."

"I'm sorry my journal pages upset you, but you have to know I didn't include everything I'd written in Scotland in my memoir. I can also take parts that include you out of my book—whatever you want. The last thing I ever wanted was to hurt you."

He bobbed his head, shuffling red curls. "I realize that now. Rose made me see that clearly, as well. I suppose everyone already knows about us. I'll leave that to *ye* to decide. Besides"—he leaned in with a quirk of a lip—" 'tis a brilliant piece of work, and I was wrong to accuse *ye*." He squeezed her hands gently. "*Ye* put *yer* heart and soul into that book. *Ye* should be proud as I am of *ye*."

She couldn't believe what he'd just said. Light filled her rib cage and expanded, and she soared with joy. "You read my book?"

"Aye, I did." Bryce tugged her closer, then brought a hand to his lips and brushed a soft kiss into the center of her palm. "I'm in love with *ye*, Brielle Finlay Hunter."

Her heart swelled and burst like a firework. Rising on her toes, she swept her lips against his. Stars sparkled under her eyelids like sparklers, exploding in the night sky. When she felt his hands cup her face, she sighed and soared as they kissed. When they finally drew apart, she gazed into his deep-blue eyes. "I'm in love with you, too. I didn't know this kind of love existed."

"Maybe *ye* just needed to come to Scotland."

Laughing softly, she nestled her head in the crook of his chin and chest, feeling the gentle rhythm of his heart. This was where she belonged.

Bryce wrapped his strong arms around her, chin atop her head. "I'm at the height of my career. I've spent the last ten years busting my arse to get where I'm at, and now, I'm ready to share my life with *ye*. I want to be with *ye*." He glided his wide hands along her back. "Will *ye* have me?"

She looked up. "What are you saying?"

"Marry me, Brielle."

Her lungs filled, and joy exploded within her; yet, the smiling faces of her children on the wall beside the entry paused her inner celebrations. Flashes of memories flickered through her mind—Phoebe and Noah playing with Bryce, hopping across stones, and running through heather, hugging Mimi good-bye as they left for LAX, and Andrea arriving at her front door with homemade pasta. "But how will this work?"

"We can live in Scotland or L.A. I should've purchased a home in L.A. before. But 'tis time, especially since *ye* and the children are here, and I'll be filming here next summer. I'll still need to travel to Scotland for *Stars* for a few more seasons, but we can make it work."

"Are you sure? Spending a holiday with us and your entire life are two entirely different things. Are you sure this is what you want? A family?" Even as the words escaped her mouth, she prayed he wanted them.

He held her hands in his. "I know 'tis going to be hard work, but I'm willing to do that work with *ye*. Marry me? Be a family with me?"

Blinking back happy tears, she gripped his strong, warm hands. Eight years ago, she vowed to Ryan they'd be together forever. Two years ago, she was devastated. A year and a half ago, she stood on her own two feet with her first job in years, her own home, and a happy family of three. Five months ago, she couldn't have imagined she'd fall in love with Bryce after a chance meeting, nor form a connection to his country, and find the missing pieces of herself she'd lost; yet, she did. Now, she had the chance to grasp that final piece of happiness.

His gaze pierced hers.

Bryce wanted her. He wanted to make a home with her and her kids. "But what about your career?"

"We film eight months out of the year, and it's a grueling schedule. But after the day's done, there's no one I want to come home to but *ye* and the children." He squeezed her hands. "I can't move to L.A. permanently, at least not until the show's over if that's what *ye* want. Maybe we can buy a place somewhere in the hills—"

"No." Brie shook her head. She pictured the outskirts of Glasgow and miles and miles of green, the castles and culture, the warm people, picturesque Glencoe, and coming home to Bryce highlighted by the golden porch light. She longed to return. "I want the kids to explore and experience Scotland like I did with you and like they did a week ago. I want to be with you."

Touching his forehead gently to hers, he feathered his hands through her hair. "Marry me, Brielle."

"You know you might never go to the bathroom alone again?"

His smile grew, twinkling his blue eyes. " 'Tis a sacrifice I'm willing to take. Do *ye* trust me?"

Brie kissed him smartly on the lips. "I trust you."

"Marry me? Make a life with me?"

"Yes. Oh, my God, yes!"

They embraced in her quaint home surrounded by pictures of her children and the life they'd built. Now, she was ready for her future. And her future was Fraser.

Epilogue

September 10

I said, yes*! The man I love asked me to marry him. The decision was as easy as breathing—I'm in love with Bryce Fraser.*

I lived in a loveless marriage for far too long and denied myself the opportunity to be happy in an adult relationship for the sake of my children. But if I decline love for them, what am I really teaching them? The greatest gift of all is love.

And, they love Bryce. Phoebe asks when he's going to come play, and Noah wants to learn how to do more outdoorsy things—Bryce taught him how to put up a tent and make a fire. And of course, they can't stop asking when we're going back to Scotland. Soon, my babies. Soon!

Ryan even agreed with the move. I still can't believe it. But as much as he travels, he figures he can see them a few times a year when he's in London with a quick flight to Glasgow and have quality vacations during the summer and holidays in L.A. Plus, he has a new baby coming. He'll have his hands full. What I realized is, we're both moving forward, and we've finally agreed on something—one another's happiness.

Bryce makes me happy. We're making our home in Scotland to create memories like he and I did as children, oceans apart. And who knows, maybe I'll discover more about myself and the Finlay clan. I've already spoken to Holly and told her the news, and we're planning a get-together once we settle in. Plus, she's asked to read my historical fantasy romance once I've finished. I've only just begun, but I'm inspired and having so much fun plotting out the story and discovering more about my characters and myself.

Years ago, my family began in Scotland, traveled to America, and now we're returning to where they started. We'll still travel to L.A. during Bryce's shooting breaks and visit with Ryan, Andrea, and Mimi during holidays. But this year, we're spending Christmas and Hogmanay together in Scotland with Andrea and Mimi flying in to join the Fraser festivities.

I already gave notice to my landlord. I'm packing belongings in boxes and arranging movers, and we're searching schools in Glasgow for the best place for the kids. We'll make it work.

This journey all started with a plane ticket to Scotland. I am forever grateful I took the leap and went on a vacation to find myself, because in the end, I did find myself, but what's more, I found love.

****

Brie gazed out the large, bay window, watching her children sprint across the jade lawn. A smile spread as joy flooded her body like the radiant sunset, warming the cloudy sky with notes of pink and orange and coloring the green mountains in golden-coppery hues. They'd been in Scotland for less than a month, and she'd already noticed a difference in Noah and Phoebe and in herself. She felt a rejuvenation to explore their new home and create a beautiful life filled with love alongside her kids and Bryce. Love was wondrous—

love gave her wings.

Glancing at her laptop, she hit Send, emailing her final, edited manuscript, and thrust her hands up in celebration. The heart-shaped diamond resting on her ring finger caught the lovely, fall Scottish sunlight and winked. She was marrying the man of her dreams. She wasn't looking for him, but Bryce found, er rather, ran into her, and she couldn't have dreamt what life with him would've been like—because her life was even better. Mornings filled with laughter, days burst with adventure, and nights radiated with tenderness. Glancing at the ring again and thinking about the promise the ring held, she smiled, her chest overflowing with love and expanding into every crevice of her being.

Hearing a honk through the open window, Brie looked up.

A four-by-four pulled into the yard, and Bryce stepped out, holding his arms wide toward their children who bounded straight into them.

She stood and strode down the porch steps.

Her heart spilled over with love and happiness. She was home.

A word about the author...

Erica Mae is the author of romantic comedies including a Christmas novella, Falling for Lemon Snowballs, and contemporary romance. She writes swoony romance with strong heroines who achieve their dreams and learn that they are worthy of love. When she's not writing, you can find her exploring with her family, on a yoga mat, or cooking up a new recipe.

Another title by the author
Falling for Lemon Snowballs